# THE

# LAST

# BEEKEEPER

BOOKS BY JULIE CARRICK DALTON

*Waiting for the Night Song*

# THE

# LAST

# BEEKEEPER

## JULIE CARRICK DALTON

TOR PUBLISHING GROUP
NEW YORK

THE LAST BEEKEEPER

A Forge Book
Published by Tom Doherty Associates / Tor Publishing Group
120 Broadway
New York, NY 10271

www.tor-forge.com

Forge® is a registered trademark of Macmillan Publishing Group, LLC.

Library of Congress Cataloging-in-Publication Data

Names: Dalton, Julie Carrick, author.
Title: The last beekeeper / Julie Carrick Dalton.
Description: First edition. | New York : Forge, 2023. | "A Tom Doherty
    Associates book." |
Identifiers: LCCN 2022041400 (print) | LCCN 2022041401 (ebook) |
    ISBN 9781250269218 (hardcover) | ISBN 9781250269225 (ebook)
Subjects: LCGFT: Novels.
Classification: LCC PS3604.A43555 L37 2023 (print) | LCC PS3604.A43555
    (ebook) | DDC 813/.6—dc23
LC record available at https://lccn.loc.gov/2022041400
LC ebook record available at https://lccn.loc.gov/2022041401

Our books may be purchased in bulk for promotional, educational, or
business use. Please contact your local bookseller or the Macmillan Corporate
and Premium Sales Department at 1-800-221-7945, extension 5442, or by email
at MacmillanSpecialMarkets@macmillan.com.

First Edition: 2023

Printed in the United States of America

0  9  8  7  6  5  4  3  2  1

*For my parents, Barbara and Ross Carrick.*
*I have had the privilege of watching my mother and father excel*
*in numerous endeavors, including puppeteering, belly dancing,*
*driving an ambulance, selling real estate, cleaning houses, writing*
*genealogy books, farming, and that super-secret thing we can't*
*talk about. You are the world's best storytellers—and even better*
*secret keepers. Thank you for filling my life with creativity,*
*entrepreneurial energy, books, adventure, tea parties, mystery,*
*love, and a lifetime supply of story ideas. I love you.*

# THE

# LAST

# BEEKEEPER

# Prologue

*M*y *bees will survive,* Sasha promised herself as she crouched in the dirt watching them die. A worker bee hauled a dead sibling to the opening of the hive and launched the body onto a pile of her lifeless sisters in the dirt below.

"Why are they dying?" Sasha whispered to her father, his head so close to hers his whiskers brushed her cheek.

He rubbed his face with stiff, arthritic hands and crawled closer to the hive. "Come here."

He put a hand on the pine box. Sasha did the same.

"What do you feel?" he asked.

"Wood?" The smooth grain gave slightly under her fingernails as she pressed harder.

"What else?"

Warmth brewing inside the hive overpowered the shade cast by oak branches.

"It's hot. And buzzing."

"Bees hum at the exact pitch of a G note, like on Mom's piano," her father said, pipe smoke infused in his shirt mixing with lavender in the breeze.

"How do they know the note?" She pressed her ear to the side of the hive, vibrations tickling the inner parts of her ear.

"They just know. They communicate with signals only bees understand."

With her cheek still flush against the hive, Sasha looked at her father and blinked three slow, deliberate blinks, scrunching her eyes tight each time.

"What are you doing?" he asked.

"Sending a signal only *you* can understand." Again, she stared at him and blinked three times.

He furrowed his brow as if concentrating. "I love you, too."

Her father placed one hand on the hive and the other on Sasha's shoulder, his callused skin chafing her sunburn. The hum disoriented her until she felt as if she hovered above the ground. The buzzing grew louder, filling her skull, telegraphing secret signals down her neck and arms to warm her fingertips.

"That note is a part of you now." His words hung in the viscous air. "It's a huge responsibility to be tuned to the pitch of a bee."

For a moment Sasha could see the air—particles, sound waves, breath—moving like liquid around her. She parted her lips to taste the sizzle of lavender and wax.

A loud chirp startled Sasha and she pulled her ear away from the hive.

"This is Lawrence." Her father answered his phone and walked toward the farmhouse, leaving Sasha alone with her bees and the vibrations destined to tremble under her skin long after the hives fell silent.

# One

Sasha stepped off the sour-smelling bus hoping the taste of chaff in the air would guide her back to the farmhouse. Every night since her father had gone to prison, she had visualized walking up the sagging porch stairs, retracing the familiar path down the hall, fingertips recounting each dent in the scuffed chair rail, every flourish in the wrought-iron heat vents.

She hadn't been this close to her childhood home in eleven years, but it had never felt farther away.

The hydraulic bus door screeched as it slammed closed. Sasha jumped sideways and the bus lurched away.

After six steps on the broken pavement, memory tingled in her feet, her knees, and the thumping space in her chest. When she first landed in state care, she used to spin herself dizzy to see if she could intuit which direction led back to the farm. No matter how long she spun, and even if she tripped or fell, she always recognized the beeline home before opening her eyes.

Flanking the desolate road, fields that once swayed with barley and rye now teemed with an untamed fervor that prodded at the dormant wildness in Sasha. She yanked up a tuft of tall grass, clotted dirt clinging to the roots. The earthy aroma, the precise mixture of life and decay that punctuated her childhood, greeted her like an old friend and conjured a longing to howl into the wind whipping her hair across her face.

4 JULIE CARRICK DALTON

Sometimes the vibrations in Sasha's fingertips, ghosts of the bees she and her father once tended, swarmed her with aggression, attacking her from the inside. Too much lost when the bees died. Too much wrenched from her tattered, younger self. Other days, the gentle hum enveloped Sasha in tender, honey-soaked memories of her father's beard and a world that had not yet come undone.

She no longer whipped her head around to chase rogue flickers in her peripheral vision. The barely audible hum of tiny, nonexistent wings hovering close to her ear rarely tempted her to close her eyes and hope anymore.

Her bees, like nearly all the pollinators, had disappeared more than a decade ago.

As Sasha trudged up the final hill toward her childhood home, the familiar buzz warmed her fingertips. She shook her hands out, forcing blood into her fingers, and clapped to dispel the phantom hum.

She shouldn't have waited so long to return home. She had aged out of the state juvenile-care system four years ago. Since then, she had relentlessly promised herself she'd return to find the research her father buried. *Soon,* she repeated in her mind every night before slipping off to sleep. *Soon.*

But she couldn't take time off work from the bike shop. The bus ticket cost too much. The walk from the bus stop was too long. Convenient reasons to avoid home made staying away an easy habit, one she could no longer indulge. Her father's first parole hearing was scheduled in less than a month and she intended to unearth the documents he buried before his release. If he found them first, Sasha might never understand what she helped him hide all those years ago. She might never understand the truth about why he chose prison over her.

The media already hummed with news of the hearing. WILL THE LAST BEEKEEPER BE RELEASED EARLY? WILL THE LAST BEEKEEPER'S DAUGHTER TESTIFY ON HIS BEHALF?

The letter from her father's lawyer requesting her presence at the parole hearing lay crumpled in a pocket of her backpack. Writing a dispassionate note on her father's behalf instead of appearing in person had been the coward's way out, but hadn't she learned that maneuver from her dad, who chose to hide behind his secrets instead of parenting his motherless child?

The first night Sasha spent in the state home, she made herself three promises, and every night since she had renewed the vow before going to sleep. *Find the research. Understand the truth. Rebuild a family.*

But now, as she took the first steps toward acting on her oaths, she worried she wouldn't find anything at the farm and would have nothing left to promise herself, other than rebuilding a family, which seemed more unlikely than unearthing the mythic lost documents.

Maybe it would be better not to try.

Dust from the road clung to the sticky saliva gathering in the corners of her mouth. Sasha adjusted the backpack on her aching shoulders and took a swig of water from a nearly empty bottle.

She stopped visiting her father in prison years ago. Not because she didn't love him, but because she couldn't take the bullying by other kids. But now, with the possibility of his imminent release, Sasha needed to know what she helped her father bury in the field all those years ago. She needed to understand why he chose to protect those documents instead of her. And more than anything, she needed to finally understand if it had all been her fault.

The weight of everything she owned thumped against her body as she swung her violin case to maintain momentum as she approached the driveway.

ABSOLUTELY NO TRESPASSING.

Hand-painted red letters on a sheet of plywood leaned against a large rock marking the driveway.

Fucking squatters.

Technically, the farm had defaulted to state ownership when her father went to prison. She had no legal claim, but this land belonged to her and she to it. Local officials wouldn't notice if she camped out for a few nights. Squatters, however, would fight.

Sasha kicked the sign, the impact on the rubber toe of her boot reverberating in her knee. This was *her* home. She kicked it again, cracking the brittle wood, but not breaking it.

Sasha didn't want a fight, but she refused to turn back.

What right did squatters have to turn her away?

She quickened her pace and passed the weatherworn barn that had once been her mother's workshop. Her eyes stung as she faced the house she had been dreaming of for years, but her dehydrated body failed to conjure tears. The garden spilled onto the driveway in a tangled mess. Shutters hung at odd angles. A dry sob stuck in her throat when she saw the silvery leaves of her mother's unruly lavender, lording over the weeds.

The tire swing she and her father used to beat like a piñata to vent their frustrations twisted in the wind, the rusty chain creaking with the familiar groan that made Sasha's knees wobble.

She drank the last swallow of water, dropped her pack to the ground, and ignored the buzz building in her ears. *It's not real. They're gone.*

She knelt on the ground and leaned her elbows on her pack, taking in the familiar but altered scene. A tower of rusty bike wheels impaled on a spike stood in front of the porch. Of all things to survive time and looters. The day she and her father moved her hives to hide them in the forest, she had marked the hives' location with the sculpture, a monument to all she and her father failed to protect.

As she ran a finger absentmindedly over the cracked leather of her violin case, something landed on the handle.

At first, she mistook the insect for debris carried by the wind, but the wind had stilled. Her throat tightened as the shiny stinger twitched.

A bee.

Her skin burned with the decades-old guilt of her role in the demise of the final bee colony. The last of their kind.

No one had seen a honey bee in the wild for eleven years.

Yet there it sat. A bee. A perfect, beautiful bee, taunting her. Haunting her.

*Apis mellifera,* her father's voice boomed in her mind.

The Earth seemed to stutter on its axis as Sasha stared at the fuzzy body, the threadlike antennae. As the bee rose into the air in front of her, the whir of its wings stirred a faded memory as elusive as a forgotten color.

The vibrato hummed in her teeth as the bee lowered itself to walk across the violin case.

She squeezed her eyes shut against the mirage summoned by her desperate need to believe some bees had survived.

She had spent her first eleven years helping her father tend bees, and every year since trying to forget the hypnotic sound of being surrounded by them.

Sasha, of all people, didn't fall for the bee-sighting hysteria. She knew the truth.

The bees were gone.

Sasha stared at the figment, willing it to dissipate. Was she so weak her mind could conjure a bee to appease the empty, aching space in her chest?

Entranced by the impossible creature—conjured by heat, dehydration, or the shock of being home—Sasha didn't notice the man emerging from the farmhouse.

"Pick up your pack and turn around," he shouted, a rifle on his shoulder aimed at Sasha's chest.

Sasha jumped to her feet, knocking her pack over.

"Pilgrims are no longer welcome here."

When she looked down, the imaginary bee had vanished.

# Two

## SASHA'S 22nd BIRTHDAY
### JUNE 6

Sasha froze as the man stepped onto the porch, followed by another man and a woman, all of whom appeared to be in their mid-twenties.

"Are you lost?" A tall woman with light brown skin and long, wavy hair walked down the stairs toward Sasha. A swath of fabric wrapped around her waist flapped in the breeze.

Sasha didn't answer.

"Our sign's hard to miss."

Sasha wiped the crust from the corners of her mouth and put her hands over her head.

"I'll get you a drink," the woman said. "Then you can move on."

Sasha picked up her bag and violin case and followed the woman up the porch stairs. The scent of lavender gathered into a thick lump in her throat. She tried to swallow it down, but her throat was too dry, and she gagged.

The two men watched Sasha as she passed them, but they didn't speak to her.

"Where do you source your water?" Sasha asked as she walked into her own kitchen. She placed her palm on the scored butcher block island, feeling the grooves carved by knives that might have been her mother's.

"From a creek in the woods. We filter and boil it." The woman poured a mug of water from a jug and handed it to Sasha.

Sasha assessed the slightly cloudy water.

"We've been here six months, and no one's gotten sick." The woman jumped up to sit on the butcher block in the exact spot Sasha's mother used to sit. *We have chairs, you know,* her father used to tease.

There were no chairs in the kitchen now. She had expected that looters would have cleaned the house out, but seeing the empty space hurt like an old wound that refused to heal. This woman seemed too comfortable in Sasha's house, sitting on Sasha's counter.

"Are you thirsty or not?"

Sasha gulped the tepid water.

"Are you allowed to be here?" Sasha asked. Shaded squares on the faded yellow wallpaper outlined where her father's watercolor paintings once hung.

"Are *you* allowed to be here? That's the question you should be concerned with." The woman folded her arms across her chest and squinted at Sasha.

"Can I stay?" Sasha clenched her jaw, wanting to yell at them, and kick them out of her home. "Just for a while."

The two men walked into the kitchen.

"Sorry, we're out of rooms," the tall guy with the rifle said. He had blond hair, high, round cheeks, and a heavy brow.

"I can pay you. Just let me stay a week," Sasha said. They could easily rob her and take all her money, but she couldn't think of another option. "I need a place to rest up, then I'll move on."

"Are you a pilgrim?" the woman asked.

"A what?"

"Did you come to pay homage to the last bees? Or are you a conspiracy theorist trying to uncover 'the truth'?" She waved air quotes as she said *the truth.*

"No." Sasha's response came out too aggressively, nearly a shout. "Who would do that?"

"You just happened to stumble on the home of the Last Beekeeper?"

Sasha dug her fingernails into the palms of her hands. If they forced her to leave, she wouldn't be able to search for her father's research, which mattered more than staking a claim on the house that should rightfully be hers. She tried to maintain a neutral, non-threatening demeanor, but inside she seethed. What did they know about the beekeeper or the truth?

"I just want a place to sleep."

The three friends exchanged glances.

"Money up front," the blond guy said. "Don't go in the bedrooms. And don't take any of our food unless we specifically offer it to you."

"You can sleep in the living room, under the piano or somewhere out of our way," the second man said, his voice a degree softer than his two friends'. His shaggy brown hair looked like it had recently been the subject of a home haircut. Stray curls popped up in random places, giving him a comical, but charming appearance.

"But somewhere we can see you." The man with the rifle shifted the gun awkwardly in his hands. Although Sasha suspected he had no idea how to shoot a gun and doubted it was loaded, she didn't trust her theory enough to test it.

"If you're staying, you need to work," the woman said. "And if you break any rules, or if for any reason we decide you need to leave earlier, that's our call, not yours. No refunds."

"Do you have any weapons?" the blond man asked.

"No." She didn't mention the knife tucked into her sock. "But I have tools. I'm good at fixing things if you have any odd jobs."

"Can you patch the roof?" said the second guy, shorter than the blond, but several inches taller than Sasha.

"I can try," Sasha said.

The bushy-haired guy smiled slightly. The one with the rifle noticed the smile and scowled.

"I'm Halle, by the way. The grumpy one is Ian." The woman

gestured toward the blond guy. "And this is Gino. Millie's some-where wandering in the woods, as usual."

"Welcome to the apiary." Gino smiled more openly this time, and raised his eyebrow at Ian, daring him to reprimand him for being friendly.

Sasha smiled back, a twinge of optimism displacing her fear. The way they backed each other up and talked each other down stirred a twitch of envy. If she fixed the roof, they might let her stay on longer than a week. If she found her father's research—or if she didn't—she had no plans for where to go next and her meager savings wouldn't get her far. And this, after all, was her home.

The front door slammed and a small woman in her fifties with a long gray braid walked into the room with wide, purposeful strides and a straight back.

"This is Millie." Halle turned to Sasha. "What's your name?"

"Sasha."

"Sasha's staying for a week."

"Short for Alexandra?" Millie squinted and tilted her head as she scrutinized Sasha.

"Just Sasha," she lied, not wanting to give away any more than she needed to. As soon as she'd aged out of the system, she legally changed her name from Alexandra Severn to Sasha Butler to escape affiliation with her infamous father.

"They gave me a week too." Millie offered a reserved smile. "A month ago."

"Maybe it's time to renegotiate," Ian said to Millie, then shifted his gaze to Sasha's bag on the floor.

"It would break your heart if I left," Millie said.

Gino tucked his chin to his chest to hide a smile.

Sasha inched closer to her pack, protecting her belongings from Ian's stare.

Millie put a hand on Sasha's elbow and Sasha flinched, pulling away. Millie nodded at her with a half smile suggesting she understood.

"Do you have a plate?" Millie asked.

"A plate? No."

"We only have four plates, but you can share mine," Millie said, then leaned closer to Sasha and fake-whispered, "Although it's Halle's night to cook, so keep your expectations low."

Millie's creamy voice, deep, rich, and smooth, put Sasha at ease. She couldn't place Millie's subtle accent. Sasha liked her and hoped Millie, being a relative newcomer, might be an ally or a friend.

A table built out of wooden pallets anchored the otherwise empty kitchen. Several drying bouquets of lavender—her mother's lavender—hung from the empty curtain rod above the sink. Beside them, bunches of drying basil, parsley, and thyme swayed in the breeze coming through the open window. Stripped of cabinet doors and light fixtures, the kitchen looked sterile, cracks in the plaster the only places for memories to hide.

Ian put a hand out, indicating he expected payment immediately.

Sasha pulled up a pant leg and opened a pouch bound to her calf. She handed Ian a few bills, not sure how much seemed fair for a week under a piano in her own house. He accepted the money and didn't ask for more. She made a point to let them see how little cash remained in the pouch. She kept the rest strapped to her lower back.

"Do you have electricity?" Sasha asked.

"I wish," Gino said.

"And no running water?" Sasha tested them again to see if they knew about the hand pump under the porch.

"If you don't like the accommodations, you can leave," Ian said.

"Give her a break. She paid her money." Gino trailed a hand across Ian's shoulder as he leaned closer to count the money.

"You said something about pilgrims? Do a lot of people pass through here?" Sasha asked.

"Not many in the first few months we were here, but recently more people have been showing up, chasing rumors the bees were back."

In the wake of the Great Collapse of the pollinators, Congress criminalized reporting bee sightings without evidence, but it didn't deter fanatics and crazies who shouted on street corners with hand-painted posters reading THE BEES SURVIVE. Most people laughed off bee sightings. Those who claimed to see bees were either lunatics, attention-seekers, cult members, or, worse, troublemakers intent on derailing the precarious food security that had taken a decade to reestablish.

"There's been a lot of chatter online, but when the police started cracking down on false bee sightings in the city, people stopped coming out here," Halle said.

Sasha's stomach tightened at the mention of sightings. Her fingertips buzzed at the memory of the bee she had imagined on the driveway minutes earlier. Her mind had conjured the hum and the peripheral flit of a wing numerous times, but never a fully formed bee. The phenomenon, labeled Apis manifestation syndrome, was deemed a contagious, hysterical product of desperate minds unable to accept that human society remained permanently altered without bees. The agricultural collapse, followed by a near economic implosion, drove distraught people to believe irrational things.

"We intentionally came to the middle of nowhere so we'd be left alone." Ian glared at Sasha as he put the gun in the pantry. "We're miles from anywhere. No car-charging stations nearby, so not many vehicles come out this way. The grid's been down for eight years, and the toxic soil scares most people away."

"It doesn't scare you?" Sasha asked.

"It's safer than living in the camps," he said. "Why are you here, if you didn't come about the bees? This place isn't on the way to anywhere."

"The bike shop where I worked closed down and I couldn't find another job. I couldn't take living in the shelter anymore, so I rode the bus as far as I could afford. At the end of the line, I started walking. This is where I ran out of water."

"No family?" Ian paced as he talked.

"I grew up in a state care facility until I aged out four years ago. Today, actually. I aged out four years ago today." She didn't mention her father. If they knew her identity, they might assume she intended to usurp the farm, which she did not. Despite their antagonistic first encounter, Sasha liked the idea of bunking with this pieced-together family for a while.

Without any warning, Halle grabbed both of Sasha's wrists. "Did you ever meet a girl named Beatrix? She's eleven now. She has a rounder face, but we look a lot alike. She's my sister."

"I wouldn't have known any kids her age. Plus, there are so many state care facilities now. I doubt we would have been in the same location." Sasha felt a pang of jealousy. No one on the outside had waited for her.

"But you were safe? They treated you okay?" Halle squeezed Sasha's wrists.

Sasha blinked hard to suppress the rush of memories she had trained her mind to forget. The constant reprimands and barely edible food. The looks of disgust from her teachers when they discovered she was the daughter of the Last Beekeeper. The searing loneliness. She wasn't opening that Pandora's box for a stranger.

"I made it out, so I guess I'm all right."

"I take the bus to visit her once a month, but when she turns twelve, in like three months, they're transferring her to a facility for older kids three hours from here. They wouldn't let me be her guardian before I turned eighteen, and now I'm legal but they won't consider a custody hearing because I don't have any income or a legal address. I need to get her out of there. Do you have any idea how many Brown girls go missing from the system every year?"

Sasha knew. Kids ran away. Kids disappeared. And if no one advocated for them, too many slipped through the cracks. As the high-profile daughter of a famous—or infamous—scientist, Sasha had never been at risk of disappearing, even when she wanted to. The special treatment didn't win her many friends.

"I heard if you squat on an abandoned Ag property for five years, you can stake a legal claim," Halle said. "But I don't want to wait five years. I'm going to get a job, find a permanent place, and get Beatrix back. Is she safe in there?"

"She's safe." Sasha worked to keep her facial expression neutral at the idea of the squatters laying a claim to her farm. "I mean, kids can be mean. School sucked most of the time, but they fed us. They didn't lock us in a dungeon or anything. But yeah, the sooner you can get her out, the better."

Sasha knew plenty of kids in the system who had *not* been fine.

"We'll find a way to bring her home." Gino put an arm around Halle's shoulder.

Halle let go of Sasha's wrists and gave Sasha a forced smile that hinted at a relentless ache. The tea-stained floral fabric of Halle's skirt, vaguely familiar to Sasha, swished as Halle rose up on her toes to reach a pan from an upper cabinet.

"I can help with dinner if you want," Sasha said.

"No thanks," Halle said, while Millie, Gino, and Ian all said "Yes" at the exact same time.

"Fine. They think I'm a terrible cook." Halle didn't seem to take offense.

"I'll bring up some more water," Gino said. Ian and Millie followed him outside, leaving Sasha alone with Halle.

"Would you really stay here for five years to establish residency?" Sasha asked. "This place is pretty run-down."

"If that's what it takes to get custody of Beatrix." Halle rummaged through the open cabinet space where Sasha's parents once kept pots and pans.

Sasha longed to peek inside the corner cabinet where her mother had sampled different wood stains. The dark walnut stain her father preferred, the amber tones of the cherry her mother wanted, and the clear coat of polyurethane Sasha liked best. In the end, they chose the cherry stain because Sasha and her father both ranked it second, thereby earning the most votes.

"Do you have anything?" Halle asked.

"You mean food?"

"Yes, I mean food."

"No." On the off chance Ian made her leave early, she needed to protect her supplies.

Halle side-eyed Sasha and hefted a large, dented pot onto the counter.

Sasha glanced at her backpack, where she had at least a dozen energy bars and a pound of jerky.

Halle measured two teacups full of rice from a burlap sack, paused, then dumped a third cupful into the pot.

"I lied. I have some food." Maybe the best way to ingratiate herself was to be honest. Or mostly honest.

"I know you do." Halle's voice softened. "It's okay."

Sasha unzipped her bag and pulled out a few strips of jerky.

"Ha, see if they make fun of my dinner tonight," Halle said as she chopped a soft onion and three limp carrots, tossing them into the rice along with some fresh herbs. Sasha cut up a fistful of jerky, which Halle folded into the rice. Preparing food beside Halle in the familiar walls of the kitchen gave Sasha the sensation of being inside a dream where everything felt familiar, yet somehow off.

They carried the pot outside and lit a fire in a pit near the porch. Halle placed the pot on a grate positioned over the fire and covered it with a flat piece of wood in place of a lid.

"Mind if I check out the house?" Sasha asked. "I'll look at the roof and see if I can patch the leak."

"I guess not, but stay out of our bedrooms. I'll keep an eye on dinner."

Sasha went inside and snooped through the kitchen cabinets. A few beat-up pans, a collection of mugs, four plates, and a tangle of unmatched silverware. Nothing she recognized.

Making sure no one saw her, she eased open the door to the basement, and crept down the dark stairs. The main level of the house no longer held any familiar smells, but the musty basement yanked her back to stolen moments when she snuck into her parents' larder to pilfer honey. A small, dirty window in the far corner let in enough light to confirm the hidden cabinet door to the larder remained in place. A casual observer would never suspect anything lay behind the wall in a dark corner.

*You're turning into a goddamn prepper,* her mom's brother, Chuck, had scoffed at Sasha's father when he had sacks of rice and dried beans delivered. Next came flour in huge, sealed cans with expiration dates twenty-five years in the future. Nuts, dried fruit, and seeds filled the larder.

*Why does it make you mad when Chuck calls you a prepper?* Sasha asked as she helped her father haul the food into the basement.

*Because he's right, I guess,* her father had said.

*What's a prepper?*

*Someone who stocks up on things because they fear the worst is coming.*

*Do you fear the worst?*

*Sometimes I do, Little Bee.*

Dusty, long-abandoned spiderwebs clung to Sasha's face and hands as she crossed the room. She pressed on the false front and held her breath for a beat, her hope mounting at the give of the spring-loaded catch.

The panel clicked and sprang open to reveal a time capsule of her father's prepper tendencies in the small walk-in room. She ran her hand over the sacks, tins, and jars, longing to read the labels too obscured in shadow to decipher. She twisted a small canister open and touched a few grains to her tongue. Salt. As the grains melted on her tongue, she tried to remember the last meal she ate in the house, the last time she might have consumed salt from this canister. She hated that she couldn't remember.

Ian seemed like the type who would claim squatters' rights to everything on the property, so she had no intention of revealing the larder to the squatters. But salt might go a long way in building their trust. She rolled the shaker between her hands, remembering the satisfying weight and gritty texture of the ceramic. She slipped the saltshaker into her shirt pocket.

She crouched down and felt along the back of the bottom shelf, holding her breath in the hope of finding her father's honey stash. Her fingers grazed a Mason jar. The airy heft of the glass told her seeds filled the container, not honey. Both of her parents had been dedicated seed savers, drying trays of seeds from the season's best crops for the following year. Five more jars of seeds lined the back wall.

Sasha did not need light to recognize the individual seeds in the jars she had played with like maracas as a girl. The ting of tomato seeds against glass, and the sandy shush of spinach. The feather weight of zucchini seeds and the flaky but substantial mass of pumpkin. The last jar weighed more than the others. Sasha rolled the jar, allowing the seeds to fall slowly against the glass. The contents felt irregular, small and sandy, heavy and clunky.

*This is a jar of hope,* her mother explained as she tossed handfuls of her carefully curated wildflower seeds along the edge of the forest above the vegetable fields.

Pebbles and scales of bergamot, black cohosh, milkweed, fireweed, and echinacea shifted around the clunkier sunflower seeds.

*You and Dad take care of the bees in boxes, and I'll look after the ones in the woods,* her mother said as she raked her seeds into the loose soil.

*Dad says they're gone.*

*But what if they come back? They'll be hungry.*

Her father always planned several steps ahead, too. He never acted without reason, although Sasha didn't always understand his reasons. When he buried his research instead of turning it over to the authorities, he made the choice to go to prison. Only eleven at the time, Sasha had faith in him and trusted he had planned a few steps beyond what anyone else could see.

She had expected him to come home to her.

Instead, he betrayed her, setting her loose into a world that did not need her.

Digging up her father's research might give her answers, even if they weren't the ones she hoped for.

Sasha held her mother's jar of hope to her cheek and rolled the smooth, cool glass across her lips, cheeks, and forehead before tucking it into a far corner of the larder. She ran her hands over the empty shelves, searching for anything that might have been left behind. Her fingers grazed a stack of papers on the back of the top shelf. Loose pages held together by a paper clip. It couldn't be this easy. Could her father have hidden his work in the larder, and not in the bunker as she had assumed?

In the dark shadows, she couldn't read the documents, but her fingers recognized the paper, not as her father's work, but her mother's. Crumpled, water warped, and crusty in places. Sasha's mouth watered as she held the pages to her face and imagined the aroma of her mother's potpies, stroganoff, and borscht. Before she died, her mother handwrote Sasha's favorite recipes and walked her through each one several times.

Sasha had been too young to cook alone, but after her mother died, she read the recipes to herself like bedtime stories, acting out the scenes in her mind. Her mother chopping vegetables. Sasha stirring. The tick, tick, tick of the kitchen timer. And the triumphant moment when a perfectly browned, bubbling-at-the-edges chicken potpie emerged from the oven.

Sasha crawled inside the larder and sat with her back to the wall. She wrapped her arms across her chest and pressed the crinkled pages to her heart.

This was Sasha's home, and she intended to stay.

# Three

Sasha squatted on the floor in the basement larder and scooped one last fingerful of honey into her mouth before screwing the lid back on the Mason jar and returning it to the bottom shelf. She sucked on her finger, tracing the outlines of calluses with her tongue. She took pride in the thick skin on the pads of her fingers created by pressing down on the strings of her violin. Evidence of hard work, her father said.

She tugged at the collar of the ridiculous eyelet dress, two sizes too big, her father brought home days earlier for her to wear to her orchestra performance. Her mother never would have asked her to wear a white dress, which made her pale, freckled skin appear ghostly. Her mother would have bought the right size. But pointing out what her mother would have done felt unkind. Her father was trying.

"Where's Dad?" Sasha asked Chuck, her mother's brother, who rested on the farmhouse porch swing with his eyes closed, moving the creaky swing as he rocked his feet from heel to toe, toe to heel. His belly strained the buttons of his blue Oxford shirt. Chuck wasn't a large man, but it annoyed Sasha that he always wore clothes one size too small.

He didn't answer, but Sasha could tell he was awake.

"Chuck, where's my dad?" she said louder, knowing he would answer this time. He hated when Sasha refused to call him Uncle Chuck.

"He's finishing up a call," Chuck said without opening his eyes. He maintained a slow, creaky swing, his body limp, but his fingers tapping rapidly on the arm of the wooden swing.

Sasha sat on the porch stairs picking at a sprig of lavender, pulling off one petal at a time until a small pile of purple scraps circled her feet. She hadn't told her father yet, but her orchestra would be performing "Flight of the Bumblebee." She wouldn't need to tell him she had lobbied the conductor for months to include the arrangement. Her father would know.

She bounced in anticipation of seeing his face in the audience when he realized his daughter had commanded an entire orchestra to play for him.

"Are you tuned up?" Her father appeared in the doorway. Sasha wished he had trimmed his half-wild gray beard, but at least he wore a button-down shirt, mostly tucked in.

"Not yet." Sasha opened the violin case, tightened the bow, and lifted her instrument. She followed her father to a hive under the enormous oak tree, one of the hives Sasha had tended and cared for since she built the boxes herself at age eight.

Her father pried the top off, cracking open the sticky layer of propolis with a hive tool.

The bees rose in smoky wisps around Sasha. Their hum moved inside her head and in her fingertips. Her bees. She put the violin to her shoulder, closed her eyes, and pleaded with herself to remember this perfect smell. Wax and honey, rosin on her bow, oil she had rubbed into her instrument hours earlier, and lavender clinging to her fingertips. The perfume of everything good in one single breath.

"You're going to make her late." Chuck hauled himself out of the swing and clomped down the stairs.

"Shhh." Her father put a hand up to keep him from coming any closer.

The bees recognized Sasha's scent, her heat. Stray bees whirred around her head and circled the hive. She held the violin to her shoulder with her chin and let go with her hand, drawing the bow across the open G. She paused to listen to the bees, and adjusted the fine tuner in search of the right vibration.

Her violin sang the tiniest bit flat. She twisted the fine adjustment and played again. As the frequency synchronized with the pitch of the bees, an electric charge coursed through her body. The hum of every bee, of every hair strung on her bow, the ecstasy of being understood, seen, heard.

As she coaxed the precise note, the bees circled closer, landing on her feet, her violin, the tip of her bow. At least twenty bees tickled her arms, drawn in by the perfectly matched resonance.

She lifted the bow off the string and waited, violin tucked under her chin, until the final vibrations stilled.

"The bees always come for you," her father said.

Sasha detected a note of envy in his voice. She held her position, violin on her shoulder, the bow one inch above the strings, until the last bee flitted off.

"Did you oil the water pump like I asked?" he said as he maneuvered the cover back on top of the hive.

"I'll do it tonight."

"You need to take care of things if you want them to work when you need them."

"I will." She had never once needed that pump.

Her father moved with slow, fluid motions around the bees, finding his own way to sync up with them the way Sasha did with her violin. They parted for him, not in fear, but out of respect. His knotted hands, stiff with swollen, arthritic knuckles, adjusted the hive lid back into place.

"I have a surprise for you tonight," Sasha said, fighting the urge to tell him about "Flight of the Bumblebee."

"Do you?"

She bounced toward the car.

Her father's cell phone rang.

"Don't answer it," she pleaded.

"This isn't a convenient time," her father said to the caller, and stepped away from the car. He paced back and forth under the broad canopy of the old oak tree that shaded the hives on one side and Sasha's tire swing on the other. He scratched his beard, and squeezed his eyes shut. "No, no, no! I didn't authorize that."

Her father glared at Chuck, but Chuck focused his eyes on his shoes and chewed on his fingernails.

"We aren't ready." Her father's voice cracked as if he might cry, which Sasha had never seen him do. The voice on the other end of the call warbled in panicked, unhinged tones.

Chuck shifted from foot to foot with increasing agitation.

"This can't happen. You have to stop them," her father shouted.

Angry tones erupted on the other end of the line as Sasha's father rubbed his beard and paced with uneven strides—short tight steps followed by long strides, giving him the appearance of someone deciding if they should make a break for it. He grabbed the chain supporting the tire and leaned on it as if he might collapse.

"Who authorized this? This is criminal recklessness," he said in a low growl that sent shivers over Sasha's skin. "Do you understand if this goes wrong, we will have destroyed our one chance? You couldn't wait a few more fucking months?"

He hung up and stomped back toward the house and up the wooden porch stairs.

"Can we go now?" Sasha's voice felt small as she called after him.

"I have to get to the office. There's an emergency." He raked his hands through the untamed mop of his hair. He stared at Sasha then at Chuck with wide eyes but didn't appear to see them.

"My concert."

Her father closed his eyes and gripped the porch rail so hard Sasha worried the wood might splinter. After a few seconds he went inside and slammed the door.

"So, we'll go ahead without him." Chuck opened his car door. "We have plenty of time. I'm sure he'll be there."

"Right," Sasha said, the tune draining out of her. Her father wouldn't be there, but she and Chuck played along with the charade. Chuck seemed to get satisfaction out of stepping in when Sasha's father failed her. In addition to being her uncle, Chuck was also Sasha's godfather, although they never made it official in a church because, as her parents often said, God lived in trees and soil and wind, not a building or a book. According to her father, Chuck had asked for the job the day after Sasha was born. Sleep-deprived and overwhelmed, her parents had said, *Sure, why not?*

On the front seat of the car lay a small bouquet of carnations wrapped in clear cellophane, the kind sold near the checkout counters in grocery stores.

"I didn't know if anyone else would think to bring them." Chuck scooped them up so Sasha could sit down, then handed them to her.

"Thanks." She held the flowers to her face and sniffed them, although carnations didn't have much of a scent. It should have been her father taking her to the concert, not Chuck, who sweat too much and always smelled like cheese. Sasha placed the second-rate bouquet on her lap and crossed her arms. She pinched at a pink petal, wishing her father could be as steadfast as her uncle.

"Why is he mad at you?" Sasha asked.

"He's frustrated. He's brilliant, your dad, but he thinks too much. It paralyzes him from taking action. He thinks everyone should always believe him, and when they don't, he writes them off as stupid. It can rub people the wrong way."

"You mean it rubs you the wrong way."

"If your father would look up from his microscope and see the bigger picture, things would be easier for him."

"But he's right," Sasha said.

"You don't know what we're talking about."

"He's always right. I know you know that," Sasha said. "And I know it makes you mad. It makes me furious sometimes."

"Having unchecked faith in a single person is dangerous, Alexandra," Chuck said, invoking her full name to annoy her. His knuckles whitened as he squeezed the steering wheel. "Even if you think you're right, you need to leave room for people to question you, to challenge you. Prove your theory, but don't ever expect people to believe you simply because you tell them to. It's arrogant."

"So, my dad's arrogant?"

"I'm just giving you tips on how to get along in this world. One of your hair things is falling out." Chuck pointed at the honey bee clip holding her hair out of her eyes. Her mom had given her the pair of barrettes the final Christmas they spent together. "I know you don't want to lose that."

Sasha refastened the clip to mirror its partner on the other side of her head.

"Are you sitting in the same spot as last time?" Chuck said. "The way the light fell on you at the last concert, it made your hair look red like your mom's."

"Same spot as always." Sasha swallowed down the lump rising in her throat. The year her mother got sick, an undercurrent of red began burning through Sasha's dark brown hair. Her mother swore the red had always been there, but Sasha remained convinced her love for her mother had manifested itself in the subtle heat of her hair color.

The collar on Sasha's dress scratched her neck every time she turned her head. She stared straight ahead on the drive to the performance hall, keeping her chin up so the itchy fabric did not touch her skin. By the time they arrived, her neck felt stiff, and it hurt to turn her head.

She reached into her backpack and pulled out a small pot of lotion made of honey, beeswax, oil, and rosemary, one of the last jars of lotion her mother had made. The balm would go rancid if she didn't use it up soon, but she still rationed it. She massaged it into her neck and stretched the knotted muscles.

"Did your mom make that?" Chuck asked.

Sasha nodded.

"I miss her too," Chuck said as Sasha got out of the car. He always got misty when he talked about Sasha's mother, his only sibling. "I'll see you inside."

The dissonant sounds of young musicians tuning instruments put Sasha on edge as she entered the auditorium. She unpacked her violin and music and took her seat. She closed her eyes and fine-tuned the strings to the vibrations still resonating in her bones. As her violin quieted, she teased out each individual instrument around her, parsing out which small note each orchestra member attempted. Depending on how far out of tune the instrument drifted, she could usually identify the musician.

Sasha sat in the center of the second violin section, not a standout. She had excellent pitch but unreliable rhythm. Alone, the musicians emitted unconnected chirps and vibrations, but together they assembled something larger than themselves. The buoyancy of the harmonies lifted Sasha out of her seat, carrying her above the acoustically paneled hall, where she could swim in the collective melody. She could never achieve such beauty alone. Nor could she escape the feeling that the music longed to soar beyond the confines of the walls.

The rosemary lotion worked its way into her muscles as she turned her head from side to side to regain her range of motion. She undid the top button on her dress and folded the annoying Peter Pan collar inside the dress so it didn't show. The loose fabric hung like a sack around her wiry frame.

Chuck sat in the front row, an empty seat on either side of him. Her father would never get to hear her play "Flight of the Bumblebee" with the full orchestra. She tried to focus on her anger and disappointment, as the chill of fear tried to creep in. She didn't want to think about what had scared her father so much.

Chuck caught Sasha's eye and half waved, the bright pink carnations glowing on his lap amid a sea of parents cradling roses. At least she had Chuck; despite his awkwardness, she could always count on him.

# Four

The wooden stairs creaked as Sasha tiptoed up from the basement, trying not to draw attention to the basement or herself. She folded her mother's recipes in half and tucked them into the back of her pants, then eased the door open and walked into the kitchen.

"What the hell were you doing down there?" Ian said.

"Just exploring. I like old houses." Sasha's heart pounded so hard it hurt. "Halle said it was okay."

"We didn't invite you into our home so you could go nosing around in our stuff," Ian said.

Gino sat on the warped kitchen counter with Ian in front of him, centered between Gino's knees. Gino draped his arms across Ian's chest from behind, his chin resting on Ian's shoulder, and rolled his eyes at Sasha, indicating she shouldn't take Ian too seriously.

"Got it." Sasha clenched her jaw, fighting the urge to inform Ian that in fact *he* was trespassing in *her* home, not the other way around.

The house had not aged well. Water stains yellowed the ceiling below the spot where the gables intersected above.

Gino followed Sasha's eyes to the ceiling. "You're looking at this all wrong."

"Looking at what wrong?"

"This house. You see an old house in disrepair."

"It *is* an old house in disrepair." Sasha skimmed a fingertip over a curling edge of brittle wallpaper.

"It's dry, for the most part, and kind of warm in the winter. And check out these heat grates." Gino gestured at the wrought-iron filigrees on the floor vents. "They're stunning."

"Here it comes." Ian relaxed his body against Gino's chest and shook his head.

"I'm serious. If you only notice what's failing, I mean, if you spend all your time crying over what's lost and broken, which, yeah, it's a lot, you miss what's still in front of you. Like these kick-ass vents," Gino said.

"Says our resident philosopher who cringes every time a squirrel gets in the attic," Ian said.

"I can find where they're getting inside and seal it. I'm pretty handy." Sasha tried to hold back a smile. Gino appreciated her wrought-iron vents, which made Sasha curious to learn more about him.

"So you said." Ian's playful tone turned sharp again. His scarlet lips and pale skin with ruddy splotches on the cheeks lent Ian the appearance of a child coming in from the cold.

She pulled the saltshaker out of her pocket and handed it to Ian.

He tapped a few grains of salt into his palm, sniffed it, and touched it with his tongue. Sasha waited for a sign of appreciation, but Ian's face remained cold.

"Nice." Gino took the shaker from Ian and tasted a few granules.

"I'm taking the salt to Halle for the rice, but it's yours to keep." She paused a moment, hoping Ian might express some gratitude, but he said nothing and returned the shaker.

Sasha took the salt outside to the fire, where Halle stood with the bottom of one foot pressed against the inner thigh of her other leg. Her skirt and her long hair fluttered in the breeze as wisps of smoke curled around her. Sasha followed Halle's gaze across the fields of swaying grasses.

"We haven't eaten meat in at least a month. Millie and the guys are going to flip over this."

The tightness in Sasha's shoulders eased as her breathing fell into rhythm with the motion of the floppy seed heads and wildflowers in the distance.

"I have salt." Sasha handed the shaker to Halle.

"Holy crap." Halle's face lit up. She had large brown eyes and a narrow face with a sharp jawline. She smiled with her whole face, her eyebrows arching high.

The wind shifted, blowing hickory smoke into Sasha's face.

From where Sasha and Halle stood, the forest screened out the hulking structure of the apiary as if the building did not exist. Sasha needed to go to the apiary, no matter how much it would hurt. But not yet. She could enjoy this meal and get a solid night's sleep first.

Sasha imagined her mother emerging from the forest, her dark red hair framing her face in haphazard spikes. She concentrated, trying to remember her mother's features, but all she could conjure was her angular posture and dusty floral scent. As Sasha stared at the woods, the trees parted and a woman's figure emerged, ducking under a branch. Her heart skipped as the woman straightened and swung her long braid over her shoulder.

Millie.

Sasha drew in a deep breath to calm her racing pulse.

Balancing a bundle of willow branches and an armful of fireweed and grape leaves, Millie walked toward the house and sat on the porch steps. She opened a pocketknife and began stripping bark from the branches in slow, rhythmic movements.

"Is someone sick?" Sasha asked.

"Why would you ask?" Millie continued working without looking up.

"Fireweed's an anti-inflammatory, and willow bark is a natural aspirin. My mom used to make willow bark tea to ease my dad's arthritis."

"Did she? These are for Ian. He's our resident apothecary. I'm helping him build up a stash of medicinals."

"Can I help?" Sasha pulled the pocketknife out of her sock and picked up a willow branch.

"Of course."

"Are those wild grape leaves?"

"The fruit didn't set, but the leaves are delicious. Packed with good vitamins. I'm going to soak them overnight and stuff them tomorrow," Millie said.

Sasha and Millie worked silently until they stripped all the branches. The smell of Halle's dinner wafted over to Sasha, causing her stomach to growl in anticipation of a hot meal.

"Dinner!" Halle shouted, a note of triumph in her voice.

Gino and Ian joined them by the fire as Halle scooped the rice mixture onto plates.

Gino passed a steaming plate to Sasha.

"I can wait. I don't want to take anyone's plate."

"I'll eat mine out of a mug. It tastes the same." Gino held the plate closer to Sasha until she accepted it.

"Damn, Halle," Ian said through a mouthful of food. "What's in this?"

"You want to tell them?" Halle asked Sasha.

"Beef jerky." Sasha tried not to appear too eager to please.

"Fucking brilliant," Gino said.

As Halle walked past to take a seat near the fire, wind whipped her skirt with a muffled snap. The sun-faded floral material fluttered next to Sasha's cheek, stirring a memory of lazy summer mornings lying awake in bed. The curtains. Sasha's eyes stung as she recognized the pattern of hydrangeas, rosebuds, and ivy. The curtain from Sasha's childhood bedroom was wrapped around Halle's waist. Morning sun through that fabric woke Sasha in a lemony puddle of light every morning her first eleven years.

Sasha turned her face from the smoke and blinked away the urge to wrap her arms around Halle's legs.

"I'd like to make a toast." Halle raised her glass of slightly cloudy water.

"Of course you would." Ian raised his glass.

"To an edible meal, and—" Halle paused to build suspense. "And to Sasha's twenty-second birthday!"

Sasha froze, an icy sting rushing through her veins. How could Halle know it was her birthday?

"Did you go through my stuff?"

"You told me you aged out of the system four years ago today, so I did the math. Am I right?" Looking pleased with herself, Halle tilted her glass in Sasha's direction.

"Right." Sasha's hand trembled as she clinked her glass against Halle's.

Before closing her eyes as she lay under the baby grand piano the first night, Sasha rapped her knuckles against the underside of the rosewood frame and held her breath as the echo reverberated in the out-of-tune wires. Under the piano might be one of the only spaces in the house she had never occupied. She prodded at her indignation, but her anger at the interlopers was already waning.

Sometime after midnight, footsteps crept down the hall from the room that had once been her father's office but now served as Millie's bedroom. Sasha pretended to be asleep, but from her nest in the far corner of the room she watched Millie sneak outside, careful not to make any noise. Millie clearly didn't want to wake anyone, either out of courtesy or because she didn't want anyone to follow. Curious, Sasha waited a few minutes and went after her.

Sasha didn't see Millie outside, so she walked toward the path in the woods she had walked hundreds of times between her home and her father's apiary. A nearly full moon offered enough light to see by and enough shadow to hide in.

The towering oaks and firs made her feel small yet part of something immense. Among the trees, Sasha never stood out, but always fit in. She ran her fingertips over the chunky bark of an oak tree. The unique yet familiar folds and gnarls told a story Sasha couldn't quite decipher. Like listening to poetry in another language. The meaning remained elusive, but the lilt, cadence, and tenderness in the bark stirred emotions words couldn't animate.

As her eyes adjusted to the darkness, Sasha scanned the forest for Millie. Ian still made Sasha nervous, and she hadn't figured Halle out yet, but she felt drawn to Gino's enthusiasm and Millie's gentleness.

*Rebuild a family.*

Only hours ago, her only goal was to find the missing documents and leave. Now, drawn in by childhood ghosts and the lure of camaraderie, she was tempted by the prospect of staying.

The trail deposited her on the edge of the meadow leading to the apiary. The hulking frame, expansive enough to house an airplane, loomed over the wildflowers reclaiming the once-gravel driveway. She waded through grasses up to her thighs to get to the metal door of the apiary office. Vines scaled the rust-stained exterior, dripping off the overhang above the door.

Wind sucked on the door, rattling the walls when she pushed it open. A tangle of bittersweet slapped against her cheek.

A film of dust covered everything in the tomb-like office. She tiptoed across the cement floor toward her father's desk, imagining the long-gone books and journals lined up like perfect soldiers.

In the desk drawers, Sasha found a jumble of dried-up pens and loose screws. She walked toward the airlock leading to the apiary, once a sanctuary for millions of honey bees.

The handle gave way without resistance. She stepped inside and the door slammed closed.

The silence inside the airlock chamber bored inside her body, muting the sound of her biology with a stillness so deep her own thoughts felt irreverent and disruptive. Although she couldn't see anything in the pitch black of the windowless chamber, she averted her eyes from the hooks on the wall where her father once kept the clean suit Sasha had refused to wear.

Sasha opened the door on the other side of the airlock and stepped into the apiary. Weak light skimmed through torn shreds of the roof fabric, casting dancing shade on the ground.

It had been so warm, eleven years ago to the day, when she ventured in, unprotected, fuming with rage, the air clotted with humidity and heat generated by hundreds of thousands of beating wings.

The apiary that once swam so thick with bees the air itself appeared to sway, now tasted stale. She walked toward a sugar trough. White ghosts of crystallized sugar collected in frozen waves on the bottom of the tray. The sugar stains reminded her of the patterns sea-foam left behind after waves retreat.

Something brushed against her neck, and she slapped at it, only to realize it was her hair. Her pulse quickened and she pushed back the disjointed memories of the bees, her bees, swarming, stinging, her throat closing. Panic climbing her spine.

*Just breathe.*

She ran to the emergency exit and pushed the door open.

She gulped down the air.

During her father's trial, his lawyer claimed Lawrence kept the last bees as a hobby, and his real data remained at his office. Prosecutors offered to reduce his sentence if he produced the documents he claimed never existed.

But Lawrence Severn stuck to his story: There had never been any data to keep.

Those last bees were pets, he said in open court, which lit up the press. The arrogance. The recklessness. Making pets of the last living bees and allowing them to die.

Or, more accurately, allowing his daughter to kill them.

Her father's secret writhed inside her with mounting urgency. The truth pulsed beneath her feet as she walked away from the apiary into the overgrown field.

The meadow behind the apiary had been lush with wild grasses and flowers when Sasha was young. Now trees and shrubs asserted themselves, clawing the land back into the hollowed-out forest. She waded through the grass, the brush of crisp, thirsty stalks swishing against her legs like a memory. Familiar, if a bit uncomfortable.

She walked toward the remnants of her grandparents' apple orchard. Two trees remained, both bent toward the ground like gnarled hags in the moonlight.

Sasha stood between the two trees and began counting her steps forward in the direction of the apiary. One, two, three. By her eighth step, she caught a glimpse of Millie standing at the edge of the forest watching her.

Maybe the wooden door to the storm cellar had melted into the ground, absorbed by the earth. Gone. Along with anything her father left behind.

Sasha pretended not to see Millie. When she got to the fourteenth stride, the ground changed from the cushion of dried soil and grass underfoot to the muffled reverberation of a buried wooden door. Her heart pounded and her fingers buzzed as she fought the urge to drop to her knees and scratch her way into the underground bunker.

Her father's bunker remained undisturbed, but under Millie's eyes, Sasha forced herself to keep walking without pause.

# Five

After Sasha had given up her seat in the orchestra, a year and a half earlier, she had shrouded her metronome with a grass-green scarf, the one her mother wore after her hair began falling out.

With concentration and patience, she could mimic rhythm with the tick of the pendulum or the flick of a conductor's baton, but left on her own, Sasha never retained the meter.

Liberating herself from the tick, tick, tick of someone else's pre-determined pattern, from the controlled acoustics of the concert hall, made her fingers itch to play her way. She wanted something different from her violin.

Sunlight shimmered through the green scarf with a cheerful burst of color, as if affirming she no longer needed mechanical su-pervision to tell her what to do and when. With her violin case in hand, she crept down the stairs and out the door.

She ran through the overgrown field where her mother once grew strawberries. The violin case thumped against her thigh and morning dew soaked her canvas sneakers. She clambered over the fieldstone wall and slipped into the woods, still shadowy in the slant morning sun.

She followed the sound of the creek, exuberant with spring melt. Water slapped against the mossy rocks, higher than at any point for the rest of the season, yet lower than the preceding years.

On the bank, she opened her violin case and dragged her bow

over a block of rosin, releasing a cloud of pine tar and beeswax into the forest.

With the violin and bow in hand, she leaped from rock to rock until she reached a broad flat stone in the middle of the creek, where she sat cross-legged on the damp moss.

Her perfect G danced against the rushing water. She played the harmonies of her second violin part to "Flight of the Bumblebee," partnering with the melody of the creek and the chattering leaves.

This was what music wanted. Wild sound waves roaming the universe, free of itchy collars, acoustic panels, and metronomes. A flush of bright purple fireweed grew along the edge of the creek, hosting three honey bees bobbing from flower to flower in time with Sasha's music. When she stopped playing, the bees flew off.

Sasha lay on her back on the rock and stared up at the clouds visible between the crown-shy umbrellas of oaks and maples. She closed her eyes and listened to the forest the way a conductor would an orchestra.

She conducted the forest with a swoop of her bow, cueing the flute of birds, and the rush of wind to stir the leaves like a papery glockenspiel.

Her violin lay on her chest, rising and falling as she breathed in the music of the forest.

"Sasha!" her father's distant voice interrupted her music. "I have a project."

*A project.* Her father's way of saying he needed her to do something she wouldn't want to do. She remained on her back staring up at the sky. His project could wait a few minutes. She closed her eyes to listen to the rush of water carving through the rocky creek bed.

A loud clang jolted her up, almost knocking her violin into the water. Her father never rang the bell in the old barn, but she had heard stories about her grandfather using it to sound the alarm when coyotes roamed among the sheep or when a twister appeared on the horizon.

That bell signaled an emergency.

Sasha tossed her violin in the case and sprinted toward the sound. Her father could be hurt, or the house might be on fire.

Breathless, she dropped her violin case on the porch in front of her father, who paced back and forth without acknowledging her.

"What's wrong?" she panted.

"We're moving a bunch of hives today." Dark circles drooped under his puffy eyes. He furrowed his brow when he saw her violin case but didn't ask any questions.

"That's the emergency?"

He ignored her and walked toward the box hives arranged in a circle under the east-facing side of the enormous oak tree that dominated the front yard.

"You're moving *my* hives? No way." She kicked a spool of mesh fabric on the ground.

"The bees aren't going to like this. I don't want you getting stung." He handed her a veil and gloves, although he didn't wear any himself.

"I won't move them. They need to be near me. Plus, my bees would never sting me." Sasha crossed her arms and refused the protective gear, which she considered offensive. Despite having grown up surrounded by millions of bees, she had yet to be stung even once.

"I'm not asking you. I'm telling you. We don't have time for this."

Sasha bit the inside of her cheek and put on the gloves and veil.

She helped him unroll the mesh and cut it into long strips, which they laid out on the ground. He tried to light a match for the smoker, but his clumsy fingers couldn't hold the matchstick. Still angry, Sasha grabbed the matches, and in one resentful strike she lit the match and the smoker.

Without a grunt of thanks, her father took the sooty box and blew into it until the puffs of smoke rose around him. He marched over to the hives and started with Sasha's favorite.

"Not that one." She ran over to stand between her father and the hive.

"We're moving them all." He puffed smoke around the hive, lulling the bees into a stupor.

Sasha had gotten used to the sadness and worry in her father's eyes, but the fear quivering in his hands terrified her. He rubbed his knuckles but couldn't mask the trembling.

They should wait until dusk, when the bees settled in the hive.

They wrapped her hive in the mesh fabric, blocking the entrance but allowing airflow. After a few minutes, the bees roused from their smoke-induced trance with mounting panic. They didn't understand she wanted to help them.

Sasha knelt next to her hive and pressed her face to the wood. "It's okay," she whispered. "It's going to be okay."

They smoked all six hives and wrapped the openings with the mesh fabric to keep the bees inside. Her father began shifting them one by one onto a trolley and rolling them up a ramp to the bed of Thunderbolt, his beloved rusty old pickup truck.

Bees gathered pollen and nectar this time of day. What would the foragers do when they returned to find their home gone? They'd be lost. Alone without their family. The smoke made her nauseous, but she continued working.

"Where are we taking them?" she asked as her father closed the tailgate with the last of Sasha's hives on board.

"Do you want to drive?" He often let Sasha drive the truck on the long driveway between the apiary and the house. Part of her wanted to deny her father the satisfaction of appeasing her, but she never passed up a chance to get behind the wheel.

*Driving a stick shift is a lost art,* he told her every time. *They don't make them anymore.* She didn't know anyone who owned a gasoline-fueled vehicle, let alone a stick shift. Every time Thunderbolt chugged out a cloud of black smoke when her father dropped her off at school, she cringed from humiliation. But, like her father, she loved the old clunker.

Sasha climbed into the driver's seat and sat on the edge so she could reach the pedals.

"We're taking them into the woods."

"Why?"

"We're protecting them. That's all you need to know."

They inched down the rutted driveway, trying not to jostle the hives any more than necessary, then drove around the barn on the tractor-access trail toward the edge of the forest.

Dark clouds gathered. They needed rain, but not now. The stranded bees would have nowhere to hide, their papery wings useless in a downpour.

They rolled the hives one by one off the truck. Her father moved a watermelon-size rock from the fieldstone wall on the edge of the forest. They deconstructed the wall, one stone at a time, until they created an opening to carry the hives through.

Wind kicked up leaves, and the temperature dropped several degrees. Sasha walked past each box and placed both hands on the cover, willing them to be safe. *Be still, little bees. Be brave.*

Her father maneuvered the first box about fifty yards into the forest. He dragged the box another few feet and turned to angle the opening eastward.

"That won't work in the winter." She pointed to a pine bough, strong enough to hold thick snow, which had been falling in fewer but heavier dumps in recent years. The branch would cradle the snow until it became too heavy, and the dense snow would pour down on the hive. Her father's eyes followed Sasha's up to the branch, and he nodded.

He surveyed the clearing, his eyes lingering on a spot protected by a boulder without any boughs overhead. He tilted his head in the direction of the boulder and raised his eyebrows.

Sasha nodded.

It took hours to rehome all six hives on safe, level ground. They camouflaged the boxes with branches and leaves, making sure the opening to each hive faced east without any obstructions.

When they finished, they replaced the stones and scattered leaves and twigs over the top and into the cracks to conceal the disturbance to the wall.

"They're going to be coming for my bees. I don't know when,

but I won't be able to stop them." Her father sat on the stone wall and rubbed his knuckles on one hand, then the other.

"Who would take our bees?"

"You know bees are dying in the wild."

"But ours aren't."

"The government wants all the remaining colonies taken to indoor managed facilities to protect them from environmental contaminants."

"That's bullshit." She had never cursed in front of her father before.

He turned his head away, but Sasha saw the corner of his mouth turn upward in appreciation of her outrage.

"I don't have a choice. Ours are the last known bees in North America. I'll still be overseeing their care, but they'll be indoors at a managed facility where teams of scientists can study them, protect them."

"Our bees don't want to live indoors." Her hives needed open territory to forage, they needed fresh air.

"When they come, they'll confiscate all the bees inside our apiary."

Sasha withdrew the curses she had been silently hurling at her father. She crouched down and put her hands on the ground, spreading her fingers out. Her father steadied himself against the stone wall and with slow, painful movements lowered himself to join Sasha. He pressed his hands to the earth next to hers, his fingers burrowing into the soil like twisted roots of an ancient tree.

"But they won't know to search for *your* bees." His chin quivered as he looked over his shoulder at the woods.

# Six

By the fifth morning, Sasha began to see patterns in the rhythm of the squatters' life on the farm. Despite her regular nighttime excursions, Millie woke before anyone else and started a fire in the pit out front, setting a kettle of water on the grate for everyone else. Ian came down next and fanned open a small block of solar panels to charge his phone, the only cell phone among them.

Halle came down next, made a cup of tea, and drew with nubs of charcoal pencils on the wall opposite the fireplace.

The smudgy mural depicted the farmhouse, the big oak tree, and the fields. Figures Sasha interpreted as Ian and Gino sat on the porch stairs, while a woman who resembled Halle lounged on the porch swing. The black lines captured warmth and tenderness. The way Gino rested his head on Ian's shoulder. The ease with which Halle's hand draped over the side of the porch to touch the lavender.

As Sasha lay under the piano, pretending to be asleep so she wouldn't disturb Halle's drawing time, she hoped to see her own likeness appear on the wall. This was her home, not theirs. Her mood twisted from a longing to be one of them to a rage that they could be so comfortable in the house her grandfather built, while Sasha, the rightful heir, slept under a piano.

She rolled over and scooched further down into her sleeping bag.

"Sorry I woke you." Halle crouched down to see Sasha.

Sunlight pouring in through the window behind Halle highlighted all the untamed curls she hadn't bothered to smooth out since waking up. She wore a different piece of paisley fabric tied around her waist, over a navy-blue tank top.

"Are you going to paint it?" Sasha stretched, reluctant to emerge from her cocoon.

Halle tilted her head to one side to see the mural from Sasha's horizontal perspective. "I would if I had paint. But for now, black-and-white will have to do. Come sit in the sun and have tea with me."

Sasha crawled out of her sleeping bag and followed Halle outside as Gino came down the stairs rubbing sleep out of his eyes.

"Any other odd jobs you need taken care of?" Sasha asked as she poured hot water over a tea bag Halle had already used.

"You could get the wind turbine working so we'd have power." Ian squinted at the rickety tower Sasha's father had rigged up decades ago as one of his many backup plans.

"I can try."

"I was kidding. You actually know how?"

"Maybe. No promises." Sasha had spent hours working on that turbine with her father, and tinkering with its twin, an identical turbine at the cabin her mother's family used to own. Or maybe they still owned. She hadn't spoken to her uncle Chuck in a decade. "I'll look at it this afternoon if I have time."

"You have other plans?" Gino asked.

"Not really." She had waited several days to get a feel for the schedules around the farm. While Gino collected firewood, Ian would read medical texts in the afternoon. Halle did yoga or knitted, and Millie, probably tired from her midnight walks, always took a late-morning nap, her defense against the hunger gnawing on them all. During the day, they each did what they could to avoid thinking about food until their evening meal together. Sasha hadn't eaten since the previous night's dinner and wouldn't again for hours.

The remoteness of the farm offered them escape from the insecurity of life in more populated areas, but the lack of jobs and money presented the risk of starvation. Sasha wasn't ready to give up her secret stash in the larder, but in a few days, they would be out of food, and she wouldn't have a choice.

"What will we do after the rice and beans run out?" Sasha floated the use of "we" to see if anyone objected to her presumption she would still be around.

"The day after tomorrow's distribution day. You're coming with us. The more people we have, the more rations they give us," Ian said.

"What rations?"

"The state brings trucks in every other week and distributes dry goods. I thought you knew." Halle touched her arm. "Oh, God, were you worried?"

Sasha resisted the instinct to pull away. Something about Halle's touch reminded her of her mother. Light but warm. Reassuring, but not coddling.

Sasha wanted to ask what would happen if they forced her to leave after seven days. Did Ian intend to keep her share of the rations? What if she challenged them and refused to leave? She could lay claim to the house, throw Ian and Gino's stuff out the window and reclaim her parents' room.

But that wasn't what she wanted.

She yearned for them to want her to stay. Even if it meant sleeping under the piano.

After everyone dispersed, Sasha went inside and waited to hear Millie settle into her room for her nap.

She picked up her violin case, snuck out the back door, and headed toward the woods. Her fingers ached to press on the strings so the vibrations would drown out the phantom buzz humming almost constantly since she arrived at the farm.

A long-dormant spring reentered her step as she walked faster, over the familiar earth, anxious to get to the creek, as if it might not be there unless she hurried. On a rock surrounded by rushing water had always been her favorite place to play music, the oaks, maples, birch, and hemlocks, the rocks, and the camouflaged creatures her audience.

Cool water churned over stones, filling the air with a familiar aroma of minerals and moss, the smell of her tears after her mother's funeral. The spot she ran to after fights with her father. The consistency of the water soothed her, hypnotized her until her breath steadied and her heartbeat eased into sync with the breath of the trees.

Sasha leaped from the largest boulder at the edge of the water and bounced to a broad flat rock, around which the water parted like curtains on a stage. Her stage, the only one she ever felt entirely comfortable on. She tightened the horse hairs strung on the bow and drew it across the dwindling block of rosin, her last block. The friction sent a puff of particles into the breeze, returning the pine tar and beeswax home.

A colony of pale purple echinacea grew around the base of an oak tree, flanked by a cluster of fireweed poking out between rocks along the bank, reminding Sasha, with a flash, of the carnations Chuck gave her at her final concert. She made a mental note to collect some fireweed leaves and echinacea blossoms for Ian before heading back to the house.

She cracked her neck and gripped the violin between her chin and shoulder so she could draw her bow with one hand and adjust the tuner with the other. Would the trees remember her? Would they judge her playing? The muscles in her neck felt as tightly drawn as the strings on her instrument.

As she adjusted the strings and the notes fell into tune, the buzzing in her fingers melted into the music. The low notes resonated in her rib cage, warming her from the inside. The song, the same song she always played, the second violin part in "Flight of the Bumblebee," filled the forest and her audience fell silent. The music trembled in the mossy rock holding her body up and in the shuddering leaves overhead.

Something moved in her peripheral vision, and she shifted her

The Last Beekeeper     45

position to see a flutter near the fireweed. The flicker hovered over a flower and bounced to another blossom. Sasha played louder, willing the vision to disperse itself, but the bee seemed to be enjoying the music. It settled onto a flower and crawled inside to suck the nectar.

No. Like the buzzing in her fingers, she imagined the bee, a manifestation of her grief and guilt.

The bee rose out of the flower and flew toward Sasha, as the music continued pouring out of her instrument, muscle memory guiding her fingers as her mind spun. She pleaded with her quivering muscles to still themselves as flashbacks of twenty-eight tiny, venomous daggers pricked her with the memory of EpiPens stabbing into her thighs.

*Be still. Just breathe.*

The impossible bee landed on the rock next to her bare thigh.

This could not be her legacy. Killed by an insect that did not exist. A creature Sasha herself had destroyed.

No. She imagined the bee, a ghost of all she had taken away from her father, and all he had taken away from her.

Her bow screeched on the strings and a twig snapped nearby. She turned in the direction of the noise and the bee rose up to hover in front of her face. She flinched and shifted backward on the stone, knocking the block of rosin into the water.

"No," she shouted, as the wooden box fell into the moving water, the last of her rosin bobbing and crashing against rocks. "No, no, no!"

Gino jumped out from behind an oak tree and splashed into the water, chasing the rosin as it spun. He slipped on the wet stones, falling into the water, but continuing until he stood up with an arm over his head.

"I got it!" Gino splashed his way back through churning knee-deep water and sat next to Sasha on her rock. He handed her the rosin, wet, but intact.

Sasha held the wood case to her face, breathing in the soothing smell.

"Can I?" Gino held his hand out and she gave him the box.

"What does this mean to you?" he asked as he sniffed the box.

"It's just." Sasha didn't know how to explain that the smell of rosin had driven out her fears at night in the state home. The smell of the forest. "It's my childhood."

She immediately felt foolish.

"I get it." Gino peeled off his soaked T-shirt and wrung the water out. "You don't have to hide in the woods, but I get it if you want some privacy. Music's personal."

"Did you follow me here?"

Gino scrunched his eyes closed and wrinkled his nose. "I saw you running toward the woods with a violin case, and well, I'm nosy."

"Thanks for jumping in after the rosin. It's silly, but it's important to me." Sasha scanned the air for any sign of the imaginary bee, but it had evaporated in the wind.

Gino balled up the wet shirt and dabbed at a cut on his shin from where he fell.

"Shit, are you okay? Here, let me do it." Sasha laid her violin in its case and took the shirt to clean Gino's wound, a minor scrape. Her eyes stopped on a thick, purple scar on Gino's side. She averted her eyes.

"Go ahead, you can ask."

"It's none of my business."

"But now you're curious, aren't you?" Gino leaned toward Sasha, daring her to ask.

"Maybe a little."

"A lion mauled me."

"Right."

"Ask anyone. I trained lions in the circus before the world fell apart."

"What really happened?"

"What are you thinking long-term?" Gino dipped his bloody

shirt in the water and wrung it until it rinsed clear. "You came here because you ran out of water. Now what?"

Sasha's pulse quickened. She had been waiting for one of them to suggest she should move on. In two days, the week she had paid for would end, and she still hadn't found a safe time to dig for her father's papers.

"I don't know yet." She closed the latch on her violin case and stood up. "Want to go foraging with me?"

"Foraging?" Gino twisted his face with distaste.

"Foraging. Let's go see what we can dig up in these fields."

# Seven

Gino followed her toward the once-contaminated field her mother used to plant. Sasha rambled through the tall grasses, concentrating on the different colors and shapes of leaves.

"What are we looking for?" Gino asked.

"This used to be a farm. Vegetables go to seed. Who knows, maybe some survived. But only pick from the upper edges of the field, near the woods." Sasha imagined the descendants of the vegetables her mother had planted coming back on their own, season after season, going to seed and fighting for soil and light and water.

Finding stragglers after all these years would be a sign, an indication she was meant to be there sharing the fruits of her mother's long-ago labors with these new friends. As a little girl, Sasha swore that food from her mother's fields tasted better than any other vegetables. Her mouth watered as she searched.

"Why not from the field?"

"Toxic soil. Anything growing up on the hill above the fields wouldn't catch the runoff, so it's safe."

Sasha surveyed the field. Shrubs and small trees popped up among the wild grasses, belying the poisons in the soil. The field folded down the hill to the edge of a forest tumbling into the valley. The wide flat valley had been mostly forested, with stretches cleared for soybean and corn belonging to a corporate farm Sasha's parents hated. Now the valley floor was almost entirely cleared, with a massive construction project underway several miles in the distance.

"What's going on down there?" Sasha asked.

"We've heard rumors it's a campus for an Agri New Deal project, probably one of the greenhouse projects."

"Great." Sasha grimaced at the idea of thousands of people flocking to the area. She scanned the grasses for anything edible or for the flit of a tiny insect. "What do you make of people claiming to see bees?"

"Oh, geez, you are one of those pilgrims, aren't you? Fuck. I swore to Ian you weren't."

"I'm not. I'm just curious about what you think."

"We have wackos show up all the time, swearing they saw a bee, so they made the pilgrimage to the home of the Last Beekeeper. They talk about him like he was some martyr, not a traitor who is rotting in jail."

Gino's words pricked at her skin. Her father was not a traitor. He might not have been the most attentive father, he might have abandoned her when she needed him, but he loved those bees and would have done anything to protect them.

"A word of advice: Do *not* ask about bees in front of Ian. If people keep coming here and claiming they see bees, eventually one of them will report a sighting. Then they'll get arrested, or at least investigated. And if the investigation brings authorities back to this farm, we'll get evicted for squatting illegally. Any mention of bees is a reminder this lovely little home we've made for ourselves could be yanked away at any minute."

"But hypothetically, wouldn't it be spectacular if bees did exist? We've changed so much in the last decade. We banned the ag chemicals killing insects. I mean, look around you." She swept her arm toward the field. "The end of monoculture agriculture—"

"You mean the end of agriculture."

"No. It's not the end. The land is healing itself. We've nearly eliminated fossil fuel use. Twenty years ago, that seemed inconceivable.

What if? I mean, don't you ever wonder? What if some bees survived? What if conditions improved and they came back?"

"Sasha." Gino looked sad on her behalf. "They're gone. And if you're hoping to stay here beyond tomorrow, I suggest you never bring this up again."

"How long have you and Ian been together?"

"Two years. We met at a camp. Super romantic."

Sasha liked being near Gino because he reminded her that happiness still existed. She fought the urge to skip as they talked.

"Tell me about it. I need a good love story."

"I got sick at the camp, and Ian helped me. I woke up staring up at those blue eyes of his. I'm a total stereotype, I know. The patient who falls for the doctor."

"Ian's a doctor?"

"Not officially, but he's the closest we have."

"What about Halle? Did you meet her in the camp too?"

"Yeah, she attached herself to us a few months after Ian and I got together. We couldn't shake her for anything." Gino laughed. "Believe me. We tried."

"Are you trying to shake me?"

"Undecided. It depends on how much food you *forage* up for dinner." Gino added air quotes around "forage."

"Just wait." Sasha intended to contribute more than she withdrew. She wanted to fit into this mismatched family almost as much as she wanted to understand her own family's secrets. "Are you going to make Millie leave?"

"Millie's Millie. It's like having my mom around. And honestly, I don't think anything could make her leave if she didn't want to. She's stronger than all of us."

Gino whistled a complicated melody as they walked. The notes rang clear and sharp, like a bold stroke of color on a blank canvas. Sasha walked a few paces behind him, allowing the notes to rise above him and rain down on her.

He turned around and walked backward in front of Sasha, the

muscles in his cheeks, jaw, and forehead tensing and quieting to animate the music coming from his lips.

"You have perfect pitch," Sasha said when he stopped.

"You would know." Gino continued walking up the hill.

"Know what?"

"Perfect pitch. I heard you tuning your violin in the woods. Damn near perfect pitch. How come you only play harmonies?"

"It's what I know."

"I get it. The world needs more harmonies."

"I don't play for the world. I play for me. Besides, I have a horrible sense of rhythm."

"This is true. I, on the other hand, have fabulous rhythm. Let me go with you next time you sneak off into the woods. I'll help."

"I don't think so." Sasha turned her back to Gino so he wouldn't see her smile. If he intended to join her in the future, maybe he wanted her to stay.

He fell in step next to her. "Come on. Let me be your metronome."

"Okay fine, but don't expect much."

"Yes!" Gino pumped his fist.

"Are you a musician?"

"I was a professional whistler, but it's a competitive racket, so I retired."

"I thought you tamed lions."

"I have many talents."

Gino started whistling again and continued up the hill.

Sasha recognized the yellowing leaves of potato plants along the edge of the forest and sprinted up the hill.

"Grab here." She positioned Gino's hands around the stalks of a potato plant. "When I count to three, we both yank them up."

"What is it?"

"One, two, three!"

They both pulled their plants up to expose two clusters of brown potatoes, nine in all.

"Potatoes!" Gino threw his arms around Sasha and squeezed

hard. The warmth of another body against hers shook loose a sob she didn't feel coming. No one had hugged her for so long her body forgot how to respond. She wanted to return the embrace, but her arms wouldn't move. She choked trying to hold back another wet sob.

"Hey, what's going on?" Gino pulled back to see her face. "Are you okay?"

Sasha shook her head and sat down with the potatoes on her lap.

"What just happened?"

Embarrassed, Sasha wiped her face and tried to steady her breathing. "I'm fine."

"You don't look fine."

"I don't have anywhere to go at the end of the week. I can pay you more money." Sasha watched a rabbit dart into the poisoned field.

Gino sat down next to her and wrapped both arms around her. "One day at a time. But I feel pretty confident those potatoes will earn you at least another day or two."

Within an hour, they gathered an armful of overgrown asparagus stalks, three onions, nine small potatoes, a few garlic bulbs, and bunches of dandelion greens.

"Halle's going to freak when she sees this." Gino sniffed the asparagus.

Ian, Halle, and Millie were sitting on the porch stairs talking when Gino and Sasha approached with armloads of fresh vegetables.

"Where the hell did you get that?" Ian jumped up.

"Sasha, it seems, has a talent for foraging," Gino said.

"If you get a fire started, I'll make dinner tonight," Sasha said.

"Thank God. It's Halle's night again," Gino said.

Halle kicked Gino on her way over to light the fire.

"You guys stay out here while I prep dinner," Sasha said.

"No argument from me. Foraging is exhausting work," Gino said.

"Do you need any help?" Millie asked.

"I'd like to cook by myself if that's okay." Sasha enjoyed Millie's company, but she wanted to be alone with her mother's vegetables in her mother's kitchen.

Millie nodded in a way that let Sasha know Millie understood Sasha wanted to impress the others.

With everyone else outside, Sasha snuck down to the larder and scooped two cupfuls of lentils and a few bouillon cubes she hoped might still have flavor.

After filling the stockpot with ten inches of water, she chopped the asparagus, onions, garlic, and potatoes and dropped them in the water with the bouillon and lentils. She finished it off with several fistfuls of parsley, rosemary, and thyme from the overgrown herb garden and added a few shakes of salt and pepper.

"Fire's ready when you are." Halle came inside as Sasha finished prepping the meal. Halle tried to peek in the pot, but Sasha blocked her view. "So, what are we eating?"

"It's a surprise." Sasha didn't want to overplay the meal, although she hoped they would like it. She needed them to be impressed.

They sat around the fire as the sun dipped lower in the sky, laughing about Sasha and Gino crawling around in the dirt hunting for onions. Ian lay with his head on Gino's lap while Gino raked his fingers through Ian's shaggy hair.

Halle lay on her stomach, propped up on her elbows, chin cupped in her hands. The light flickered in her dark eyes reflecting the glow of the flames. Sasha wanted to know more about her new acquaintances but didn't want to expose herself to their questions. Who had they been before the Collapse? How had they all ended up in this place? And most important, could she trust them?

"If you could do anything, be anyone, what would you choose?" Sasha asked as the stew simmered. "If you could go back to school, have any job in the world?"

Halle poked at the fire with a stick. "I'd take Beatrix and run off to Ecuador. We went there when she was a baby, to visit my father's family. They live in a tiny village in the Andes. It took forever to get there. Beatrix screamed the whole way. I complained they didn't have internet. My grandmother grew tons of food in her garden. She would take me with her to walk to the foot of a volcano every morning and leave her cow to graze with all these other cows. In the evening we'd go back to bring her home. They had fresh milk. They kept pigs and chickens too. I thought they were backward. I wanted to get back here the entire time."

"So why do you want to go back?" Ian asked.

"Because when everything went to shit, my grandmother kept growing food in her garden and walking her cow to that volcano. They didn't take more than they needed. Everyone grazed their animals on communal land and took care of each other. I used to think a volcano was the most dangerous place in the world to live. I couldn't figure out why anyone would choose to stay there. Now I'd give anything to take Bea back there. I'd paint that gorgeous volcano every single day."

"Sounds amazing," Sasha said.

"I haven't heard from my grandmother since their grid went down the first time. I sent letters for years, but I don't have a return address. I choose to believe they are still living the same life I remember. But the truth is, even if I heard from my grandmother, I'd never be able to get there. You have to be a millionaire to fly and hitching my way to South America with Bea isn't an option."

Halle poked at the fire, sending a burst of orange sparks skyward.

"How about you, Sasha?" Ian asked.

A flutter of hope stirred in Sasha's gut every time Ian initiated conversation with her. If she could win him over, the others would let her stay.

"I always wanted to be a farmer. With chickens. I'd grow tons of food, and I wouldn't have to pollinate anything by hand. In my fantasy, the bees do all the work."

"Oh, the bees. It all sounds lovely." Millie sat cross-legged a few feet from the fire and unbraided her hair as they talked. Dark streaks gave way to varying shades of silvery gray as her hair unfurled in gentle waves. Millie combed through it with her fingers and rebraided it.

"My parents used to take me into the mountains to a cabin my mom's family owned," Sasha said. "My dad called it the Backup Plan because it was so remote and off the grid. If the world fell apart, we could escape to live in there. We picked berries, apples, and hazelnuts. Everything smelled like woodsmoke from the cookstove. We couldn't get a cell signal, but we had a ham radio and we used to get on it for hours and chat up truckers passing through the region. I haven't been in years, but I swear I remember every turn on the long ride there, every rock, every tree, even the angle of the sun hitting the mountainside. If I could do anything, I'd go to the Backup Plan and start my own homestead."

"How come you didn't go there when everything collapsed?" Ian asked.

"My dad had a falling-out with my mom's family, so we stopped going after my mom died." Sasha left out the part about her father being in prison. "Now it's just a pleasant memory."

"Where's your dad?" Gino asked.

"I haven't talked to him in, well, in forever. I'm on my own."

"Do you think you'll ever see him again?" Millie asked.

"I don't know. He's the only family I have left, other than my mom's brother, but I don't talk to him either." Sasha wished she hadn't mentioned her parents. "How about you, Ian? What would you do?"

"Ian wants to be a doctor," Halle and Gino said simultaneously.

"I would have been, but after the Collapse, some wacko conned my parents into joining a cult. They gave him all their money, including my college money. I lived on the commune with them for a few years, but when I turned sixteen and wouldn't commit to turning over any money I made to the cult leader, my parents told me I had to choose: worldly possessions or salvation. I said, 'Fuck salvation.' They won't talk to me now. I trained as an EMT, or at least I made it most of the way through training. I couldn't afford to finish, but I'll go back one day."

Sasha crawled over to the fire, moved the pot of soup to the edge of the circle, and folded the dandelion greens in to wilt.

"Gino?" Sasha said.

"I'd return to being an explosives expert for the military. Free-lance, of course. Or I'd go back to my true calling, being a champagne taster. I have a very discerning palate."

Halle rolled her eyes.

"What? It's not like the two are mutually exclusive," Gino said. "Don't be so judgy."

"How about you, Millie," Ian said.

Millie continued braiding her hair and stared into the fire. "I wish I'd been a better mother. I hope to set things right one day."

No one said anything for a while as they all stared at the fire, watching their what-ifs rise with the sparks in the night.

Sasha sent up a silent thanks to her father for being a prepper. She hugged her knees closer to her chest, trying to keep her expectations in check. The smell of bubbling stew teased of another life, either ahead of her or behind her, Sasha couldn't decide.

Sasha ladled stew into mugs and handed them out. The earthy aroma filled her with hope. An air pocket in one of the logs crackled and burst, sending a spray of sparks up into the night air.

"Are these lentils?" Halle held a spoonful close to her face to examine the soup. "Have you had these all this time?"

"It takes time to build trust," Millie said, still staring into the fire.

"Damn, this is outstanding." Gino slurped up a mouthful, waving his hand in front of his face as he burned his tongue. "It tastes like . . ." He let his sentence trail off unfinished.

"Home," Millie said. "It tastes like home."

Gino continued staring into the fire. His spoon fell from his fingers into the dirt.

"Gino?" Ian put his soup down and crawled over to his partner. "Hey, Gino, can you hear me?"

"Shit." Halle jumped up and pulled her sweater over her head.

Gino's mug fell from his hand, splattering hot soup on Ian, who didn't react to the burn. Gino's eyes fluttered and he didn't respond to Ian, his arms tensed, folding close to his chest, his fingers curling into rigid claws. Halle and Ian worked together to transition Gino from the rock where he had been sitting to lie on his back on the ground. His body stiffened and jerked as if being shocked by electricity.

Sasha put her food down and started to crawl toward them, but Millie grabbed her arm and held her back. "It's okay. He's having a seizure. Ian knows what to do."

"We're here," Halle said as she rubbed Gino's arm. "We're here."

Ian wiped drool from Gino's cheek and stroked his hair as the tremors quieted. After about two minutes, which felt like an hour, Gino's body stilled, but he did not open his eyes.

Without speaking to each other, Halle and Ian rolled Gino to one side, placing Halle's sweater under his head and positioning his top arm to fall across his body with his hand under his cheek. Ian pulled Gino's top leg forward to angle his body so he lay on his side, leaning slightly forward.

"Is he going to be okay?" Sasha asked.

"For now, he'll be fine." Ian knelt on the ground and rubbed Gino's back. "That was a long one. Second time this month. He needs to get back on anti-seizure medication."

"Why isn't he on it now?" Sasha asked.

"We can't afford it," Halle said.

"We need to find work. We can't keep living off government handouts and foraged food. This isn't a life." Ian rocked back and forth as he spoke. Another air pocket in one of the logs exploded with a loud crack as it sent a plume of sparks into the air. "We're in a fucking holding pattern and it's killing him."

Gino opened his eyes and looked up at Ian.

"How bad was it?" Gino asked.

Ian lay down on the ground facing Gino. He took both of Gino's hands in his, brought them to his face, and kissed them. "Nothing we can't handle."

# Eight

Sasha sat on the porch steps her sixth morning on the farm, watching the sky morph from pale yellow to a tangerine glow above the treetops. Millie had already built a fire, heated a pot of water, and disappeared on her morning walk. Sasha poured water over wild mint leaves and held the mug to her face so the steam rose around her cheeks and warmed the tip of her nose.

Wind moved through the big oak tree, swaying the chain supporting her tire swing, more of an oval now than a circle after years of sun, heat, and gravity distorting its shape. The air felt unnaturally flat compared to the riot of chirping warblers and the bubbly trill of killdeer that once colored mornings on the farm. Her mother's favorite, the veery, had vanished years earlier as the insect population plummeted.

Queen Anne's lace intermingled with the lavender next to the porch stairs. Her father would have yanked out the Queen Anne's lace, whose nectar tainted honey by adding a whiff of body odor that overpowered the floral notes.

She closed her eyes to squeeze the image of the bee out of her mind. Her father would be ashamed of her for losing herself to hallucinations. *Think like a scientist,* he always told her. Sasha's stomach knotted as she remembered his parole hearing was scheduled to start in a few weeks and she still hadn't searched for the missing documents.

She needed more time.

The longer she spent with this found family of squatters, the more she longed to stay with them. Her whole adult life had been dedicated to finding the truth. But digging up the evidence, possibly exposing her family history to her housemates, would likely destroy her chance to stay.

The idea of her new friends knowing about her father made Sasha's pulse bounce. Living in anonymity for the first time freed her from the constant judgment of others. She couldn't give that up.

Sasha absentmindedly took a sip of her tea. The hot liquid seared her tongue, and she spit it out.

With no one around, she decided to peek under the porch and check if the pump still worked. She put her mug on the porch stairs and crawled on her knees through the overgrown lavender and weeds. She pulled a tangle of vines off the latticework door and wiggled the rusted latch back and forth until it released, and the panel creaked open.

The pump appeared intact, but would it work? The cold metal handle covered in chipped green paint fit in her hand exactly the way she remembered.

She tugged on the handle, but weather, wind, rust, and dirt fixed the lever in place, leaving only a few millimeters of wiggle. Pumping it up and down for several minutes, she created enough give to convince her she could get the water flowing, as long as the water table hadn't dropped too far.

The creak of the pump reminded her of fetching water at the Backup Plan cabin. Did the cabin still exist? Did Chuck still own it? She pictured herself skinny-dipping in the river, floating on her back with the sun warming her naked little-girl body as she listened to the rat-a-tat-tat of woodpeckers.

She knelt on one knee, using the other foot for leverage, and rocked the handle up and down, gaining more range of motion with each pump. Again and again, she pulled the lever until air sputtered in the pipe, and a burst of cloudy water gushed out.

With each gritty, stuttered motion, the water ran a bit clearer. Mud soaked her shoes and pants. The air hung heavy with the scent of lavender as she emerged from under the porch. Right after her mother died, Sasha's father tended the lavender with attentive care, but work soon distracted him. Left alone, the lavender, like Sasha, survived on its own.

She and her father could have had so many more wonderful years in this house if he had agreed to give up the documents he claimed did not exist. Her anger, once again, morphed into festering resentment. Why hadn't he turned over information that would have cleared him? How could the contents have been worse than going to prison for twenty-five years and leaving his motherless daughter alone?

She had a right to know why her childhood had been disposable to the person she loved most.

A long-handled shovel, possibly once belonging to her family, leaned against the house. She ran one hand up and down the well-worn wood searching for something familiar in the smooth grain.

Even if it meant jeopardizing her chance to stay with Halle, Gino, Ian, and Millie, she needed to know what hid in the bunker. She picked up the tool and walked toward the path leading to the apiary and to the answers she had been avoiding. It felt reckless to search in daylight, but it was day six, and she might not find another chance.

The idea of leaving tightened the knot in her gut.

Halfway between the farmhouse and the apiary, a squirrel jumped from branch to branch, sending a flurry of leaves raining down on Sasha. She clicked her tongue at the darting creature.

It leaped to the ground and paused to scrutinize Sasha.

She took a half-eaten ration bar out of her sweater pocket and broke off a small piece, which she tossed toward the squirrel. "Go ahead."

The squirrel hesitated, then snatched the morsel, shoved it into its pouchy cheeks, and bounded away. Sasha stayed crouched on her haunches listening to the forest chatter.

"Do you have enough extra food to be feeding rodents?"

Startled, Sasha jumped up as Millie walked down the path behind her.

"I know it's stupid. But I love squirrels."

"It's not stupid." Millie glanced at the shovel in Sasha's hands but continued to walk past her. "Why are you so muddy?"

"Did you know there's a spigot under the porch? I got it working. It'll be a lot easier than hauling water out of the woods."

"How did you know to look under there?"

"Lots of old houses had pumps, so I figured I'd check."

"Do you think it's potable?"

"Probably, but we should boil it."

"Walk with me." Millie's gray linen pants swished. She kept her hands in her pockets, her back long and straight, making Sasha self-conscious of her slouch.

The trail ended at the edge of the woods with a full, wide view of the apiary, looming as a constant reminder that bees did not exist, that this was where they ceased to exist. Several sections of the fabric membrane stretched across enormous horseshoe arches had been cut and removed, the heavy-duty material probably used for tents or sold on the black market. The exposed steel hoops arched like picked-over ribs on a decaying carcass.

Sasha turned away, shamed by the downfall of her father's pride.

Something about Millie's ease in the absence of conversation reminded Sasha of her father. He never needed to fill the air with unnecessary words. Millie's respect for silence felt like a kindness.

The wind kicked up around them, hinting at a coming storm, although the sky above them remained clear and blue.

"How long has it been?" Millie asked after a few minutes.

"How long has what been?"

"It seems a bit convenient you discovered a hidden water pump when no one else noticed it after living here for months."

"I notice things."

"So do I." Millie spoke with a hypnotic tone that soothed Sasha as much as it unnerved her.

Millie walked closer to the apiary. Sasha followed, her pulse fluttering.

Not now. The more time she spent with this family of squatters, the more Sasha longed to remain with them. She found comfort in their squabbles, loyalties, and idiosyncrasies. They made her laugh, allowed her to feel safer than she had in years. It was the closest she had felt to being part of a family or a group since entering the state care system.

Sasha and Millie walked through a tear in the fabric that opened like a curtain to a grand stage. As they stood inside the once-magnificent structure, Millie tilted her head back and stared up at the sky through a gash in the ceiling. Wind flapped the fabric with a roar that shook the membrane in rolling waves.

"It's a remarkable structure. Although it never made sense to me why anyone would keep bees indoors."

The sand floor shifted under Sasha's feet.

"They were dying. He wanted to protect them," Sasha said, an old wound ripping open. She gripped the handle of the shovel tighter, imagining the bee stings in her hair, on her face and neck, remembering the air humming with bees around her in the exact spot where she now stood.

"You're his daughter, aren't you?"

A sliver of blue sky winked at Sasha as the roof flap opened and closed. Her stomach tightened, and she leaned on the shovel for support.

"The beekeeper's daughter."

Sasha didn't respond.

"You look an awful lot like the pictures I remember. You have his eyebrows."

Sasha sipped her tea and didn't look at Millie. Her tongue hurt from where she had burned it minutes earlier. She longed to put down the burden of her family history. But she also needed the truth. She needed to stay.

"I won't say anything to the others, but I see you. You're hurting and I can't tell if it's because you've been away for so long, or because you're back."

"Maybe it's both." Admitting her identity to Millie felt foolish, but necessary, as if denying her name might make the happy memories fade. Sasha had been forcing herself to visit the tender memories, which meant wading through difficult bits to get to the smell of bike grease and lavender and beeswax.

"Do you want to talk about it?" Millie stepped closer. She smelled like cinnamon and moss.

"About what?"

"Whatever you want to talk about."

"There's nothing to talk about." Sasha dragged the shovel across the sandy ground, making a circle around herself. "He went to prison. I survived. I didn't have anywhere else to go, so I came here."

"Do you have any other family?"

"An uncle, but we had a falling-out years ago and haven't talked since."

"What are you going to do?"

The grasses outside the apiary swayed in hypnotic waves. Sasha felt herself swaying, too, as her eyes lost focus on the grass to take in the vastness of the field.

"I want to stay here, but . . ." She intended to find answers to all the questions her father never gave her, but she couldn't search for them with so many people around. If they moved on, she could search the property without distraction. But she didn't want them to go and leave her alone.

Wind whipped a flap of fabric on the roof with a slap. Ghosts of Sasha's family wandered this farm, but, at least for now, real people walked among them.

"If you want them to trust you, you need to trust them first," Millie said as if reading Sasha's mind.

Sasha let the shovel drop to the ground and cradled the tea mug in both hands, trying to eke out any residual warmth. She wanted answers, but even more, she wanted people.

"What's the shovel for?"

"Oh, nothing." Sasha struggled to find a believable answer. "I'm going to start a garden."

"It must have been painful. Losing your father, the trial. And all so publicly."

Sasha stared across the open field at the apple trees she used to climb as a girl. A couple of hundred yards away, the land dipped and flattened, a change so slight it would go unnoticed to most eyes. But not to Sasha's.

"I watched your testimony. I'm sorry you went through that."

No one had ever said that to Sasha before. People asked if the lost documents existed or why she broke into the apiary. No one ever acknowledged how difficult the trial had been for Sasha.

Millie watched Sasha with gentle eyes. No accusation, no prying.

Frayed strips of fabric whipped in the wind, occasionally creating a low howl as gusts curled inside the long tunnel.

"Are you alone too?" Sasha asked.

"Sometimes, but not today." Millie rested a gentle hand on Sasha's shoulder.

"Do you think it's possible bees still exist out there somewhere?" Despite her certainty that she hadn't actually seen a bee, the mirage haunted Sasha, prodding her to wonder, *What if?*

"Yes. I believe," Millie answered.

"Really?" Sasha had expected Millie to repeat some version of the warning Gino had given her the day before.

"We owe it to ourselves, to the world, to have hope. If we don't have hope, what do we have to fight for?"

"I have hope too." Sasha's heart pounded as if she and Millie had committed a crime. Standing in the apiary, the last place she had seen bees before the Great Collapse, the day after seeing an actual bee in the wild seemed like too much of a coincidence. It had to be her imagination.

"Do you want help with your garden?" Millie asked.

"Sure." Although Sasha had lied about intending to plant a garden, the idea now appealed to her. Tending seeds implied she would be there to gather the harvest.

"Does this mean you're planning to stay for a while?" Millie asked.

"It depends on Halle, Ian, and Gino, I guess. Are you going to tell them about my father?"

"It's your story to tell. Not mine." Millie took both of Sasha's hands in hers.

Sasha hadn't felt cared for in so long she didn't know how to reciprocate the kindness. Maybe she would be okay here. She could start over and never look back.

"But, Sasha." Millie squeezed both of Sasha's hands firmly. "The truth always finds a way of coming out. And it will be a lot easier if they find out from you."

# Nine

## SASHA, AGE 10
### OCTOBER 3

Ever since the night of Sasha's last orchestra concert, a year and a half earlier, her father had been too distracted to pay attention to anything Sasha did. Phone calls late at night, long days in his office, longer nights in his study, or clandestine visits to the bunker.

He gave up the pretense of parenting, making cold cereal for dinners they ate without speaking. Sasha interpreted her father's comfort sitting in silence as a manifestation of their shared grief, a gesture of solidarity. He no longer coddled her with the charade of cooking hot meals.

Something vast and formidable loomed over her father. The fact that he made little attempt to mask his panic prodded Sasha to be brave on his behalf despite her escalating fear.

During Sasha's first seven years, the three of them—her mother, her father, and Sasha—had been a team. Her parents married late and were shocked when, at age forty-seven, her mother became pregnant. By the time Sasha came along, all four of her grandparents were dead.

No cousins. No family gatherings. No birthday cards with checks in them. Just Chuck, her mother's brother, always hovering in the background.

Sasha's small world, however, felt enormous. Her parents included her in everything, treating her like a fully functioning adult. They shared the family finances and asked her opinion about everything from what crops to plant to whether they should delay getting a new roof for one more year.

Roaming free-range on the two-hundred-acre property, Sasha managed her hives, tended her own garden. When she sold vegetables at a local farm stand, she contributed part of her earnings toward the family finances, even though no one asked her to.

"Are we enough?" she had asked as her mother carved a roasted chicken when Sasha was six. In her mother's hands, the knife sliced gracefully through the tender breast, creating perfect slices. When her father carved, the meat came off in mangled chunks. "Is three people enough? Everyone else has more people than we do."

Without a word, her father plucked a piece of chicken from the platter, ate the juicy bit with his fingers, then stood up from his stool. Slowed by arthritic aches, he climbed up on top of the stool and stood. He stomped one foot on the seat and climbed down with creaky, awkward movements.

"A three-legged stool can hold you up as long as all three legs bear their weight." He flipped the stool upside down so the three thick legs extended up toward the ceiling. "You, your mom, and me." He tapped one of the legs with each name. "Nothing can destabilize a three-legged stool."

He flipped the stool right side up and banged his fist on it. Sasha pounded her fist next to his so hard her hand hurt for a week. The stool, like their small but mighty family, did not wobble.

At the time, her father's metaphor satisfied Sasha, but when her mother got sick, the legs on their tripod felt less stable. After her mother died, her father said they were a ladder, with two strong legs that would take them as high as they wanted to climb.

Now the ladder felt unsteady, filling Sasha with icy dread every time her father slammed the door to his study, leaving Sasha on the other side.

Sasha tolerated school, preferring the company of the fields and forest, which stubbornly clung to summer foliage although it was already October.

She ran through the field to check on the potatoes she had planted months earlier along the edge of the woods, far beyond the borders of the contaminated field. The crusty earth had fought her the day she'd scooped and chopped at the soil with a rock until she formed a long, shallow trench to plant the tubers.

The leaves had now browned and curled, indicating the potatoes were ready to harvest, but she left them under the earth to multiply for the next season and the season after that.

She climbed over the stone wall and wandered until she found the closest hive, sitting in a sunny puddle of light between two birch trees. Bees spun around the opening of the wooden box. Sasha knelt a few feet from the hive, relieved by the furious activity. Pollen packed the haunches of incoming foragers, and busy workers unpacked the loot.

"Sasha!" Her father's voice boomed from the direction of the farmhouse. She curled her knees against her chest and covered her ears with her hands. The bees flew in. They dashed out. Her father yelled louder, the tremor in his voice penetrating Sasha's attempt to block him out, but once again, she sensed panic in his voice.

She didn't stop running until she got to the front yard, where her hives had stood in a cluster days earlier. After weathering two years of icy winters and mushy spring thaws, each square box had left behind a deep footprint in the hard, crusty soil. The yard resembled a mouth full of gaping wounds where teeth had been yanked.

"Make it look like we never kept hives here." He scratched his beard and paced.

"Why?" She trotted next to him as he walked in a widening circle. Most of the time, Sasha appreciated when her father spoke to her like an adult, trusting her to make good decisions and complete any chore he gave her, but this time she wanted guidance.

"Just do it." He walked inside without giving further instructions.

His words stung like a slap. She wanted to run inside and tend her wounded feelings, but her father's fear now showed plainly in his bloodshot eyes, his gray skin, and the tremors in his hands. His inability to hide his anxiety startled Sasha. Shouldn't he at least be pretending for Sasha's sake?

Whatever loomed over her father now hung over Sasha, too.

The yard looked off-balance without the hives, as if the farm's center of gravity had shifted. She dragged a rusty rake across the yard, allowing the metal prongs to bounce on the ground, sending dissonant vibrations up the wooden shaft into her hand.

As she started to rake over the footprints, she noticed scattered bodies on the ground. So many dead bees. Too many to be part of the natural life cycle. Stragglers who returned home to find their hives gone, she guessed. Sasha bit the inside of her cheek, trying to push away images of her lost bees circling the yard with nowhere to find shelter.

Sasha ran inside to grab a spoon and a plastic container. She scooped up the bees and sealed them in a box for her father to employ as treatment for his arthritis. Weaning himself off the venom would be difficult when the bees eventually disappeared.

They never talked about the death of the pollinators in their home. Discussing it felt disloyal to her father. But Sasha knew. Everyone knew. They studied the extinction of pollinators in school, talked about it on the bus. Sasha always excused herself or put headphones on and closed her eyes before someone directed questions to her.

She scratched the rake over the caked ground, clawing at the squares, but if anything, her attempts accentuated the raw wounds. She moved potted plants from the porch steps and clustered them over one square. Sasha lay on her back in the middle of the circle where the hives had been and watched the clouds drift overhead in blue-gray swirls that curled like smoke.

A squirrel leaped from branch to branch overhead. Above the branches, clouds contorted into ocean waves and mountains that rose and fell like time moving in fast-forward. If only she could morph the imprints of the hives into something else.

If she dug them up, the freshly turned soil would draw attention. They needed to become something new.

A single bee flew above her head and Sasha felt a sharp pang in her chest. She wanted to clasp her hands around the tiny creature and escort it to its new home in the woods.

Sasha walked toward her mother's workshop, a graveyard of unused farm tools, mechanical parts, and discarded bits.

As she approached the tire swing, Sasha picked up her pace, leaping to grab the chain and landing with one foot in the curve of the rubber tire. The momentum carried her in a wide arc across the yard. She leaned back and bent her knees, pumping, again and again, to build momentum until she soared almost even with the branch from which the swing hung. She held on with one hand and opened her other arm and leg to feel the air rush across her skin and through her hair.

Sasha could fly like a bee.

As the swing slowed like a pendulum, Sasha jumped to the ground and sprinted to the workshop. She filled a wheelbarrow with six rusted bike-wheel hubs from her mom's junk pile. Clouds hung a bit lower as she huffed her way across the yard pushing the cargo. She stacked the six wheels on top of each other to form a teetering, Seussical tower over one of the squares left behind by a box hive.

She dragged over an empty broken hive from the barn and placed two milk crates on either side to form a sitting area and table over the scar left from another now-absent hive. She covered the remaining hive footprints with rust-eaten water barrels she rolled over from behind the barn.

By the time the clouds started to break, the yard resembled a junky-chic sculpture garden with no trace of the beehives.

She watched the path between the house and the apiary, waiting for her father to come back. He would appreciate her work. They were a team.

Several bees flew by as she waited. Lost. Panic flickered.

A beehive must be moved less than three feet or more than three miles from its original location; otherwise the relocation will confuse the bees' celestial compasses, which allow them to memorize and navigate territory based on landmarks and their relationship to the sun. The new location in the forest fell in the danger zone. Countless bees would not find the hive and would die, lost and alone.

Her father wouldn't put the bees at risk unless the alternative was worse. But what could be worse than jeopardizing some of the last surviving bees?

# Ten

SASHA, AGE 22

JUNE 13

"That was our best ration haul ever." Halle bounced as she walked backward in front of the others on their three-mile trek back from the ration-distribution station. Halle had doled out orders. Ian hunted down dried soybeans, Gino found a sack of brown rice, Halle carried a sack of garbanzo beans, and Millie carried a bag full of cooking oil, flour, tea, and baking powder. Sasha, who had been assigned to find produce, filled her bag with squash, onions, sweet potatoes, apples, and carrots.

The bounty felt decadent, but it needed to last two weeks.

Halle skipped next to Sasha and put an arm through Sasha's to link elbows. Sasha squeezed Halle's arm with hers. Being part of a team felt good. Individually, they couldn't have pulled such a variety of foods together, but when they pooled their resources, they had more. They needed Sasha, too.

"I'm going to make chickpea patties with chopped onions and carrots tomorrow," Gino said. "Sasha, can I use your salt?"

"It's yours. Use as much as you want."

The rush of air from a passing truck blasted their faces with dust and debris, but the burst of air invigorated Sasha as if a valve had blown open. She wanted to yell as the truck blew by, to release the question exploding in her chest: *Can I stay?*

"You know what I'd really like for dinner?" Halle said. "A cheeseburger."

"With fries," Sasha added.

Ian scowled as if disapproving of children playing a silly game. He had been quieter than usual on the walk to the ration station, more pensive, which worried Sasha. Maybe he was planning how to tell her it was time to move on.

"How about you, Millie?" Gino asked.

Millie stopped walking as she pondered the question, as if her answer carried important weight. The others paused to wait for her. "I'd like more of that soup Sasha made."

Millie was advocating for Sasha, and the gesture caught Sasha unprepared. The need to be wanted swelled in her chest with such force, Sasha couldn't speak in response. Her voice would crack, or worse, she might cry.

No one mentioned that Sasha had burned through her seven days. She already planned her speech if they asked her to leave. She had as much right—which meant no right at all—to be on the farm. They couldn't force her out. If they insisted she leave, she might tell them the truth, that her grandfather built the house, her father had been born there, and so had she.

Metallic gray clouds hovered on the horizon, hinting at a storm. It hadn't rained in months and the parched land crackled in anticipation.

"We're stopping at the market," Ian said.

"We don't need anything else." Gino looked surprised.

"There's someone I need to talk to." Ian blinked rapidly as he spoke.

Millie pressed her lips into a tight line but didn't say anything.

"I love the market," Halle said. "They always have weird stuff and weirder people."

"I'd like to go." Sasha tried not to sound too eager.

"Fine, you all go," Millie said. "Leave the food with me in a shady spot by the road, and I'll wait for you. I don't like crowds."

The market had started out as a swap shop, but as more vendors popped up to hawk used housewares and clothing, mechanical parts and baked goods, the market became the only community gathering place in the agricultural region now deemed unsafe for agriculture.

The market reminded Sasha of a sadder, drabber version of the county fair her parents took her to. Instead of the piped-in music of the fair, the melancholy of a wailing harmonica welcomed them as they approached the old movie theater parking lot now strewn with rows of tables and vendors.

Halle stopped at the community message board at the entrance to the market. Flyers tacked to the board fluttered with faces of the missing. HAVE YOU SEEN MY DAUGHTER? Pictures of the elderly, beloved spouses, young children. Halle touched each flyer, as if acknowledging the pain behind each disappearance.

When the power grid outside the city failed eight years earlier, and never came back online, the disruption of communication separated families and friends. Most people left rural areas for the city, which maintained power. How many had already been found? How many never would be?

Inside the market, dozens of tables lay strewn with used cutlery, pots and pans, food, and dinnerware. Farm tools, used clothes, blankets, sleeping bags, work boots.

HAVE YOU SEEN BEES? REPORT THEM TO US, NOT THE GOVT, read a hand-painted sign propped up against a wobbly table. Halle looked past a woman who tried to give her a brochure, but Sasha couldn't resist meeting the woman's eyes.

"Do you get many reports of bees around here?" Sasha asked the woman.

"Come on, Sasha, keep moving." Ian tugged on Sasha's arm.

"More than you'd think." The woman handed Sasha a pamphlet.

"Don't encourage them," Ian said when they were out of earshot. "They're a cult, a bunch of nutjobs who believe bees are going to come back and save us. They come by the farm every now and then as if the bees are going to suddenly rematerialize in the apiary. I'm pretty sure they're on some kind of watch list. We don't need the attention."

Sasha couldn't afford to be associated with anything related to bees. But were these people really delusional? And if they were, did that mean Sasha, too, might be losing her grip on reality? She crumpled the pamphlet and shoved it in her pocket to use as kindling.

The smell of freshly baked bread permeated the air. A young woman picked a banjo from under a canopy, gifting the market with a carnival-like atmosphere.

Sasha stopped to inspect a bike propped against a sign that read OCTAVIA'S BOOKS AND BIKE PARTS. The front wheel flopped to one side, and rust spots dotted the fire-engine-red paint. The bike stirred a nostalgia for soaring down the hill at the end of her driveway with her arms outstretched like wings, the wind whipping through her hair.

"Are you Octavia?" Sasha asked a Black woman sitting behind a counter covered with boxes of books interspersed with crates of assorted bike parts.

"I am."

Halle wandered off to a used-clothing booth. Gino and Ian had already disappeared into the crowd.

Sasha leaned down and rotated the pedals.

"The gears are a mess and the front wheel's bent." Octavia had dark skin and short-cropped hair. She wore a sleeveless green top and frayed jeans. She crossed her thick arms over her broad midsection and stood up while Sasha examined the bike.

"You aren't a very persuasive salesperson." Sasha crouched down to examine the tires. The treads were worn, but in better shape than the mechanical parts. She pinched the rubber and pressed down on the seat to check if the tires held air.

"But I'm honest."

"How much are you asking?"

"How much do you have?"

"I don't have any money. I want to find a job so I can make some cash, but I can't find a job because I don't have transportation."

"The vicious cycle. You need money to make money. Take it," Octavia said. "If you think you can get this bike working, take it."

"I don't have anything to give you."

"I've been lugging that bike to market every week for three months. You're the only person who has ever shown the slightest interest. You'd be doing me a favor."

"Seriously?"

"No one else wants it, and it's a pain in my ass."

"If I get it working, I'll come back and pay you something when I can. I don't know when that will be. But I will." Every time Sasha made a plan or a promise, she believed more fiercely in the future.

"Deal." Octavia stood up and extended a hand. Her palm, rough with calluses, yet tender and warm, reminded Sasha of her mother's hands.

Sasha picked up a book from the end of the counter and flipped through the copy of a novel she had read numerous times. She ran a finger along the spines of the books lined up in crates, finding several of her favorite authors.

"I don't get your theme. Bike parts and science fiction?"

"I've also got a bunch of literary titles in there and some random romances. We all need a love story now and then."

"Have you read this one?" Sasha held up a worn paperback.

"Oh, please, I can practically recite it by heart. I've read all the books I sell. I used to teach speculative literature at the university before it closed down. Most of these are from my private collection."

"And the bike parts?"

"They came from my husband's fix-it shop. He died a few years ago and I found myself sitting on a pile of books and bike parts, but no job." Octavia bent over to move something under the counter. "So here I am."

"You have great taste in books." Sasha rummaged through the boxes.

Octavia held up a warped clothbound book coming apart at the seams.

"Like I said, I don't have any money on me."

"I dropped it in a creek. It's too damaged to sell."

"I like to read by the water too," Sasha said, thinking back to the moss-covered rock in the woods.

Octavia waved to a tall man with medium-dark skin and loose curly hair. He wore a white button-down shirt and tan pants, nicer and newer than most people in the market wore. He nodded at Octavia as he finished a call on a bright purple cell phone.

"Let me guess, you finished it already?" Octavia said.

"Yep." He plunked down a worn paperback called *A Rotten Blond* held together with layers of yellowing tape.

"Have you read that yet?" The man gestured toward the book in Sasha's hand.

"Yeah, but I'm going to read it again."

"It's one of my favorites too," he said.

"Bassel's one of my best nonpaying customers," Octavia said, and turned to Sasha. "My new friend here needs a job."

Sasha didn't appreciate Octavia sharing her unemployment status with a stranger, especially not this one. He looked a few years older than Sasha and had one of those faces that made her want to stare. Dark eyes and animated eyebrows, a wide smile, and heavy cheekbones.

Sweat soaked the small of his back, but he kept his sleeves rolled down. He wore expensive-looking brown leather sneakers with red laces that appeared new, or at least well cared for.

Sasha turned to rummage through a box of books to stop herself from staring at his long eyelashes.

"The ag department's building a bunch of greenhouses a couple miles beyond the ration station. They're hiring a ton of people to hand-pollinate vegetables. Not a glamorous job, but it's a job." Bassel didn't look like he needed a job.

"Do you need experience?" Sasha tried not to appear too eager.

"Hand-pollinating plants? Unless you have some past-life experience as a bee, I can't imagine what would be relevant."

Sasha felt a blush rising up her neck and pretended to cough.

"There's a table set up at the end of the next row. I think you can apply over there," Bassel said.

Sasha craned her neck to see Halle and Gino filling out applications under a banner that read AGRI NEW DEAL.

"What's with the sparkly purple phone?" Octavia asked Bassel.

"If you worked in a government office surrounded by this"—he pointed to his white button-down shirt—"you'd want some color in the room too. They all hate my phone, which makes me like it more."

Octavia laughed.

"I brought you a gift." Bassel pulled a copy of a slick-looking science fiction paperback Sasha didn't recognize out of his bag and dropped it in front of Octavia. "I have mixed feelings about the ending."

Octavia turned the book over to read the back. "I'll let you know what I think."

Sasha tried to get a better look at the book without being too obvious, but Bassel's shoulder blocked her view.

"If you get that bike to work, maybe I'll let you take a peek too," Octavia said to Sasha without looking up at her.

"See you next week?" Bassel asked.

"You know where to find me," Octavia said.

"Nice meeting you," Bassel said to Sasha. "Maybe I'll see you around?"

"Yeah, maybe." Sasha tried to think of something clever to say so he might stay longer, but her mind froze.

"I know I can fix this bike," Sasha said to Octavia as Bassel walked away. "And I'll pay you whatever you think is fair as soon as I can. I'll be back, I promise."

"I know you will."

"How do you know?"

"Because you want to see what other books my friend over there likes." Octavia gestured with her chin in the direction of Bassel as he walked away.

"All I'm looking for is a bike." Sasha's face reddened.

"Ummm-hmmmm." Octavia selected a bike chain from a tangled pile in a crate and put it in a paper bag. "You'll need a chain."

"Bike parts and books. I think we'll be great friends," Sasha said.

"Don't go printing hand towels with our initials on them. It takes more than admirable taste in books to be my friend."

"Noted. I'll let you know how the repairs come along. Thanks," Sasha said.

Ian joined Sasha at the counter and nodded apathetically at her.

"I was told to see you about setting up a booth at the market," he said to Octavia.

"What kind of booth?" Octavia put a hand on her hip and narrowed her eyes.

"A first-aid station. Basic wound care, herbal remedies. I'm not a doctor and I'm not pretending to be one, but I have some first-aid experience, and I don't think there's any medical care around here." Ian spoke faster than normal and fidgeted with a bike pedal he'd picked up from the counter.

"We could use medical help, but I don't want a quack making people worse or making promises you can't keep." Octavia bit her lower lip as she considered. "Most people around here don't have much money."

"Neither do I. I'll accept bartered items. Food or housewares if they don't have money," Ian said.

Octavia lifted a box onto the counter and began arranging books in stacks that didn't seem to have any logic or theme from what Sasha could decipher.

"I'll give you one month of Saturdays as a trial," Octavia said. "Then we'll talk."

"Deal." Ian beamed. "I'll be here Saturday morning."

"That's fantastic." Sasha turned to congratulate Ian, but he had already walked away.

Sasha wandered in and out of the booths, her stomach rumbling at the smell of bread curling around every corner. She paused at an unattended booth with a sign that read FREE STUFF. She rummaged through the piles of damaged clothing and linens, gathering up three large sheets, stained and ripped. She knotted them into a ball and fixed them onto the handlebars of the bike.

Sasha passed Bassel standing in front of the community board. He covered his mouth and chin with one hand and rocked back and forth on his heels. Sasha considered talking to him, but his previously cheerful demeanor now looked pensive and stormy. She opted to leave him to his thoughts as he scanned the faces of the lost.

Sasha met up with the others at the table with an Agri New Deal banner, where they all set up online accounts and filled out the job applications Bassel told her about.

"Can you believe this? If we got jobs and could stay on the farm . . ." Halle grabbed Sasha's hand. "We need this so bad."

"You can use Ian's phone," Gino said when Sasha paused at the contact-number box.

"Millie should fill out an application too," Sasha said as they walked toward the exit of the market.

"She won't do it," Ian said.

"Why not?"

"She never goes into the market. She hates crowds."

"Where is she?" Sasha scanned the roadside, a flutter of panic rising. Someone could have robbed Millie. They shouldn't have left her alone with so much food.

Halle pointed to a large boulder at the edge of the forest flanking the road. Millie's tan shirt and gray hair blended into the background. As they walked toward her, Millie stood up and waved.

The five of them lumbered back to the farm, weighed down with sacks of food and a bike with one warped wheel.

Halle had found a purple wool sweater with one sleeve missing in a freebies bin. Holding a sack of rice on one shoulder, she swung the disfigured garment by its intact arm over her head like a helicopter as they walked home.

"I've never seen anyone advertising for jobs around here. Maybe things are about to change." Halle skipped as she whipped the sweater through the air.

"I get that it's free, but what are you going to do with a one-armed sweater?" Gino asked.

"Unravel it and knit a scarf for Beatrix. Purple's her favorite. I'm taking the bus to see her next Tuesday. I should be able to finish by then."

"Okay, so hmmm, Halle gets free yarn and Sasha finds a free bike, but *you*—" Gino pointed to Ian. "You are supposed to be the responsible one. I can't believe you spent actual money on a first-aid kit. We need food, not gauze."

Ian hadn't told the others about his conversation with Octavia yet.

"This isn't just *any* first-aid kit. It has two military-issued tourniquets, a suture kit, scissors, a scalpel, antiseptic, an EpiPen, and a lot more. I got a great deal." Ian's bright blue eyes lit up as he described the contents of the small kit enclosed in a metal clam shell. "One of the two EpiPens is missing, but one is better than none."

Sasha shuddered, remembering EpiPens jabbing into her thigh as she fought for breath. One EpiPen was not enough.

"Can I eat anything in your first-aid box? I don't think so," Gino said. "We can't spend money on bandages when we need food. They're reducing rations starting next week, you know."

"I'm setting up a first-aid booth at the market. I have a decent supply of herbs, and the fireweed astringent works pretty well. I know how to treat basic injuries. I've sewed up wounds before. And it's not like there's any other medical care around here."

"Is that legal?" Halle asked.

"Is anything legal anymore?" Ian said. "I could have been a doctor, you know."

"We know," Halle and Gino said in unison.

"You'll get paid?" Gino asked.

"Hopefully, even if it's just in bartered items. But it's not just the money. People in the camps are sick and no one's helping them. I can at least try."

"I'm proud of you. You'll be an amazing doctor." Halle stopped swinging her sweater and kissed Ian on the cheek. "And thanks."

"For what?" Ian said.

"Sometimes I feel like I don't know why I'm bothering to fight to bring Beatrix home. I think how shitty everything is. Maybe she has it better in there, you know? Then someone—" Halle nudged her shoulder against Ian's. "—*someone* reminds me of the good in the world and I remember why I'm bringing her home. I believe this world can be better. That's what I want for her."

Ian tucked his chin down to hide a blush.

"What are you going to do with those sheets?" Millie pointed to the bundle on Sasha's bike.

"I'm going to tear them into strips, then wash and boil them to sterilize them."

"What for?" Gino asked.

"To make bandages for Ian's first-aid station."

Ian smiled, just barely, but Sasha noticed.

"You really think you can fix it?" Ian gestured toward Sasha's bike.

"Of course." Sasha couldn't wait to get back to the farm and take her mother's tools into the workshop.

"It will come in handy if any of us gets a job. That greenhouse campus is five miles away," Halle said.

Sasha didn't point out that she would be taking the bike with her if she left.

"Don't get your hopes up," Ian said. "The military surplus guy told me there are already thousands of people setting up tent camps north of the campus. They're expecting ten times the number of applicants as they have positions."

The farmhouse, located miles beyond the ration station, gave them a buffer from passersby, for the most part. After the ration station and the market, the land opened up to an expanse of nothing but abandoned farms with no power, no water, and fields laced with toxic chemicals. Most residents had abandoned the land, but now, with so many people flocking to the greenhouses, Sasha worried about the encampments pushing closer to the farm, forcing them to defend their stake.

"Shit," Halle said. "So, I guess we hope at least one of us gets a job."

"It will probably be me," Gino said, shifting a sack of garbanzo beans from one shoulder to the other. "With all the glass on those greenhouses, my experience as a professional window washer will make me an irresistible candidate."

With rations being slashed, people would be increasingly desperate, which meant more competition for jobs and resources in their quiet corner of the world. Sasha didn't want to be one of the desperate people in the camps. She squeezed the rubber grip on the handlebar to hold back the familiar rising panic.

*Please let me be the one to get the job,* Sasha pleaded silently. *Please let me be indispensable.*

"Hey, don't look so grim. I bet one us of will get a job. I can feel it," Halle said to Sasha as they approached the top of the driveway. "Who was that guy at the bike stall?"

"Just some guy looking at books," Sasha said.

"He's cute," Halle said. "In a nerdy kind of way."

"I didn't notice," Sasha lied.

"Oh please, I saw you gawking at him," Halle said. "No judgment."

"Oh my God, Sasha's blushing," Gino said. "Our little Sasha has a crush."

Sasha's face and neck burned, but she didn't care. If Gino thought of her as *our little Sasha,* then he couldn't turn her out with no place to go, could he?

Sasha caught Millie smiling at her and could tell Millie was thinking the same thing.

# Eleven

The following morning Millie and Sasha cleared a patch of ground for a kitchen garden up the hill from the farmhouse. Sasha transplanted some herbs from around the house and asparagus she and Gino found while foraging. She planted rows of spinach seeds she found in the larder, the only seeds she could plant this late in the season. In the spring, if she was still there, she would scatter her mother's wildflower seeds along the edge of the forest.

The soil scratched with a satisfying grit under Sasha's fingernails. The rustle of Millie shifting positions, the way she stutter-stepped to keep her balance as she tugged a stubborn weed free from the ground, her soft, guttural sigh. Those noises—Millie noises—became part of Sasha's morning.

"How did you end up here?" Sasha stretched her neck and shoulders.

"I was on my way back to the city. I have family nearby. But I wanted to see it for myself."

"The apiary?"

"Yes."

"Do you blame me?" Sasha stabbed at the fledgling compost pile with her shovel, folding the dry top layer into the spongy underlayer.

Millie stood up and brushed her hands off on her pants. "You were a child. This is *not* on you."

"Sometimes I still feel the buzzing in my fingertips."

"You're lucky. Few people carry such memories." Millie rubbed the tips of her thumb and forefinger together.

"When people figure out who I am, they want to hear about my father, about the trial. Kids at school were the worst. They picked up on the stories about me breaking into the hive without a clean suit, and that the colony died afterward. They were already dying. Before that day, they were dying."

"They *were* already dying." Millie's words, her kindness, her presence soothed like a balm. "You didn't kill those last bees. We all did."

Sasha wanted to believe Millie's words, the same words she told herself over and over. But every night, when she was alone in the dark, the guilt gathered like a cloud. Like a swarm.

By 10:00 A.M., the sun burned strong, and Millie stood up, dusted her hands off, and went inside for her nap. With Millie asleep, and the others nowhere to be found, Sasha grabbed the shovel and headed toward the apiary.

It had to be now. It was day eight and she didn't have any time to waste.

As she stepped onto the path in the woods, an urgency simmered in her gut, as if, after all these years, she needed to hurry. She quickened her pace to a slow jog, then a run. She broke through the edge of the woods and didn't pause as she sprinted through the knee-high grass toward the apple trees, the brush of crisp, thirsty stalks swishing against her leg like a memory. Familiar, if a bit uncomfortable.

Leading up to his trial, her father spent countless hours working in the storm shelter, taking his meals there, sometimes sleeping on the cot in the back corner. Now the memory of the underground storm cellar felt like a dream, like a story she had told herself.

Sasha positioned herself between the apple tree and the stone wall, with her back to the apiary, and paced out the steps as she had days earlier. Dried weeds and thistle crunched under her boots. On the fourteenth step, the ground hardened as her boot landed on the buried door to the bunker.

Decades' worth of sinewy growth thatched a thick weave together over the hatch to her great-grandparents' storm cellar. She yanked at the weeds, and clawed away the layer of moss and dirt. She traced the edges of the decayed synthetic mat she helped her father cover with several inches of soil. Her father—the one he used to be—felt close.

The edges of the woven mat disintegrated in her hands as she rolled it back and expose the doors to the storm cellar.

"*Little Bee*," the shush of grass seemed to whisper.

After she cleared the hatch, she stood to the side and yanked on the handle. The iron ring, stiff in its socket, resisted, then stuttered and creaked. The door eased open with a groan to reveal the familiar cement stairs. Her feet left prints on the dusty treads as she descended into the darkness. The lack of sound disoriented her.

Musty air triggered a sneeze, and particles of dust swirled in the column of light on the stairs.

The bunker still smelled of beeswax and honey, which seemed impossible until she saw the boxes lined up against the back wall. Perhaps her own young hands had built these hives, which appeared to have been used years ago. She laughed out loud at the thought of her father saving her box hives the way any other parent would collect crayon drawings.

Dusty light poured down the cement stairs into the ten-foot-by-ten-foot space, untouched in eleven years. In the shadows, Sasha made out her father's desk, the cot where he often napped, and the slouching silhouette of his microscope, still draped in the linen cover. Stacks of his journals and binders lined the back of the desk.

Her father's gravelly voice whispered in her memory, *No one can ever know about this place. This is the most important thing I'll ever ask of you. The most important thing anyone will ever ask of you.*

Sasha sat on the dust-covered bed to take in the room.

*No matter what they promise you, or what they threaten you with, you must never tell.*

Even at age eleven, scared and confused, Sasha had understood the enormity of what her father asked. Whatever her father hid in this cell suddenly felt dangerous.

She should run back to the farmhouse and confess everything. Would they want her to stay? Would they shun the Last Beekeeper's daughter the way the kids at school had?

She resisted the urge to leave.

Her hands shook as she picked up a stack of journals, the documents her father believed to be so important that he went to jail to protect them.

She flipped through the first notebook, which contained nothing more than observations of his hives, numbers, temperatures, the weight of honey produced in individual hives.

Nothing of particular interest. What had she expected? A great revelation? A confession? An apology?

She picked up another notebook filled with tidy penmanship in the first several pages that devolved into larger letters, shakier words by the end. Sasha remembered the year his handwriting changed due to his arthritis. He maintained his distinctive, left-leaning slant, but the once smooth lines became erratic and the pressure on the pages grew heavier and more desperate.

A loose sheet fell out of the worn journal. The page appeared to be the first page in a longer document titled "GMO *Apis mellifera:* A Study in Enhanced Resilience."

Her father wrote about bees the way other people bragged about their children. "Tough and resilient in the face of rising temperatures and drought, and less affected by environmental contaminants, they outlasted almost all the pollinators in North America. They thrive on a wide variety of pollen sources but can also survive with a single source."

*If we can save them, they can save us,* her father told her more than once.

Sasha had thrown her arms around her father and buried her face against the worn flannel of his shirt to hide her tears.

As Sasha flipped through the journals, she found another

loose page, which appeared to be from the middle of a personal letter.

". . . should have told you in Geneva. I won't bother to ask your forgiveness. Specimens with enhanced resistance to pesticides, but also with all the environmental resilience of the natural bees, were released with the goal of encouraging crossbreeding. They are indistinguishable without genetic testing. Our intention was to establish the safety over many generations in a controlled environment, then inform the international community before their release."

Sasha traced the large, awkward handwriting with the pad of her finger, imagining the pain in his knuckles as he gripped the pen.

"They had been showing impressive resistance to chemical pesticides. We planned to release the findings and share the data with other countries. We thought we could change the world, but instead . . ."

The letter stopped midsentence at the bottom of the page, suggesting it continued. Sasha shook all the notebooks searching for the rest of the letter but could not find the next page or the previous one. Who had the letter been intended for?

Touching his writing, reading his words, made her father feel present.

*Did I really see a bee? Should I tell anyone? Am I losing my mind? Tell me what to do, Dad. Please.*

Being in this space overwhelmed her with the memory of her father's dedication to the bees. The hours, the nights, the sleeplessness. It couldn't have all been for nothing.

On the inside cover of one journal, in faded pencil, she made out faint words. "If only she understood what she has done. If only she knew."

Was he writing about Sasha, talking *to* her? The back of her neck prickled.

Her father's accusation felt cruel, as if he had planted the message for her to find and remind her of the damage she caused. As if she needed reminding. She understood. She destroyed his final chance to save the bees. What else should she know?

*If only she knew.*

Her fingernails dug into her palms as the relentless taunts from the other kids flooded back. Her father had destroyed the world by killing the last bees. He was an evil scientist who created killer bees. Sasha had contaminated and killed the last bees, which was why so many people were dying. New rumors emerged every school year. No one wanted to eat lunch with the girl who destroyed humanity's last chance to save the bees and prevent mass starvation.

Sasha flipped through the ledger, searching for something that might explain why the numbers in his journals mattered so much.

As Sasha thumbed through the notebook, a shadow darkened the cellar door.

Millie stood on the stairs, her jaw hanging open.

"Is this . . . ?"

A wave of nausea slithered up Sasha's throat, and she swallowed hard. She should have been more careful. "Millie, you can't come in here."

"It's been here all this time? And you knew?"

"I didn't know what he left down here. I still don't." Sasha stood up to block Millie from getting near the journals. "This is his private property."

"What are you going to do with all this?"

"Nothing. I'm going to seal this place back up. I never should have dug it up in the first place. Can you forget you ever saw this? It doesn't matter anymore. The bees are gone. My father's in prison. None of this matters now."

Millie picked up a journal and opened it. Sasha tried to take it from her, but Millie turned her back so Sasha couldn't reach it.

"Are you going to report this? It will stir everything back up. I'm finally on my own, trying to start a new life," Sasha pleaded. "And think about Halle, Ian, and Gino. If you say anything, they will send teams in to confiscate everything, they will tear the house apart looking for more research. They'll evict us all. You know they will."

Sasha sat on her hands to stop the trembling. She rocked back and forth and practiced the breathing exercise a therapist in the state facility taught her. Breathing in for five counts. Out for five counts.

"It's okay. I won't tell anyone."

The room spun around her, the walls closing in. In for five counts, out for five counts.

Millie stood up and took both of Sasha's hands. "We're going outside, okay?"

Sasha allowed Millie to guide her up the stairs. Breathing in. Breathing out. Her eyes burned at the change of light as she crawled up the last few stairs and sat with her head between her knees. *Just breathe.*

Millie sat beside her and rubbed her back the way Sasha's mother used to.

"If you're going to tell them, please be honest with me so I'll be prepared." Sasha sat up.

"I won't say anything. You should tell them yourself. Not necessarily about this shelter or the research, if you don't want to, but tell them about your father. They deserve the truth."

"I'll try."

"Being lied to by people you care about hurts." Millie flattened the hem of her shirt as she spoke, her finger working the worn fabric over and over in the same spot.

"Who lied to you?"

"That conversation is for another day," Millie said. "Do you want to read through the notebooks together? You shouldn't be alone right now."

"No, but thanks. They're full of charts and notations about temperature and death rates. Nothing of interest." Sasha didn't mention the letter.

"Did you know about this place when you testified?"

"You remember my testimony?"

"Everyone watched the trial of the Last Beekeeper."

Sasha groaned and folded over to put her face in her lap, her arms covering her head. She closed her eyes and breathed in the lingering scent of honey mixed with mildew in the journals.

"I've been planning for years, ever since the trial, to come back here and find out why he wanted me to lie about it, why he chose to go to jail. And now it feels like it doesn't matter. I've spent most of my life circling around a hole in the ground. But no matter what's in these notebooks, none of it changes anything. He left me. Why can't I let it go?"

"Maybe you needed to dig it up so you could confront it, so it wouldn't haunt you anymore. Now you can control what you do next. Do you want to go backward?" Millie tapped the journal on her lap. "Or forward?"

Sasha thought about sleeping under the piano. The comfort of hearing Halle's, Gino's, Ian's, and Millie's footsteps on the creaking floorboards. The smell of a fire first thing in the morning and working side by side in the garden with Millie.

Her future waited aboveground. What had she expected to find? A letter of apology? A detailed explanation? Whatever secrets these journals held, if any, could only cause her more pain. There would be no magic moment of closure or understanding. Only dredged-up regrets.

"Will you help me cover it up?"

"Of course," Millie said, the maternal note in her voice striking a tender spot in Sasha's chest.

# Twelve

## SASHA, AGE 10
### OCTOBER 5

Sasha assembled a potpie to surprise her father at dinner. Her mother had taught her how to make the family favorite and left her a handwritten collection of the recipes Sasha would miss most. Sometimes when she cooked, Sasha talked out loud to her mother, asking questions the recipe didn't answer.

*We're out of butter. Can I use oil?*

*Is it weird to use extra green beans and leave the peas out? I never told you, but I've always hated peas.*

While dinner cooked, Sasha sat on her bedroom floor plucking at the strings on her violin. She dragged her bow back and forth on the well-worn block of rosin, watching the dust particles cloud around the hairs on the bow and catch in the evening sunlight. She pulled the rosin into her lungs and held her breath.

When the musicians rosined their bows before a performance, the scent settled Sasha's nerves. Over the years she had worn down several translucent amber blocks until only scraps remained in the corners of the wooden cases.

She put the violin to her chin and dragged her bow across the G and D strings, both of which skewed flat. The discord clawed at her ears like fingernails on a chalkboard. She played louder and gritted her teeth to absorb the dissonance.

The floor beneath her feet rumbled as if the Earth itself might be reacting to the sound, to the sadness of her displaced bees.

The rumble stopped and started again. She put her violin down and peered out the window. A long line of official-looking trucks lurched up her driveway, pausing at the fork and turning toward the apiary.

They were coming for the bees.

"No, no, no!" She ran down the stairs. The aroma of potpie wafted through the house.

She sprinted to ring the bell in the old barn. Her father would hear it at the apiary. Chuck pulled into the driveway and ran toward her, catching her before she made it to the barn door.

"The trucks. I need to warn Dad." She tried to sidestep Chuck, but he grabbed her hand. Sasha wriggled free. "They're coming to take his bees."

"There's nothing you can do."

"We need to warn him."

"He knows." Chuck clamped his arms around Sasha. "He's been expecting them."

"Why are you letting this happen?" Sasha thrashed against him but couldn't break his hold.

"Our *Apis mellifera* recovery group has the authority to take them to a safe location where they can care for them and try to protect them."

"You should be *giving* the bees to Dad to take care of, not *taking* them." Tears streamed down Sasha's face. "You're killing them."

"If he fights them, your dad will go to jail."

"Stop saying 'them.' *You* could stop this if you wanted. I know you could. You *want* him to lose his bees, don't you? Mom used to say you try to use power you don't have, but you're afraid to use the power you *do* have."

Chuck drew in a sharp breath and his arms slackened as Sasha hurled his dead sister's words at him.

She wanted him to hurt. He had the power to help her father, to help the bees, but he chose not to.

"Congress passed a law prohibiting private individuals from

keeping bees. Your father, just like every other citizen, is required to hand over any remaining bees to authorities. It's nothing personal toward your father."

Would they come for her hives hiding in the forest?

Chuck released Sasha, but she buried her face against his chest, wishing she could take back her cruel words. He ruffled a hand through her hair and touched a finger to the side of his nose, the gesture her mother had always used to indicate all was forgiven, a kindness Sasha didn't deserve, but one Chuck always extended.

Chuck guided her toward the house.

A whiff of burning pie crust greeted them as they entered the foyer seconds before the smoke detector blared. Sasha startled at the noise, but Chuck didn't flinch. His cheek pressed against Sasha's head, he whispered something. Sasha felt the heat of his breath, but the wailing alarm drowned out his words.

Her anger at Chuck's refusal to help her father mixed with her shame and the acrid smoke of a ruined dinner to form a bitter charcoal taste in Sasha's mouth. She spit on the floor. Chuck went into the kitchen, where he grabbed a broomstick and rammed the alarm over and over until bits of plastic rained down into his thinning hair and the house fell silent.

# Thirteen

## SASHA, AGE 22
### JUNE 15

The morning after uncovering her father's bunker, Sasha woke early, as planned, to work in the garden with Millie. The failure of waiting her entire life to find her father's work, to finally unearth it, and to realize she didn't have the courage to read it hung like a stone around her neck. She had convinced herself her father's secrets must be significant and worth the sacrifice. But what if they weren't? What if he'd abandoned Sasha for nothing? She couldn't face it. Not yet.

Ashes from the previous night's fire sat cold. No water brewing for tea. Sasha expected to see Millie already working, but the garden was empty. Sasha lugged two-gallon jugs of water up the hill to water the herbs and spinach. The morning chill held fast to the damp air, sending a shiver up Sasha's spine as water sloshed against her legs.

Maybe Millie did blame Sasha and no longer wanted to help her with the garden. Maybe she was inside telling Ian, Gino, and Halle everything.

Sasha dropped the jugs of water and sprinted back to the house.

"Millie." Sasha banged on Millie's door, but she didn't answer. "Millie, are you in there?"

"What's going on?" Ian came downstairs.

"Have you seen Millie?"

"She's probably out walking."

Sasha pushed past Ian and opened the door into the empty

room. Millie's bedroll, her clothes, her backpack, everything was gone. Including Millie.

"Millie!" Sasha ran through the house. She couldn't have left without saying goodbye.

Ian chased after Sasha as she looked in the kitchen, the basement, and up to the second floor.

"Did you know?" Sasha burst into Halle's room.

"What's wrong? Did I know what?" Halle sat up, still bleary from sleep.

"Millie left."

Halle looked past Sasha to Ian behind her.

"She took all of her stuff," Ian said.

Sasha ran down the stairs and outside. She jogged down the driveway, although she knew she would never catch Millie. She could have left in the middle of the night and caught a morning bus to the city. She could be anywhere.

Ian followed Sasha to the end of the driveway. They looked down the narrow road in both directions and saw nothing but broken pavement and overgrown fields.

"She never intended to stay long," Ian said, his voice low and soft, a shift from his usual sharp tone.

"She didn't even say goodbye." Sasha's words came out in sobs. She couldn't explain to Ian why she took Millie's disappearance personally. The betrayal stung; the loss of friendship and companionship blocked out what she didn't want to acknowledge. The fear. The terror that Millie could expose her identity, go public with her father's research, and put her new friends at risk of eviction. Sasha paced in the middle of the road, not bothering to restrain the sobs rising up from the long-buried parts of her she wished she could ignore.

Ian stood in front of Sasha and put a hand on each of her shoulders.

"She should have said goodbye." Ian pulled her in to his chest and held her as she sobbed. "But you're okay, Sasha."

Ian's shirt, which he had worn for several days in a row, smelled of dried sweat and smoke from the fire.

"We're all going to be okay," Ian said, and kissed the top of her head.

Halle and Gino ran up the driveway to where Ian and Sasha stood in the middle of the road.

"She's really gone," Gino said, and folded around Sasha and Ian, joined by Halle. They stood in a tangled knot in the center of the broken road until Sasha's heaves calmed and her breath quieted. Without a word, the four walked back to the house hand in hand.

Halle lit the fire and made Sasha a cup of tea with a fresh tea bag. As she sipped the tea, Sasha's grief over losing Millie morphed into shame, then dread, and rage.

How could she have been so careless, so stupid?

"I'm going for a walk. I'll be back in an hour," Sasha said.

"Want some company?" Gino asked.

"No. I need to walk this off alone."

Dew sparkled on the grass and leaves with a cheeriness that exacerbated Sasha's cheerless mood.

Millie befriended Sasha, mothered her, and waited for Sasha to crack.

As she cleared the woods the apiary came into view. The steel ribs of the once-mighty structure stood like a giant monument to all the regrets Sasha had accumulated.

Millie had been planning to leave. Maybe it had nothing to do with Sasha.

But the closer she got to the bunker, the more certain she became.

Millie set her up.

She followed the path of trampled grass toward the apple trees. Unable to tell if Millie had been back since they covered the bunker together, Sasha cursed herself for not leaving a marker or cairn to alert her if anyone had disturbed the bunker.

She cleared off the mat with bare hands, tossing rocks and

sticks aside and sweeping piles of dirt with her forearms. The wind kicked up, swirling loose dirt into her face.

She rolled the mat back to expose the wooden door, surprised once again that it existed, that it hadn't all been a dream. She heaved open the groaning door and descended the stairs. The damp cellar chilled her, and she wrapped her arms around her waist, in part to warm herself, but mostly to stop her body from trembling.

She had to be wrong. Millie wouldn't.

Her eyes adjusted to the darkness, and a damp chill settled over Sasha. She traced a streak on her father's desk where Millie had run her finger through the dust the day before. A bold rectangular outline stood out on the dusty surface, marking the spot where her father's research had sat for more than a decade.

Her father's journals were gone.

She searched the corners of the small room, on the floor, the cot, but Millie had taken them all. She would probably sell them to the highest bidder. Sasha imagined the headline: THE LAST BEEKEEPER'S SECRET RESEARCH UNEARTHED: HIS DAUGHTER KNEW.

"Fuck you, Millie," she yelled. The heat in her throat felt satisfying, and she released another howl, no words. Her voice tore at her throat until she choked on a wet sob.

Millie could implicate Sasha, and everyone would know she had covered for her father and lied under oath. Could she be charged with perjury? She had been a child at the time, but she'd known exactly what she was doing. Millie said all the right things to Sasha, spoke in gentle words. She listened and pretended to care.

Sasha had returned to the farm with the intention of unearthing answers, and now, with any hope of finding answers gone, she felt rudderless. The driving force that guided her for eleven years stolen from her by someone she trusted. Sasha sat in the dark, unsure how to function without the story she had told herself every night since her father went to prison. What if the parole board released her father and he came back for his papers?

Where would she go now? She had no family, other than Chuck, whom she would never turn to for help. And she had no real friends, no home. Except the farm and the people squatting on it. This land anchored her, and with each passing day, these new friends tugged on her a little more.

A sharp pang in her gut reminded Sasha that Halle, Gino, and Ian faced eviction from the farm if officials came looking for the bunker. They would blame Sasha. They would not want the Last Beekeeper's daughter to follow them when they left the farm.

Sasha would be, once again, alone.

Millie would likely sell the journals and stir up a new wave of accusations and scandal. Now, as an adult, Sasha would not be able to shield herself from her past and her lies.

With her father's parole hearing approaching, the revelation of the research would impact whether the parole board agreed to release him early. How could Sasha have been so reckless?

Lying awake in her shared room at the state home, Sasha had soothed the ever-present ache in her chest by reminding herself she had a future. She had plans. *Find the research. Understand the truth. Rebuild a family.*

Those demands she placed on herself the first night in state care now felt impossible. She'd found what she came looking for but let it slip away.

Something important lurked in those journals. Her father wouldn't have abandoned her for anything less than an urgent cause. But now, because of Millie, she would never know what, if anything, her sacrifice had been for.

Sasha sat on the creaky cot in the dank cellar, peeled the dusty quilt back, and pressed her face to the flattened pillow, searching for traces of her father.

Everyone she had ever cared about had left her, betrayed her, or both.

The pillow smelled of mildew and dust. Nothing more.

She rolled onto her back and stared up at the cracked ceiling. If she stayed down here, no one would know where to find her. She could disappear into the ground and avoid the inevitable headlines.

The idea of pulling the bunker door closed and barricading herself inside calmed her. She closed her eyes.

Bright light poured down the stairs when she woke up. She couldn't tell if she had been asleep for minutes or hours. Her head pounded and her stomach growled with hunger.

While she slept, her grief had morphed into anger, tempered, as Millie suggested, with a guilty tinge of relief. The research haunting her for the past decade was no longer her burden to carry.

*It's okay to grieve for the things we've lost, but it's more important to protect what we still have. Look around you. What do you love?* Her father's words felt close in the bunker.

"What *do* I love?" she whispered back to him. She curled her knees up to her chest as she contemplated the truth that maybe she didn't love anyone, other than her father. And her recklessness might have destroyed his only chance for parole if Millie turned over the documents before his hearing.

Gino and Ian had each other. Halle had Beatrix. Millie had family out there somewhere. But if Sasha disappeared, would anyone care?

Sasha could go after Millie. Leave the farm. Forget about Halle, Gino, and Ian. Now that the research was gone, why stay? Even as she imagined ways to track Millie down, Sasha did not intend to leave. Although her chance to learn the truth about her father had evaporated overnight, she still had a shot at fulfilling the last vow she made as a young, lost girl: *Rebuild a family.*

She needed to convince Halle, Ian, and Gino to want her to stay on.

Sasha stepped out into the blinding sunlight and closed the door to the bunker. She smoothed the disintegrating mat over it, and covered it with a thick layer of soil, grasses, and stones.

With the last shovelful of soil, Sasha promised herself never to reopen the bunker. The missing journals ached like a phantom limb she couldn't touch or soothe.

When Sasha returned to the farmhouse, Halle, Gino, and Ian sat on the porch stairs. They stopped talking as she approached.

"You okay?" Gino asked.

"I'm fine. I'm pretty sure I saw some beets along the edge of the forest near those potatoes we dug up. It's my night to make dinner."

"We can make dinner tonight if you need some time," Halle said.

Sasha didn't answer and walked toward the field. She approached the edge of the forest where she transplanted the potatoes and asparagus as a child. She dug up four large potatoes and crawled on her hands and knees in the rocky, overgrown soil looking for wayward carrots, garlic, and onions among the asters and timothy grass.

She hated that she missed Millie's company.

Sasha had allowed herself to believe they shared a connection, that Millie saw her and forgave her. Forgiveness, even from one person, had been a huge weight lifted from Sasha's shoulders. But it had been a lie and the weight now hung twice as heavy.

Millie promised not to tell anyone about the research, but Sasha didn't trust her. Had she been playing Sasha the whole time, waiting for Sasha to lead her to the bunker? Maybe her friends huddled around Ian's phone that very moment, reading about Millie's discovery of her father's research.

With six beets, one garlic bulb, several onions, two large Jerusalem artichokes, and two carrots in her bag, Sasha headed back to the farmhouse.

She paused at the garden to clip some parsley and dill before entering the kitchen. Inside, she spread the vegetables out on the butcher block, mentally deconstructing her mother's borscht as she cleaned and prepped the ingredients. Would vinegar be a satisfactory tang in place of the sour cream her mother used?

"Caught you red-handed." Gino jumped up to sit on the counter next to Sasha's pile of diced beets.

Sasha waved her crimson-stained hands in his face.

"I'm going to keep an open mind. But really? Beet soup?" Gino sniffed a beet and grimaced.

"Beets help build up your blood and have tons of vitamins." Ian joined them in the kitchen. "But let's be honest, they taste like dirt."

"Withhold judgment until you try it." Sasha didn't tell them about the baked potatoes.

Ian's phone chirped, and he looked at the screen for a few minutes.

Sasha held her breath. Was it Millie, warning the others about Sasha's deception?

Ian ignored the message.

"Give us a shout when dinner's ready," Ian said as he and Gino left the kitchen.

Sasha scrubbed the potatoes, poked holes in them so they wouldn't burst, and rubbed them with olive oil. She placed the potatoes in a small metal toolbox from her mom's workshop, which she had scrubbed clean. She closed the lid, and placed it in the hot coals of the fire pit.

Sasha drained two cups of white beans she had soaked overnight and added them to the stockpot with water, chopped beets, a few bouillon cubes, onion, garlic, carrots, chunks of Jerusalem artichoke, a generous splash of vinegar, and salt and pepper.

After the soup simmered over the fire for an hour, Sasha adjusted the salt and pepper, and added parsley and dill with another splash of vinegar to offset the sweetness of the beets. The soup bubbled with a syrupy viscosity. She stabbed a knife in to test the potatoes, then moved the box to the edge of the fire.

She felt her housemates watching her through the living room window as she monitored the soup. They were talking about her; she could feel it. Sasha's week had more than passed. They had her two-week portion of the rations. And after her emotional outburst, why would they want to keep her around?

Millie's deceit underscored the lesson Sasha had learned too many times. Betrayal hurt. She needed to get in front of the truth before it got in front of her. It was time to tell her new friends about her past.

This meal needed to be spectacular.

Sasha ladled the soup into mugs and opened the box of potatoes, the skins crisp, but not burnt.

"Are you kidding me?" Ian said when he saw the baked potatoes.

"I simmered some garlic and salt in olive oil to put on the potatoes. It's not butter, but it's not bad."

The moon rising over the trees on the horizon, and the gentle breeze teasing of the dropping temperature to come, paired well with earthy soup and baked potatoes.

Sasha watched Ian as he tried the borscht. He drew out the moment, refusing to react as he scrutinized a mouthful.

"It's brilliant," he said in a voice so low Sasha had to lean forward to hear him. "You're a fucking magician."

Halle cleared her throat as if she wanted to make an announcement. "Sasha, we want to talk to you about something." Halle sat with crossed legs, her back straight.

Sasha swallowed down a rising panic.

"The three of us have been together for a long time. We're a team," Ian said. "We trust each other."

They were cutting her loose.

"Oh, my God, just say it." Gino kicked Ian's foot.

"Look, I—" Sasha tried to interrupt. They couldn't make her leave. She needed them.

"Ian is trying to say we want you to stick around," Gino said.

Sasha stared at her knees. She felt like she was listening to the conversation from far away.

"Sasha?" Halle said.

The truth lodged in her throat. She could tell them everything and jeopardize their invitation. Or keep her secret and secure her place with this family.

"Do you want to stay?" Halle said.

She swallowed the truth trying to spill out and choked on her breath.

Halle put an arm around Sasha's shoulder. "You're home, if you want to be."

"Give the girl some space." Ian pulled Halle back. "She hasn't said if she *wants* to stick around."

"I do."

"Then let's put a ring on it," Gino shouted.

Sasha pulled her knees closer to her chest to hide the tremors racking her body. If she let go of her legs, she might come undone. She felt like she had been holding her breath for hours, for years, too afraid to come up for air.

The familiar lines of the farmhouse felt less like a ghost from her past and more like a promise of a future.

The smoky sweetness, tempered by the earthiness of the beets, swirled in the air.

"Just so you know, we decided to ask you to stay before you cooked this meal," Gino said. "But if there had been any debate, the baked potatoes would have sealed the deal."

As they ate and talked, Sasha took in all the details. The way Gino hummed under his breath when he thought no one listened. How Ian's sharp features turned tender when he smiled at Gino, and the way Halle braided a strip of Sasha's old curtains into her hair. The perfect balance of sugar and acid in the soup. She wanted to grab every bit of this moment and bind it to her heart.

They wanted her to stay.

These friends could handle the truth about who she had been and who she was now. She rubbed her palms on her thighs to warm her hands.

"If I'm going to stay, I need to tell you—" Sasha began.

"Damn." Ian jumped up, reading the screen on his phone. "It's the beekeeper."

Sasha sucked in a sharp breath.

"Our generous host was denied parole," Ian said. "They cite lack of remorse, belligerence, and unwillingness to cooperate with authorities."

"I thought the hearing was in a few weeks," Sasha said, trying to keep emotion out of her voice.

"They held the hearing early to avoid the media frenzy," Ian said.

"Wait." Ian continued scrolling through the story. "There's more. It says they denied parole, but they are transferring him to a low-security prison hospital."

"He's sick?" Sasha tried to stay calm. She should have visited. She should have agreed to testify in person. "Why is he going to a hospital?"

"It says he has been suffering from dementia for a few years, but his situation has gotten increasingly worse, and doctors no longer think he can function in a general population. He's being transferred to a federal medical facility."

"Where?" Sasha asked.

"Who knows." Ian turned off his phone.

"Sucks for him, but at least we know he won't be coming back here laying some false claim on the farm," Gino said.

"He forfeited the property to the state when he went to prison. We may not have a legal right to be here, but neither would he," Halle said.

*But this* is *his home,* she wanted to yell. *This is* my *home.*

Sasha tried hard to avoid news about her father, although the national obsession with him made it difficult. It had been easier to ignore him, change her name, try to forget. Suddenly, six years had gone by since she had seen him, and her lump of hot anger had morphed into burning shame over abandoning him.

"They went too easy on him, if you ask me." Halle slurped soup from her mug. "And now he gets to live in some cushy white-collar facility with three meals a day while we squat in his broken-down house digging up wild fucking beets for dinner? It's bullshit."

A wave of nausea hit Sasha. She stared into the flames, trying to keep her dinner down.

"No offense, Sasha," Halle said.

Sasha froze as they all stared at her. Had Millie told them? Were they toying with her by offering to let her stay? The beets churned in her stomach.

"Why would I be offended because you hate the beekeeper?" Sasha's heart pounded so loud she could barely hear over the rush of blood in her ears. The beets rumbled in her gut.

The edges of her vision unraveled in threads. She blinked hard and tried to focus on a single ember at the edge of the fire.

"I think she meant 'no offense' at insulting your beets." Ian laughed.

Sasha tried to laugh, but it came out in a garbled moan.

Gino crawled over to Sasha. "You okay? Halle was kidding. The soup's fantastic."

"I don't feel well." Sasha stood and walked toward the woods, trying to focus her narrowing field of vision strewn with tiny flashing specks. As soon as she made it to the edge of the driveway, she dashed toward the woods, the soup rising faster than she could run.

She dropped to her knees a few feet from the edge of the forest and retched until bloodred beets pooled on the ground in front of her. She rocked back and forth, twisting a blade of grass around her finger, torn between who she was and who she could be if she shed the yoke of her father's legacy.

"Hey, I wasn't insulting your cooking." Halle knelt beside her and rubbed Sasha's back as another bout of retching seized her. "And if you don't want to stay, we understand. We weren't trying to pressure you."

Halle's calm voice melted over Sasha as she scratched at the soil and dug up a fistful of earth. She squeezed the soil, paying close attention to the grit, the pebbles, the clay of home.

"I want to stay."

She stopped fighting her body as it evicted the last of her loyalties to the past.

# Fourteen

Sasha moved from under the piano to her father's former office the day after Millie disappeared. The first several nights in the office, she dreamed about Millie turning her father's notebooks over to the authorities, about police showing up to evict them, about Halle, Gino, and Ian blaming her. She dreamed about visiting her father, but he never recognized her.

Each day with no news about the stolen research sharpened the edge of Sasha's anxiety. Every time Ian opened his phone to read the headlines Sasha's pulse fluttered. The dread of loneliness penetrated her bones, icing her to the marrow. No matter how many layers she wore or how close she sat to the fire, she could not stay warm.

Halle, who had taken up lighting the morning fire in the weeks after Millie left, offered Sasha a mug of hot tea made from dried mint and lavender. Her hair hung loose, falling halfway down her back in messy tangles.

Sasha hugged the mug with both hands as the warmth calmed the hum in her fingers. She sat on a rock next to Halle, the chill of the stone penetrating her flannel pants. Dew clung to the grass, glistening like sequins in the apricot glow creeping across the lawn and up the porch stairs.

A brown haze hung above the distant fields between the farm and the greenhouse construction site. Scaffolding and glass panels rose out of the abandoned farms with unexpected speed, giving Sasha hope at least one of them might find a job soon.

Between the greenhouses and the farm, rewilded fields and forests relaxed in the morning light, comfortable with their untamed selves in a way Sasha envied.

"They moved her," Halle said, turning so Sasha could she her swollen, red eyes. "I was supposed to visit Bea on Saturday, but Ian got a message this morning telling me that due to a transportation mix-up, the bus moving her cohort left yesterday afternoon. She's four hours away."

"We'll find a way to get you there," Sasha said.

"How? We barely have enough to eat. I don't have money for the bus ticket. If there is a bus. And I'd probably have to stay overnight, which I can't afford, so I'd end up sleeping on the street and probably get killed. So, no. I won't be going anytime soon."

Sasha scooted closer and draped her arm around Halle's shoulder.

Trees at the highest elevations on the other side of the valley flashed early hints of crimson. As the temperature dropped, they spent more time collecting firewood and kindling ahead of the unpredictable winter.

The reality of Beatrix's relocation and Gino's lack of medication, along with the increasing reports of thefts and home invasions, gave the chill a sharper bite. Halle and Sasha both pulled their sweaters tighter around their waists at the same moment to block the wind.

Halle spun one of the rusty bike wheels impaled on the spike Sasha had arranged where her beehives once stood. "There's something sad but kind of beautiful about this, don't you think? There's a story here and we'll never know what it is."

Sasha swallowed hard as she watched the wheel slow its spin and settle into place.

"The fall spinach will be ready soon." Sasha tried to sound cheerful.

Halle forced a weak smile.

Deer used to feast on her mother's spinach, prompting her to try deterrents from hot peppers to coyote urine to metallic ribbon, but the deer usually ruined a third of the crop. Deer, however, had vanished from these woods years ago, leaving Gino as the creature she needed to protect her greens from most.

The asparagus Sasha transplanted from the field had taken to the new soil enthusiastically, promising an early crop the following spring. Every day as she checked on her plants she offered a quiet plea to the trees, the soil, the sky. *Please let us be here together in the spring when the asparagus breaks through.*

Sasha stood up and stretched.

"Morning walk?" Halle asked.

"Come with me."

"Nah, you go ahead. I'm going back to bed," Halle said as she plodded up the porch stairs.

Sasha had taken up a habit of going on long morning walks to collect flowers, herbs, bark, and roots for Ian, whose first-aid stall at the market had grown popular, even if it didn't bring in much money. Sasha accompanied him most Saturdays, managing the lines and assessing need.

At the edge of the field, she climbed over the stone wall and stepped into the forest. A sensation of being underwater but able to breathe enveloped her. Heavy pine branches muted sounds yet made them sharper at the same time. The creak of branches, the shush of leaves. Sasha swam through the soupy air, gulping down mouthfuls of floating golden particulates.

As she padded through the clearing where she and her father once hid her hives, moving steadily toward the creek where she'd seen the phantom bee weeks earlier, Sasha's past and present folded in on each other, entangling the hopes and fears of her childhood self with those of the new self she was trying to hold on to.

Gathering herbs for her mother. Gathering herbs for Ian. Tending bees with her father.

As a child, she didn't flinch when bees landed on her skin and walked across her bare toes. Her father paused every time he got stung and closed his eyes for a few seconds, offering a silent memorial for the bee who died. The memory simultaneously warmed and chilled her.

She sat on the ground and pressed her back against an oak tree, inhaling the aroma of mossy earth.

Something brushed against her hand.

She squeezed her eyes closed, tried to control her breath. *Don't move. Don't panic. Breathe.* She opened her eyes to find a leaf had fallen on her hand.

Just a leaf.

But the terror had worked its way inside her, coursing through her veins, adrenaline propelling a cocktail of disappointment and relief through her pounding heart.

She shuddered to think of the countless times she had scratched stingers out of her father's skin, never fearing the bees or their venom. The bees had been playmates, friends, not something to be feared—until the day they almost killed her.

Yet the longing grew until she could barely breathe.

She could never break the tether, the pull of the hive, the hum under her skin. Her body ached to be near them again.

Using Ian's phone, she occasionally searched a local message board for mentions of bee sightings, monitoring the recent uptick of unhinged believers.

She hummed, mining her memory for the perfect G until the familiar note settled in her sinuses, rattling in the back of her throat like an old friend, and her body fell into sync with the rhythms of the forest. Next to Sasha a cluster of fiery tiger lilies craned their necks toward the patches of sun sifting through the swaying hemlock and the bony shadow of a dead slippery elm.

Sasha felt invisible, part of the billions of molecules making up the forest. The earthy stew of mulch and decay loosened the tightness in her chest.

A doe walked into the clearing, so quiet Sasha wondered for

a moment if she had conjured yet another illusion, but the deer's twitching, caramel-colored ears and fleecy breath filled the clearing with proof of the impossible. A twig snapped under Sasha's thigh and the deer bounded out of sight, leaving a metallic sizzle and the whiff of a memory she couldn't bring into focus.

# Fifteen

In the afternoons, after she collected herbs for Ian, Sasha went into her mother's workshop to work on the red bike Octavia had given her.

She wanted to go back to the market and impress Octavia with her handiwork. She had already sanded down the rust, cleaned and reassembled the gears, patched the tires, tuned up the brakes, and hammered out the warp in the fender.

After working on the bike, Sasha climbed the ladder to the hayloft and allowed herself one chapter of the most recent book on loan from Bassel. Some days she read the chapter three times, but never more than one chapter.

She intended to return to the market on ration-distribution day, as she had for the past three months, hoping to see Bassel. Their leisurely book chats had become a reliable event she looked forward to.

She unrolled her mother's tools on the work surface and inhaled the earthy scent of worn leather. Sasha wanted to get the bike in working condition so she could visit her father in the hospital.

The workshop, a barn used by her grandparents to keep sheep and goats, smelled like generations' worth of expectation. Grease stains from the workshop, which had displaced livestock decades earlier, marred the thick-cut wooden floorboards.

Although her parents had never kept animals in the building

during Sasha's lifetime, she caught whiffs of livestock when the wind curled through the cracks in the walls. Sawdust, compressed and broken down over decades, filled in the creases where walls met floor.

Back in her mother's workshop years later, the ghosts felt close.

*It's important to take care of our belongings*, her mother had said as she taught Sasha basic bike maintenance. *People are too quick to throw things out if they aren't perfect.*

Some days she felt closer to the memory of her mother than she did to her father, whom she'd spent more years with. Her mother remained fixed in her memory, while her father shifted shape between the loving parent she remembered, the hero she wanted him to be, and the villain everyone else imagined.

Sasha struggled to reconcile the different versions of herself as well. Did the carefree child still exist? Was she doomed to be the Last Beekeeper's daughter, the heartless girl who sent her father to prison? Or could she abandon her former self and be Sasha Butler, a woman with no history?

*The truth always finds a way of coming out. And it will be a lot easier if they find out from you.* Millie's warning crashed into her mind at unexpected moments. Was it already too late? Had her prolonged silence morphed into an unredeemable lie? At night as she lay in bed, Sasha had practiced her confession. She intended to tell her friends the truth about her father that night. It was time.

She took the front wheel off the bike and mounted it on a vise built into the counter, imagining her mother's hands guiding hers as she adjusted the spokes.

"I forgot to tell you Bassel texted Ian last night." Gino startled her as he walked into the workshop. "He wants to know if you finished the book he gave you, and he said something about getting lunch to talk books?"

"When did he text? Did he say when he wanted to meet?"

"I don't remember." Gino smirked at her.

"What?"

"Nothing. He texts you a lot. Ian's going to start charging you a messenger-service fee."

"Should I tell him to stop?"

"No, I'm messing with you. We'd never stand in the way of young love."

"We're friends." Sasha wanted to change the subject.

"How's the bike coming?" Gino ran a finger over the handlebar.

"It's almost finished." Sasha cupped her hands in front of her face and breathed on her bare fingers to warm them against the cooling air. The draftiness felt comforting in the summer months, but soon the cold would creep into their bones, their fingers and toes, and their minds.

"Statistically, it's unlikely one of us will get a job, let alone all of us." Gino leaned on the counter.

"One of us will get a job. And whoever gets the job can use my bike."

"How'd you learn to fix bikes?"

"I used to hang out with my mom when she fixed stuff in her workshop." Sasha's mouth felt full of cotton. The truth warmed her with a long-simmering heat rising up from her belly.

"I can imagine you pulling off a teenager-in-coveralls-with-grease-on-your-cheeks aesthetic with style." Gino cocked his head to one side. "You never talk about your parents."

The weight of the memories pressed on Sasha with an urgency that had been building ever since Millie left. The words began collecting and taking on mass before she gave them permission, as if she no longer maintained power over the truth.

"My mom fixed my first bike right here after I crashed into that tree learning to ride a two-wheeler." She pointed to a linden tree on the edge of the driveway, visible through the window.

"You mean, here? Right here?" Gino squinted at her and cocked his head to one side.

*It will be a lot easier if they find out from you.*

Sasha sucked in a deep breath fortified with mildew, sawdust, and the memory of sheep she never met. The wrench trembled in her hand.

"I grew up here. In this house." She watched her words settle like dust. "He's my father."

"You're . . ."

"I didn't have anywhere else to go. I was afraid to tell you when I first got here, and I didn't plan to stay long. It felt liberating, for the first time in my life, to not be that girl."

Gino pressed the heels of his hands into his eyes for a few seconds, then looked at her as if seeing her differently.

"I wanted to tell you. I tried. But you invited me to stay, and I wanted to be part of this family, so I didn't say anything. After a while, this new life started feeling like the truth and I got scared."

"Of us?"

"Of losing you." Sasha's knees felt rubbery. She walked over to the workbench and jumped up to sit on it, her feet dangling in the air. "I didn't want you to think I was trying to claim the house. I wasn't. I'm not."

"If—when—people find out the Last Beekeeper's daughter is here, it's going to draw attention to us." Gino cracked the knuckles on both hands. "Which could get us kicked out."

Gino paced in front of Sasha, his feet always staying inside the pool of sunlight on the floor. "Ian's going to flip. Fuck. He's going to want you to leave."

"No, he won't." She tried to convince herself. "Ian's my friend."

"Which is why he's going to be mad you lied to us."

After her mother died, Sasha felt closest to her memory in the workshop, as if the essence of her mom existed in the air, the grease stains, and the rusted hinges on the door.

She gulped down the air, swallowing it, absorbing it. Beams of light poured in through the small window in the hayloft, lighting the swirling dust as if it had mass and shape.

"Sasha, hey, look at me."

She couldn't get enough breath in her lungs. Her fingers tingled with light and her muscles stiffened. Her fingers coiled inward, her wrists winding like the scroll of a violin.

Sasha felt something over her face. She kicked as Gino whispered in her ear, "Slow your breathing, Sasha. Slow breaths. In and out. In and out."

She wanted to fight him, but also wanted to stop fighting. If she closed her eyes, she could disappear into the column of dust and light.

The sun framed Gino's face like a halo when she opened her eyes to see him hovering over her. She didn't remember lying down on the floor.

"You're okay. I think you had a panic attack."

As the room came into focus, she shivered, although the air felt warm on her skin. Her fingers tingled.

*Slow your breathing, Sasha. Slow breaths. Slow breaths.*

The bike chain lay on the floor next to an empty paper bag.

"You hyperventilated. I learned the paper-bag trick from Ian."

Sasha started to stand up, but Gino pulled her back. "Sit a little longer."

"Are you going to tell them?" Sasha wanted to retract her confession.

"Your story belongs to you. Not to me. Not to Ian." He scooted next to her so both of their backs leaned against the cabinet where her mother once stored tools.

"This was my mom's workshop. See that two-person saw in the rafters? My granddad used it to cut down the trees they cleared to build this barn. My family named the saw Uncle Buzz. I'm not sure why. But we always took it with us to that cabin in the mountains. We'd pack up and my mom would yell, 'Don't forget Uncle Buzz.'"

Gino looked around the barn as if trying to visualize her memories.

He hummed quietly, the air reverberating in his throat like an entire orchestra living inside him. It wrapped around her like warm tea on a cold night.

"How do you do that?"

Gino kept the music coming, filling the workshop, invisible notes dancing with the dust and the light. His shoulders rose and fell, his fingers twitching as if conducting his breath. After he finished the song, he sighed deeply and slapped his thighs.

"What I'm going to tell you is only for you. No one else, okay?"

"Okay."

"I sang. No lion training, no bomb defusing. I sang opera. It was my whole world. When things started falling apart, I couldn't find work. I ended up on the street, then in a shelter." He looked up at the hayloft as if seeing the inside of the barn for the first time. "This one night, I was singing to myself, not loud, but three guys came back to the shelter drunk off their asses. They'd seen me have a seizure once and pegged me as a weird, queer loner they could kick around. That night my singing set them off and they jumped me."

Sasha caught the aroma of Halle's dinner-in-progress slipping through the cracks in the walls.

"I grabbed the closest thing I could find, and I swung. Hard. And I kept swinging." Gino put a hand to his side where the jagged scar hid under his shirt.

"I remember hearing glass break and the guys yelling and punching at me from different sides. Then, they were gone.

"I was bleeding pretty bad. One of them cut me." Gino rubbed his side as if reliving the memory. "After a minute I realized one of the guys lay on the floor gushing blood. I'd slashed his throat with a broken bottle I don't remember breaking. The glass, my hands, everything was covered in blood. He died before the police arrived. I stayed in the hospital for a few days. I never got charged with anything. They treated me like a victim, like I hadn't killed a human being."

"You didn't have a choice," Sasha said.

"I haven't sung since. I can't. It's like every time I think about it, I see that guy coming at me and my throat tightens. I know it's stupid, but I feel like he took my voice. Maybe I don't deserve to get it back. How do you ever settle up with the universe after taking a person's life?"

"You defended yourself."

Gino shrugged.

"Does Ian know?"

"Neither of them do."

"I won't tell them." Sasha put her head on Gino's shoulder.

"The Last Beekeeper, huh?"

"He was everyone's villain when we needed one. But he's also my dad. He used to call me Little Bee. The world hates him, but I miss him."

They sat in silence for several minutes.

"Why haven't you told Ian what happened to you?"

"I don't want him to know that part of me exists."

"Why'd you tell me?"

"Our stories belong to us, not to anyone else. But they're heavy. We can help carry each other's shit."

Sasha sat on her hands to stop them from shaking. Her muscles felt stiff, as if she might never be able to move them again, anchored to the floor, the barn, the farm, with a bond she could never break, whether she wanted to be free or not.

"Maybe no one's here." An unfamiliar voice came through the open window in the workshop.

Gino held a finger to his lips, indicating they should stay quiet.

"Just get the food and whatever else we can sell and then get out," another man said.

Sasha crept closer to the window and peeked out.

"Six men. Two have baseball bats," she whispered. "We need to warn Halle and Ian."

"How?" Gino whispered.

"The bell." Sasha pointed to the rusty dinner bell in the loft, a dry-rotting rope extending down and tied to a hook.

Gino nodded, and Sasha yanked on the rope several times. Clanging filled the barn and reverberated inside her head.

"It worked. Ian's at the door with the rifle," Gino said.

After she had shown her housemates the larder, which she had pretended to stumble on by accident, they had moved all their food stores into the secret room, along with their valuables and money. If looters showed up and tried to rob them, their belongings would stay safe behind the secret panel.

Halle insisted they leave some food and some cash in the kitchen to give looters something to take so they would move on. They had been robbed twice before Sasha arrived, but no one had shown up since to test their strategy.

Sasha and Gino walked up the driveway behind the intruders as Halle joined Ian on the porch.

"You can put the gun down, Doc," a man in a dirty jean jacket said. "Everyone knows it's not loaded, and even if it was, you don't have the balls to fire it. Aren't you the healer from the market? Do no harm and all that shit?"

The men ignored Ian and walked up the steps. Ian stepped between the intruders and Halle. Under different circumstances, Ian would have loved being recognized as the healer from the market. His stall, positioned next to Octavia's, had become so popular that queues of patients waited for him when he arrived. Every week he came home with an odd assortment of food, clothing, and housewares as payment, and sometimes a little cash. But Sasha knew he would do the work for free. She also knew the intruder was right. Ian would never intentionally hurt anyone.

"What do you want?" Halle asked.

"Food, money, anything we can eat or sell."

Ian kept the gun trained on the man in the jean jacket but didn't speak. Sasha and Gino stood with Halle and Ian.

"You keep an eye on them while we look around," the guy in the jean jacket said to a barrel-chested man with a baseball bat.

The living room was empty, other than the ratty sofa and a pile of bike parts Sasha had been trying to salvage.

"We don't have much," Halle said, her eyes flitting in the direction of the nearly empty sacks of rice and lentils left strategically on the counter next to two molding onions. Beside the food lay three burlap ration sacks that once held black beans and barley.

"What the hell do you guys eat?" the guy in the jacket said as he rummaged through the empty cabinets.

"That's all we have," Halle said.

Ian cracked his neck and adjusted his grip on the rifle, aimed at the men in the kitchen.

Gino started to walk toward the intruders, and without warning the barrel-chested guy turned and swung the bat with a sharp motion, pounding Gino across the stomach with a thud that knocked him to the ground.

"Gino!" Sasha dropped to her knees next to him.

"I'm fine," Gino groaned.

"Stay behind me." Ian's nostrils flared as he positioned himself between Sasha and the man with the bat. Muscles in Ian's neck twitched.

Everyone knew the gun wasn't loaded, but Ian refused to give up the charade.

Gino stood up, his eyes flickering around the room until they landed on three empty wine bottles on the table holding stubby candles with wax dripping down the sides. He swallowed several times and caught Sasha's eye. He gestured with his head in the direction of the bottles.

"I found cash." A tall, skinny teenager with tan skin and gaunt cheeks pulled a small wad of bills out of a mug Halle had strategically left in a cabinet.

"Leave half of the cash and take the food. We won't give you any trouble," Sasha said.

"Yeah, I don't think so." The guy in the jean jacket grabbed the money from the teen's hand and shoved it in his pocket.

"Check this out." The teenager pulled Sasha's violin case out from behind the sofa.

"No!" Sasha lunged to grab her violin, but the barrel-chested man grabbed her and pinned both arms behind her back. He smelled like he hadn't bathed in weeks. The stench of tooth rot and gum disease on his breath made her gag.

"Take the money and food but leave the violin." Ian tightened his grip on the rifle.

The man in the jacket swung Sasha's violin gleefully as they walked toward the door.

She would never be able to replace it. She would never play again.

Gino wrapped his arms around Sasha to keep her from chasing her instrument.

After the intruders left, Ian waited about ten seconds and followed them outside.

"Ian, don't." Halle tried to grab his arm, but he shook her off.

"I said leave the violin," Ian shouted at the men on the driveway.

The guy in the jacket spun around and took three belligerent strides back toward the house. "What are you going to do, Doc, shoot me?"

Ian glanced sideways at Sasha and drew his lips into a tight line, his breath shallow and sharp. His finger trembled on the trigger as he closed one eye and centered the intruder in the sight.

Sasha felt his panic rising. Ian had never confirmed the rifle wasn't loaded. He let them assume. As the sweat beaded on his forehead and his trigger finger twitched, Sasha understood it had been loaded all along.

"Ian, please don't," Sasha whispered.

The blast rattled the windowpanes. Gino, and Halle, and most of the men on the driveway dropped to the ground. The man with the violin stood frozen as a bullet whizzed past his shoulder and thunked into a tree behind him.

A flicker of relief passed over Ian's face, morphing quickly into a rage Sasha had never seen in Ian's eyes. He descended the porch stairs slowly and pumped his weapon, ejecting a brass casing with a clatter.

"*That* was a warning shot." Ian lowered the weapon to aim it at the man's arm. "I could shoot your arm off, or you could put the violin down and walk away. Either way, the violin stays. You just need to decide if you want to keep your arm."

The other men scrambled backward down the driveway, some crawling, some standing with their hands over their heads. The man in the grimy jacket slowly bent over and placed the violin on the ground.

"Now get the fuck off our land." Ian took another step toward the men.

"That thing's been loaded all this time?" Halle sputtered as the men sprinted down the driveway.

"You know how to shoot?" Gino whispered.

"No, I've never pulled a trigger before." Ian rubbed his shoulder.

Halle ran toward the violin case, picked it up, and placed it next to Sasha's feet.

Gino took the gun from Ian and leaned it against the wall. He placed one hand on each of Ian's cheeks, cupping his chin, and kissed him. "You okay?"

Ian pressed his forehead against Gino's and let out a long, ragged sigh.

"We need to be better prepared. The people I treat at the market are desperate. They're starving. Almost everyone I see—whether it's a cut, a rash, infection, fever—they're hungry. It's turning us into monsters."

Ian looked at Sasha and swallowed hard, an unspoken promise passing between them. Ian had not intended to miss his target, and Sasha would never tell.

Sasha opened the violin case and held the rosin to her nose.

"No one messes with my family." Ian's voice quavered, but his words landed hard.

Sasha looked at each of their faces, their solidarity fortifying her weak knees. This was the thing she had been chasing her whole life. The feeling of being loved. Of being home. Of belonging, which, for the first time, felt more important than being safe.

Sasha's relief and the fear in Ian's voice tumbled around in her chest until they erupted as a nervous laugh, which quickly spread to her companions. They laughed because they had to. The alternative meant acknowledging how the scene might have played out and what lay ahead in their uncertain future.

# Sixteen

Sasha shuffled into the kitchen late in the morning several weeks after the trucks drove away with her father's bees. Without his hives, her father seemed to have disengaged from time. He woke and slept at odd hours. Some nights they ate dinner an hour after she got home from school, other nights they didn't sit down until eleven. Sasha released herself from everyone else's circadian rhythm and mimicked her father's unpredictable schedule.

Morning sun poured into the empty kitchen. No coffee in the pot, no dishes in the sink. He hadn't gotten out of bed yet. Sasha didn't bother getting ready for school, making it her fourth absence in a month. Eventually they would have to recalibrate, but for now, she drifted through the days on her father's time.

She walked down to the basement and opened the larder. She picked up the half-empty jar of honey they rationed for special occasions. They never used to ration honey.

She put the jar in her backpack next to her mother's well-worn copy of *The Swiss Family Robinson* and went outside.

She climbed the ladder of small boards she had nailed onto the broad trunk of the oak tree in the front yard and settled onto her favorite branch, where she could see the whole yard but no one could see her.

From her vantage point in the tree, her sculpture garden, which she had been so proud of months earlier, looked like piles of junk.

How had she imagined herself clever to stack bike wheels on top of each other?

She opened the honey jar and tilted it toward her mouth. The slow ooze of honey inched toward her lips, as sunlight filtered through the jar, highlighting an array of tiny air bubbles trapped in amber.

As soon as the cheerful, linden-infused honey hit her tongue, Sasha laughed out loud. The six-year-old honey vintage triggered a flashback of wobbling on a two-wheeler while her mother ran beside her under a shower of the season's spectacular linden leaves.

Sasha ran her finger around the lip of the honey jar and sucked until the pad of her finger grew soft and the tangy sweetness dissipated. She put the jar away and took out her book, but before she finished the first page her father walked out onto the porch, his silver hair in a mad-scientist disarray.

"Sasha! Where are you?" her father shouted. He walked over to her sculpture garden and straightened the crates she'd positioned as seats next to the hive turned makeshift table.

Sasha froze so she wouldn't give away her hiding spot on the branch above his head.

He adjusted the stack of bike wheels and stepped back to survey the sculptures from ten yards away. Sasha held her breath.

"You did impressive work out here. Now come on down. I have another project for us."

"How'd you see me?"

"We have to move the hives again." His bloodshot eyes darted wildly around the yard.

"Are they coming for my bees?"

"I don't know, but we can't leave them in the woods anymore. It's not safe."

"Are you going to get your bees back?" she asked.

"No."

Sasha sucked in her lower lip so her father wouldn't notice the quiver.

"It's okay to grieve for the things we've lost, but it's more important to protect what we still have," he said. "Look around you. What do you love?"

Sasha loved her tire swing, the farmhouse. She loved the curtains in her bedroom and the stone wall at the edge of the forest. She loved her bees. And her father. But she said nothing.

"If we get lost in mourning what's already gone, we'll be paralyzed. Allow yourself to fall in love with what is real, with what exists, with what might exist. And fight for it."

"My bees are real."

"Exactly. So, we fight for them." He walked over to the truck and started the engine. They returned to the spot where they had unloaded the hives and reversed the entire process by deconstructing the stone wall, maneuvering the hives out, and rolling them up the ramp onto the flatbed.

By the time they had loaded the first hive on the truck, darkness had settled in and the November air chilled Sasha's fingers.

"Can't we finish this in the morning?"

Her father, who held a flashlight in his teeth, shook his head, sending a beam of light careening across the ground.

"Where are we taking them?" Sasha bit down on her cheek, allowing the spike of pain to block her tears from coming.

"To the apiary. They won't look there. They think they already confiscated all our bees," he mumbled around the flashlight. The bags under her father's eyes hung heavier than usual, his shoulders more stooped.

"They don't want to be inside."

Her father scratched at his beard. "I know. But it's not safe for them to be out here anymore."

A bat swooped low over their heads, giving Sasha a wisp of courage. She used to sit on the porch swing with her mother watching throngs of bats dart through the purple night sky. Bats didn't fly by their house anymore. There weren't many left.

The beautiful bat dipped close to their heads. Sasha squeezed both hands into tight fists. *I will fight for you.*

As they finished loading the fifth hive up the ramp into the truck, a car pulled into their driveway. She tapped her father's arm and pointed to the headlights. Her father turned off his flashlight and motioned for her to be still.

They crouched down next to the truck, which wouldn't be visible from the driveway, the dark green paint folding into the high grasses and the stone wall.

Her father knelt behind Sasha and wrapped his arms around her, holding her back up against his chest. Sasha felt his heart rate ratcheting up with every breath.

"Stay quiet," he whispered.

The ethereal lisp of a veery, her mother's favorite songbird, called out from the edge of the forest. Every time she heard a rare veery's trill, she imagined her mother calling to her.

A man got out of the sedan and walked up the porch stairs. Sasha let out a sigh of relief as she recognized the familiar shuffle.

"It's just Chuck." Sasha tried to stand up, but her father pulled her down.

"He can't know we're out here."

Chuck cut a slouchy silhouette against the moonlit night. He paced on the porch steps for several seconds before pounding on the door and yelling, "Lawrence, where the hell are you? We need to talk."

Sasha's father held her tighter. She closed her eyes and imagined him holding her the way he had when she was little. Rocking her to sleep, reading to her on the porch swing, tucking her into bed.

She tried to sink into the comfort of his embrace, but the thumping of his heart against her back made Sasha want to protect him instead of the other way around.

"We'll be okay, Dad."

"I don't mean to frighten you."

Sasha put a finger against the side of her nose to indicate all was forgiven.

They sat in silence for twenty minutes after Chuck gave up and drove away and her father's pounding heartbeat slowed to a steady rhythm.

Something deeper than silence greeted them when they entered the long tunnel of the apiary, which had housed millions of bees months earlier. Sasha felt like she had walked into a freeze-frame where she was the only thing moving while the rest of the world stood frozen. She kept her breaths shallow, afraid if she inhaled too deeply, the silence would slither inside her and make a nest.

She hummed a low steady tone.

Tired, and achy, Sasha and her father spread the six hives out in the giant space. Troughs of sugar water and an array of droopy flowers and bushes replaced the buffet of flowers outdoors.

She pressed her ear to one of the hives. Something sounded off. As if in their panic the bees had recalibrated to a G sharp instead of a G natural.

"They hate it here. We need to take them back outside," she said.

The beekeeper knelt next to his daughter and pressed his ear to the hive too, his head facing in the opposite direction from Sasha's so the backs of their heads touched.

"They'll be okay. They have to be." Her father stroked the pine box.

Sasha lay down on the earthen floor and watched the enormous fans at the end of the tunnel, churning fast enough to keep the air from being entirely stagnant, but not enough to cool her sweaty skin.

"I should have tried harder," he whispered.

The background noise grew louder as Sasha focused on following a single spinning blade, but she could never keep her eye on a single blade, no matter how hard she tried.

As she focused her vision on the fan, Sasha's body felt lighter, as if she might float away like a wisp of pollen. The whirring of the motor, the hiss of air whipping against the fabric membrane roof, dizzied her.

Her father fumbled with the matches to light the smoker, but this time, Sasha did not help him.

He dropped the first match and did not attempt to pick it up. He gripped the second so tightly between his stiff fingers it snapped as he dragged it across the textured strip on the box. The third match flared in the darkness.

He lit the smoker and calmed the bees so they could unwrap the mesh and release them. A few stragglers thrashed with their tiny feet and wings entangled in the mesh. Some clung to the fabric, already dead.

He dislodged a dead bee from the mesh and pinched it to expose the stinger.

"The world's fragility makes it beautiful." He stabbed the stinger into the tender space between his thumb and forefinger. He sucked in a sharp breath and closed his eyes as he rubbed the red welt to distribute the venom, soothing his arthritis. "We need to *see* the beauty, not just look at it. You'll remember that?"

# Seventeen

## SASHA, AGE 22
### SEPTEMBER 20

Sasha leaned her newly refurbished bike against a chain-link fence outside the medical prison where her father had been transferred. Unlike the prison he had been in for the previous eleven years, the facility was accessible by bike, although it took an entire day to get there and back. She would be racing the sun home.

Sweat drenched her shirt. She drained her last sip of warm water and sat back to catch her breath. Her hands fumbled with the lock Octavia loaned her for the trip. How would she explain to her father why she hadn't visited in years?

The weight of his name nearly crushed her as a child. Over time the shame twisted into writhing, pulsing anger. He abandoned her. If she pretended her past did not exist, she could move forward in the world like everyone else. She could build a new life for herself.

Except she couldn't move forward, because underneath the rage, she missed him.

She smoothed her windblown hair, drank a few swallows of water, and pressed the buzzer at the entry. As her body cooled down, the fall air chilled her damp skin, sending a ripple of gooseflesh over her arms.

The entryway smelled like a sour sponge left to ripen in dirty dishwater.

"I'm here to visit Lawrence Severn." She spoke softly, hoping her voice wouldn't carry. The women at the reception station both jerked their heads up.

"Is he expecting you?" the older receptionist asked.

"No."

"Your name?"

"Sasha."

"Last name?"

"Severn." Claiming the name she had relinquished felt dangerous.

"Relationship?"

"I'm his daughter."

The receptionists exchanged glances, both pursing their lips in synchronized judgment. The older, gray-haired receptionist didn't bother to hide her delight as she scanned Sasha's face for traces of the infamous smile, which Sasha had no intention of performing for their amusement. Older kids at the state home taunted her for years. *Do the smile. Do the smile.* She always refused, which won her no friends.

"Sign here." The gray-haired receptionist handed her a clipboard. "Take a seat and I'll see if he is available."

Scattered mauve chairs, muted by a gray patina of age and wear, sagged in the middle of each cushion, compressed by the backsides of uncomfortable family members waiting, waiting, waiting.

The proportions of the visitors' room mocked the lack of visitors. Too little furniture in too large a space. The seats pressed against the perimeter of the room, all of them facing into the center, as if a tight ring of chairs had been pushed outward until they hit the walls, unable to escape.

Sasha gnawed on her raw cuticles. The room reeked of body odor and canned meat.

Would he be angry at her for staying away so long? Or would he ignore her absence? Her sweaty clothes stuck to her body in the stuffy room. She had tried hard not to imagine how time and the onset of dementia might have changed her father. News reports of his transfer to the medical prison gave little information about his condition. Would he recognize her? Would he remember abandoning her to protect his research? Would he remember why it had been so important?

A door at the far end of the room opened and an attendant wearing pale green scrubs pushed a wheelchair into the room.

"Sasha Severn?" he said loudly, as if he needed to distinguish her from the multitude of nonexistent visitors.

She stood up and the attendant rolled her father over to a table near Sasha. She had never seen her father in a wheelchair.

"Alexandra?" the attendant asked without a flicker of recognition or judgment, which made Sasha like him immediately.

"Sasha."

"You sure you want to hang out with this one? He's a con man and a pickpocket." The attendant winked at Sasha's father and fist-bumped him. "If you've got food on you, he'll swipe it without you ever knowing until later you reach in your pocket for your chocolate and find it's gone, gone, gone."

Her father laughed.

"I'm messing with him. I sneak him candy sometimes, but if he gets caught with it, he promises to say he stole it, so I won't get in trouble."

The attendant was white, about forty, and stood more than six feet tall, with a tattoo of a vine wrapping around one forearm.

"Okay, Mr. Severn. You have thirty minutes. If you need me sooner, Candace will buzz me." He threw a mock salute in the direction of the receptionists. "I'm Hugo, by the way. It's a treat to meet the famous Alexandra."

"Right," Sasha said, irritated that Hugo had deployed the famous-daughter reference.

"I've heard so much about you." Hugo did not take the hint.

"The whole world thinks they know me. You don't."

"I didn't mean anything." Hugo appeared hurt. "I'm happy to meet you after hearing him talk about you all this time, is all. I'll leave you two."

"Shit. Wait, I'm sorry. People give me crap about the trial, my dad, and well, everything."

"I'm not here to give anyone shit." Hugo put his hands up in surrender. "He said you had a lot of spunk."

"Look, I'm sorry."

"We're good. Enjoy your visit." He fist-bumped Lawrence again and walked away whistling a song Sasha recognized but couldn't place.

Sasha had never seen her father fist-bump anyone.

His once sun-leathered skin now hung pale and papery around his jowls and neck. When he saw Sasha, his face lit up with a huge familiar smile.

"Hi, Dad."

Lawrence winced in pain as he opened his arms to her.

"Are you hurt?" Sasha hugged him gingerly.

"I'm fine. These damn joints." He pulled her close. The strong institutional detergent on his clothing hadn't washed away the sweet linger of beeswax infused in his beard.

"I'm sorry about the other night," he said.

"The other night?"

"About your concert. I'm sorry I missed it. I'll be there for the next one, I promise."

Sasha masked a dry sob by pretending to cough. Did he still see a little girl when he looked at her? She squeezed his hand, willing him to see her, to remember.

"Dad, I don't perform anymore. I haven't in years."

"Right, right, right. Of course, I know that." He brushed nonexistent lint from his sleeve and rubbed his swollen knuckles. "How's school going?"

"Fine." There was no point in explaining that she'd graduated years ago and couldn't afford college. "I need to talk to you about something."

"Of course." He leaned over the table, propped his chin up on both fists, more at ease than she remembered, softer around the edges.

"Why did we bury the bunker?" she whispered. "What was so important?"

The smile on his face froze in place for half a second, then melted away. His eyes darted around the room.

"Who told you to ask me that? Was it Chuck?" He slammed a hand down on the table, causing Hugo to glance over at them. Her father waved him off with an irritated dismissal.

"No one told me to ask you anything. I need to understand what I helped you bury, and why."

He sat back and folded his arms across his chest. "Your uncle only cares about himself. Jealous, conniving bastard."

Sasha had worked hard to distance herself from Chuck, not bothering to check in with him when she aged out of the system. He climbed the ladder in the Department of Agriculture while her father wasted away in jail.

*Last chance,* Chuck had said the last time she saw him.

After her father went to prison, the court forced her to live with Chuck, despite his betrayal of her father. When she ran away the third time, Chuck came to pick her up at the police station weeks before his scheduled transfer to DC. Sasha didn't want to move. She couldn't live so far from her father and from the farm, even though the state had taken ownership of the property.

She convinced her social worker to reevaluate Chuck's guardianship, saying he was never home. He forgot to pick her up from school. He neglected her.

In truth, her father had done those same things, but Chuck made a poor substitute for her father.

"If you cared about me, you wouldn't move," she shouted in the busy police station waiting area. "You wouldn't take me away from him."

"Alexandra, this promotion is important." He took her hand, but she yanked it away. "I'm not going to force you to come with me. But I want you to."

Sasha folded her arms across her chest.

"Last chance," he said as he left Sasha with the social worker.

She had been twelve at the time and Chuck hadn't put up enough of a fight to keep her. Who allows a twelve-year-old to decide who she lives with? Sasha cursed him months later when she found herself trapped in one of the many juvenile-care facilities that popped up in the wake of the Great Collapse.

She hated Chuck for forcing her to live with him. She hated him more for letting her leave.

"Chuck doesn't have anything to do with why I'm here."

"Don't let him find you. And don't let him find those bees." Her father's eyes widened.

"What bees?" Sasha leaned closer. Maybe he knew something about the recent sightings.

"Our bees."

"That was a long time ago. Those bees are gone."

He seemed confused for a moment, taking in the room and looking closely at Sasha's face.

"Right. They're gone." He rubbed his eyes and tried to disguise his confusion.

How many times had he relived that same revelation?

"Why did you protect your research instead of me? You chose this." Sasha gestured around the room. "Instead of me. I deserve to understand why."

"Leave it alone, Alexandra." He spoke with an articulated clarity he had lacked moments earlier.

She had wanted to believe she and her father protected something noble, something worth their sacrifice. As the years passed, Sasha's childish naïveté transformed into doubt and the gnawing question: Had she been conned?

"You've been locked up for eleven years while I've been trying to get by in a world where no one can forgive the daughter of the Last Beekeeper. Do you have any idea what it's like living with that? Don't tell me to leave it alone."

He cringed as her words hit a tender spot.

"You don't understand." His face morphed from a wounded expression to a stern one. "You need to stop asking about it. Forget the bunker ever existed."

With the research gone, only her father held the answers Sasha sought, and his own memories appeared to be slipping away, taking all the secrets with them. She wanted him to parent her, reassure her.

"It's dangerous." Anger seeped into his voice. Hugo looked over at them.

"Dangerous for who? For you?"

"For all of us. The less you know the better." He gripped the edge of the table. "It's not time yet."

"Time for what?"

"You'll know when it's time." He leaned close to Sasha and put his hand on hers. Fear rumbled in his bones. "You must leave this alone. It all stays buried."

Did real danger lurk in the pages of the journals Millie stole, or was her father delusional?

"I'm sorry I haven't visited in so long. I . . ."

"I'm glad you're here now, Little Bee. Is your mother coming?"

Sasha's throat tightened. She shook her head, unsure whether she should remind him her mother had died nearly fifteen years ago, or let him blissfully forget.

A light flashed, indicating her visit was over. She needed more time, time to touch his hands, catalog the new lines in his face. Time to understand what motivated him and what he had involved her in.

Mostly, she wanted more time to be with him.

"I love you, Dad." She leaned over and hugged him, letting her head rest against his shoulder. Less flesh covered his bones now, but pressing her face against his body, listening to the beat of his heart, Sasha felt safer than she had in years.

"Second chances only come along once," he whispered. "We can't mess it up this time."

"Second chances for what?" Sasha asked as Hugo guided her father away.

On her ride home, Sasha averted her eyes from the sea of greenhouses rising up in the distant folds of the hills, now brown, as the last flush of autumn color had dissipated. She didn't want to get her hopes up. According to the news, the Department of Agriculture planned to open fifty enormous greenhouses by the end of the year, with another two hundred and fifty coming online over the next three years as part of the Agri New Deal.

In the three months since they'd applied for greenhouse jobs, none of them had received a response, although they checked the status every week. *Application pending.* Always pending.

Colorful dots of tents and campers popped up in clusters on the perimeter of the greenhouse campus, more commonly known as the glass farm. Encampments expanded every day as desperate people showed up to compete for the jobs Sasha, Halle, Ian, and Gino needed.

Makeshift shelters spilled over into fields of abandoned farms once owned by her childhood neighbors. How would all these people survive winter? Water and food would be scarce. Sanitation would become a nightmare.

Ian's first-aid booth had plenty of customers who supplied them with odd bits of food and cast-off items, but it wasn't enough to feed Ian, let alone all of them.

With rations being slashed every month, Sasha worried they would have to fend off more intruders at the farm. The first several nights after the break-in, Sasha had moved upstairs and slept on the floor in Halle's room, not wanting to be alone on the first floor. But after Gino set up noisy trip wires around the perimeter of the house and Ian bartered to get Sasha a baseball bat, she returned to her own room.

The world felt on edge, as if the barely stable economy might crumble if the wind changed direction. However, despite the relative instability of the rest of the world, Sasha hadn't felt this settled since she was eleven. She had friends, a home, something worth holding on to, worth fighting for.

Lying awake at night in the state home, Sasha had turned her father's words over like finely polished stones.

*We can rebuild,* he promised her before they dragged him from the courtroom. *We are not the last.*

Sasha spent the next decade analyzing those words. What would they rebuild? Their broken family? The bees? Or did he literally plan to rebuild the decaying farmhouse?

As her father disappeared through the courthouse doorway, Sasha had vowed to rebuild it all. A family. The house. And what if, she allowed herself to imagine now, what if the bee had been real?

But to rebuild, she needed to stay.

Telling Gino about her past had felt like a dangerous but necessary step. She trusted him to keep her secret, but the longer she stayed with this new family, the more she wanted to be honest with them all before Millie exposed her.

Would her new friends turn her out for lying to them? And if they evicted her, could she survive in the overcrowded camps begging for food, alone, once again?

*Please let me be the one to get a job.*

She needed to be needed. To be indispensable.

# Eighteen

On her way home from visiting her father, Sasha stopped at the market to return the bike lock to Octavia and scavenge for parts at the end of the day, when vendors started giving away items they couldn't sell. The unwanted bits were Sasha's favorites.

Octavia stood behind her counter, leaning over to collect books in a box as she prepared to close up shop for the day.

"Damn." Octavia stood up and walked a circle around Sasha and the bike. She pinched the tires, squeezed the brakes, and leaned in close to examine the gears.

Octavia shook her head, as if trying to evaluate what made Sasha tick.

Sasha grinned.

"Excellent work. There's a huge market for bike repairs around here. You think you can fix these up?" Octavia gestured with her head in the direction of four bikes in varying states of disrepair leaning up against Octavia's counter.

"Absolutely." Sasha tried not to let her excitement show. "How much would it cost to buy another one, as is?"

"I'll tell you what, I can't pay you cash, but if you can fix up the two nicer ones, like you did your bike, I'll let you take the other two to do what you want with. I can't move broken bikes. I'll provide what parts I can, but you'll need to be creative. On the edge of the parking lot, you know that area with a bunch of broken-down cars and appliances? There's a huge pile of car tires. Sometimes you can find bike tires mixed in. You might find useful stuff over there."

"Deal." Sasha dropped her bike to the ground and threw her arms around Octavia's broad shoulders.

"Whoa, there. I am not going into business with you if you're going to bring that kind of energy," Octavia said in a gruff voice, although Sasha caught a slight smile when she released her from the embrace.

"Sorry." Sasha crouched down to examine the bikes. "I love working on bikes, and I need some for my housemates. We applied for those greenhouse jobs. They're going to need transportation too."

"She had a knack for fixing things too. At least that's what I hear." Octavia lowered her voice.

"Who?" A chill rushed over Sasha's arms.

"Your mother."

"My mother died a long time ago." Sasha put down the gears she had been examining.

"I know. You look a lot like your dad. But you have your mom's hair."

"I think you're confusing me with someone else. I should get going." Sasha stood to leave.

"Hey, beekeeper's daughter."

Sasha's fingers went cold.

"I'm not going to tell anyone."

"But I'm not—"

"My husband knew your—"

"Sorry I'm late." Bassel jogged over to the counter, sweat glistening on his forehead.

"It's about time," Octavia said, and raised her eyebrows at Sasha, suggesting they would finish the conversation later.

Sasha smiled at Bassel and smoothed her hair and her shirt. Octavia caught her eye and smirked.

"I got hung up at work. Did you get it? It's all I've been thinking about all day," Bassel said.

"Of course I did." Octavia put a hand on her hip, looking pleased with herself.

Sasha forced a partial smile at Bassel, unable to put words into a coherent sentence. If Octavia knew who her father was, did other people know? Would Octavia use it against her? How long had she known? Bassel gave her a crooked smile, which amplified the pounding in her chest.

The ground under her feet felt unstable, as if it were sand being washed away by retreating waves.

"Hey, Sasha." Bassel stood up straighter and put a hand in his pants pocket, then pulled it out and leaned on the counter.

"Picking up a new book?" Sasha managed to say over the pulsing in her ears. *Just breathe. Slowly, with control. Breathe.* She liked that Bassel appeared flustered by her.

Octavia raised her eyebrows to see how Bassel would answer.

"I, umm." He looked back at Octavia.

"You can trust Sasha. She and I are going into the bike-repair business together. She's good at keeping secrets, just like I am." Octavia held Sasha's gaze for half a second, pulled out a brown paper bag with something inside, and set it on the counter in front of Bassel. She took a step back and crossed her arms.

Bassel stared at the bag.

"If you're not going to look inside, I will." Sasha started to reach for the bag, but Bassel picked it up first.

He peeked inside and grinned. He had a wide smile with one front tooth overlapping the other in a charming way. Her quieting heart rate spiked again.

"Go ahead, try it," Octavia said.

Bassel reached inside the bag and twisted open a container. He stuck his face over the bag and inhaled deeply. His grin morphed into a scowl.

"It's fake." Bassel rubbed his eyes and pinched the bridge of his nose. "It's fake."

"You haven't tasted it," Octavia said.

Sasha inched closer.

Bassel stuck a finger in to scoop something up. As he brought his hand out of the bag, the smell of sugar water made Sasha want to gag.

Bassel stuck his finger in his mouth and spit the goo onto the ground.

"I paid good money for that," Octavia said. "Do you have any idea how many contacts I had to go through?"

"You got ripped off," Bassel said.

"How do I know you aren't trying to rip me off by saying it's fake so you can pay less?"

"Because I'm not giving you anything for it."

"Let's see what Sasha here thinks." Octavia nudged the bag closer to Sasha.

She caught a scent of fresh ink and mint as she leaned closer to Bassel to peek in the bag.

Honey. The golden color made Sasha want to believe it could be real honey, but the viscosity suggested corn syrup. The saccharine smell lacked complexity, no floral notes or citrus accents.

"This isn't honey. But I think . . ." She smelled it one more time. "But it might be cut with real honey. Can I taste it?"

"What the hell. Go ahead." Octavia threw her arms up in the air.

Even though the texture wasn't quite right, the feel of the imitation honey made her hands shake. She scooped up a fingerful and touched it to her tongue. Under the heavy cut of corn syrup, she detected a hint of lavender in the grossly diluted syrup.

"It's probably fifteen percent honey," she said, and handed the jar back to Bassel.

He tasted it again and closed his eyes as the imposter melted on his tongue.

"Lavender?" he said.

"How could you taste that?" Sasha said, surprised that Bassel, who looked about five years older than her, could discern individual floral notes in honey, which had become a rare delicacy by the time Sasha was eight.

"I remember." Bassel handed the jar back to Octavia.

"So do I." Sasha held Octavia's stare.

"What am I supposed to do with this now?" Octavia sniffed the contents. "Smells like honey to me."

"Do you want to grab a bite or something?" Bassel asked Sasha.

"Yeah. Sure." Sasha wiped her sweaty palms on her thighs and tried to act casual.

"Oh, thank God. It's about time you two stopped pretending to randomly meet up at my stall," Octavia said.

"I do no—" Sasha protested.

"Oh, please, and you're just as bad," Octavia said to Bassel. "He asks about you all the time, Sasha. I'm running a business here, not a dating service. I do not have time for this. Go get a drink. Go get a room for all I care."

Sasha's face burned with heat.

"I was thinking more of grabbing a snack." Bassel smiled, looking as embarrassed as Sasha felt.

Octavia reached under her table and heaved a thick hardcover medical book titled *Wound Care* onto the counter in front of Sasha. "I found this in a recycling bin. I grabbed it for the doctor. Can you take it to him?"

Sasha flipped through the glossy color photographs and grimaced at the images of open wounds and oozing infections.

"Ian better remember this if I ever need stitches." Octavia frequently offered gifts perfectly selected for the recipient. But with each gift, she extracted the promise of a favor to be delivered someday in the future. Sasha didn't know of a single instance where Octavia had called in any of these favors, but everyone owed Octavia something, making her the richest, most influential, and most beloved person at the market.

"Tell the doc if he sets up for a few hours on Sundays, too, the vendors' association agreed to pitch in a little bit from each booth to pay him a salary. We know he treats people even if they can't pay. He's the only medical care out here."

"You know he isn't a real doctor, right?" Sasha said.

"He's the closest we've got. And everybody loves him. He's great with people, especially the elderly. He treats folks with dignity and—"

"You're talking about Ian? Grumpy Ian?"

"He's not grumpy with patients. I'll even throw in lunch if he agrees to Sundays, too."

"I'll tell him. And I'll be back with the bike when it's fixed." Sasha grabbed the handlebars of the beat-up green bike. Bassel took Sasha's red bike and walked beside her.

She wanted to ask him about the honey but didn't want to appear too eager. She had spent the last eleven years dodging conversations related to beekeeping.

"Octavia isn't very subtle." He looked sideways at her. "But she isn't wrong. I have been looking for you."

"Why?" Sasha squeezed the handlebars of the bike.

"I don't know. We like the same books. I bet we have other things in common."

"Like honey?" Sasha's heart beat so fast she wondered if Bassel could see it through her shirt.

"Like honey."

They walked around the stalls as the shopkeepers closed down their booths for the night. Vegetable vendors put out their less de-sirable produce in boxes they left at the gates for the stragglers from the camps who didn't have money. Shopkeepers traded mostly in cash, but most businesses bartered, and almost all the food vendors fed the hungry at the end of the day.

"You were going to spend a lot of money on that tiny jar."

"It wasn't for me."

Sasha's stomach tightened. Had she misread the situation? Maybe Bassel just wanted a friend to discuss books with.

"My mother's missing. We don't always get along. We have, well, philosophical differences. I haven't heard from her in almost two years. She disappears every now and then. But this time . . ." Bassel looked down at the ground. "It's been a long time."

"And the honey?"

"It's her favorite thing in the world. We fought before she left. I thought it would have made a nice peace offering when she comes back. If she comes back."

"What did you fight about? Wait, sorry. None of my business. You don't need to answer."

"It's fine. My mom's an anarchist. When I took this job with the ag department, she went nuts, telling me I was brainwashed, a sell-out. She can't let go of the world that used to be. She's obsessed with whose fault it is, but I want to focus on the future, like how can we move forward? How can we rehabilitate the soil? How can we feed people? We had the same fight over and over, and then one night she stormed out and I haven't seen her since."

"Must be hard not knowing." Sasha looked him in the eyes for the first time since leaving Octavia's booth. "I hope you find her soon."

Bassel skimmed the flyers on top of flyers tacked to the community board. Everyone had lost someone or was lost themselves. The ache in Bassel's eyes stirred a pang of regret for the years she had avoided visiting her father.

"Hey, we're organizing a protest at the greenhouse complex." A teenage boy startled Sasha as he jumped in their path and tried to hand her a paper.

*What are the feds hiding?* The flyer listed details for an upcoming meeting.

"Not interested," Bassel said as they walked past the boy.

"So, what exactly do you do?" Sasha asked.

"I'm a soil regulator. I'm stationed here to monitor the recovery of contaminated agricultural land in this sector."

"I applied for a greenhouse job, but I'm not holding my breath. I hear they're flooded with applicants."

"True, the odds aren't great, but you never know," Bassel said.

Sasha squinted at the setting sun. "I'd love to hang out, but I have to push two bikes home in the dark. I should head out in a few minutes."

"I could drive you. With the seats down in the back, I can fit both bikes."

"You have a car?" Sasha didn't know anyone who owned a car. Getting in a car with Bassel felt reckless, but something in his smile, in the way he talked about his mother, made her feel safe.

"A quick bite?" He crinkled his nose and smiled, showing the overlapping front tooth Sasha couldn't resist. "I'm buying."

"That sounds good." Her stomach rumbled. "How do you know Octavia?"

"Before I got settled in government housing, I stayed in her boardinghouse for a few months."

"Octavia runs a boardinghouse?"

"Did you think she supported herself selling used paperbacks and bike chains? I think she runs the shop because she likes having a place to go and a way to keep track of everyone's business. Besides, the market would collapse without her. She has her hands in everything and she knows everyone's secrets."

"Now that I know you're buying, I'm starved." Sasha had no interest in talking about all the secrets Octavia kept, because one of them was hers. As she walked next to Bassel, she wondered what secrets of his Octavia hoarded.

# Nineteen

## SASHA, AGE 22

### SEPTEMBER 20

After a quick meal of noodles at the market, Bassel drove Sasha home. As they approached the driveway to the farm, Sasha braced herself for him to recognize the apiary and comment about her living in the home of the Last Beekeeper, but he didn't mention it.

"Do you mind letting me out here? If you pull in the driveway, Ian, my housemate, will see the headlights and come out with a rifle. We've had some uninvited guests recently."

"Can you manage both bikes? I could walk you up if you want."

"I've got it from here. Thanks for the ride. That would have been brutal with both bikes." Sasha put a hand on the door but didn't open it. Sitting in the car with moonlight pouring onto their laps reminded her that possibilities existed beyond the farm.

Bassel got out of the car and helped her get the bikes out. The moon behind Bassel backlit his curls, and Sasha dug her fingernails into her palm to resist reaching up and touching his face.

He helped her steady the bikes, one on either side of her, and stood in front of her. He put a hand over each of hers on the handgrips. She caught the smell of ink again, mixing with pine wafting in from the woods.

"Good night, Sasha Butler." He stood there without moving other than a soft squeeze of his hands over hers. Moonlight kissed his profile, highlighting the bow of his upper lip, which twitched nervously. He drew in a breath as if to say something but didn't speak. He backed up slowly and walked toward his car. She didn't move until his car pulled away.

Sasha had never told Bassel her last name, she realized, as his taillights disappeared over the rise in the road. Maybe he really had been asking about her.

The bikes clunked over potholes shadowed in gauzy moonlight as Sasha made her way toward the house. The pedals slammed into her shins, digging into her skin every few steps.

How could a person's eyelashes be that long?

When Sasha approached the curve in the long driveway, a scream—undeniably Halle's—cut through darkness, followed by a howl from Gino. Sasha froze, unsure whether she should run in the direction of the screams—or away. When Ian, always the quiet, stoic one, yelled something incoherent, but charged with fear, or rage, Sasha dropped the bikes and sprinted toward the workshop.

Flashbacks to the barrel-chested man beating Gino with the baseball bat clouded Sasha's vision. Had the looters returned with weapons?

Halle yelled again, words Sasha couldn't make out. Sasha's heart felt like it was clad with spikes, stabbing her chest with each violent heartbeat. When fights broke out over squatters' rights, houses always went to those willing to use violence.

They had been lucky last time. But if word had gotten out that Ian kept a loaded rifle, intruders might return with guns of their own.

Sasha didn't see signs of anyone else on her way up the driveway, but the shouts grew louder as she rounded the bend and saw Halle, Gino, and Ian in the shadows on the front porch.

Inside the workshop, she searched for a makeshift weapon. She grabbed the largest wrench from her mother's tool belt, took a deep breath, and sprinted from the workshop toward the house. Her three friends moved as a tangle of arms and legs, holding each other, tripping over each other's feet, howling.

"Sasha! Where the hell have you been?" Gino called. "Get over here."

"Are you hurt?" Ian pointed at the blood trickling down her legs where the bike pedals had pummeled her skin.

"You're okay?" She turned in a circle to make sure no one lurked behind her.

"Are you planning to bludgeon someone?" Gino pointed at Sasha's hand, frozen over her head with a tight grip on the wrench, ready to strike.

"You were yelling. I thought . . ." Her face burned with rage, even as it became apparent no one threatened her friends.

"You came running here to defend us?" Gino put a slow-moving hand on Sasha's shoulder, and with his other hand gently pried the wrench from her hand.

"You're shaking." Halle took her sweater off and draped it around Sasha's shoulders. "We're fine. Are you okay?"

Ian knelt to examine the cuts caused by the bike pedals.

"I'm fine. I'm fine." She closed her eyes and took three slow, deep breaths to calm her heart rate. "Why were you screaming?

"Happy screaming. We got jobs at the glass farm!" Halle said.

Halle's words, meant to be joyful news, landed like a stone in Sasha's gut. They wouldn't need her. They wouldn't be impressed with the banged-up bike. They had real jobs that paid real money.

She should be happy for them, but the math was clear. If all three of them landed jobs, statistically she couldn't have. She would now be using more resources than she contributed.

Her mouth felt dry from thirst, from running. From fear.

"Aren't you going to say anything?" Halle grabbed both of Sasha's hands. "Don't you understand what this means?"

"That's great. I'm happy for you." She forced a smile.

The tire swing twisted in the breeze, letting loose a low groan as the rusty links rubbed against each other. It was going to be a chilly night, the beginning of a cold fall and a freezing winter. Sasha shuddered, thinking about the encampments.

"Oh, baby girl. You don't get it," Gino said, his eyes open wide with excitement. "You got a job too. We *all* got jobs!"

Sasha's body went numb as they waited for her reaction.

"How do you know?" she asked.

"I hacked your account after we got our notifications." Ian held his phone out for her to see the letter addressed to her.

"Say something," Gino said.

Halle wrapped her arms around Sasha so hard Sasha's ribs ached, but the invisible bands around her chest loosened.

Gooseflesh rose on her skin as the wind churned up the scent of lavender.

"There's more," Ian said, his voice breaking through the noise in Sasha's mind. "Congress passed a temporary moratorium on evictions of people squatting in abandoned properties or encampments surrounding glass farm campuses. The Department of Agriculture committed to building barracks to house greenhouse workers who need it, but in the meantime, there won't be any more squatter evictions."

"We're going to be okay," Halle whispered. "We're all going to be okay."

Sasha felt as if she were floating a few inches off the ground. Arms folded in around her, and she let her body melt into the family she intended to hold on to with everything she had. At least for now, they could stay at the farm. They could pool their money to get Gino's medication and help Halle bring Beatrix home.

Sasha dropped down to sit on the porch floor. The moon had shifted, casting a shimmer on the pile of rusted bike tires impaled on the spike.

"Do you want to see your job offer in writing?" Ian held his phone out for Sasha to read.

*Dear Sasha Butler,*
*It is with great honor and gratitude that we offer you a position in the newly established Pollination Corps of the United*

*States' Agricultural New Deal. In the face of the ongoing agricultural crisis, our country is learning to rely more and more on our hand pollinators to feed the nation. Your role as an employee of the Department of Agriculture will serve a vital national interest. We thank you for your contribution to the effort to stabilize our food security.*

*As you know, the national unemployment figures have remained above 22 percent for three years. Food systems have not recovered from the Great Collapse of our pollinators. You have the opportunity to help your country and feed your fellow citizens. Two out of three families in the United States reported not having enough food within the last three months. With the massive rollout of the greenhouse systems, we aim to boost employment and restore food security for all.*

*You have been selected from an enormous pool of applicants. We had to turn away 93 percent of the candidates. You are among the first of a historic corps of workers. There will be many more hires in the future. But your cohort will be the first. Congratulations.*

*Your country thanks you for your service.*

*Sincerely,*
*Charles Skinner*
*Assistant Director*
*US Department of Agriculture*

Uncle Chuck.

*Don't let him find you.* Her father's warning echoed in her mind. *And don't let him find those bees.*

A chill rushed up Sasha's spine.

# Twenty

## SASHA'S 11th BIRTHDAY
### JUNE 6

Sasha lay awake in bed staring at the amber water stain on the ceiling from last winter's ice dam above the gable. Now the paint darkened whenever it rained. The more rain, the wider the circle. The stain resembled the cross section of a tree with visible rings marking each rain event. Six misshapen rings showed, although there should have been twenty downpours since the roof started leaking. Good for the ceiling, bad for the dry, dusty land.

As the sun smeared pink through Sasha's bedroom window, her father's slow footsteps lumbered down the stairs, more weight on his right foot as he leaned on the stair rail.

"Can I go with you?" Sasha leaped out of bed and followed him. Her father hadn't allowed Sasha in the apiary to check on her bees since the day they moved them from the woods to the indoor facility. He gave her updates, but they usually weren't positive. Just like the bees in the wild, her hives were dying off, although at a much slower rate. She liked being part of her father's secret. Not even Chuck knew her father still kept bees at the apiary.

"Not today."

"But today's different." Sasha dropped a hint, expecting her father to remember her birthday. He shook his head and kept walking.

"They're my bees."

"They do not belong to you, to me, to anyone. A far as you or anyone else is concerned, those bees no longer exist." He spun around faster than Sasha had seen him move in months. "Don't you understand? They're dying. All of them, and I can't stop it. This is not about you."

Sasha's forearms prickled with fear. He rarely raised his voice to anyone. If anything, he whispered too often, especially when he mumbled to himself. She went back into her room and slammed the door.

Hadn't she tended them? Hadn't she always left more honey than they needed to make sure they had enough food for winter? Maybe the reason her bees survived when the others died was because Sasha was a better beekeeper than her father, better than any of them.

Her bees.

She flung herself onto her bed and screamed in her pillow until she fell back asleep. She dreamed of her mother opening her bedroom door and walking across the room with a steaming stack of pancakes drowning in honey. Her mother cupped one hand around a single lit candle in the middle of the stack.

Sasha woke in the empty room but allowed the waking dream to unspool.

*Happy birthday, sweetheart,* her mother would have said as Sasha blew out the candle.

Each with her own fork, Sasha and her mother would have eaten from opposite sides of the stack. Sasha would run her finger around the perimeter of the plate to scrape up every last drop of honey.

*What should we do today? Anything you want.* Her mother would have tucked Sasha's hair behind her ear.

*I want to see my bees.*

*I know, sweetie.*

*I can help him. You know how good I am with bees.*

*It's not the right time.*

Even in Sasha's waking dream, her mother's cheekbones started to hollow, shadowing her face with a green-gray cast.

*Potpie or stroganoff for your birthday dinner? I have ingredients to make both. Whichever one I don't make tonight, we can have tomor-row. Double the celebration.*

*I don't care.*

*You have to pick one.* Her mother would have pressed her as if the future of civilization hung on which meal Sasha chose for her birthday dinner.

*Potpie.*

Her father banged on the door, dissolving Sasha's fantasy.

"I have a lot of work to do." He stuck his head inside her door. "Why don't you make some spaghetti tonight and we'll eat together after I finish up work. We can celebrate then."

Why should she make dinner on her own birthday?

"Fine."

She pulled a pillow over her head, and closed her eyes, trying to bring back the image of her mother, who wouldn't come into focus now that she was fully awake.

*Don't be angry. This is hard on him. It's his life's work,* her mother would have said.

*I changed my mind. Stroganoff.*

*Of course. It's your birthday. You can have whatever you want.*

Sasha smelled her mother on the lavender breeze drifting in through the floral curtains.

At dinner, she would force a smile and play the perfect birthday girl, then make the case that she could be her father's hands, help with the things he struggled with. She swallowed down the knot of anger. She would swoon over whatever birthday gift he offered even if he gave her another science book to add to her shelves full of science books.

At five fifteen she started dinner and set the table.

Sasha couldn't complain to anyone about her father's obsession with the bees in the apiary because he was keeping them illegally. She couldn't even tell Chuck, who she knew would coddle her and sympathize with her neglect. He would also report her father.

The fact that her father wouldn't let her see her bees made it worse.

She slammed silverware on the table and went upstairs to put on the white eyelet dress her father had bought for her recital two years earlier. Although she still hated the dress, at least it fit properly now. She would do whatever it took to charm her way back into the apiary.

*I'll dress for dinner too,* her mother would have said. *How about my purple dress?*

Sasha's mother hated dresses. With short, spiky red hair flecked with white, her mother looked most beautiful in a T-shirt and jeans. She'd had large green eyes and dramatic cheekbones. As a little girl, Sasha used to smear grease on her cheeks to emulate her mother the way other kids experimented with their mother's lipstick. But Sasha looked nothing like her mother. She favored her father, with heavier bone structure, a thick jaw, and dark eyebrows. Months before her mother died, Sasha had cut her hair short like her mother's only to realize her face couldn't pull off the style.

*I think I'll break out my black heels,* her mother might have said in preparation for Sasha's birthday celebration. Her mom hated high heels, but she loved doing the very thing everyone least expected.

Sasha's father was predictably late.

Dinner grew cold as she waited alone on the porch swing.

At six o'clock, Sasha paced on the porch. The pasta congealed into a lump.

All his talk of beauty—*See the beauty in the world*—was bullshit. He didn't see his daughter on her birthday. If he couldn't examine something under a microscope, it didn't matter. It didn't exist.

At six forty-five she called her father for the tenth time. No answer.

*Be patient, Sasha,* her mother would have advised, holding a finger to the side of her nose, their family's signal that simultaneously meant *I'm sorry* and its response, *All is forgiven.*

At seven, Sasha stomped down the porch stairs, feeling unsteady in the high-heeled shoes she had taken from her mother's closet for her birthday celebration. She stumbled toward the trail in the woods leading to the apiary.

Branches whipped across her bare shins, exposed by the ridiculous white dress. A twig caught the hem and tore the bottom edge, as she wiped the tears streaming down her cheeks.

The humid breeze tasted like grass. She wanted to chew the air into a ball, spit it out, grind it into the dirt. Her mother's shoes rubbed the backs of her heels, forming blisters, but she didn't slow down.

Her face burned from exertion, anger, and tears when she burst into the empty apiary office. She wanted him to feel bad, to see her hurt.

The sound of her mother's heels on the cement floor echoed off the aluminum walls.

"Dad," she yelled in the angriest voice she could conjure.

She pushed open the airlock separating the office from the indoor apiary and turned on the light. Since moving Sasha's bees indoors, her father had instituted new protocols. He began wearing a clean suit to prevent bringing any contaminants in contact with the bees. He installed a new air-filtration system.

She passed the clean suit hanging like a ghost on a hook. She considered putting it on, but the one-piece suit would have hung off her and dragged on the ground. Besides, her bees had spent their whole lives around Sasha. They crawled on her skin and tiptoed over the tops of her feet.

Bees did not need protection from Sasha.

She turned the doorknob, feeling the suction break as she pushed the door open. Her ears popped. The new fans churned with a louder groan than the old ones.

"Dad?"

The long, cavernous tunnel was empty, other than hundreds of thousands of bees flitting through the air. The row of flowering bushes and wilting flowers looked less appetizing than the wildflowers and lavender they preferred. Her eyes stung with fresh tears at the sight of her bees sucking up sugar water from a tray. Her bees. Full-grown bees drinking sugar water instead of foraging.

"Dad!"

The door slammed shut behind her and the buzzing around her grew louder. Sweat dripped down her neck. How could her father stand wearing a clean suit in this heat?

The new fans churned louder as they switched to a higher gear. Giant fan blades churned the thick air with a hypnotic grind. No other noises, as if the rest of the world had fallen away. That must be what if felt like to her bees. Their whole world reduced to a vaccuous space.

A wave of jealousy rushed up her chest and neck, burning her sweaty skin. Why did her father have to spend so much time with the bees? The oblivious insects flitted around the sad bushes, sipped on the sugar water. Had they forgotten the wildflowers? Had they forgotten Sasha?

The fans changed speed again as she walked toward the closest hive. The pitch of the gears clashed with the hum of the bees.

Her eyes on the fan, her ankles burning as her mother's shoes cut into her heels, she walked toward a hive. An unsettling urge to flip the box fluttered in her fingertips. After years of her tender care, they had forgotten the lavender, the honeysuckle, and settled into this trap working for her father.

She clamped her jaw closed as the urge swelled. To punish her father, punish the bees.

Sasha took a decisive step toward the closest hive, one of her high-heeled shoes sank into the sandy flooring, and she tripped. As she stepped forward to recover, her shin smacked against a shallow trough of sugar water. Warm syrup sloshed upward, drenching the front of her torn dress. A flurry of bees leaped from the tray where they had been sucking the cheap imitation nectar.

She wiped the sugar water from her shins as the flustered bees sputtered around her, following her as she stepped back, drenched in sugar.

*Never make sudden movements. Be calm. Always calm.*

But the bees swarmed closer, drawn to the sugar soaking her dress. Bees crawled up her shins, tangling their tiny legs in the wet lace of her dress and triggering a distress signal to the other bees.

The first stinger sank into her forearm. The second on her neck as she swiped at her throat, smearing her skin with sugar. The rest came too fast, from too many places at once. Her tongue felt thick.

It felt as if the air was being sucked out of the apiary. Not enough oxygen. Her lips felt swollen. What was happening to her?

"Dad," she tried to yell, but her breath emerged as a croak.

Allergic. The realization amplified her panic.

How was it possible that after living with bees her whole life she was allergic? She had never been stung and had assumed she never would be.

She needed air. Her throat tightened. The red of the exit sign over the emergency door pulsed in her peripheral vision. The alarm. She could trigger the alarm.

She stumbled toward the door, her vision fraying on the edges. Her heart felt too big in her chest, forcing blood to move too fast. And the burning.

Clawing at tight skin on her neck and chest, she tripped, falling face-first in the dust. Her mouth full of dirt, she couldn't conjure enough saliva to spit. On all fours she crawled toward the door, the pulsing red light throbbing in sync with her heart beating in her throat. EMERGENCY EXIT ONLY. She pulled herself up on the door and pushed it open.

Leaning on the open door as the fresh air washed over her face, she tried again and again to swallow. She coughed to clear her airway, but the air in her lungs barely squeaked out.

The emergency alarm wailed yet sounded far away. A cloud of bees rushed out the door. A thick, syrupy mass, they kept coming. The swarm moved like melting chocolate, swirling and folding over itself above Sasha's head as she fought to get air through her tightening throat, and struggled to keep her swollen eyelids open. The skin on her lips stretched tight like it might peel open.

Stings on her neck, face, and arms burned, the heat crawling up her torso, neck, and scalp as she lay in the tall grass outside the apiary.

"I'm sorry, Sasha." A voice hovered over her.

The bees would never hurt her on purpose.

"I'm so sorry."

She felt her body being lifted in the air. The bees came back for her.

Her body thumped against something soft and warm, safe and familiar.

She forced her eyes open and saw the swarm disappearing into the woods without her.

"Stay with me, Little Bee."

It wasn't his voice but his smell that yanked Sasha back. Her father ran through the tall grass, over the gravel driveway, his waxy breath falling heavy on her face.

"I'm so sorry," he said. "Hang on. Please hang on."

Her father tossed her onto a cushioned surface infused with the smell of old socks that haunted her father's pickup truck.

She stopped fighting the tightness in her throat and chest. She no longer needed oxygen. She felt light and heavy at the same time. Thick like dough, yet the air blew through her as if she were made of lace.

A stabbing in her thigh jolted her back to her surroundings, and she screamed an airless, silent scream. Her father's head pressed against her chest as he waited, listened. A second stab set her other thigh on fire. Heat burned in her leg and up her torso, erupting in a cough.

He touched his rough hand to her face and tilted her chin up. She could no longer see the swarm, but their collective relief washed over her, warm like honey, as they rushed into the wild.

"Breathe, Little Bee." He slapped her cheeks. "Breathe."

# Twenty-One

## SASHA'S 23rd BIRTHDAY
### JUNE 6

When the asparagus burst through the soil the following spring, nine months after she accepted the greenhouse job, the flash of tender green reopened wounds Sasha had worked hard to heal. She pushed away thoughts of Millie's hands working alongside her own as they uprooted plants from the field, separated the crowns, and replanted them.

It had been almost a year since Millie disappeared with the research Sasha found in the bunker. As far as Sasha could tell, Millie had kept her promise of not telling anyone about the papers, but Sasha's anger and fear flared at unexpected moments.

Once, while chatting with Bassel at the market, Sasha imagined she saw Millie watching them. When she read an article that speculated about the decade-old mystery of the beekeeper's lost papers, her rage toward Millie overwhelmed her.

But other days, when Sasha sat reading on the porch next to Halle as she knit, relief was the only emotion she could conjure. If Millie hadn't taken the documents, if Sasha had reburied them as she intended, the notebooks would have haunted Sasha, summoning her always. Eventually, she would have dug them up. She would have gone through each journal page by page, obsessing over every word in search of the reason why her father so desperately wanted to protect his work.

Maybe Sasha would have exposed her father's research and gotten them all evicted from the farmhouse if the authorities swooped in to sift through the bunker and the house.

Millie had done her a favor, she tried to convince herself. The lost research was no longer her burden to carry, yet it hung over her like a hammer poised to drop at any minute.

The emergence of the asparagus reminded Sasha that dormant possibilities can fight their way toward the sunlight. Sasha knelt in the damp soil and dug up a thick crown of asparagus, and she disentangled the roots into three clumps. Each section looked diminished and frail without its family to hold it up. But next season each third would expand into a robust cluster that in a few years would again need to be broken apart and replanted. Sacrificing part of this year's harvest in anticipation of next year's bounty required faith.

Separating the crowns felt like an investment in their uncertain future on the farm. A prayer, a sacrifice. *One more year. Please let us have at least one more year.*

She dug holes and replanted the three parts of the plant.

"You got this," she whispered to the displaced stalks as she pressed the soil into place and doused them with water from a milk jug. "You'll be okay."

Sasha resisted looking at the driveway again. Halle should have been home from her shift at the greenhouse fifteen minutes ago.

Sasha sat back on her haunches and burrowed her fingers into the loose soil of her garden. The texture, the spongy clumps of damp earth, the improving ratio of sand and grit, always sent a shiver up her arm. She was winning the battle to bring vitality back to this patch of earth. The dark soil in her garden stood in sharp contrast to the sterile hydroponics in the greenhouse where she worked ten hours a day, five days a week.

Miracles grow out of barren soil and chemicals. But Sasha didn't want a miracle. She didn't want a genetically modified tomato the size of a grapefruit, like the ones in the greenhouse where she worked. She wanted something she could nurture, count on, cherish, and hold.

It infuriated Sasha the greenhouses dedicated valuable space to growing tomatoes, which could be pollinated by the wind when grown outdoors. But tomatoes brought a reliable price, which helped fund the more nutrient-dense produce, most of which sold for prices the workers couldn't afford.

The motto of the glass farms, Feeding the Nation, didn't apply to the hungry poor.

Sasha crawled over to check on her tomatoes, descendants of seeds her mother saved years earlier.

She pinched a limp tomato leaf and looked up at the hazy, gray sky. The heat made it impossible to keep up with the water her plants demanded. The acrid zest of crushed tomato leaf reminded her of her father's hands after they had worked in the garden together. Dirt, sweat, wax, and a sweet hint of tobacco.

A few hundred yards away, Halle soared down the driveway on her green bike, going too fast as usual, the tail end of her skirt whipping behind her. The tension in Sasha's shoulders relaxed a degree. Halle's shift at the greenhouse ended an hour after Sasha's. It was the quietest hour of Sasha's day, long enough to stir a pang of relief when Halle came home. A cloud of dust kicked up behind the bike as Halle slammed on the brakes in front of the porch and let her bike clatter to the ground.

Halle skipped up the hill toward the garden and pointed at Sasha. With her tangle of hair knotted on top of her head, Halle planted her feet in a wide stance and sucked her cheeks in to suppress a smile.

"They say it's your birthday." Halle sang off-key and strummed an imaginary guitar. "Well, it's my birthday too."

"It's not your birthday," Sasha said.

"But it's yours," Halle shouted in a singsongy voice. She kicked off her shoes and skipped barefoot across the brittle grass.

More than her birthday, Sasha wanted to celebrate the day marking a full year since she had arrived back at the farm, since she met Halle, Ian, and Gino and found a home. They had been able to stash away a tiny nest egg with the goal of finding a permanent home together, a place the state would find suitable for Halle to bring Beatrix home to.

After food, most of their combined income went toward Gino's medicine, but it wasn't enough to maintain a regular supply. His seizures hadn't stopped, but they hadn't gotten worse in recent months. They rarely talked about it, but the housemates always remained alert, watching Gino and praying he would stay healthy until they had enough money to maintain his med supply.

For the most part, they were safe, and they were together, which was more than Sasha would have dared dream a year earlier.

Ian purchased another rifle, and Sasha installed bolts on the doors. Their deterrents might slow desperate invaders but wouldn't stop them. Sasha worried whether they could survive another winter on the farm.

Halle skipped over to the asparagus patch where Sasha worked.

Sasha stood up and dusted her knees off, careful to make sure the soil fell back into her garden. She worked too hard on her compost to let the nutrients disappear into the wind.

"I got you a present. They replaced a bunch of doodads in Greenhouse Eight's filtration system. I stayed after my shift ended and picked through the piles before they sent them to Reclamation." Halle reached into a slouchy bag slung across her chest and pulled out a metal clamp meant to mount on a counter, perfect for working on bike parts. "I thought you could use it in your workshop. It needs to be cleaned up, but it's in decent condition."

"You're a goddess." Sasha tossed the clamp back and forth between her hands. The weight of the small metal object felt satisfying, full of promise.

"It's going to be a great sunset. I'm going to go start dinner, but I'll be back for the light show. Are you serenading your veggies again?" Halle nodded toward Sasha's open violin case on the ground. "Not that I'm judging."

"My mom used to swear talking to her plants made them grow better, so who knows, maybe they like music, too."

"Play me something." Halle clasped her hands under her chin.

Sasha dusted the loose dirt from her fingers and put the instrument to her chin. She had been trying to teach herself the song Gino liked to whistle. She didn't quite have it, but she was getting close.

A gentle wind swept across the grass, fluttering Halle's skirt and the tops of the asparagus. Sasha closed her eyes and imagined the music weaving in and out of the vegetable rows.

When she opened her eyes, Halle was halfway back to the farmhouse, skipping to the melody. Sasha didn't know what the song was about, but the way Gino embodied the music made Sasha simultaneously sad and hopeful. She held the last mournful note longer than usual and nodded at the asparagus.

Sasha's stomach churned. She hadn't eaten anything but sprouts and bread for lunch. What she wouldn't give for a ripe strawberry, so plump its juice would roll down her chin. Her saliva glands pinched, and she swallowed hard. In September the apples from the two gnarled apple trees near the old apiary would come in. She and Gino had climbed the trees in April to hand-pollinate every flower they could reach. Tiny green knots now weighed down the branches with the promise of a robust harvest. They would roast slippery apple slices over the fire and sing songs from their childhoods. She could wait for the apples, an indulgence few people could hope for these days.

After the greenhouses opened and the federal government reduced—then eliminated—the food rations, some of the tent camps cleared out. The few with jobs barely scraped by on meager salaries, and violence flared in the greenhouse barracks. The food she and the other pollinators grew were shipped off to cities where people of means outbid each other for baskets of mealy produce.

Sasha dipped her pollinating brush into the remaining squash and cucumber blossoms as the sun fell lower in the sky. The tedious chore made her grateful for the potatoes, carrots, beets, and asparagus, which didn't require facilitated pollination.

She shielded her eyes from loose dirt swirling in a gust of wind that bent a tussle of echinacea and bergamot on the upper edge of her garden. Four tall sunflowers bobbed, casting cartoonlike shadows.

Sasha's vegetable patch, her tiny corner of the world, gave her hope, even as the rest of the world grew increasingly unstable. The field in front of her garden unfurled like a quilt tufted with scraggly low brush and wild grasses.

They had failed the land, and now, beyond her small bit of earth, the land was failing them. The greenhouse model was meant to be a bridge to a new model of agriculture, but so far, no one had delivered on that future. The Agri New Deal served the few and broke the many.

Sasha felt the underpinnings of the greenhouses quaking. Employees whispered in corners. Strikes failed because replacement workers clung to the chain-link fences, waiting for the chance to fill a vacancy. Their fragile illusion of stability felt more precarious every day.

Sasha sat with her knees pulled up to her chest and blew at a fluff of pollen floating by.

As she watched the fluff settle on the ground, a honey bee rose from an echinacea blossom and landed on Sasha's bare knee, inches from her face, its tiny feet touching her skin.

Real feet. Touching her.

Every muscle in Sasha's body seized. Her throat tightened, her airways constricted, as she watched the swagger of the insect, its shiny stinger twitching from side to side.

She squeezed her eyes closed and opened them to see the creature still staring up at her.

A bee. Inching across her skin, challenging her this time to believe.

*Believe.*

If all the other bees had been her imagination, this moment confirmed that Sasha was losing her mind—or was proof that bees still existed.

Either prospect terrified her.

*Don't move.*

Flashbacks of bee stings frequently tormented her dreams. Twenty-eight tiny daggers full of venom, her airways closing, the inescapable knowledge she was dying, dying, dying. Sasha survived that day twelve years earlier. The bees, however, did not. Her skin burned with the guilt of her role in the demise of the last colony.

The paintbrush slipped from her fingers as the bee rose into the air in front of her. The whir of its wings stirred a faded memory, as if she had rediscovered a forgotten color.

A single bee creates a shadow of the sound a hive makes, a nearly imperceptible hum. But Sasha had been finely tuned to internalize the pitch of a bee's wings beating the air at two hundred and thirty beats per second. The tiny bones in her ears and the cavities in her sinuses received the vibration like a secret language. A message.

The bee lowered itself to sit, once again, on Sasha's leg. Adrenaline surged through her veins, filling her with a soul-unzipping awareness that something long-awaited, yet inconceivable, stood in front of her.

*Just breathe. Be still.*

Phantom bee stings on her face and neck burned and itched as she fought to stay calm. The memory of EpiPens stabbing into her thighs triggered a twitch in her leg, and the bee lit off. Gone before she could catch her breath.

"Come back." Sasha fell backward, crushing a cucumber vine on one of her most productive plants. She crawled through the dirt, clawing her way to the edge of the garden, searching the sky for the bee. "I believe you."

If this bee existed, others must have survived as well.

*Believe.*

The sky looked miles higher than it had seconds earlier, as if Sasha could now see the layers of the atmosphere, the strata of particulates and unexpressed moisture. Clouds above her swelled with hoarded condensation. Her chest felt like it couldn't contain a fierce swell of the long-absent sensation: hope.

"Who are you talking to?" Halle said.

Sasha's breath came fast as if she had been running upstairs.

"You okay?" Halle asked.

"Just talking to myself." She touched a finger to the skin where the bee had landed.

*Second chances only come along once.*

Sasha considered telling Halle about the vision, but the encounter—real or not—felt too intimate to share. Down in the valley, the greenhouses shimmered in the sunlight. It wouldn't take much to shatter them.

Halle looked at Sasha with wide eyes, unaware that Sasha might have witnessed a miracle. Or that Sasha might be losing her mind. Halle lifted one foot off the ground and pressed it against the knee of her opposite leg to stand, as she often did, in a tree pose. Her toes and heel rooted into the dirt, anchoring her to the land.

"Hey, birthday girl," Gino called. He and Ian came down the porch stairs and walked toward the garden. Gino broke away from Ian and sprinted toward Sasha. He picked her up in a twirling hug.

"You almost missed it." Halle gave Gino a chiding punch in the arm.

"We're here now," Gino said, glancing back to make sure Ian followed.

Ian stepped up beside Sasha and nudged his shoulder up against hers. "A whole trip around the sun. And we're all still here."

"We need to do something about your hair." Ian fingered Sasha's split ends. "After dinner I'm giving you a trim. Consider it a birthday gift."

"I'm not letting you near my hair after that last cut." Sasha swatted his hand away and examined the fuzzy ends of her hair. In most light, her hair appeared dark brown, but against the backdrop of the setting sun, the deep red embers glowed through the brown.

"It's almost time." Halle looked over her shoulder at the sun drooping low in the sky. "Wishes ready?"

Gino stepped behind Ian and threaded his arms around Ian's waist, resting his chin on Ian's shoulder.

In moments like this, when they gathered together, tired and reeking of the organic fertilizers that sloshed around the greenhouses where they all worked—in these moments, unexpected waves of gratitude swamped Sasha and threatened to knock her to her knees. It had taken so long to find her way home.

She should forget she ever saw that bee. She should wish to forget.

But the touch of tiny feet on her skin, physical contact she could not deny, had already burst through her defenses. She could no longer deceive herself into unseeing them. The bee in the forest had also been real. She had allowed herself to deny its existence too long, and she could no longer look away.

*The bees always come for you.* Her father's words returned to her.

As the sun slunk lower, a peachy burn bubbled up from the horizon.

"It's time." Halle wrapped her arm around Sasha's shoulders and squeezed.

The sunset, as seen from their hilltop farm, lacked the heroism to turn heads, but a secondary light bouncing off the array of greenhouse roofs in the valley set the horizon on fire when the conditions were right. The scaffolding of the greenhouses had gone up so quickly it had seemed like a new structure grew from the ground each week for several months the previous summer. The light shows began the week the first glass panels were installed. First one house, then five, then twenty.

A last burst of light from the slumping sun glanced off the greenhouse roofs, causing them to blossom from gray to a smear of vibrant orange, pink, and purple. Sasha filled her lungs and held the air in. Next to her, Halle sucked in a deep breath and smiled behind puffed-out cheeks. Gino and Ian filled their lungs, and they all waited, their eyes on the light as they made their wishes.

One, two, three seconds and the orange glow melted into pink.

At six seconds, the pink blaze morphed into a dusty purple shimmer.

The air in Sasha's lungs burned to get out.

*Believe.*

On ten, Halle emptied her lungs in a forceful stream of air, as if blowing out a birthday candle.

The skin on Sasha's leg burned where the bee had touched her skin.

*Believe in the bee.*

"Today's the day, Sasha. All your wishes will come true," Halle said.

Sasha held the hot air in her chest. If the bee was real—it couldn't be real—it could upend the security she strove to create. That bee could smash the glass of the greenhouses in the distance and destroy this fractured semblance of stability.

Or—she released the air in a forceful blast—that bee could save them all.

# Twenty-Two

## SASHA'S 23rd BIRTHDAY
### JUNE 6

"No dishes on your birthday." Halle reached for Sasha's plate as Sasha started to stack their plates after dinner.

"Tonight's my night." Sasha held on to her plate for a moment, then released it to Halle.

Rituals gave shape to their lives. Ian's rules and Halle's need to bend them provided a rhythm to their patchwork existence on the farm.

A steady breeze chattered in the wind turbine Sasha had repaired months earlier, creating enough electricity to power lights in the kitchen and family room and to charge Ian's phone.

The nearly full moon rose from behind the windmill. Sasha moved her head to the side until she centered the pale orb around the center of spinning blades and the moon lit up the middle of a sunflower crowned by rotating leaves. A heavy humidity hung in the air, teetering between comfort and chill.

Ian and Gino sat with their legs dangling over the edge of the porch.

"I chilled the beer in the creek." Ian stood up and walked backward toward the woods.

"I'd *love* an ice-cold beer." Gino grimaced at Ian.

"Stop making faces. This batch is going to be fantastic."

"Mmmm-hmm. Let's go get this amazing beer." Gino followed Ian.

"Want to practice for your interview?" Halle swung in a wide arc on the porch swing.

"They'll either want me or they won't." Sasha tried to downplay her nerves, but they all knew the bump in salary would be enough to get Gino back on the medicine he needed.

Halle plucked a stem of lavender poking through the stair railings and tossed it to Sasha. No matter how hard Sasha tried to desensitize herself, the smell of lavender always hit hard. Images of her mother crashed in. Bouquets drying on hooks in the pantry, the pale petals steeping in a jar of honey. Her mother had surrounded the farmhouse with lavender to attract bees. The perfume saturated the corners of Sasha's memory.

Sasha caught the flowers Halle tossed at her and held them to her face, pressing on the wound. One day it would stop hurting. One day it would simply be lavender.

Sasha picked up Ian's phone, which he'd left on the porch stairs, and began scrolling through the day's headlines.

"Are you worried they'll overturn the eviction moratorium?" Sasha asked.

"It will never pass. And if they did overturn it, no one could ever get us out of this house. It's our home." Halle's knitting needles clicked faster as she worked on a scarf for Beatrix. "You can't spend every waking minute looking backward or worrying yourself sick over the future. Just for today, look around you and be happy."

But Halle's optimistic words couldn't mask her worry. Every stitch reminded her she had not seen Beatrix in months and had no idea when she would see her next.

Sasha traced the path the bee had walked on her thigh hours ago. Vibrations of the bee's wings echoed in her memory, whispering something urgent. This time, Sasha was ready to listen.

Gino and Ian emerged from the woods, each with a hand on a wooden milk crate rattling with bottles of beer. In their other hands they each held an open bottle.

"It's not terrible." Gino took a swig as they walked. "I think he's finally done it."

Ian beamed.

"What if some survived?" Sasha said. "What if they've been hiding?"

"Who's hiding?" Halle asked.

"The bees." Her housemates exchange concerned looks.

They did not discuss bees at the former home of the Last Beekeeper. It was one of the unwritten rules of their small family. They didn't bring up Beatrix unless Halle did. They pretended to believe Gino's stories about how he got his scar. No one ever mentioned Ian's family. They had rules.

"Care to elaborate?" The creak of the swing halted as Halle planted her feet on the ground.

"What if the pilgrims were right all along?" Sasha strained her ears to listen for the frogs that should have been singing from the creek. Their throaty voices had all but disappeared in the past few years. She rubbed a finger over the well-worn grain of the floorboards, remembering the sensation of dragging her bare toes over the pearlescent knots as a child.

The snap and hiss of a beer bottle opening next to her ear startled her. Ian picked up Sasha's hand and folded her fingers around the cold, wet bottle.

A lone frog sang in the distance.

"I think they're out there somewhere." Sasha clinked her bottle against Ian's. "And I'm going to find them."

# Twenty-Three

S asha's head pounded as she struggled up the first hill of the five-mile commute to work at the greenhouse. Halle and Gino fell out of sight as they crested the hill on their bikes. Ian hung back with Sasha.

"You're dragging," Ian said.

"Maybe, but it's your fault. What's in that home brew?"

"It's a secret recipe. Come on." Ian stood up on his pedals and sped up.

Sasha loved their commute to the greenhouse. Some days they rode in silence. Other days they laughed, talked, or raced. The ritual gave Sasha's days predictable shape.

Halle opted to stay an hour later than the other three so she could have a lunch break to meet with a group distributing flyers with pictures of Leah, the missing woman from Greenhouse Fourteen, as well as of other women who had disappeared in recent months. The hour before Halle returned became a time of respite in which none of them interacted. Sasha cherished their communal silence, yet never relaxed until Halle pulled into the driveway.

"Why the new interest in bees?" Ian said as Sasha caught up with him.

"No reason."

"For what it's worth, I don't think it's possible."

"Forget it." Sasha pedaled harder and Ian matched her speed.

"You're the one who brought it up."

"It was stupid. I shouldn't have said anything." The view of acres of greenhouses opened up as they soared down the hill.

"We don't need anyone overhearing you say you believe in bees. Crackpots will flock to the apiary, police will get involved, and we'll get kicked off the property. People disappear after claiming they saw bees. I know you know that."

"Fine. There are no bees." The combination of the late night, the beer, the bright sun, and Ian's questions made Sasha feel nauseous.

"What's going on with you?" Ian said.

"Nothing. I'm nervous about the interview."

"Bullshit. There's something else."

"I'm not obligated to share every detail of my life with you." Sasha's words came out harsher than she intended. She stood up on her pedals and broke away, leaving Ian behind.

Gino and Halle waited for them at the bike rack, cluttered with hundreds of bikes belonging to other greenhouse workers.

"What?" Halle looked from Sasha to Ian and back to Sasha. "What happened?"

"Nothing," Sasha and Ian both said at the same time.

Every day when Sasha left the campus for the farm, she gave thanks that their little family didn't live in the overcrowded ag barracks. She would never do anything to jeopardize their stability at the farm.

"Sasha!" Bassel jogged toward her from across the parking lot.

Bassel worked out of an office on the other end of the greenhouse campus, and she rarely saw him near her building.

As Bassel jogged toward them, a young woman who looked like she had been crying pulled Ian away from the group. Gino watched as Ian consoled her.

"I got you a birthday present." Bassel beamed as he handed her a small package wrapped in newspaper. "Sorry it's a day late."

Sasha ignored Halle and Gino making exaggerated swoony eyes

at each other and hoped Bassel didn't notice. Behind Bassel, Ian embraced the woman.

Bassel chewed on his thumbnail as Sasha slowly tore the paper to reveal a bright purple cell phone. She turned it over in her hand.

"Your phone? I can't take your phone."

"It's not a big deal. I got a new one for work, paid for by the department. My old phone's already prepaid for three months. I know you've been wanting to get one, and if you want to keep it after three months, you can reload it." Bassel bounced slightly as if he had practiced his speech.

"I don't know what to say," Sasha stammered. "Thank you."

"Does this mean your boyfriend won't have to text my boyfriend to pass you notes anymore?" Gino said to Sasha.

Sasha's face flushed. She and Bassel had never been on a real date, although they often met up to exchange books. At first, Sasha hoped Bassel might have an interest in something more, but in months of friendship, he had never made a move.

"Oh, I got you something else, too." Bassel reached into his bag again and pulled out a book-shaped package wrapped in newspaper.

Sasha ripped off the paper to see a copy of *Ethanol Candy,* the third installment in a series she loved.

"Are you kidding?" She threw her arms around Bassel's neck. "This is amazing."

"Call me later and tell me how the interview goes. It's today, right? I programmed my new number into the phone. I have to get to work. Happy birthday." Bassel jogged back toward the parking lot.

Sasha had mentioned the interview over a week ago, and Bassel remembered. Sasha hugged her arms around her waist.

"No one just casually gives their pal a *phone,*" Gino said.

"When are you going to stop pretending you aren't in love with the guy? He's clearly into you too," Halle said.

"We're friends." Sasha slipped the phone into her pocket, fingering the shiny edges, worn smooth by Bassel's fingers.

Sasha, Halle, and Gino lined up, as they did every day, to be patted down before passing through the gate to make sure no one brought in contraband that might contaminate the plants in the greenhouses. They would be patted down again on the way out to prevent anyone from stealing fresh produce.

Most workers spent their days surrounded by rows of lush vegetables they couldn't afford to eat. Sasha often witnessed her coworkers pinching off leaves and small fruit to eat when no one watched, but Sasha rarely did. Except for the strawberries. Some days the smell overpowered her.

Ian joined them in line.

"What was that about?" Gino asked.

"I treated a four-year-old kid two months ago for a broken finger. I set it the best I could. It healed fine. But the finger wasn't his problem. The kid was severely malnourished. He died last night. That woman was his aunt."

Gino put a hand on Ian's forearm. "I'm so sorry."

"Look at this fucking place." Ian gestured to the greenhouse. "We produce tons of food. But the people in the camps are starving to death. Why are we even doing this?"

"Because we don't have a better option," Gino said.

A tattered banner reading A GRATEFUL NATION THANKS YOU! fluttered above the expanse of double doors leading into a two-story glass atrium with a security check, and two corridors: one leading to the offices, the other to the greenhouses. A community bulletin board overflowed with flyers advertising items to trade. Employees were forbidden from advertising items for cash sale, so they bartered. Vegetables for a mattress. Haircuts for a bike chain.

Missing posters, some brand-new and others worn, dotted the board. An ad for a mattress in exchange for dried beans covered the face of a young woman who had gone missing weeks earlier. Sasha recognized her face from the greenhouse where Halle worked.

"Damn it." Halle leaned over Sasha's shoulder to move the ads from covering a flyer of her friend Leah's face. "You would think they care when their own employees go missing. This is the third person to disappear this quarter. It's easier to replace them with another expendable body."

Inside the atrium, silent screens flickered above the mass of workers feeding into security-check stations. Images of the Carolina coast after yet another hurricane filled the screens. Acres of broken glass that had once been greenhouses sparkled like glitter in the aerial shot. Those shards would scar the sand for decades, sinking and churning with tides until they reemerged, turned and polished by the sea and smoothed over in the bellies of sea creatures before breaking down and becoming sand once again.

The muted news shifted to a report of a bee sighting in North Carolina, where more hurricane-ravaged greenhouses lay strewn across beaches. A man in a white button-down shirt talked to a reporter. He smirked as the reporter asked him questions. Sasha didn't need the closed captions to decipher the condescension in his muted voice. Another government talking head with all the answers. Bees did not exist. *Why must you humor these fools?* his sneer suggested.

Bile churned in Sasha's gut as she watched the official scoff at the North Carolina bee sighting. A tremor of solidarity heated her belly.

Ian looked from the TV to Sasha. She scowled at him and got in the security line behind Halle. The lobby smelled of humid bodies and desperation.

Sasha scanned her ID badge, and a red light flashed on the monitor.

"They want to talk to you upstairs," the attendant said. "Room sixty-three."

"Am I in trouble?" Sasha tried to keep the panic out of her voice. Her job interview wasn't scheduled for hours.

"Big trouble." He squinted at Sasha.

Not today. God, not today. Being reprimanded on the day of her interview wouldn't bode well for her chances or for her confidence.

The attendant, whose name tag read CHAD, laughed. "How the

hell would I know if you're in trouble? Go to room sixty-three and find out. Next."

"Asshole," Gino hissed as he scanned his badge behind Sasha. Halle flipped Chad off.

"Gotta keep this job interesting when I can, you know?" Chad called after them.

Sasha took a deep, slow breath to calm her nerves. A steady stream of pollinators hurried past them as they pressed against the wall at the base of the stairs leading up to the managers' offices.

"Want me to walk up with you?" Ian asked.

"No. I'm sure it's nothing," Sasha said. "They probably just re-scheduled my interview or something. I'm sorry I acted like an ass earlier. And I'm really sorry about the boy."

"Me too," Ian said. "But right now, you need to focus on your interview."

"Find us later and let us know what's going on." Halle's attempt at encouragement looked more like she was battling a painful cramp. "Good luck. Not that you need it."

Sasha waved as she opened the door to the stairwell. She took the flight two steps at a time and opened the door on the second floor to a blast of cool air. Temps in the greenhouses often soared above ninety-five degrees, while the bosses blissed out in air-conditioned offices. Sucking in a deep breath, she pushed down her resentment and paused outside room 63.

*Don't panic.*

She smoothed her shirt and wiped her face to dry the damp sheen left over from the bike ride.

She faked a confident smile and knocked.

# Twenty-Four

## SASHA'S 11th BIRTHDAY
### JUNE 6

Sasha woke up in the emergency room attached to an IV line with an oxygen tube in her nose, machines beeping and whirring around her.

Chuck slept in a chair in the corner of the small room, his head resting on his arms folded across a counter. Sasha lifted her hand to reach for him and noticed the welts on her hand, so swollen her skin looked like it might burst if she bent her fingers.

Three police officers stood outside her door talking to her father.

"Can't we do this after my daughter recovers?" Her father rubbed the knuckles on one hand and then the other as he paced in a small circle.

"Sir, this is serious," an officer said. "You are being charged with a federal crime. Keeping bees outside of an authorized facility has been illegal for several weeks. You willfully violated the pollinator preservation statutes. We have to take you in now."

"But my daughter."

"Sir, the doctors said your daughter is stable. She's going to be fine. Mr. Skinner offered to stay with her."

Sasha wadded the sheet in her stiff fist. The coarse fabric snagged on the calluses on her fingers.

"We can cuff you if you don't cooperate, or we can do this quietly. It's your choice."

Why would they be arresting her father? Sasha tried to call to him, but her words came out as scratchy, squeaks. The machine monitoring her heart rate recorded jagged spikes as she choked out another attempt to call her father.

"At least let me say goodbye." Her father caught Sasha's eye and tilted his head back and cracked his neck, something he always did before tackling a difficult challenge.

An officer escorted him to Sasha's bedside then stepped outside the room.

Her father leaned close to kiss Sasha's cheek and whispered in her ear. "This is important. Never tell anyone those bees escaped. Never. You never opened the emergency door. I found you inside the apiary, okay?" His voice rattled in her ear. "This is important. No one must *ever* know any bees escaped. Do you understand me? They confiscated all the bees left in the apiary, but they have no way of knowing some escaped."

Sasha couldn't answer.

He squeezed her wrist hard until it hurt. "I need you to promise. No matter what they say about me. If they threaten me, if they put you on the stand in a courtroom, if they put me in jail. You *never* opened the door. I need you to trust me. This is more important than you realize."

She wanted to ask what he meant, but his grip on her arm told her to stay quiet.

"No bees escaped." The heat of his breath hissed against her ear as he took one of her hands in both of his. "You can tell the truth about moving the hives to the woods, to the apiary. But not about the bees escaping or about the bunker. No one can know the bunker exists. And, Sasha, you must never, ever tell Chuck what happened. Never tell Chuck any of this. Do you understand?"

She nodded her head so hard the oxygen tube slipped off. Her father replaced it and held her stare, transmitting a fear-stoked message. Her father had never once asked her to lie. Now he wanted her to lie to the police and to her uncle, the one person who had never let her down. She shivered in the thin hospital gown and pulled the covers tighter around her to conceal the tremors.

She wanted to apologize for releasing the bees, but she remembered her promise. She never let the bees out. She never opened the emergency door.

After a long silence, the police officer came back into the room and cleared her throat. Chuck stretched in the chair in the corner, his face brightening when he saw Sasha awake.

"Thank God, kiddo." Chuck smoothed his messy hair to cover a balding spot on top of his head.

Her father glared at Chuck.

"I'll call your lawyer." Chuck's lips drew into a puckered knot. He straightened his back as if steeling himself for something he had long been expecting.

Her father gave Sasha a final nod, loaded with desperation Sasha interpreted as not from fear of being arrested, but an impassioned plea for Sasha to keep her promise. Sasha longed to tell him she loved him, and she would die before giving up his secret. Instead, she blinked hard three times as the police officers, one at each of his elbows, guided her father out of the room.

Chuck took Sasha's hand in hers, and she squeezed hard.

The seams holding Sasha's life together stretched and pulled until she felt the first thread snap and the unraveling began.

# Twenty-Five

## SASHA, AGE 23
### JUNE 7

"Come in," a man's voice called from the other side of the door to room 63.

Instead of her pimply supervisor, who she expected to see, a colorless, toad-shaped man hunched over the empty desk. His mass had expanded, and his once-brown hair now swept across his scalp in a sad, gray comb-over, but the wide jaw, the gray eyes drooping under heavy lids, were unmistakably Chuck's.

"I'm sorry, I think I'm in the wrong place." She bowed her head, hoping he wouldn't recognize her as she turned to leave.

"Alexandra, don't tell me you don't recognize your uncle Chuck."

Sasha's heart pounded at the rush of courtroom memories of Chuck grinning his sappy smile at her as she sat on the stand, his betrayal still raw after all these years. She had hoped changing her name meant her uncle wouldn't be able to find her, but he appeared to be expecting her.

"You've been doing impressive work." He motioned for her to sit down.

She took one step closer but remained standing.

"I think I'm in the wrong place."

"No, come in. I asked to see you."

The air-conditioning screeched. Sasha wanted to run. After Chuck testified against her father, he rose through the ranks until he was appointed assistant secretary of agriculture.

Sasha hadn't been in the same room with her uncle since the day her social worker removed her from Chuck's custody after she ran away from his home for the third time.

"I'm reviewing candidates for the greenhouse efficiency manager position." Chuck's chair sat too low, giving him the appearance of a child at the adult table.

"Isn't that below your pay grade?"

"I like to be involved." He gestured toward the chair again. "Sit."

Sasha perched on the edge of the stiff fake-leather chair.

Chuck put his tablet down and tented all ten fingertips on the desktop as if preparing to leap across the desk.

"I know we had a rough patch, but I've always cared about you, you know that, don't you?" Chuck leaned back in his chair, crossing and uncrossing his arms. He crushed and twisted a paper napkin stained with grease from his breakfast.

"I know, Chuck." She smiled as he tried to cover a wince when she refused to call him "Uncle." "Why did you want to see me?"

Being cordial to Chuck, when she longed to crawl across the desk and shove the greasy napkin down his throat, demanded all her willpower. She wanted this promotion, and she refused to let her uncle derail her.

He wiped his face again with the wadded-up napkin and tried to raise his chair. The buttons on his too-tight shirt looked like they might burst open from the effort.

"I read over your proposal to improve efficiency in the greenhouse water-filtration systems." His chair hissed and shrank again. "With increasing water scarcity, we need ideas like this. If we scale your plan to all the greenhouses, we could save billions of gallons of water a year."

Sasha dug her fingernails into the fake leather of her seat cushion.

"You have vision, like your mother." Chuck blinked repeatedly as he held her stare. "The pay raise and the signing bonus are quite generous, I made sure."

"Are you offering me the job? I didn't interview yet." Chuck's smug suggestion that he helped secure the position with an insider connection drained the satisfaction out of her victory.

"This should help, don't you think, with your roommate's medical bills and whatnot?"

He knew too much about her. She wanted to tell him where he could stuff the job. But she needed the promotion, and for whatever reason, Chuck wanted to make sure she got it.

If anyone found out her mother's brother, who happened to be the assistant secretary of agriculture, handed her the job without an interview, she would be shamed and ridiculed. But did it matter? She deserved the position.

"I expected you to be more excited about this." He wrinkled his brow. "Don't you want the details?"

"Yes, of course."

He handed Sasha a piece of paper with a formal job offer, which included a 60 percent increase in her salary and a substantial signing bonus. Sasha took a deep slow breath and tried not to let her uncle see how much she wanted it.

"We need minds like yours. What we're doing here matters. We are saving lives. I designed the plans for the glass farms all across the country because I knew if we could feed the nation while giving people meaningful, satisfying work everyone would benefit."

The more he puffed himself up, the lower his chair shrank. He pumped the lever under the seat again, trying to elevate his position.

"There are a few papers to sign, boilerplate stuff. We will need the contract back one week from today. You will have access to sensitive information, so we ask for your commitment and discretion. I trust you are still proficient at keeping secrets?" He tried to catch her eye as he handed her a folder, but she didn't look up.

If anyone knew Sasha could keep a secret, it was Chuck.

Sasha had worked hard to prove she didn't need a college degree to work in facilities management, yet she had been passed over for a promotion twice in the past nine months. Her supervisors often turned to her with mechanical questions, then took credit for her solutions. But coming from Chuck, the promotion felt tainted and suspicious.

"I can have the paperwork to you tomorrow." Sasha didn't need a whole week to decide. She needed this job. She wanted this job. She had *earned* this promotion.

"I like the enthusiasm. But I don't want to see you back at work until Monday. I talked to your supervisor, and we think you deserve a few days off, paid, of course. You take today and the next three days. Show up on Monday bright and early and you can start straightaway."

Sasha cringed at the smear of satisfaction on Chuck's face. A shiny gold pin with the Department of Agriculture insignia glistened on his rumpled lapel. Chuck probably spit-shined it every morning right after fixing his comb-over in place.

"The days are paid? My supervisors know about this?"

"Yup. Paid at your old salary rate, of course, but paid in full. I'm so glad I could be here to deliver the news in person." Chuck spoke at an annoyingly slow pace, as if afraid of making a mistake. He was still the same man who followed her father around like a puppy dog, always seeking approval.

But Chuck had also played an important role in her childhood. He had shown up for Sasha when no one else bothered. He cried with her when her mother died. Sasha wanted to believe he had been sincere, that he hadn't doted on Sasha as a power play against her father.

She had never been sure how to feel about him as a child, until he tried to turn her against her father. Could she trust him now?

Part of her wanted to fall back into the role of his niece and tell him about the bee, to speculate about what it meant. Chuck understood how much she suffered when the bees died.

Although she had spent the last eleven years distancing herself from her past, she often longed to talk to someone with shared memories, someone who remembered what bees smelled like and how the hum of a hive gave her the sensation of floating.

Sasha searched his face for hints of whether he would believe her or laugh at her if she hinted that she had seen a bee. Would he praise her or fire her? Help her or have her arrested? She squirmed under the power Chuck wielded over her, but she also sensed in his eagerness that she maintained power over him as well.

He looked like a prop behind the bulky desk, empty except for his tablet. A generic clock on the wall ticked off long seconds in the windowless room. Cool air blew from a vent over Chuck's head, causing his meticulously arranged hair to flutter.

"I almost forgot. This will be your office, air-conditioning and all." He planted his elbows on the desk and laced his fingers into a giant fist. Chuck rearranged his hands to put the other one on top, then changed his mind and reconstructed the fist. He rested his chin on his fidgety hands and leaned forward in anticipation of Sasha's reaction.

"Thank you," she said with as much apathy as she could conjure. Her own office. Air-conditioning.

"It's a shame about your father. He was a brilliant man."

"He's still a brilliant man, Chuck."

He winced again as she said his name.

"Right, right. I didn't mean to disrespect him. Whatever happened in the past, I will always count him as a friend, as family. And you, too, Sasha. Promise you'll reach out if you ever need anything."

Sasha dug her fingernails deeper into the fake leather and tried to appear appreciative.

"This is important work we're doing. The glass farms are producing hundreds of thousands of tons of food each day. We reduced hunger by thirty percent since the first greenhouses came online. You and I are part of the greatest public works project ever undertaken."

Sasha stood and extended her hand.

Chuck jumped up from his chair and walked around the desk. "Family doesn't shake hands, now, do they?" He pulled her into a sticky embrace. He still smelled like cheese. "It's wonderful to see you, Alexandra."

As she walked down the hall toward the stairwell, Sasha wiped her hands on her thighs. She would accept this job, but she didn't owe Chuck anything. Not gratitude, not love, not the admiration he craved.

She opened the door to the stairwell, and a blast of humid air announced the end of the air-conditioned section of the building. Heat in the unventilated stairwell exacerbated the stale odor of cement steeped in the breath and sweat of workers gasping in hope and exhaling fear.

She flipped through the paperwork searching for a catch, but all she found was a confidentiality agreement, which she had already agreed to when she signed on as a pollinator, a renewed pledge not to disparage the government and the Department of Agriculture, in particular, and reminders that associating with "hostile agents" would be grounds for dismissal. Nothing she didn't expect.

She wanted to feel excited about the job, but she couldn't shake the lingering feeling that Chuck was waiting for her to make a mistake so he could expose her and all the secrets she had been keeping. Between Octavia, Gino, and Millie knowing the truth about Sasha's identity and now Chuck reemerging in her life, Sasha felt a mounting urgency to tell Halle and Ian the truth before someone else did.


A n unexpected twinge of nostalgia tugged on Sasha as she pressed open the heavy metal door to Greenhouse Six clutching Chuck's offer letter in her hand.

Each greenhouse, with its own specific cocktail of nutrients depending on what grew inside, gave off a unique smell. Greenhouse Six was a network of six connected structures growing the same produce at various stages of development. Seasons did not exist at glass farms.

Numerous glass panels had been replaced due to cracks, hail damage, or broken seals. The newer panels didn't match, lending the ceiling and walls a patchwork quality. Nutrient seepage stained and gummed up the tubing. Months' worth of bodies and breath, pollination and photosynthesis, had accumulated into a grime darkening every crevice in the once-shiny fixtures.

These seasonless Frankenfruits grew not from soil and rot and decay and sunlight, but on a diet of panic and false hope. The enormous tomatoes, bright red and bursting with juice, crushed pithy in the mouth and melted to slush with a touch of heat.

Sasha spotted Gino pollinating rows of tomatoes with his no-nonsense precision. Paintbrush in, swirl, next flower, with consistent rhythm and grace. She walked through the twenty yards of tomato trays, increasing her speed to a jog, then a sprint. Gino saw her coming, dropped his brush, and ran to meet her. His eyebrows danced up and down with questions.

The air felt more oppressive than usual, thick enough to chew on. Sweat darkened Gino's armpits.

"What'd they want?"

"I got the job." Sasha opened the folder with the offer letter so Gino could read the details.

"This is huge." Gino's eyes widened as he read. "But I'm going to miss sexing up plants with you all day. Who am I going to gossip with?"

Condensation dripped from the ceiling and splashed onto Sasha's cheek as Gino hugged her, lifting her feet off the ground.

"Your meds," Sasha whispered.

"I know." Gino buried his face in Sasha's hair. "I know."

"Do you think it's enough?"

"Before you blow your bonus on me, you should get some new pants or something. Your wardrobe could use an update."

"What's wrong with my pants?" Sasha scrutinized her favorite jeans, faded and stained, but soft as flannel.

"I'm proud of you. You worked so hard for this."

Sasha felt a pinch of guilt, unsure if she had earned the job entirely on her own.

"Will you tell Halle and Ian? They gave me the rest of the day off, plus three more days—with pay. I'm going for a long bike ride."

"A bike ride? You just got a life-changing promotion, and you celebrate by biking?" Gino stepped back and squinted at her. "Is there something you aren't telling me?"

"How do you always know? I'm going to go visit my dad. It takes nearly a whole day to bike there and back. I haven't seen in him months, so I figure today's the day."

"Wow. Okay. I'll just say you went for . . . a bike ride?"

"Thanks."

"Why am I more excited about this job than you are? Is there a hitch? Are they making you do something illegal? Oh, my God. Are they forcing you to be a spy? Or worse, do you have to wear a suit?"

"I'm shocked, I guess. I'm going to stop by the market on the way home and pick up something for dinner. Tell Ian he's off the hook for cooking tonight."

"We deserve to celebrate." Gino hugged her again.

Liquid fertilizers sloshed through miles of tubing snaking up and down the endless rows of soilless growing racks spilling over with green. The stench of the chemical soup had gagged her when she first started, but now she didn't notice it. The odor clung to her hair and clothes after leaving the greenhouse every day, as it did to Halle's, Gino's, and Ian's. She sucked in a lungful of the humid, putrid air and swallowed.

Condensation dripped down the walls like tears. Industrial fans whirred in a bass growl, and Sasha wondered if all the greenhouse fans hummed at the same pitch, like the bees, or if each fan had its own individual calibration.

# Twenty-Six

## SASHA, AGE 23
### JUNE 7

*You'll know when it's time.*
Nine months earlier, when Sasha had asked her father about the buried research, he'd told her it wasn't time yet. She'd played the conversation over in her mind a thousand times.

Time for what?

During subsequent visits, her father hadn't remembered the conversation. How would she know when the time came if she didn't know what she was waiting for? Had she ruined whatever her father expected of her when Millie walked off with his journals?

Sasha biked the twenty miles from the glass farm to the prison hospital fueled by a tangle of excitement about the promotion, distrust of Chuck's motives, and the need to understand what her father had meant.

Was it time?

With her arms outstretched for balance, she pedaled down the middle of the neglected road to avoid potholes pocking the pavement from the edges inward. Her hair whipped into her mouth, and she let out a howl. The sound rumbled up and scratched at her windpipe, tearing its way out of her. She roared again, letting the wind carry her voice away.

She tried to clear her mind of Chuck's smug smile, the same smile he'd offered her as she took the stand at her father's trial. An I-know-what's-best-for-you smile. An I-won smirk.

Fuck him and his need to reconnect.

Sasha yelled again into the wind, shards of dread and guilt slicing into her with a thousand tiny cuts.

A loud horn wailed from behind her, startling her out of the sinkhole of her thoughts. A tractor-trailer approached from behind. For half a second, she considered not moving out of the way and challenging the truck to swerve. She was tired of moving out of other people's way.

The horn blasted again, this time so close the bellow reverberated in her throat. She cut hard toward the uneven shoulder and skidded out. Gravel tore at her shin and forearm as she slid across loose stones and chunks of broken pavement. The truck spit hot air, dust, and sand into her face as it sped past.

She lay on the side of the road, cursing her recklessness. Her precarious life left no room for mistakes. No injuries, no infections, no damaged bikes.

As she lay on the ground assessing her scrapes and bruises, a wild whooshing filled the sky. The melodic base tones grew louder and an enormous swan flew directly over her. *Thwomp, thwomp, thwomp,* synchronized with the beating of Sasha's heart.

Although she had seen a swan once as a child, Sasha thought of the enormous bird in the category of mythic creatures like unicorns and fairies. Too beautiful and magical for this broken world. Where had this survivor come from?

The swan circled three times; its wings, spanning at least six feet across, ripped through the air with slow, rhythmic pulses until it straightened its path and disappeared into the horizon. Sasha held her breath as the final, waning whisper feathered into the wind.

Her quads ached as she climbed the final slow-burning incline before reaching the prison hospital. The road rash on her leg and arm stung, and her rear fender rattled from the crash.

Sasha locked her bike to a bench and walked around the parking lot a few times to settle her breathing before buzzing in.

While she waited, seated in a sagging mauve chair, Sasha picked at a pebble embedded in her palm from the bike accident. Momentum from the crash had driven it under her skin, where it bulged up like a shiny pearl. She would save the extraction for Ian, who relished the opportunity to perform minor surgeries.

Hugo grinned at Sasha as he wheeled her father over to the seating area.

Lawrence reached out for her hand and Sasha leaned over to hug him. His bones felt so close to his skin.

"I'm sorry, Little Bee."

"About what?"

"About missing your concert. It was important to you." Papery skin draped around his powder-blue eyes, his only unchanged feature.

Sasha absolved him yet again, but he never remembered, as if he lived forever in a loop of guilt. But why, of all things, did missing her violin concert haunt his faulty memory?

"That was fourteen years ago, Dad. I'm not angry anymore."

"Right." He straightened his back.

"How have you been?" she asked.

"The food stinks." His voice sounded thin and diminished, veiled in a phlegmy cough he couldn't clear. He surveyed Sasha as if trying to decipher clues about where they were in time. His eyes stopped on her shin, the fresh wound glistening with blood droplets. "You're hurt."

"I skidded out on the gravel on the way here. I'm fine."

"Is your bike okay?"

"Nothing I can't fix."

"That's my girl." He leaned back in his chair and tried again to clear his throat.

He was missing a tooth on the lower right and the gap startled Sasha.

"How's school?"

"Great." Instead of correcting him, she allowed herself to slip into the role of daughter. "How are you feeling?"

"Okay, but the arthritis won't let up." He held up his hands to show the thick knots locking up his joints. "They won't give me my medicine."

She shuddered at the memory of her father self-medicating with bee venom.

"Nothing else helps."

"Do you think any still exist?" Sasha's pulse fluttered. Speaking about the bees with her father felt dangerous.

"Of course."

"You remember bees were declared extinct, right?"

"It doesn't mean they aren't out there." He rubbed the knuckles on one hand in a rhythm, suggesting the habit soothed him.

"Do you remember telling me not to dig up the bunker because it wasn't time yet?"

He furrowed his brow. "I never said that."

"You told me I would know when it was time. But I don't understand. Time for what?"

"I have no idea what you are talking about." His eyes darted around the room, and he rubbed his knuckles harder.

"I saw a bee." Sasha leaned her head close to her father, keeping her voice low.

Lawrence stopped rubbing his knuckles and tightened his hands into fists that wouldn't close all the way. He leaned toward her and whispered, "When?"

"Yesterday. And maybe last year. I wanted to believe I imagined it. But they're real," she whispered, glancing over Lawrence's shoulder to the receptionists. "How can I track them to find out if there's a hive?"

"Who have you told?" Her father's eyes darted around the empty room.

Hugo leaned on the front desk and laughed with the receptionists.

He spoke with animated gestures, telling a story his audience apparently found hilarious.

"No one. I want to find proof before I tell anyone. How can I track it?"

"You already know the answer. Bees always know how to find their way home. They always travel in a straight line. You need to find the line."

"But how do I do that?"

"It's hard to find something that doesn't want to be found. Offer them something they want."

Hugo walked over to Sasha and Lawrence. "How are we doing over here? Would you like any water?"

"No," Lawrence said sharply.

"No thanks," Sasha said.

Hugo lingered as if waiting for them to resume their conversation.

"I got a promotion at work today." Sasha fumbled to fill the silence as Hugo hovered too close for them to discuss the bees.

"Humph." Lawrence crossed his arms. He stared out the window for several minutes without speaking, although his lips moved as if he were replaying a conversation in his mind. Sasha shifted in her seat and Lawrence startled as if he'd forgotten she was there.

He coughed several times.

"I'll get you some water." Hugo walked down the corridor.

Her father patted Sasha's hand with a reassuring pressure that gave Sasha the fleeting sensation her father could make everything okay. She wished she could curl up on his lap the way she had as a little girl.

"You need to find Dr. Maher."

"Are you feeling sick?" Sasha started to stand up, but he grabbed her arm.

He shook his head, drew in a long breath, and cleared his throat. "You really saw a bee?"

"Yes."

"Find Dr. Maher. She can help you. No one but her." He spoke with the gravelly edge Sasha had been accustomed to as a child. Stern and resonant. She used to love pressing her ear to his chest to feel the thick vibrations when he spoke.

He looked more like himself, his eyes focused and clear.

"Who is she? Where do I find her?" Sasha asked.

"I wish I could talk to your mother about this."

"She's gone, Dad."

"I know that," he yelled. "I said I *wish* I could talk to her."

"Me too." Sasha wanted to push him for more information, but he was retreating from the present.

They sat in familiar, comfortable silence staring out the window. A row of crisp brown hedges, all dead, bordered the side yard. The scraggly twigs, bare of all leaves, stood out against the brown grass, reminding Sasha of her father's twisted fingers pointing at her.

His eyes softened and his shoulders dropped into a comfortable slouch, as if observing nature calmed him, even the sad state of the nature outside the prison window.

Sasha envied his ability to forget this world and slip into a comfortable past where she was a little girl and her mother was alive.

"I'm going to be a manager in one of the greenhouses. The pay is a lot better."

"The greenhouses?" He spoke with an edge of panic in his voice.

"I was a pollinator, but now—"

"Don't tell Chuck anything." Lawrence jolted up and grabbed Sasha's wrist, squeezing hard.

"Dad, that hurts." She tried to pry his fingers off, but he clamped down harder.

"Those bees never should have been released. It never should have happened."

Sasha pulled her hand away, stung by her father's rebuke. She hadn't meant to let the bees out.

Hugo appeared in the doorway and waved. Her father released his grip.

"How was your visit?" Hugo asked.

"Great. Can we have a few more minutes?" Sasha said.

"Sorry, but he has a physical therapy appointment."

"I'll come back soon, okay?" Sasha touched her father's hand, knowing her words might be a lie. If she pursued the bee and got arrested, she might not see him again for a long time, if ever. She consoled herself with the sad truth that as soon as she left, he would forget her promise to return. "I love you, Dad."

"Dr. Maher. No one else." Fear flickered in his eyes.

# Twenty-Seven

## SASHA, AGE 11
### JUNE 7

Chuck stayed by Sasha's side in the hospital room after the police took her father away. Unlike her father, Chuck did not understand the communal nature of silence. He filled the tiny, beeping room with empty words. His breath floated around the cubicle, tripping on wires, and filling in spaces between the irregular chugging of the blood pressure cuff on her arm.

Chuck said he would stay at the house with her. What did she want for breakfast? Did she want him to go to the grocery store? What time did she wake up for school? Did she drink coffee? No, of course not, he answered himself. Was she cold? Should he call the nurse for an extra blanket?

He prattled on for hours, only stopping when Sasha closed her eyes and pretended to sleep. She wanted to know when her father would be home, why they took him away. Did he blame her? Would they arrest her, too? Asking Chuck questions would invite unwanted conversation, so she let the unanswered questions spin in her head as he talked about nothing, and she feigned sleep.

He chattered as they waited for discharge papers and on the entire ride home, although later, Sasha couldn't remember a thing he said, only the droning of his voice.

"Hungry?" he asked when they walked into the empty farmhouse. She wanted to say no and go to bed, but her stomach rumbled. "How about pancakes?"

"It's midnight," Sasha said.

"Pancakes taste great at midnight." Chuck surprised her with his familiarity with their kitchen and the ease with which he whipped together pancakes from scratch without a recipe. The kitchen floorboards creaked at a different pitch under Chuck's feet, as if the house knew he did not belong.

The kitchen soon smelled of vanilla and the generous dash of cinnamon Chuck folded into the batter at the last second. He placed a lopsided stack of golden pancakes on the table with a jug of maple syrup and gestured for Sasha to sit. Sasha preferred honey to syrup, but she didn't say so.

Chuck sat in her mother's chair as he folded a wad of pancakes in his mouth and smiled with his mouth partially open.

The pancakes were fluffier and sweeter than her father's rubbery attempts. After gobbling down five pancakes, she took her plate to the sink.

"I'll clean up. You need to get some sleep," he said.

She wrapped her arms around her uncle, holding in all the words she wanted to say. He gave her a syrupy smile.

She scratched at the raised welts on her neck and arms.

"The doctor said not to scratch."

Sasha resumed scratching as soon as she turned the corner to go upstairs. She listened for the clatter of dishes in the sink as Chuck cleaned up the midnight pancakes, but instead he left the dishes and walked down the hall into her father's study.

Her father hated other people being in his office.

Sasha tiptoed back down the stairs, stepping on the edges of the stairs closest to the wall so they wouldn't creak.

The sound of drawers opening and closing and papers rustling came from the study. Sasha ran a light finger along the wainscoting in the hall to steady herself as she inched toward the study door. Melting into the shadows in the dark hall, she peeked in.

Chuck sat at her father's desk, yanking open drawer after drawer.

He rifled through files and pulled books off shelves with reckless urgency. His normally pink skin glowed red and a vein in his forehead pulsed.

Sasha balled up her fists and forced herself to stay quiet. Maybe he sought information to help the lawyers bring her father home.

Sasha broke into the apiary, not her father. If anyone should be in trouble, it was her.

Chuck opened the cabinet where her father kept his art supplies. Sasha dug her fingernails into the soft pine of the doorframe where she hid in the shadows as Chuck flipped through half-finished sketches of bees, hives, and flowers. He pulled up a watercolor of Sasha as a little girl, but tossed it aside, uninterested.

Sasha's heart jumped to her throat. She didn't know her father had ever painted her likeness.

Chuck's shirt stuck out from his pants, and his tie hung loosely around his neck. Sasha watched him go through every drawer, every shelf, every book, for more than half an hour, fighting the torturous urge to claw at the bee stings burning her face, neck, and arms.

Chuck flung himself back in her father's desk chair and covered his face with his hands. His frustrated sigh almost made Sasha feel sorry for him, until he noticed Sasha lurking in the shadows.

"Where is it, Alexandra?" He slammed his fist on her father's desk, rattling her grandfather's stained-glass lamp. Chuck's red-rimmed eyes darted around the room, his hair flopped in all the wrong directions, and sweat dripped down the side of his face.

Sasha ran up the stairs and slammed her bedroom door shut. Her heart pounded so loud she couldn't hear anything over the rush of blood in her ears.

Sasha sat on the front porch with a pile of shredded lavender petals on her lap when the police car pulled into the driveway the morning after her father's arrest. She jumped up, and the dusty perfume swirled in the air, reminding her of running barefoot in the summer.

The officer got out and opened the back door to let her father out.

Sasha held her hands to her face and inhaled the fragrance, trying to summon a memory of security. She scooped up a handful of petals and rubbed them against her skin until they rolled and tore. The aroma would ease her father's burden when he ran from the car to hug her.

Her father emerged rumpled and unshaven, wearing the same clothes he'd worn the day before.

Their three-legged stool toppled when Sasha's mother died. Her father claimed he and Sasha were now the two legs of a sturdy ladder. They could climb high as long as they had each other.

The apology she had been practicing tumbled around in her mind, slippery and inadequate. Her heart throbbed in her throat.

She forced herself to stay put and resist the urge to run to him, wrap her arms around him, and beg his forgiveness. She would wait until he came to greet her, and she would envelop him with her lavender memories.

He walked toward her without smiling, his gait stiff as he accommodated a clunky monitor around one ankle. Chuck had warned her about the device meant to ensure her father didn't leave the property while he awaited trial. Sasha averted her eyes to preserve his dignity.

"Feeling better?" He brushed her tangled hair aside and examined the welts on her neck, still caked in a paste of baking soda and meat tenderizer. His skin felt rough, but his touch was warm.

"Just a little itchy."

"I'm starved." He walked into the kitchen and cranked open a can of soup.

"Can I see it?" Sasha asked.

Her father froze with a wooden spoon hovering above the pan on the burner.

"Does it hurt?" She curled her toes over the smooth, familiar wood of the threshold between the kitchen and the hall.

Her father turned around and put his foot on the seat of a chair and pulled up his pant leg to reveal a black cuff with a pinprick of a red light that flashed every few seconds.

"Can they hear us?" she asked.

"No."

Sasha stepped closer and put a hesitant finger to the metal cuff. She pulled back quickly, afraid of being shocked.

"I have a project for us after lunch."

He ladled out two bowls of soup and sat down next to Sasha. Halfway through their meal, punctuated only by slurps and clinks of spoons on ceramic, he sighed and let his shoulders slump.

Sasha straightened her back and sat tall. She could be strong for them both.

Her father picked up a cloth napkin and folded it over his hand, tucking in the edges to form a puppet with a mouth, his favorite restaurant game when Sasha was little.

"Crackers?" he asked with a straight face.

"Don't."

He picked up two crackers in the mouth of the napkin monster, and just before dropping the crackers in Sasha's soup, the napkin monster chomped on them, sending bits flying into her bowl and across the table as he made Cookie Monster chomping noises.

"I'm not a baby anymore." Sasha picked bits of cracker off the table and dropped them in her soup.

"I know you're not."

"Chuck made me pancakes at midnight."

"Did he?"

"He also went through your desk and all your files."

"Did he say what he was looking for?"

"No. I don't think he found what he wanted. He was angry."

"Did you tell him any bees escaped?"

Sasha shook her head, too ashamed to speak.

"Charles Skinner is dangerous." He put a hand on each of Sasha's shoulders and squeezed. Her father never referred to Chuck as Charles. Hearing him refer to her uncle by his formal name made Sasha feel like they were talking about a stranger. "No matter what he says, you cannot trust him."

Sasha felt as if her father had dumped a bucket of ice water over her head. Chuck often reminded her of a bumbling cartoon character. Annoying and awkward. But not dangerous.

After lunch Sasha followed her father through the woods toward the apiary, trying not to stare at the ankle bracelet bulging out from under his pant cuff.

They both carried long-handled shovels, although Sasha didn't know why. Dark purple bruises marred her shins from where she had bumped against the sugar water tray the night before. The swelling from the bee stings itched and burned with increasing intensity the closer they got to the apiary.

"We're going to bury the bunker. Permanently."

"Why?"

"There's going to be a trial. And I'm going to go to prison."

Her father spoke in the same matter-of-fact tone he might have used to ask about the weather. Sasha stopped walking. Her feet refused to obey. The shovel slipped from her hand, clanging as it landed on a rock.

"I don't want anyone, especially not Chuck, getting into my stuff while I'm away." He didn't pause to wait for Sasha. "He doesn't know our bunker exists. No one does."

She picked up the shovel and hustled to catch up.

"This land is unsuitable for agricultural use for three generations, so I don't think anyone will poke around in an overgrown field, at least not during my lifetime. And after that, I don't give a shit what they find."

"I don't give a shit either."

Her father gave her a sideways glance but didn't reprimand her for cursing.

They trudged through tall weeds, pampas grass scratching Sasha's already injured calves. They walked the long way around to the opening of the bunker, as they always did, staying twenty feet apart from each other so they didn't tread on the same path. Her father had trained Sasha not to trample grass near the bunker so their tracks would never form a noticeable path.

They approached the storm cellar from a different angle every time.

A few yards from the bunker door her father maintained a pile of branches and underbrush. Every time he closed the hatch, he shoveled dirt to cover a woven rubber mat and scattered the grass twigs and rocks over the surface.

"Today we seal the bunker up for good. You can never come back."

She imagined someone decades, possibly centuries in the future uncovering her father's lair and wondering what secrets it held.

Her father brushed the pile of branches and dried grass to the side and rolled the mat back to reveal a heavy wooden door centered over a cement foundation.

"My father rode out three tornadoes down here." He told her the same story every time he brought her out to the bunker. "Do you remember where their house used to sit?"

"Right here." She stomped her foot on the ground and looked at the gnarled apple trees once visible through the kitchen window of a house she had never seen.

"That house stood here when your mom and I took over the property. I hated tearing that place down, but it was falling in on itself. As much as we try, we can't stop time. But I made sure we saved the storm cellar."

Sasha followed him down the dark cement stairs, lit only by the sun pouring through the open door. The cool, damp air sent goose bumps across her skin. Her father turned on the lamp fashioned out of a flashlight inverted in a glass jar.

He sat down on the small cot where he often took afternoon

naps and stared at the diagram of a bee's wing hanging over his desk.

"Did you know Australia and New Zealand declared four thousand more species of Hymenoptera extinct yesterday?" she said, the damp cement walls flattening her voice. She suspected the porous concrete sucked up their words and stored them in the walls forever.

"I know."

She would never smell the damp waxy air, the musty odor of the flattened pillow, the pine of the box frames he often used as a work surface. She summoned the images into her mind, where she etched them into her memory.

"Can I keep the microscope?"

"No. Everything stays."

"But your journals."

"Nothing in here is backed up anywhere. Only my handwritten notes. No digital files. Like the cabin, this is a backup plan."

"Backup for what?"

"I'm not sure."

As her father scratched out some final notes in one of his journals, Sasha scanned the room for a souvenir to take but found nothing. Instead, she unfastened a barrette holding her overgrown bangs out of her eyes. A tiny bee painted with yellow and black enamel stripes perched on the end of the clip. She left the matching clip in her hair.

She placed the barrette on the desk next to the microscope, which her father had already draped in a dust-cover shroud.

Sasha took one last look down the stairs before her father slammed the door shut. He rolled the mat out over the door, as he had done so many times. He handed Sasha a shovel, and they began tossing dirt onto the woven fabric. Each scoop came from a different location, so they wouldn't leave a conspicuous hole that might draw suspicion.

The sound of soil against the wood door hit with the same hollow thud as the dirt Sasha and her father had tossed on her mother's coffin after they lowered her casket into the earth.

Her father paused every few minutes to rub his knuckles.

"What are you going to do without the venom for your arthritis?"

"Live with the pain."

When they had covered the entire mat in several inches of dirt, her father pulled a small bag out of his pocket and handed it to Sasha. "Grass and wildflower seeds." He stepped back from the patch of fresh dirt into the tall grass.

Sasha sank her fingers in the sack of slippery seeds. She churned them with her fingers, noticing the different sizes and textures. She tossed a handful of seeds up high to let them shower around her. Her father smiled and scattered seeds in her direction with a dramatic flourish.

The sky, which had been a milky gray hours earlier, now burst with an ironic, cheerful blue.

They tossed rocks, branches, and tufts of moss over the loose soil. Weeds, grass, and flowers would soon fill in, but until then the secret lay exposed like an open grave. Her father took a step back to scrutinize their work and let out a long, hitched sigh. The bunker was his hideout, the place he went to be alone, to discover things no one else understood. The weight of his loss pressed on Sasha's shoulders, making her feel small.

"We should say something," Sasha whispered.

He nodded as if he expected her to do it.

"You were the best secret hideout in the world. I'll miss that weird basement smell like mud and wax." Sasha cleared her throat and stepped closer to her father. "And I'll miss the poster of the bee's wings and looking at stuff under the microscope."

She already longed for the shared silence inside the cement walls. But those weren't the things she would miss most. Her father's hand guiding hers as she adjusted the microscope. The snuffles of his half snores as he napped on the cot.

"I'm sorry, Little Bee." Her father touched the side of his nose.

A lump rose up her throat as she touched her nose in response. *All is forgiven.*

Sasha counted her footsteps as she walked away in a straight line, not bothering to disguise her path. Fourteen steps from the edge of the bunker door to the spot centered between the apple trees.

"Never come back here, and never tell anyone this place exists, understood?" he said.

Sasha nodded, already fighting the urge to return.

# Twenty-Eight

## SASHA, AGE 23

### JUNE 8

As soon as her housemates left for work on the first of Sasha's paid days off, she took the long-handled shovel and marched through the woods and across the field to the apple trees. She measured her paces, cleared the debris, and yanked open the heavy wooden door she once promised her father, and then promised herself, never to open again.

When she opened the chamber nearly a year earlier, the day Millie found her, Sasha had entered the space seeking answers. And when Millie robbed her of those answers, she vowed never to walk into the dank bunker again.

But now she opened the storm cellar for a different reason. She came searching for guidance on how to track the bee. Maybe in her anger at having lost the journals, she overlooked items that might help her now.

She remembered seeing a few old box hives when she was in the bunker with Millie. At the time, they seemed like bits of unwanted nostalgia from her past, but now they might prove useful. If she found the bees, she could transfer the colony into one of the boxes.

She closed her eyes and tried to remember the scratch of her father's beard against her cheek when he helped focus the microscope. He should be there now, helping her track the bees.

But Sasha had no one to blame but herself for the fact that her father had gone to prison.

She walked down the dark stairs and waited for her eyes to adjust to the shadows. Mildew and a gummy-sweet scent of wax clung to the walls.

*We will never come down here again.*

She should have listened to him. She shouldn't have opened the bunker a year ago and led Millie to his research. But now, as she stepped once again into the sealed chamber, her fingers buzzed with urgency, tinged with fear. But more than fear, Sasha felt a growing tremor of hope, a longing to believe in the destiny her father had implied.

*Second chances only come along once.*

Maybe this was Sasha's second chance.

Afraid of alienating her new friends, terrified of being exposed by Millie, Sasha hadn't explored the corners of the bunker when she opened it a year earlier. She hadn't been ready.

The nails securing the pine boards in the box hives had been driven in at odd angles, not precise the way her father worked. These were Sasha's hives, the ones she built when she was eight.

She tried to pick up the closest box, surprised at the weight. Her stomach fluttered as all the possibilities ran through her mind. Were more of his notebooks hidden in the box hives? How could she not have looked inside them? Or had her father hidden something else? For a moment she allowed herself to imagine opening the hives to find them filled with cash, which made her laugh out loud. If her father left anything behind for Sasha, it wouldn't have been money. Using a hive tool sitting on one of the boxes, she pried open the top of one of the hives.

The tacky propolis sealing the hive resisted until the waxy glue cracked, and she peeled off the lid to reveal wax-filled frames hanging in the box. Chipping away at the wax and glue, she worked a frame loose and pulled it out. Propolis adhered to her fingers and palms, reminding her of the dark splotches that perpetually covered her father's hands. Sasha used to trace the sticky residue on his hands like continents on a map, his calluses and swollen knuckles rising like mountains, the cracked skin and deep lines forming rivers and land formations.

Four honey frames hung in the pine box. The smooth-capped honeycomb stored at least three gallons of honey, possibly as much as five gallons.

Her chest ached as she admired the perfect hexagons filled with honey and sealed to protect it from the passage of time.

Honey had taken on a mythical quality in Sasha's mind, a fabled delicacy that couldn't possibly exist beyond her memory. Pollen from flowers that bloomed when Sasha had been a child hung suspended in the viscous gold in front of her. Nectar from trees she once climbed filled the cavities. A botanical time capsule of the year Sasha longed to forget.

Her pulse quickened as she imagined how much she could sell it for. Real honey. She could sell off chunks of the honeycomb or extract the honey and sell it separate from the wax, which would bring a substantial price on its own.

She scraped a curl of wax from the edge of a honeycomb with her fingernail and worked it between her fingers until it softened. She rolled it into a bean and put it on her tongue and flattened it against the back of her front teeth.

Sasha uncapped a single cell, pressed her lips to the dusty wax, and sucked. She uncapped three more. Six more, working the viscous sugar into her gums, fighting the urge to swallow until she could no longer resist. The sweetness of honey and lavender seeped into her bloodstream.

She wanted to run without direction, stare up at the clouds and spin until she collapsed from dizziness. To climb the old apple tree for no reason other than to consume the familiar view from a slightly altered perspective.

Light poured down the cement stairs, but most of the small room hid in shadow.

An outline in dust marked the empty space where her father's journals sat when she first opened the chamber a year earlier. A

212 JULIE CARRICK DALTON

new layer of dust had settled in but couldn't cover up the absence of the stolen research.

She tried to push Millie and the missing journals out of her mind.

As the sun moved higher in the sky, light reflected off something under the cot. Sasha dropped to the gritty floor and lay on her stomach to see a long metal locker pressed against the back wall. The heavy box screeched against the cement as she slid it out. Rust laced the surface after years of it sitting on damp cement.

Inside lay a beekeeping veil, gloves, and a smoker. Sasha shivered at the creeping sensation she was in conversation, in partnership, with her father, doing exactly what he expected her to do.

It felt as if her father had anticipated this exact moment and left the equipment for Sasha to find at precisely the right time. The nylon mesh of the veil felt stiff from age, but she didn't see any holes. Under the veil lay a small wooden crate filled with tubes of oil paint, ink, pens, charcoal pencils, dozens of paintbrushes, and stacks of art paper of varying weights sealed in shrink-wrap. On the bottom of the box, she found several paintings of bees and honeycomb and a painting of her younger self similar to the one she had seen when she spied on Chuck in her father's study all those years ago.

The paper, damp from sitting on the cold floor, showed mildew stains creeping along the edges, but the chubby face was unmistakably Sasha's, her messy hair grazing her chin, her mouth open in a wide grin, the deep red of her mother's hair catching the light in Sasha's brown curls. Sasha stroked the warped paper, touching the joy trapped forever in her rosy cheeks and round chin. Her mother had been alive, her father home, the bees buzzing the day he painted this image of his daughter. She longed to embody that child again, to melt into the worry-free joy shining in her eyes.

Several glass vials full of preserved bee corpses lay on a copy of *Time* magazine, the cover featuring her father holding a wooden frame covered in honeycomb and crawling with bees. He looked at the bees covering his forearms as if marveling over a child, his pride and joy. The headline LAWRENCE SEVERN: THE LAST BEEKEEPER hovered above his head.

Under the art supplies, she found three journals similar to the ones Millie took.

She sat in the dank, dark bunker, decades later, a little girl again, scared and confused.

*If only she knew.*

In the corner of the desk, Sasha found a tiny hair clip with a bee on it. A wisp of her eleven-year-old hair clung to the fastener. She fingered the smooth face of the cheerful enamel bee and clipped it in her hair.

Sasha ate another chunk of honeycomb and carried three honey-filled frames, the art supplies, journals, microscope, and beekeeping gear up the cement stairs. Sunlight blinded her as she stepped back into the present.

She leaned the frames against an apple tree, closed the door to the bunker, replaced the mesh, and covered it with dirt and rocks. It took four trips to carry everything through the woods to her mother's workshop.

Once she had hauled everything up the ladder to the loft, Sasha allowed herself a quiet minute to marvel at all she had discovered. A time capsule left behind by her father. How could she have missed this the last time she opened the bunker? Maybe she hadn't been ready to look a year earlier. Now, she couldn't turn away.

Sasha sucked honey straight from the wax and opened another cell, then another. The taste washed away her exhaustion. She floated the wax caps on her tongue, sucked out the traces of honey, and chewed the flaky wax into a ball. Honey coated her teeth and throat, knocking loose the memory of honey-drenched pancakes on Sunday mornings.

She felt like a feral beast as she clawed at the wax with her fingernails, devouring at least twenty cells. Fragments of wax clumped in the ends of her hair. Honey smeared her lips, and a warm drizzle slid down her chin, as she pressed the waxy bits against her teeth with her tongue. The jolt of sugar sent a shiver over her skin.

Honey flowed through her like a river of memory. Notes of sunshine and lavender nectar. The wax tasted like the catch in her father's laugh, a sound she had forgotten about. After indulging to the point of near delirium, Sasha covered the frames with a tarp and hid them in the back corner of the hayloft.

Pinching the pads of her thumb and forefinger against each other, she sealed her fingers together with sticky propolis, then peeled them apart. Again and again. The satisfying pull of the adhesive on her skin made a gentle snapping noise, a quiet summons to the bee.

Feeling invigorated by the sugar spike, Sasha made herself comfortable in her reading spot, comprised of an old quilt stretched over a pile of disintegrating hay, and opened the first notebook.

Numbers, dates, temperatures. The figures held no meaning for Sasha, but the handwriting revealed the trajectory of the progression of her father's arthritis. As she flipped through the pages, his handwriting got larger, less steady. The last several years of entries looked like a kindergartner's scrawl. Sasha touched the lettering, feeling the ache her father must have felt as he forced himself to write those last entries. She rubbed her knuckles.

The meticulous, tender cataloging of data felt like an affront. Christmas morning, her mother's birthday, they all passed through his fingers with no mention other than recordings of temperature and body counts. She ran her finger over the angry indentations his pen had carved as he recorded increasing death rates. His frustration lingered in the ink.

On the inside cover of the last journal, the Last Beekeeper had scrawled a note, an inscription: *For Alexandra.* He only called her Alexandra when he was angry. Seeing her formal name written in his journal stirred a pang of shame, as if her father were reaching out to her from the past with an unforgiving reprimand.

*Alexandra.* She could hear the gravel in his voice. The angle of his lettering in the inscription did not share the harsh lines of the data he recorded. He wrote her name with an understated flourish, almost decorative, but not dramatic. Unlike his normal script, yet distinctly her father's hand.

She thumbed through the pages, searching the neat columns for a reason he might have inscribed the notebook to her. Every number meant something. It had to.

Downward trends transitioned into losses of hives. As the numbers trailed off approaching the day she released the bees, her father's pain became visible in the shaky lines of his penmanship, as if he knew what lay ahead.

Tears clouded her vision as she witnessed the beginning of the Great Collapse unfurl through her father's eyes.

Three days before Sasha broke into the apiary, her father recorded the death of another queen. He always took the death of a queen hard, because with her death came the likely failure of a hive. Her father used to purchase replacement queens, but when keeping bees became illegal, he had to rely on his bees to requeen their own hives. In most cases they failed.

"Bees can create a new queen by feeding a baby bee a special diet." He had shown her how to extract royal jelly from the forehead of a honey bee. "There used to be companies that created queens to send out to beekeepers like me. But the Department of Agriculture took over and now we produce the queens."

"Why can't companies make queens anymore?"

"Without the queen, a hive dies, and without hives, humans face food shortages. So, the president issued an executive order moving all production of queen bees to facilities run by the Department of Agriculture so we could closely monitor and regulate them. Queens used to live three or four years. Now they rarely live more than one year. It's vital that we replace dead queens immediately."

"Is this what you do all day at work? Squeeze goo out of bees' heads to make queens?"

"Not me personally, but yes, there are people who do this all day every day." He held the tiniest dab of a clear gel on the tip of a lancet. "This is the most powerful substance in the world. It can transform a regular bee into a queen."

"If I eat it, will I become a queen?" she asked.

"Try it." He handed her the lancet.

"Eeewww. I'm not eating bee brain goo."

"What do you think honey is?"

"You squeeze honey out of bees' heads?" Sasha cringed.

"Honey is how bees preserve nectar. They ingest it and turn it into honey, then regurgitate it, dehydrate it, and they save honey for winter."

Sasha sat up straight. Bees vomited honey?

"You like honey, don't you?" He nuzzled his cheek against hers, his day-old scruff rubbing like sandpaper on her skin.

She pulled away from him.

"It's no different from drinking milk from a cow."

"Cows don't puke up milk." She crossed her arms, furious for having been deceived for so long.

"Royal jelly has healing properties." Her father examined the lancet, turning it in the light to marvel at the wonder his bees had created. "Doctors used to prescribe it for certain ailments."

"I wouldn't eat goo squished out of a bee's head even if I was starving." Sasha had boycotted honey for a week, vowing to never eat bee vomit again. She broke down, however, when her father placed a chunk of honeycomb on a plate with some dried apricots and nuts for a snack after dinner.

Her saliva glands stung as she watched the golden honey ooze onto the plate in slow motion. At first, she only ate an apricot. Then another apricot that had touched the honey. And the boycott ended.

Her father had laughed as she gobbled up the honeycomb.

So many nights as Sasha lay awake in the state home, she wondered if her life would have been different if she had eaten the royal jelly. What would it have transformed her into?

Her father had trained her to think like a scientist. But now, when it mattered most, she didn't understand his notes or what they meant. She tried to remember the last time she sat with her father at his microscope, only weeks before he was sentenced.

"Can you tell the difference?" Her father had coached her to differentiate the two bees under magnification. Her neck ached as she switched the slides back and forth, trying to isolate a difference in their anatomy.

Sasha adjusted the lens to sharpen the lines defining the stained-glass window of a bee's wing. And then she saw it. The edges.

"The wing on this one has curvy edges. The other one has a smooth edge!" She had sat up straight with a jerk and hit her father on the chin with the back of her head. When she turned around to face him, her father's lip bled from where she had whacked him, but he smiled as if he didn't feel it.

"Yes! Yes!" He pulled her tight to his chest.

He smelled like rosemary and beeswax lotion her mother used to make to soothe his arthritis.

"The ones with the straight edges, those bees are the ones we want to see." He held her close as he spoke.

"What's wrong with the other ones?"

"Those other bees never should have existed." The sadness in her father's voice reminded Sasha of the way he talked to her when her mother died, when he tried to explain difficult truths with honesty.

She wanted to be a bee with straight-edged wings, one of the good ones.

Now, she closed her eyes and tried to picture the bee crawling across her knee in the garden. Did it have straight-edged wings?

Sasha flipped through her father's notebooks, slowing down as she approached the date of her eleventh birthday, terrified of the harsh words her father would have used to record the day she broke into the apiary and ruined everything.

But he recorded nothing on her birthday.

The omission of her transgression felt more shameful than if he had documented it in detail. The next day he cataloged the losses in a single column. No mention of body counts or temperature or volume of sugar water. "They confiscated all that remained."

A single line in finely controlled script ended her father's final entry. "I hope someday you understand what you really did." An echo of the line from the journal Millie stole.

His anger cut through the words on the page. The sugar in Sasha's stomach turned sour.

The sympathy she had conjured for her father dissipated. How could he blame a child? Why hadn't he yelled at her? Was she not worth the effort of reprimanding her?

She picked up the *Time* magazine featuring her father's picture. She wanted to tear the cover off and shred his image, burn the pages and never have to see the famous image again. But the photograph drew her in, as it always had.

"This is obscene!" he had yelled when he first saw the magazine cover. "I am not the last. The world is burying them before they are gone."

But Sasha had seen him scrutinizing the cover when he thought no one watched him. He liked the photograph. She could tell by the way he pressed his lips together and wrinkled his chin with masked pride.

"We are not the last," he had whispered aloud as Sasha hid in the darkened doorway to his office. He stroked the bees covering his forearm in the picture. "We are not the last."

As he spoke, the floorboards under Sasha's feet creaked and her father looked up to catch her spying on him.

"We are not the last," he had repeated with slow, deliberate words as he straightened his back resolutely.

Sasha closed her father's notebook. She needed a break from the anger suspended in his shaky handwriting. She left the honey frames, journals, and microscope in the hayloft, covered by a tarp, and walked toward the house.

As much as she longed to keep the honey for herself, it would bring a lot of money at the market. Scarce jars of honey popped up occasionally, selling for exorbitant prices. This honey, twelve heavy frames, would go a long way, but Sasha needed to be smart about how she sold it. She would slip jars in slowly and quietly, test the price, observe how they sold and to whom.

As she walked into the empty farmhouse, the weight of a lifetime of secrets seemed to double. She had tiptoed through the last twelve years, always fearful people would uncover her past and judge her for her role in the death of the last bees.

She needed to make things right. For her father, for herself. For the bees.

But first, Sasha needed to tell her roommates the truth. All of it.

# Twenty-Nine

## SASHA, AGE 23
### JUNE 8

Fueled by a honey-induced energy spike, Sasha stood on her bike pedals and sprinted the entire way to the market later that morning after discovering the frames. If she could sell them, the two jars of honeycomb in her backpack might bring in enough to buy a month's worth of anti-seizure drugs for Gino.

Octavia waved as Sasha approached her booth. "Hey there, beekeeper's daughter, why aren't you at your new job?"

"They gave me a few days off before I start." Sasha had grown used to Octavia calling her "beekeeper's daughter." It felt like an endearment, a secret Sasha trusted Octavia to protect. But given recent developments, hearing Octavia refer to her father out loud made her nervous. She looked around to make sure no one listened. "Can you sell something for me?"

"Is it legal?"

"Of course." She retrieved a jar of honey from her bag and handed it to Octavia.

Octavia rolled the jar around in her hands, watching the honey slide against the glass and ooze over the wax. "This is real?"

"One hundred percent." Sasha couldn't swallow her glee at the smile spreading over Octavia's face.

"Where'd you find this?"

"Will you sell it? Discreetly?"

Octavia raised one eyebrow at Sasha.

"Look at you, all cloak-and-dagger. I'm not selling anything that might land me in trouble."

"It's not illegal. I swear. And I have more. A lot more."

"You know I'm bike parts and sci-fi, right? Not a grocery store."

"Okay, I'll give it to someone else."

"How much are you thinking?" Octavia asked.

"How much were you going to charge Bassel for the fake bottle?"

Sasha reached into her bag and pulled out the other jar and held one in each hand. The honey felt warm through the glass after being in her pack under the beating sun.

"A lot of folks are reporting bees these days. Do you know anything about Leah Haas from over at the glass farm? She reported finding a bee and two days later, she went missing." Octavia folded her arms across her chest and leaned back in her lawn chair.

"She's a friend of Halle's. What do you know about it?"

"Leah isn't one to make stuff up. Or to run off without telling anyone." Octavia gestured toward a Missing poster like the one Sasha had seen at work, taped to the inside of her awning. "I know other folks who swear they saw the dead bee Leah found. There are people who believe, you know."

"Believe what?"

"That bees still exist. That there's some big conspiracy to kill off the stragglers."

"What would anyone get out of killing off bees? You don't believe that, do you?"

"I just report what I hear." Octavia tightened her arms across her chest. "I know you were a kid, but did your father ever talk about a genetics project?"

"No, why?" She remembered the notes in her father's journal referencing a GMO project and cursed herself for allowing Millie to steal the research.

"You never heard him mention a genetics experiment?"

"I had no idea you were a conspiracy theorist."

"They say he designed some kind of superbee."

"The only superpollinator my dad created was me." Sasha had heard rumblings about a genetics project. She had also heard rumors that her father intentionally killed off the bees and the guilt had driven him mad. Stories circulated about him being a foreign spy sent to sabotage the US agricultural system. Sasha had dismissed all the stories, but the mention of GMOs in her father's journals now made her question how much she had ever understood about his work. And thanks to Millie, she never would know.

"Where'd you say this honey is from?" Octavia asked.

"I didn't say."

Octavia rolled the jar and watched the chunk of honeycomb turn in slow motion.

"I have one condition. I don't want anyone knowing the jars came from me. Given my family history, I don't want to be linked to the honey."

"I'll work my ironclad discretion into the price. Give me a few days and I'll see if I can move it."

The purple phone Bassel gave Sasha buzzed in her pocket, startling her. She hadn't gotten used to having a phone yet. She pulled it out and read a text from Bassel.

*I had an incident on my bike. Damage doesn't look too bad. Can I bring it by your place to fix?*

"Is that Bassel's phone?" Octavia side-eyed her.

"His office gave him a new phone, so he gave this one to me."

Octavia laughed and shook her head.

"What?"

"You two are ridiculous. Just sleep together and get it over with."

Sasha looked up from the phone and shot Octavia a mind-your-own-business glare.

*I'll be at the farm in an hour. Bring your bike by,* she texted Bassel. She would be home in thirty minutes but wanted time to get cleaned up before he came over.

Sasha removed her mother's leather-wrapped tools from their hiding place in a back corner and unrolled the bundle on the counter in the workshop. The tannic aroma of well-worn leather rose up. She forced herself to ignore the tug of nostalgia as gravel crunched on the driveway outside.

Bassel stuck his head inside the open door and grinned when he saw Sasha. He wheeled in a blue bike with a bent wheel, some of the spokes sticking out.

"Doesn't look too bad." Sasha crouched down to examine the damage. "Steady the bike while I take the wheel off." She knelt to loosen the bolt securing the rear wheel. Her shoulder bumped against his leg as she worked the wrench, but he didn't back away. She leaned into him for leverage a beat longer than she needed to.

Bassel sniffed the air and looked around the old barn, tilting his head up toward the hayloft.

Sasha leaned the bike frame against the wall and brushed a pile of crumbled leaves off of the counter with her open hand. Particles clung to the propolis on her skin. Sasha tried to brush the crushed leaves off with her other hand, also covered in sticky residue. She wiped them against her thighs, but the leaves adhered to her skin.

"What the hell?" Without any warning, Bassel grabbed one of Sasha's hands and pressed his fingers into her palm.

"What are you doing?" Sasha pulled away, letting the wheel drop to the floor.

"How could you possibly have propolis on your hands?" He stopped talking, suddenly aware he had scared Sasha. "I . . . I'm sorry. I didn't mean to scare you. But . . . propolis? How is that possible?"

Sasha backed away from him.

Bassel put his hands up in surrender. "But it is propolis, isn't it?"

"Why would you think I have propolis on my hands?"

"I can smell it." He leaned toward her and sniffed. "And honey, not the fake stuff."

"That's not creepy at all. Asking me to fix your bike, then *smelling* me while I do it? How could you know what propolis smells like, anyway?"

"My parents kept bees. I grew up covered in propolis. I haven't smelled it in, geez, a long time."

"Where did your parents keep bees?" she asked.

"In Egypt. My family kept bees for generations. Mom used to make all sorts of creams and ointments from honey and the wax." He inhaled deeply. "God, that smell."

"What kind of bees?"

"*Apis mellifera.*" His eyes lit up the way her father's used to when he talked about bees. Bassel looked around the workshop searching for the source of the aroma. "But how do you have propolis all over your hands *now*?"

*Lie,* she pleaded with herself. *Make something up.*

"I found an old frame in the apiary." *Stop now,* she told herself. *Don't tell him anything else.*

"Can I see it? I won't touch it." He ran a hand through his hair and shifted his weight back and forth from one foot to the other as if he were trying hard not to jump up and down. He bit down on his lower lip to tamp down a smile he couldn't suppress.

As hard as Sasha tried, she couldn't help enjoying his excitement at the prospect of smelling propolis.

"Do you remember the smell in a hive?" Sasha asked.

"How could I forget? It's in my blood. I can't escape it. Sometimes when it's quiet, I swear I can hear the buzzing. I know that sounds crazy."

"It's not crazy. I hear it sometimes too." *Do not say another word.*

"You knew bees too, didn't you?"

Sasha cupped her hands over her nose and mouth and inhaled the sticky, musty aroma. Bassel would understand her longing to hear the bees, to smell the hive, to taste that first sample of honey fresh from the comb. Maybe Octavia had told him about her family.

"I grew up on this farm." She stepped back, preempting the inevitable recoil, but Bassel's face didn't change. If anything, it softened.

"He was your father?"

"The Last Beekeeper."

Bassel took her hands again, gently this time, and held them to his face. His fingers felt exactly the same temperature as hers. She pressed her palm to his warm cheek, so her skin adhered to his, and eased her hand away, liking the way their skin resisted separating.

"You're lucky you have this place to remind you." Bassel watched the light sifting down from the hayloft.

"Remind me of what?"

"The bees, home."

Sasha's heart raced. She wanted to pull her hands away from his, but she couldn't move.

"We lost our last bees a few years before North America. It almost destroyed my mother. Her job and her identity were tied to the bees. Then a colleague trashed her research about how to protect the last species. She lost a lot of academic credibility and pretty much went off the deep end." Bassel released her hands.

Sasha could barely make out his words over the rush of blood coursing through her ears. Bassel could expose her to everyone. Ian and Halle would be furious at her for lying to them about her past. Bassel could report them for squatting illegally on the farm. But something about him made her feel safe. He had loved the bees too. She could tell by the way his eyes lit up as he talked about them.

"We moved to the States when I was six, but we never stayed anywhere very long. I don't have a place like this, full of memories. Every time we moved to a different city, a different apartment, my mother would try to make it a home. She'd always make a big pot of soup. And every time when we sat down for a first meal in a new place, she would say the same thing. 'This is home.' And I honestly never could tell if she meant the new place was home, or if she sort of believed the soup was home, which sounds ridiculous."

"It's kind of sweet," Sasha said.

"Was there honey in it?" Bassel shook off his somber tone, tilted his head to one side, and smiled.

"In what?"

"The frame you found."

"No, just an old frame."

"I smell honey."

An entire lifetime lived in the smell of propolis and wax and honey. Sasha's fingers tingled at the memory of her skin pressed against the hive. Bassel's fingers twitched by his side.

"You smell propolis, not honey."

"I loved getting propolis on my hands and then pressing them into the ground so the dirt stuck." Bassel laughed. "My mom got so annoyed at me."

Sasha placed the wheel from Bassel's bike in a clamp on the workbench and began adjusting the spokes to realign the wheel. "There isn't much damage here. I'm going to tighten the spokes to flatten the wheel. The chain's easy to fix. It won't take long."

"How are you so calm about this?"

"I've fixed plenty of bikes."

"That's not what I meant."

"This is a pretty fancy bike. How old is it?" Sasha kept her eyes on the wheel, turning slowly to tighten the spokes one at a time.

"Two years."

"You don't ride it much." Sasha fingered the well-defined treads on the tires.

Bassel stepped closer to her to examine the rubber.

"Are you smelling me again?"

Bassel backed up a step, but she could feel his eyes examining her fingers and the sticky gray splotches on her skin. She would have to scrub them with soap and sand several times to get it off.

"Can I at least see the frames?"

"No." She longed to invite him up to the hayloft, show him the honey frames and watch his face light up when she offered him a bite of honeycomb. The smell would unlock a lifetime of memories for him the way it had for her. The urge to tell him she had honey burned in her throat. She licked her lips, lingering on a trace of sugar, and pressed her palms together, pulling them apart as the stickiness bonded her skin.

She worked silently on the bike, imagining how Bassel might react to seeing the honeycomb. She imagined his smile, crooked in a charming way. But he might ask questions she did not want to answer.

"You have one in your hair." Bassel pointed at Sasha's head.

"One what?"

"A bee, right there." He stepped closer and pushed a few strands of her hair away from her face.

"A bee?" Sasha froze.

"Your hair thing."

Sasha had forgotten about the hair clip from the bunker. She tried to calm her pounding heart, but the longer Bassel stood close, the faster her pulse raced. He smelled of ink and paper. She forced herself to turn away, although she wanted to examine the curl in his eyelashes up close.

Hoping he wouldn't notice the blush rising up her neck, she turned back to focus on the bike. She worked for another twenty minutes, constantly aware of where Bassel was and what he looked at.

Sasha tightened the last spoke and spun the wheel to test the symmetry. Part of her wanted to prolong the work so Bassel would linger. But she also wanted him to leave so she wouldn't cave in to his request to show him the frames.

"All set." She released the wheel from the mount and started reattaching it to the frame of the bike.

"What do I owe you?"

"On the house. It was an easy fix."

"Then let me take you to dinner. We're the last of our kind. The beekeepers' kids. I feel like we have a lot to talk about."

She shouldn't have confided in Bassel before telling Halle and Ian, but having someone to share memories with stirred a flutter in her stomach.

"I won't tell anyone about your dad."

"What exactly does a soil regulator do?"

"I test soil samples to monitor how quickly the toxicity in agricultural soil is breaking down. I have no interest in getting you in trouble. Let me take you out to dinner." Bassel looked down at his fancy brown shoes, which looked more scuffed than usual. "I mean, like really take you out."

"Like a date?" *Do not say yes. Do not say yes.*

"Would that be weird?"

"I guess we could try it and find out." She had an urge to press her palm to his cheek again but instead grabbed the handlebars of Bassel's bike and walked it toward the door.

"Is that a yes?"

"One dinner." Inside her head, Sasha screamed, *Yes!*

"I almost forgot. I brought you something." Bassel pulled a well-worn paperback copy of *Koala Named Lit* from his messenger bag on the ground and handed it to her. "Octavia told me you asked about this book. I found one in a used bookstore during a work trip last week."

Sasha accepted the book, the paper cover adhering to her skin.

"Thank you." She tried to suppress the smile exploding up from her chest.

Bassel rocked back on his heels, looking pleased with himself.

"I remember it too," Sasha said.

"Remember what?"

"The smell of a hive."

# Thirty

## SASHA, AGE 23
### JUNE 8

"Hi, honey, we're home," Ian shouted as he walked in the front door after work. He dropped onto the sagging sofa in the living room. A scant puff of dust rose from the cushions. Halle and Gino followed him in.

"I worked through lunch so I could get home early. There's a lot to catch up on." Halle flopped down next to Ian, sending up another cloud of dust. Halle picked at a curl of wallpaper pulling away from the wall.

The floral paper detached itself from the drywall in loose scrolls where the paper met the moldings and window frames. Sasha's mother hated the wallpaper, a remnant from when Sasha's grandparents lived in the farmhouse. But the older it got, the more Sasha loved the stuffy pattern, because it reminded her of how annoyed it made her mother. She worked hard to remember all the expressions her mother wore. Annoyed and indignant were Sasha's favorites to envision, in part because they didn't come to her easily. But when the irritated curl of her mother's upper lip came into focus, Sasha felt closest to her mother.

"Did you enjoy your day of leisure?" Gino asked.

"Absolutely. Bassel came over. He crashed his bike and needed me to fix it." She wanted to ease into the difficult but necessary conversation ahead of her.

Sasha waited for Halle to make a suggestive comment about Bassel coming over, but she didn't say anything. Halle's knees bounced, and she smiled so hard it looked like her face must hurt.

"What's going on?" Sasha asked.

"Halle apparently has 'the most amazing news ever.' She refused to tell us until we were all together. I think she might explode if she doesn't unload immediately," Gino said.

Halle stood up and squeezed her hands into one fist under her chin. She scrunched her nose up. "I have a court date. They've agreed to consider my petition to take custody of Beatrix. I've had consistent employment for six months, and steady housing. Because of the eviction moratorium, I can legally claim this place as a permanent address. Those were the biggest barriers."

"You never gave up." Gino hugged Halle. "I wish I'd planned a more exciting dinner."

"You could serve dirt tonight, and I'd love it," Halle said. "I wouldn't have a shot at this without all of you. You're my family as much as Beatrix is."

Joy entered their home in unforeseen, staggering moments offering glimpses of a better future. In these fleeting bursts of happiness, Sasha imagined her mother's reassuring hand on her shoulder.

Beatrix already occupied a place in the farmhouse. She existed in Halle's stories, in the overflowing box of hand-knit gifts Halle made her sister. Sasha often imagined she caught the flutter of a younger version of Halle dashing around a corner.

Sasha occasionally envisioned her mother in the house among her friends, admiring Ian's steadfast logic and Halle's craftiness. Her mother would have especially loved Gino, with his fierce loyalty and sharp humor.

"I'm going to need all of you to testify as character witnesses," Halle said. "My work record is perfect. I've never been in legal trouble, and neither have any of you. I have a shot at this."

Sasha squeezed her knees tight to her chest and struggled not to make eye contact with Gino, who shifted uncomfortably on the arm of the sofa. If Sasha testified, it could open her up to a background check and expose her family history. It could be worse for Gino.

"This is amazing!" Ian scooted closer to Halle on the couch and hugged her.

Gino put a hand to his side and gave Sasha a small shake of his head indicating he was not ready to tell the others about his past.

"I'm going to sketch Bea into the mural before she gets here." Halle walked over to the half-finished painting on the wall, tracing her finger over an open space in the wild grass, the perfect place for a young girl to run. "I want a better world for her to grow up in. I can't deliver that, but I can paint her a brighter future."

"Speaking of your mural, I have a present for you." Sasha lifted the box she had hidden behind the couch and placed it on the floor in front of the couch. "Then I have a breaking news story of my own. I have a date tomorrow."

"Please tell me it's Bassel," Gino said.

"I'll tell you all the details, but first I want Halle to open this." Sasha drew in a deep breath. "And I have some explaining to do."

Halle knelt on the floor next to Sasha.

Sasha pulled out several unused pads of matte paper. Halle's lower lip twitched, but she did not react.

Sasha laid out boxes of watercolors, unopened tubes of oil paints, and a cigar box filled with brushes of varying sizes, a few used paint palettes, and a tightly bound scroll of canvas.

"Where'd you get all this?" Halle caressed the rough surface of the paper and pinched it between her thumb and forefinger. She closed her eyes and opened them with a pop, shaking her head to see the art supplies still there.

"Don't worry, I didn't spend a cent on it." Sasha's pulse ratcheted up. She needed to do this. She needed to tell them everything.

"I don't believe for one second that someone gave you all these art supplies for free." Halle rolled a fine-tipped brush back and forth between her forefinger and thumb.

"I dug them up from an underground bunker out by the apiary." Sasha pressed her palms against her eyes and took a deep breath. "They were my father's. He buried them with some beekeeping gear and a few other things."

No one spoke. She had to tell them everything. She owed it to them. "Some of his journals were in there, too."

"Wait. You mean . . ." Halle dropped the brush in her hand. "Your father . . ."

"He was my dad."

"You never thought to tell us this?" Ian squinted, anger collecting in his heavy brow.

"I was afraid—"

"*I* told her not to tell you. Whatever Sasha's father did or did not do, it's not Sasha's fault," Gino said.

"You knew?" Ian shouted.

"The journals?" Halle said.

"The mythic missing research. I found some of it, but not much." Sasha stopped short of telling them Millie stole most of her father's documents.

"And you waited until today to dig it up?" Ian said.

Halle opened a tube of paint and sniffed.

"Let her be." Gino touched Ian's arm. "Sasha doesn't owe you any explanations. You have no idea what kind of baggage she's been carrying."

"How could *you* not tell me?" Ian said to Gino.

"Because I knew you'd react exactly like this," Gino said.

"We've worked so hard. So damn hard." Ian's chin quivered in anger. "We found work, we built a home together. For fuck's sake, we took you in. And all this time you've been a ticking bomb, just waiting to go off, waiting for someone to figure out who you were and derail everything."

"Think about it from Sasha's perspective," Gino said.

"Some of us didn't have the perspective you have to *think about it* because you kept the truth from us." Ian turned to Halle in search of solidarity.

Halle dumped the box out, fingering the tubes of paint and brushes like they were religious artifacts. "These belonged to him?"

"He had other talents besides keeping bees. He isn't just the man in *Time* magazine. He's my father."

"What about the research?" Halle asked. "Can you understand any of it?"

"Those journals must be worth a fortune," Ian said. "If we're going to be forced off the property, at least we can sell the research and make enough money for a fresh start."

Gino punched Ian in the arm.

"I can't make much sense of his notes yet, but I'm *not* selling my dad's journals."

"It's your history. You don't owe the world or us any details," Gino said.

"We could use the money," Ian said. "Think about Gino's meds. We could—"

"For God's sake, don't make this about me," Gino said. "If she doesn't want to sell her father's stuff, she doesn't have to."

"It's not like her dad can do anything with them," Ian said. "Why keep them? At this point, they're historic documents."

"There's something el—" Sasha said.

"We could auction them off. We might get enough to find a stable, permanent place to live. A place we won't be at risk of getting evict—"

"Stop it!" Sasha shouted. "Will you shut up for a second. There's something else I need to tell you."

Halle rubbed the hairs of a fine paintbrush over her lips.

"There's a reason I dug up my father's things today. I was look- ing for beekeeping gear." She had rehearsed the conversation sev- eral times, but her words felt clumsy.

"Are you going to a costume party?" Gino asked. "God, remem- ber costume parties? When I was a kid I loved—"

"Let her finish," Ian said in a low, deliberate tone.

"I need the gear because I saw a bee. And I'm planning to track it to the hive."

A squirrel skittered inside the walls upstairs, unleashing a familiar dread in Sasha. When the squirrels snuck in—and they always snuck in—they died inside the walls, flooding the house with the slow rot of death for ten days.

"You're serious, aren't you?" Ian said after a prolonged silence.

"You can't be sure," Halle said. "Our brains deal with stress and grief in crazy ways. Apis manifestation syndrome is a real thing, you know."

"I'm not imagining things. If anyone knows how to identify a bee, it's me."

The squirrel rustled inside the wall behind Halle's mural. An unexpected rage bubbled up as Sasha's eyes settled on the image of Millie at the edge of the woods.

"You haven't mentioned this to anyone else, have you?" Halle said. "You'll get yourself fired or arrested."

"Did you find the gear you were looking for?" Gino asked.

"Yeah."

The squirrel chatter grew louder, suggesting more than one rodent had taken up residence in the wall.

"You know Leah swore she found bees too, right?" Halle stood up. "And now she's missing. I have a hard time believing it's a coincidence. She went to meet some blogger who tracks bee sightings. I have no idea who or where, but she never came back. We've been putting posters up, filed a missing person report. But she just vanished."

"I know what I saw. And if there's one bee, there's a hive. And if there's a hive, there could be other hives. I'm going to find them."

"Aren't you famously allergic to bees?" Ian asked.

"That's why I was looking for protective gear."

"There are so many reasons this is a terrible idea." Halle paced as she talked. "Okay, first, it wasn't a bee. Second, if you did find a bee, you're allergic. Third, what if you find evidence then turn it in and go missing like Leah? I can't handle another missing person in my life. And, not to be selfish, but if anyone finds out you think you saw a bee, they'll want to know where, which will expose us here on the farm and I could lose my chance to get Beatrix back."

Sasha sat on the floor and pulled her knees up to her chest.

"You're missing the big picture here," Gino said. "What if Sasha really did see a bee? What if Leah and the others did too? What if they aren't extinct after all? That would be incredible."

"The bees aren't all of a sudden back." Halle twisted the frayed edge of her shirt. "That's not how extinction works."

"If it isn't real, then why did Leah disappear as soon as she reported seeing a bee?" Gino asked. "If finding a single bee was a fluke, or unimportant, why would it be illegal to report them?"

"Why'd you wait so long to dig up your father's work?" Halle asked.

"After I got here, and you invited me to stay, I started wanting to be part of this family more than I wanted to understand my past."

"What changed?" Halle asked.

"She convinced herself she saw a bee." Ian shook his head.

"I'm going with you," Gino said to Sasha. "Just in case you find something."

"I can't believe you're encouraging her." Ian threw his hands up in the air and slumped on the couch.

"Thanks, but I'm searching tomorrow morning. Bees are only active between sunup and sundown. You'll be at work."

"Don't you think it's a bit of a coincidence *you* of all people would be the one to rediscover bees, I mean, given your history? I believe you *think* you saw a bee." Halle's face contorted as she spoke, reflecting how hard she was trying to sound supportive. "I'm finally in a position where I can imagine a future with Beatrix again. Please don't do this. Not now."

"I can't pretend I didn't see it." How could Halle not understand how important this was to Sasha, how important it should be to everyone? She wanted to be right, to prove to the world bees still existed, that she hadn't killed them.

"I'm going to figure out how the squirrels are getting in." Sasha stood up and walked toward the front door.

"Wait, Sasha. What's the other big news? What about your big date?" Halle called after Sasha as the door slammed behind her.

# Thirty-One

## SASHA, AGE 23

### JUNE 9

The following morning, Sasha trailed her fingers along the molding in the hallway as she emerged from her room, allowing the ridges and divots she once knew by heart to rise to the surface. For the past year, Sasha had resisted indulging her nostalgia because she worried her housemates would notice the memories fluttering against her fingertips.

Now, with no reason to hide her attachment, she summoned the creaky floorboards, the rattle of the loose banister. Her bare toes curled over the smooth oak threshold leading to the kitchen. Her body, more fully itself, molded back into the shape of the house.

She went outside and sat on the porch swing, allowing the gentle motion and creak of the swing to lull her into a trancelike calm.

Halle joined her on the swing. The grind of the rusty chain links changed pitch under the added weight of another person.

Sasha stared ahead while Halle examined her face, probably searching for traces of the little girl from the infamous newsreels.

"Please be careful. Talking about bees creates risk for all of us, especially considering your history."

"I can't ignore this."

"I know." Halle sighed. "I'm just scared."

They swung in silence for several minutes.

"Have you seen my other shoe?" Gino shouted from inside the house.

"I'm not your mother," Ian answered.

Halle and Sasha both smiled at the recurring saga of Gino losing his shoes.

"Is it Bassel?" Halle asked.

Sasha tried not to smile but couldn't hold it back.

"I knew it." Halle tilted her head back to stare up at the porch ceiling. "You'll be careful? You'll wear protective gear the whole time?"

"With Bassel or the bees?"

"Both, if necessary." Halle laughed.

"I thought you didn't believe me."

"I don't want to believe you." Halle leaned her head on Sasha's shoulder.

Ian joined them, looking as if he hadn't slept much the night before.

"Mind if I talk to Sasha alone?"

Halle gave Sasha a reassuring hug and went inside.

Ian handed Sasha a small box. "There's only one EpiPen here. You should have two. This is not, by the way, an endorsement of your plan."

"Thanks." Sasha reached for the box, but Ian didn't release it.

"It must have been hard. Living here with us in the house where you grew up."

Sasha nodded, afraid her voice might crack if she spoke.

"I'm still mad you didn't tell us." He released the box to her.

Sasha stood up to face Ian. She deserved whatever he had to say. The long-buried fears of being discovered, of being turned away, rejected by the people she loved, roared in her head. Her pulse sped up until she could barely swallow over the pounding heartbeat in her throat.

"But I'll get over it, Sasha." He opened his arms to her. When she didn't move, Ian pulled her to his chest and wrapped his arms around her.

Sasha's knees buckled under the weight of relief as Ian held her until her tears stopped.

Sasha waved from the porch as her housemates mounted their bikes and left for work.

A breeze rippled through the big oak tree, causing the tire swing to spin as if nudged by an invisible hand.

Knowledge of the hidden bunker had thrummed under Sasha's feet since the day she and her father buried it, but now its pulse shook the ground, calling to her, forcing her to confront its contents.

After twelve years of her curating a protective barrier against those jagged memories, her guilt reemerged fresh and raw, overshadowed only by her resolve to find answers.

The dust kicked up from her housemates' bikes settled on her tongue as she walked toward her mother's workshop.

Something on the ground in front of the workshop glistened in the morning light. She couldn't identify the shape, but it had not been there when she closed the workshop the night before.

The journals. Maybe Bassel came back, convinced he smelled honey, and found the notebooks. Pushing away flashbacks of Millie's betrayal, Sasha sprinted the last thirty yards to the workshop. A small glass jar filled with wildflowers sat in front of the door.

A folded piece of paper stuck out from among the flowers.

*Thanks for fixing my bike. See you tonight. Bassel.*

She ran inside and climbed the ladder.

The frames, beekeeping gear, microscope, and journals lay hidden under the tarp, exactly as she left them. Sasha pinched off a wedge of honeycomb and sucked on it.

She reread Bassel's note and held the paper to her mouth, tracing the indent of his pen against her lips.

Released from hiding her past, convinced of the existence of the bee, and filled with anticipation of spending the evening with Bassel, Sasha felt invigorated, activated as if she were waking from a long, foggy sleep.

She flipped through her father's journals again, hoping something would make sense to her, but the data did not reveal any secrets or suggest how Sasha could track the bees.

*You need to find the line,* her father had instructed her. She licked her sticky fingers as she read the pages again and again.

*If she only understood what she has done. If only she knew.*

His words, suspended in time, stung as if he sat beside her, whispering in her ear.

She nibbled on honeycomb, hummed the way she had as a child, and waited for the perfect G to sizzle under her skin.

As a young child, Sasha had blamed the bees for the loss of her father; as a teen she blamed her father for the loss of the bees. Under the shield of her anger hovered the fear that her father, all this time, had blamed Sasha. The tremor now rumbled like a waking beast.

The air in the hayloft grew stagnant as the sun baked the asphalt roof.

How would she find the bees?

*Offer them something they want,* her father's words whispered in her memory.

The honey.

Sasha tossed the beekeeper's suit, veil, and gloves over the rail of the loft to the floor below. The mesh of the veil caught the air and billowed like a jellyfish as it drifted to the floor.

She dropped the journals onto the cushion of the protective gear and slid down the ladder to find something to put the honey in.

She snapped a picture of the jar of flowers and texted it to Bassel.

*Thanks! Where should I meet you?*

*I'll pick you up at 6,* Bassel responded.

She licked her lips, lingering over the remnants of honey as she gathered the flowers from Bassel's bouquet, which she tied with the stem of a daisy and hung upside down in the window over her workbench to dry. She poured out the water and dropped a generous piece of honeycomb inside the jar.

Tucking the beekeeping gear and the journals into her backpack, she set out for the woods with the open jar of honey in her hand.

She ran, her pack thumping against her back with each stride, resisting the urge to check on her newly replanted asparagus as she passed by the garden. At the edge of the field, she climbed over the stone fence and slipped into the forest.

It took a moment to acclimate to the sounds of the trees, the gentle harmony of chattering squirrels, leaves shifting in the breeze, the creak of heavy limbs sighing under their own weight.

She focused on her breath, steadying it, calming her heart rate so she could fall into the silent rhythm of earth being turned by worms and the slow-motion stretching of tiny roots below her feet, trees reaching upward, buds unfolding. Even at its most quiet, the forest heaved with motion.

Sasha meandered between oaks and hemlocks, trying to visualize the direction the bee had traveled as she scanned the spaces between branches for a flash of movement, a whir of tiny wings.

After a few minutes, the edge of the field blurred into the forest. The relative darkness cast the trees in a richer green. She dropped her bag to the ground and unpacked the beekeeping suit, veil, and gloves, then took a stick and scooped out a glob of honey, which she spread on a flat stone.

Sasha slipped one foot then the other inside her father's protective suit—her father's skin—and zipped it tight. She wrapped rubber bands around the bottoms of the pant legs and her wrists and pulled on the gloves. Last, she put the plastic case holding Ian's epinephrine shot in the side pocket of the oversize beekeeping suit.

Body heat and breath stewed in the suit, overwhelming her with fear that she might run out of air. *Just breathe.* After half an hour she stood up and shook out her arms and legs. It would be easy to drift off to sleep in the cocoon.

*You have to find the line.*

This clearing where she sat did not cross the beeline.

She moved a hundred yards north and settled on a patch of soft moss and placed the honey-smeared stone a few yards away.

Time slowed as her body slipped into a meditative cadence with the maternal comfort of the forest. After Sasha's mother died, she often crawled into the woods and curled up against the trunk of a pine tree, allowing the low branches to skim her shoulders and caress the top of her head.

Even in the cool shade of the forest, the afternoon heat accumulated in the bee suit as Sasha waited for a flicker in the calm.

Sweat trickled down her back, but she refused to take off the veil or unfasten the suit. If she believed bees existed in these woods, she needed to protect herself. Taking off the gear meant admitting bees did not live in this forest or any other.

Sasha didn't realize she had fallen asleep until her head jerked up at the sound of a chipmunk chattering. The sun had moved from the height of noon to midafternoon. She twisted her neck from side to side to ease the stiffness.

Sweat soaked her shirt, her sticky fingers clung to the inside of the gloves, but she couldn't risk exposing her skin.

She fixed her eyes on a single area of open space as she waited for the flash of a tiny body darting through the sky. Ghosts of the twenty-eight bee stings emerged in her hair, on her neck and face. She clenched her teeth, refusing to scratch at the phantom histamines.

Waiting in one spot seemed futile. Wandering aimlessly made even less sense.

She stood up, removed one glove, and held her bare hand to the air in search of a silent vibration.

"This is ridiculous," she said aloud as she extended her fingers toward the treetops. Sasha once believed her father had tuned her to the pitch of a bee. Years later when she realized her father invented the story, that humans could not be tuned, Sasha felt cheated, betrayed. Yet part of her still believed.

She held her hand to the sky for a few more seconds, then crouched to press her palm against the forest floor, waiting for what? For bees to summon her?

She leaned back against the tree and looked up to the sky peeking through the crowns. Her fingers rooted into the ground, pressing through the crumbly soil, scratching at the pebbles in her way.

At first, she mistook the flutter in her peripheral vision for a leaf fragment caught in the wind. She froze and waited. Another flicker near the honey-covered rock. Hot breath filled the veil as she waited, motionless except for the pounding of her heart.

A bee landed on the edge of the rock. It turned from side to side and sampled the honey.

Sasha's chest ached as if it might burst open. She longed to peel off the veil and crawl over to the tiny miracle. Allowing the bee to see her in protective gear felt like an admission that she wasn't one of them and never had been.

Another bee joined the first, and soon six bees gathered near the honey. Tears streamed down Sasha's hot cheeks.

*Oh, Dad, I wish you were here.*

After several minutes the bees, drunk on honey, flew off into the woods, heading home.

Sasha grabbed her pack and the honey stone and followed. She lost them almost immediately, but more bees would come. Those first bees would return to the hive and tell their sisters.

She put the honey stone down and waited.

Eight bees, then ten. Soon the stone crawled with honey bees. She left the stone in place and followed the slow but steady stream of bees. Again, she lost them, but smeared honey on another stone, then another, and worked her way deeper into the woods, following the line.

*I found the line. Please tell me what to do now, Dad?*

A discovery this huge required witnesses, yet the significance of the moment demanded intimacy. They had been hiding, waiting for her. Hadn't she been hiding all this time, too? They were the survivors. When most of the other primary pollinators died off decades earlier, *Apis mellifera* outlived them. The bee her father hung his hopes and dreams on when the wild bees, beetles, and butterflies disappeared. For a while, they seemed invincible, unaffected by the heat, the droughts, the agricultural poisons.

And then they, too, were gone. But not gone. Waiting.

All the years spinning herself dizzy to prove she could always point herself back to her hive.

"I'm here," she whispered. "We're home."

She sat again and waited.

A bee landed on the honeycomb and sucked the honey until it could hold no more and darted off.

The sun would be setting soon. She must be close. Her fingertips buzzed.

They began to appear in pairs and clusters. The high-pitched hum near her ears woke her body, her skin. Her fear fell like scales to the forest floor.

Miracle or illusion. Vision or premonition. The bees began to converge from different directions.

As she stepped toward the convergence, the sound filled her head. The bees ducked, one after another, into the opening of a hollow tree. They flickered like the mesmerizing flames of a campfire. She longed to stretch her bare hands out and warm her fingers over the flutter of the gathering wings.

The opening in the tree yawned to expose a deep hollow. She stepped an inch closer.

The faint linger of balsam clung to the veil. How many times had her father worn the headgear she now wore? She inhaled the mist of his breath embedded in the fabric.

The hum of the hive crescendoed as she got closer to the tree. A perfect G. She held her breath, remembering the ecstatic moment when her violin matched the hum of the bees.

The resonance of the hum coming from inside the hollow tree intoxicated Sasha. The magnificent om of the universe. Dangerous and beguiling.

She held her ear to the bark of the tree and pressed her gloved hands against the trunk, listening. The hum grew louder. The vibrations penetrated her bones until the sound came from inside her own skull.

Bee after bee landed on the opening to the hive, their haunches loaded down with pollen. Others approached from inside the cavern and unpacked the pollen. They moved with precision, with an innate understanding of the needs of each other and the hive. Each returning bee, relieved of its burden, aimed its rear end toward the trees and wiggled.

The dance felt private, as if Sasha should avert her eyes. But she couldn't look away.

Her father taught her about the bees' geolocation prowess, about how they aimed their rear ends and gyrated their hindquarters in tiny circles, transmitting the precise distance and location of bountiful pollen and nectar sources to their peers.

Bees always knew their exact location. Their celestial compasses always guided them home.

Clusters of bees now clung to her sleeves and torso.

*Breathe. In and out. Don't panic.* Slowly, slowly, she peered into the hole in the tree. The bees fanned the aroma around her veiled face. Honey-saturated humidity filled her head and her lungs.

Without thinking, she reached for her father's hand.

She had envisioned a grotto overflowing with golden honey, but instead she found irregular masses of pale yellow honeycomb clinging to the walls of the hollow tree, hanging from the top and rising up from the bottom like stalactites and stalagmites in a cave.

Sasha's breath inside the veil grew steamy, and she gasped to fill her lungs. Her neck and arms itched, her skin prickling hot and cold at the same time.

A clump of bees collected on the side of Sasha's veil. She fought the urge to swat them. *Calm. Always calm.* The mass of bees slid down her veil, oozing toward her shoulder like melting chocolate. She held her arms out to her sides like a cross as she stepped backward in slow, fluid movements. Bees dripped off in clumps.

By her feet, Sasha found a cluster of dead bees under the opening to the hollow tree. Bees, such tidy housekeepers, carried the dead out of the hive to keep them from decomposing indoors and contaminating the hive. With slow movements, she opened another Mason jar from her bag and nudged a pile of dead bees into the jar. Proof.

Sasha backed away until at least thirty feet separated her from the hive. As the buzz around her diminished, she realized she was humming and had been for a long time. She ran her gloved hands over her pant legs and her arms, over the veil and the folds in the mesh draping down her shoulders to dislodge any remaining bees.

She held her breath, listening for any residual buzzing, swooning with a mix of joy and terror, as she stumbled out of the woods. A frothy warmth swelled in her chest.

She had planned to wash up before her date. The thought of seeing Bassel added a giddy rush to the slurry of emotions coursing through her body.

Judging by the angle of the sun, it was almost six. He would be at the farm soon. She cursed herself for not watching the time more carefully. She considered texting Bassel and canceling. How could she sit across from him at dinner and make small talk while holding on to the most enormous secret of their time?

But she wanted to see him. She wanted to know about his childhood and his bees. How did his family cope with the loss? She considered telling Bassel about the hive, but only for a second. She didn't know him well enough to trust him yet. And she owed it to Halle, Gino, and Ian to tell them first.

After her date with Bassel, Sasha would gather her housemates together. They would be hungry for details about Bassel. She would surprise them with news of the hive. Despite their fears, they would understand the enormous implications. What if the bees could come back in meaningful numbers? Their existence could alter the pessimistic trajectory of global food security.

She was getting ahead of herself.

She squinted as she stepped out of the shade of the forest. The world seemed brighter, the colors crisper, the edges of the house, the clouds, the trees, more defined. She covered the Mason jar of honey with a flat stone and left it at the edge of the forest.

Her phone rang in her pocket inside the beekeeping suit.

Not wanting to miss a call from Bassel, she quickly ran a gloved hand over the bee suit, brushing every fold of the veil in search of any straggler bees. The fresh air invigorated her sticky skin as she took the headpiece off and pulled out the phone.

The caller ID read MOM.

Her heart thumped. So many times, Sasha had longed to talk to her own mother.

She answered the call but didn't speak.

A woman spoke in a language Sasha did not recognize.

"Sorry, you have the wrong number," Sasha answered, an ache pressing on her chest.

"Sasha?"

The faint hum of a bee buzzed near Sasha's ear a fraction of a second before the stinger plunged into her neck, and she dropped the phone.

# Thirty-Two

## SASHA, AGE 23
### JUNE 9

Sasha slapped at her neck, but it was too late.

She scraped the stinger out with her fingernail and tried to calm her heart rate. Every beat propelled the poison further into her body. Her airways constricted; her face grew hot. Minutes to think.

The beekeeping suit, although unzipped, felt like an oven. She dropped to her knees, searching the thick grass for the phone, grateful for Bassel's choice of sparkly purple, which caught the light.

*Need hospital allergic reaction can't breathe,* she texted Bassel, and stumbled in the direction of the workshop.

The expanse of her mother's overgrown field between her and the driveway appeared endless, an impossible distance without oxygen. Her tongue thickened, and she scratched at her neck, her windpipe tightening until she could barely manage thin wisps of air.

She fumbled with the zipper on her bag and opened the EpiPen Ian gave her. She stabbed the needle into her thigh, through the suit and her pants. The pain barely registered as she struggled for air.

She needed the missing second dose.

Bassel's car screeched into the driveway, sliding over gravel as he slammed on the brakes.

She waved to him and gasped for breath. A sensation of doom tightened around her chest. Bassel would never see her from so far away.

A blur swam closer as her vision darkened.

No one would ever know about the bees, she thought, as she collapsed.

*I've got you, Sasha,* her father's voice whispered as he gathered her in his arms and ran, as he had so many years ago. *I've got you.*

*You're okay.* He laid her across the back seat.

*You're going to be okay.*

S he woke in a hospital bed, connected to an IV with an oxygen tube in her nose. She put her hand to her neck. The sting burned hot to the touch. She wore a faded green hospital gown.

Where was the beekeeping suit? Her backpack? The jar of dead bees? Sasha jolted upright to find Bassel sitting next to her in a folding chair, his forehead resting on fists propped up on his elbows. The small space, fitted with a makeshift blue curtain, barely had room for Bassel's chair wedged between the hospital bed and a counter.

Bassel put a finger to his lips, indicating she shouldn't speak. He pointed at the curtain, which revealed two pairs of feet standing on the other side.

"What the fuck?" he mouthed without uttering a sound, staring at her with wild eyes.

Her tongue felt thick and cumbersome, but her breath moved easily now.

"Excellent, you're awake." A middle-aged doctor pushed the curtain aside and joined them in the small space. A paunchy white man with graying hair and a bulbous forehead, he spoke without looking at either Sasha or Bassel.

"Your fiancé says you accidentally ate something with nuts in it. You gave yourself the first injection of epinephrine, and he rushed you here. Is this how you remember it?"

"Her nut allergy's terrible." Bassel lifted his eyebrows high and gave Sasha a hard stare.

"That sounds right." Sasha's words came out raspy and dry.

"You did the exact right thing." The doctor patted Bassel on the shoulder on his way out of the curtained room. "This one's a keeper."

Bassel grimaced.

Sasha touched her face. Her skin felt tight and hot, her lips swollen.

Bassel shifted from one foot to the other, staring down at his shoes.

"Fiancé?" Sasha whispered when the doctor left the room.

"They weren't going to let me stay with you because I'm not family, so I told them we're getting married in the spring. It's a lovely time for a wedding, don't you think?"

"Where's my father?" Sasha looked around the small space and into the hall. Several monitors and an IV line tethered her to the bed.

"What do you mean? He's in prison, a hospital, or whatever. I don't think he can visit."

"My dad found me." How had Bassel not seen him?

"I found you, Sasha."

"But I heard him."

"There wasn't anyone there but me."

*I've got you, Sasha.*

Bassel stepped closer to Sasha and lifted her hair off of her neck to inspect the bee sting. Sasha put her hand to the hot welt.

"They didn't see it?"

"I let your hair down to cover it up, and no one looked for it because I told them you had a reaction to nuts. They gave you the same meds as they would for a—" He mouthed "bee sting."

"Do you want a cold cloth or something to put on it?"

"No. Someone might notice."

"Does it hurt?"

"No. It itches like crazy though."

He smiled sympathetically, his long, thick eyelashes curled up with a dramatic swoop.

"Are you going to tell me what happened?"

"Not here. Nobody knows?"

Bassel shook his head. He pressed his lips together.

"Ian's texted you at least twelve times. They're pretty worried. I almost responded, but I didn't know what to tell them."

"They must be freaking out. Can you hand me my phone?"

Bassel reached into her backpack and grabbed her phone from an inside pocket. He appeared familiar with the interior of her bag. The neatly folded beekeeping suit and veil filled out the backpack. He must have slipped it off her.

"If you didn't want to have dinner with me you could have just told me," he said.

"This isn't the best date I've been on, but you definitely get points for saving my life."

He sat on the edge of her bed, his hip against hers. She could have scooted over to give him more room, but she liked the heat of his body next to hers.

The doctor came back with some paperwork.

"You are free to go, but I need you to fill in your address and contact info for follow-up." He handed the clipboard to Bassel.

"You need my address too?" Bassel asked.

"I thought you lived together."

"I said we're engaged. But we're very old-fashioned," Bassel said with a straight face. He took Sasha's hand in his.

"I'm saving myself." Sasha bit the inside of her cheek to hold back a laugh.

"I shouldn't make assumptions." The doctor turned red. "But, yes, we need your information too, sir."

Bassel maintained a serious face while he filled in the paperwork. Sasha texted Ian to let her friends know she was okay.

What the hell is going on?" Bassel said as soon as they got in his car. He gripped the steering wheel so hard Sasha thought it might snap off the steering column.

"I'm sorry you got caught up in this."

"Bees?"

"They're in the woods." Her pulse raced from the adrenaline they had given her. Her throat hurt and her head pounded. More than anything she wanted to sleep, to not talk, and to process what had happened alone.

"How long have you known?"

"I've suspected for a while, but I didn't know for certain until today."

"I saw the dead bees in your backpack."

"You went through my stuff?"

"I saved your life."

"That doesn't give you the right to go through my stuff."

"I wanted to know what was going on so I could help you."

"I don't need your help."

"It kind of looked like you needed help when I found you unconscious."

"I'm sorry. It's just . . . I found a fucking beehive. What am I supposed to do?"

"You found a whole hive?" Bassel's eyes lit up like a child's before they blew out birthday candles.

"Filled with honey." Sasha couldn't hold back a small smile. Bassel understood.

"You need to be careful who you tell. I work for Soil Reclamation, but I have access to a lot of internal stuff. There's an entire team dedicated to discrediting people who make public claims about finding bees. They destroy people's reputations, prosecute them, wreck their lives." Bassel tapped a nervous finger on the steering wheel.

"Why wouldn't this be good news?"

"It is, on a macro level. But for you, for us, it's dangerous."

"I have proof, so I can't be charged with making a false claim. I know the assistant secretary of agriculture. I could reach out to him, although I hate doing that. He's an asshole."

"I wouldn't do that yet. Once authorities know, you put yourself at risk."

"I feel responsible for this hive. I'm worried about getting my friends evicted, but I'm also worried about these bees. What will happen to the bees if I report them? What will happen if I don't?"

"I don't know."

Bassel started the engine and wove his way through the hospital parking lot. She rolled her window all the way down. The smell of asphalt mixed with the sterile linger of itchy hospital linens clinging to her skin.

They sped past abandoned farms, many occupied by squatters. Faint yellow lights flickered in a few scattered windows. Candlelight, and some electric lights powered by makeshift windmills and solar panels.

Sasha took pride in the electricity she'd rigged up at the farmhouse. But she rarely had the opportunity to see lights from other squatters' homes at night. She smiled in solidarity as the lights flickered past.

*Don't ever get complacent about the grid*, her father had shouted down from a ladder as he adjusted the blades on the turbine at the Backup Plan, the cabin owned by her mother's family where she spent her childhood summers. *The grid's going to collapse one day, and we'll be the only folks left with lights on.*

Sasha faced an impossible decision. If she reported the hive, they would likely be evicted from the farm. They would have to move into barracks and be split up. Her garden, the wind turbine, her bike-repair business would all disappear. Halle wouldn't have an address to claim in her custody hearing.

But did she have the right to hold back an important discovery with global ramifications?

She put her arm out the window and let her cupped hand ride the current. The closer they got to the farm, the sooner she faced making a decision. She stuck her head out, allowing the wind to rush through her hair and billow her cheeks. Air roared like a train in her ears.

"Can we pull over for a minute?" Sasha said.

"Are you sick?" Bassel slowed down on the shoulder of the poorly maintained road. Chunks of asphalt had broken loose on the edge of the road, making the car bounce as it slowed.

"I'm fine. I just need a minute before I go home."

Sasha got out of the car and walked over to a wire fence meant to keep people out of one of the many fields left fallow to remediate from chemical contamination.

"Section A-146," Bassel said.

"What does that mean?"

"This area is classified by the Office of Soil Reclamation as A-146. It's one of the most densely contaminated sectors in the state. We closed down fifty-six farms in this area."

"Including my family's." Sasha crouched down to climb between the fence wires.

"What are you doing? This field's toxic." Bassel followed her.

"If I ate the grass every day for a year, maybe. But walking in it for a few minutes won't hurt anyone. You know that better than anyone, Mr. Soil Regulator."

Tall grasses with heavy-loaded tassels swished across her thighs as she walked away from the road.

Sasha lay down in the tall grass and lost sight of Bassel.

"Where are you?" he called in the darkness.

"Follow my voice."

After a few seconds, Bassel approached where Sasha lay on her back.

"Don't step on me. I'm down here."

"Let's go back to the car." He extended a hand down to Sasha to pull her up.

She took his hand but yanked him down instead. He resisted at first, but reluctantly gave in and lay down on his back beside her.

"This is going to affect my housemates. When officials discover there are bees on the property, they'll evict us."

Bassel stared up at the enormous sky in silence.

The grasses swayed all around them, occasional chaff drifting down and landing on them. The Milky Way stood out against a viscous purple with barely a sliver of a moon to dim the universe.

"I'm not leaving until I see a shooting star." As soon as she spoke, a light flashed across the sky with a pale, blurred tail.

"How about three shooting stars?" Bassel turned to face Sasha.

"I appreciate that you saved my life and everything, but you don't need to get involved." Sasha scanned the sky, desperate for another star, another wish.

"You can't expect me to walk away from this."

Sasha rolled over on her side to face Bassel.

"I covered up the bee sting. I could have told them the truth at the hospital, but I didn't."

Another shooting star sliced through the sky, leaving a brief but luminous tail. They both sucked in a muted gasp at the same time as the flare burst forth and dissipated into a shimmer.

"It's bigger now," Sasha said. "The sky at night. In the daytime it looks the same as it did before. But at night . . ."

"I think about that a lot." Bassel rolled on his side to face Sasha. "All those stars dimmed by our light. But they were always there. Like these bees. They've been there the whole time."

Sasha wanted to reach up and grab his breath before it ascended to merge with the showering stardust.

"I've spent my whole career trying to determine how to rehabilitate our agricultural lands, how to learn from our mistakes and do better in the future. For us. For the wildlife we haven't lost yet."

"That sounds more like a good story than science."

"I believe in both," Bassel said.

Sasha smiled in the dark.

"There's something I need to tell you." Bassel drew in a deep breath. "I knew who you were before Octavia introduced us. I wanted to meet you."

"Why?"

"I wanted information."

"About what?" An owl hooted in the forest flanking the field where they lay.

"About your father."

"You and everyone else." She sat up, his words landing like a stone in her chest. "I'm ready to go now."

"You said three shooting stars."

"That was before I knew you were a stalker."

"Hear me out, please. I wanted to talk to you about my mother. She's an entomologist like your dad. They were friends. They worked on UN projects together. But right before the Great Collapse, your dad turned on my mom. Remember when I told you a colleague lied about my mom and discredited her work? It was your father. He destroyed her career. It devastated her professionally and personally. She spent years trying to clear her name, but the world moved on. The bees died off. Your father went to prison."

"And you never considered mentioning this?"

"I thought about it all the time, actually. I didn't think you'd talk to me if you knew."

"What do you want from me?"

"At first, I wanted information. Now, I guess I care less about the past and more about—" Bassel paused. "About the future."

"Then I envy you. I wish I could stop obsessing over the past."

"I should have told you. I didn't ask you out so I could get information from you. I asked you out because I like you."

"Did it ever occur to you my dad discredited her because her work was flawed?" Sasha tried to maintain an annoyed tone as heat rushed up her neck.

"I've gone over her work a dozen times looking for errors. Your father lied."

"So, you came here to exact revenge on my father through me?" She should feel scared. Alone in an abandoned field with a man carrying a vendetta against her family. She looked sideways at Bassel, who stared up at the sky. His black curls fell in a tangle beneath his head. Despite all the reasons he should, Bassel didn't scare her at all.

"They were friends. Why would your father go so far out of his way to destroy my mother?"

"I have no reason to believe he lied about anything," Sasha said, although her father was quite capable of lying.

"I had heard maybe . . ."

"Oh, right, the mythic missing research."

"Is there any truth to it?"

Sasha didn't respond.

"I'm not trying to hurt you or your dad. I just want answers."

Chaff floated on the breeze. Sasha blew a puff of air to keep it from landing on her face. Clotted earth clinging to the day's heat warmed her back through her shirt as cooling air chilled her bare arms. Her pulse fluttered at the residual adrenaline from the IV medication. She hugged her arms across her torso and gripped her elbows to stifle the tremors.

"If you know anything that might help me understand, I'd appreciate it. She's convinced your dad was involved in a secret government experiment. The obsession is destroying her."

"What's she doing now?"

"I don't know. I haven't talked to her in a long time. She dropped out of the science community and started chasing down conspiracy theories. She won't take my calls. Every couple of years she comes up with some new wild idea. She tries to get me to leave my job and join her. I never do, and she storms out and disappears for another year."

"Wait. I think I talked to your mother." Sasha bolted upright.

"What are you talking about?"

"I forgot. Seconds before I got stung, a call came in on the purple phone from a caller ID that read 'Mom.' It's your phone. Your contacts. It had to be your mom." Sasha felt a pang of disappointment remembering the split second when she wondered, what if, impossibly, it had been her own mother. "She knew who I was when I answered. Could you have told her about me?"

"I haven't had any communication with her for nearly two years."
Bassel put his hands over his face. "This doesn't make any sense."

"Could she be spying on us?"

"There's no way my mother would ever work for the government.
That's part of the reason she and I don't talk. She thinks I betrayed
all my morals to go work for the Department of Agriculture, which
participated in your father's smear campaign against her. She refuses
to give me room to be my own scientist. I believe we can rehabilitate
agricultural land more quickly than most people think. She didn't
want to hear any of it. She wanted me to rehabilitate her reputation."

"But if she knows who I am—"

"She wants answers. Not revenge. Besides, you didn't do anything to her, your father did."

Sasha sympathized with the consuming need for answers.

"Do you think your mom's right?" She tried to ignore the heat of
Bassel's shoulder next to hers.

"I don't know. But I'd like to prove her right—or wrong. Anything to give her closure. This obsession ruined her life and I worry
she's going to keep chasing it and I'll lose her for good."

"What's her name?"

"Kamilah Maher."

"Dr. Maher?"

"You know her?"

"My dad told me to find a Dr. Maher. He can't mean your mother."

"He's definitely talking about my mom. Where is she?"

"I have no idea. I'd never heard her name until I talked to my
dad. I asked his advice about how to track a bee. He got agitated
and told me to find your mother, only your mother, to tell her about
the bees."

Bassel lay down and stared up at the sky again.

"Why would my dad want me to talk to your mother if he knows
she hates him?" Maybe Bassel, via his mother, had been working
Sasha this whole time.

"He knows she cares about the bees. We go back at least six

generations, the beekeepers in my family. She and I moved to Utah when I was six so she could consult on an international pollinator project. We planned to move back home after a few years, but the bee populations collapsed in the Middle East and North Africa before they collapsed here, so we stayed. My mom couldn't face going home without the bees. But she also hated staying here. She hated the way Americans commodified bees, put them in boxes, and used them until they broke."

"You didn't use box hives?"

"We used clay tubes stacked on top of one another in a wall."

"I've seen pictures. The stacks look a lot like a giant honeycomb. Are they more efficient?"

"My mom would say so, but her definition of 'efficient' isn't the typical Western definition. I think she would say the tubes served the bees better. But we lost our bees just like the rest of the world to varroa mites, climate change, pesticides. I don't think it ever mattered what shape the hives were."

So much had depended on those bees her father harbored in the apiary. Sasha hadn't understood. She had been so angry. She scrunched her eyes shut, trying to block out the vision of the swarm of bees hovering over her head, escaping.

"Did you know Egyptians were the first beekeepers in recorded history?" Bassel asked.

"And we were the last."

Bassel slipped his hand into hers.

"Maybe we can figure this out together. The first and the last," he said.

"Will you help me find your mom? She tried to call you today. She must be ready to talk." It felt reckless to trust Bassel, but their shared history felt significant, as if they were meant be on this journey together.

"Of course. If the bees survived, even one hive, it would mean everything to her."

"One more star before we go?" Sasha said.

"One more star." Bassel inched closer so his shoulder pressed against hers until two stars slashed through the inky sky in concert. She wanted to believe in him. She wanted to believe in so many things.

Halle, Ian, and Gino sat on the front porch when Bassel and Sasha pulled into the driveway. Halle sprinted down the stairs and hugged her. "I was so worried." Halle's mouth pressed into Sasha's hair so that Sasha could feel her friend's ragged breath. "So fucking worried."

"I'm okay, I promise."

Sasha gestured for Bassel to sit on the porch swing.

"I'm getting the vodka," Ian said, and walked inside. "Do *not* start telling the story until I get back."

The sting on her neck itched with writhing heat. She pressed her hand against the welt, trying to quiet it.

The last time Sasha got stung, she lost everything. Her home, her family, her future. She didn't owe the world anything. She should forget the hive.

But Sasha could never forget the bees.

Ian came back with the five glasses and poured a few fingers in each glass.

"I've been saving this for a long time. But this seems appropriate. To Sasha being okay." Ian raised a glass.

A lump swelled in Sasha's throat. These friends, this family, this home, meant everything to her. But how would they handle her revelation about the bees in the forest?

"And to Bassel for saving her," Halle said.

The vodka soothed Sasha's raw, scratchy throat. She took another sip, waiting for the gentle buzz that might make the unavoidable conversation a degree easier.

Sasha focused on the porch floorboards but could feel Halle, Gino, and Ian staring at her, waiting.

"Since when do you have a nut allergy?" Ian asked.

"I don't." Sasha took a deep breath. "But I'm allergic to bees."

Sasha lifted the hair off of the back of her neck and Ian crawled over to examine the welt. He touched her inflamed skin tenderly and sat back, staring at her with wide eyes.

"You got stung by an actual bee?" Gino leaned in to get a look.

"I'll get my fireweed salve." Ian went inside and returned with a homemade ointment, which he dabbed tenderly on her neck, soothing the irritated skin.

"What did they say in the hospital? I bet they haven't seen a bee sting in decades," Gino said.

"Did they report it? Shit, you need to be careful," Halle said. "I told you what happened to Leah."

"No one knows I got stung. Bassel told them I had a reaction to nuts, which they treat the same way. I don't want anyone else to know until I figure out a plan."

"A plan for what?" Gino said.

"To protect the hive. I have the name of someone who might be able to help if I can find her." Sasha glanced at Bassel. "Until then, everyone goes to work as usual, we don't say anything to *anyone*. No discussion of bees."

"So, this is real? They're back?" Gino said.

"I don't know." Sasha imagined her younger self, barefoot and unprotected, surrounded by the swelling hum of a hive. "But if they are back, this could change everything."

# Thirty-Three

They called it today," Sasha's father said as he buttered his toast at the dinner table one week before his trial was set to begin.

"Called what?"

"The last three of North America's twenty primary pollinator species are officially extinct."

"How can they possibly know that? Did they search every forest?" Sasha said.

"It was too much, even for our bees, the last of the last."

"That's not true and you know it." Sasha crossed her arms. Her bees were out there. She saw them disappear into the woods weeks earlier.

Sasha scraped the burnt crust off of the edge of her toast. Sasha hated when her father scraped his toast, but the sound never bothered her when she did it herself.

"We used to hear crickets out here at night." He leaned his head back and closed his eyes. "They used to irritate me."

"Do you think the cicadas will ever wake up again?"

"I hope so."

"Me too." Sasha had been waiting her whole life, or at least since she read about the cicadas emerging every seventeen years. She looked forward to the screech in the air, the crunch underfoot, evidence that time could move slower for one species than another, that one life-form could take a seventeen-year nap while others recklessly raced through time.

Would the cicadas experience a collective sadness as they emerged into a world where 95 percent of insects had gone extinct? She imagined waking up one day to find herself alone, the last of her kind.

"We know something they don't. Why can't we tell them?" she asked.

"The cicadas?"

"No, the people who claim the bees are gone. We should tell them."

"No." His voice turned sharp. "I told you we can never discuss this. The bees are gone."

"But they're out there. What if they need us?"

"Stop it!" he yelled. "You never opened the door. Tell me you understand."

"I understand." She shrank back from his unexpected outburst.

"This is the most important thing I've ever asked of you or anyone else. When they put you on the stand, you tell every detail of what happened. But you leave out the part about opening the door."

"I know." Her words fought their way up her constricting throat as she fought back tears. If one tear fell, she wouldn't be able to stop the rest.

"I don't care what they say about me. I don't care if I go to jail. We protect those bees."

She wanted to scream *What about me?* I *care if you go to jail.* Even the bees, somewhere in the forest, had each other. But Sasha would be alone. A bee without a hive will die.

Her father walked down the hall to his office and closed the door.

The lemony kitchen wallpaper Sasha associated with tenderness took on a squeaky brightness. The open spice rack on the wall needed replenishing. A coriander bottle sat empty, as it had ever since her mother died.

Why did her father seem more concerned about the bees than about her? Where would she go if he went to prison?

Sasha picked up the three-legged stool her father had stood on years earlier and carried it out to the driveway. She held the stool by two legs over her head and brought the seat down as hard as she could against the gravel. The seat cracked, and the legs loosened. She smashed it again and again, until the crossbars near the bottom broke free. Over and over, she battered the broken stool, screaming as it splintered against the ground.

The impact stung her hands and burned in her shoulders. Placing both feet on the seat of the upturned stool, she wrestled a leg free.

They were not a three-legged stool.

They were not a ladder.

If her father went to jail, Sasha would be alone. A single spike.

Her father stood at his office window, his forehead pressed against the glass, watching. Sasha tossed the circular seat like a Frisbee in the direction of the old oak tree. Carrying one leg of the dismembered stool, Sasha ran toward the tire swing and smacked it with the leg. The impact reverberated up her arms. She hit the swing again and again, timing her blows as the tire spun and swung.

Sweat trickled down her neck. The piece of wood, no longer part of a chair, felt powerful in her hands, thicker than a baseball bat with a satisfying rough-hewn finish. She backed up a step and hit the tire again, this time allowing it to swing wide and return to her. She whacked it again, summoning more force with each blow.

Her father marched down the porch stairs, anger bursting from each collision of his heavy boots and the warped boards of the porch.

The hairs on Sasha's neck stood on end as he approached. She did not face him; instead she beat harder on the tire, projecting her guilt on each blow as it landed on the rubber.

*I'm sorry I ruined everything.*

She beat the wood against the tire.

*I'm sorry they took your bees.*

Her father stood behind her, not moving, but breathing like an engine revving up too quickly, about to explode.

*I'm sorry I entered the apiary.*

Her father stepped up next to Sasha, his breathing ratcheted up, his face red with rage, fear, and grief.

*I'm sorry I opened the door.*

He extended his hand to Sasha, and she handed him the leg of the stool and held her breath, waiting for him to finally yell at her, punish her, shame her. She needed the reprimand. She needed him to release her from the prison of her guilt.

He gripped the stick and held it over his shoulder, his brow crinkled with deep lines, his eyes squinting so tight they almost appeared closed. His first swing landed with a noncommittal thud on the tire. Two squirrels scurried the length of the bough overhead as if they sensed the brewing storm.

He choked up on the stool leg and pivoted sideways, waiting for the arc of the swing to slow. His lips pressed together and his nostrils flared with each breath.

As the chain rattled, the tree itself seemed to hum, sending tremors into the ground and up through the rubber soles of Sasha's sneakers.

Her father pounded on the tire; his breathing grew thick and strained, silent apologies landing with each blow. Sweat dripped down the side of his face as he dropped the stick, placed a hand on Sasha's shoulder, and walked back into the house.

Sasha crouched to the ground and picked up the stool leg, still hot from the rage in her father's grip, and shimmied under the flailing swing.

She lay on her back watching moonlight filter through branches as the tire swung like a giant pendulum above her face. The chain creaked and strained, slipping in pitch with each progressively smaller arc until it stilled itself to a gentle sway and a whimper.

# Thirty-Four

## SASHA, AGE 23
### JUNE 10

Sasha woke up with a pounding headache, either from the medication they gave her in the ER the night before, Ian's vodka, dread, or, more likely, from a combination of everything.

Bassel lay on the floor in the corner of her room with a thin quilt to cushion the hardwood floor.

She vaguely remembered Bassel helping her up to her room. The details remained fuzzy, but she remembered wrapping her arms around his neck and pulling him toward her bed, the taste of vodka on his lips. His face hovered above hers, but he pulled back and made a bed on the other side of the room.

Sasha's cheeks flushed at the memory. Maybe he wouldn't remember.

Upstairs, Halle, Ian, and Gino puttered around getting ready for work. Sasha crept out of her room and to the bathroom. Months earlier Sasha rigged a dry sink with a hand pump sucking water up from a five-gallon tank of fresh water that splashed into the basin and drained into a gray water tank.

She smoothed her hair down, gave her teeth a quick brush, gargled with water, and pinched her cheeks to brighten her hangover pallor.

Bassel sat up and stretched when she reentered her bedroom.

"How'd you sleep?" Sasha avoided looking him in the eye.

"Not bad. I called in sick to work today. I tried calling my mom's number, but she didn't answer."

"I'm going to go talk to Octavia to see if she has any contacts who might help us find her. She knows everyone. Vendors start setting up around ten."

"I'll go with you. I know this isn't at the top of your priority list right now, but I'd still like to take you to dinner sometime if you're still interested. I mean, you seemed kind of interested last night."

"I was hoping you didn't remember that." Heat rushed up Sasha's neck. "I drank way too much."

"If something's going to happen between us, which I'd like, I want you to remember it." Bassel stepped closer to Sasha and lifted the hair off the back of her neck to inspect the bee sting. "Does it hurt?"

He touched the welt lightly with the tips of his fingers. Down the hall in the kitchen, Halle, Ian, and Gino shuffled around the kitchen.

"It's a little sore." A shiver rushed across her skin.

Bassel leaned in closer to inspect the sting. He kissed her neck below the welt, his day-old scruff rough against her skin. She wrapped her arms around his neck. His breath fell hot on her skin as his lips moved up her neck. One hand buried into her hair; his other moved down the small of her back, pressing her closer.

The kitchen door slammed shut as her housemates left for work. Sasha wanted to disappear into Bassel's arms and forget the bees, her father, his mother.

"Want to get breakfast at the market?" Bassel kissed her softly.

Her phone buzzed on the floor next to her bed.

"It could be your mom." Sasha scrambled to get to the phone, which showed a text message from an unknown number, not from MOM.

*I'm sorry you aren't feeling well. Uncle Chuck.*

Sasha tossed the phone onto her bed as if it might burn her.

How did Chuck know about the ER visit? And how could he have her number, which until a few days ago had been Bassel's number?

"Are you sure no one in the hospital recognized the bee sting?" she asked.

"I was with you the entire time. No one saw it."

Who told Chuck she was in the hospital? Was he concerned about her? Or was he, too, fishing for information?

When Sasha broke her arm in third grade after falling out of a tree, her father didn't answer her call, but Chuck picked her up right away. He left work and drove her to the ER. He held her hand while they set the bone and bought her a giant swirled lollipop and a purple teddy bear from the hospital gift shop.

Sasha couldn't hold both versions of Chuck Skinner in her mind. Her father's coworker and friend. Her mother's brother, her godfather. The man who attended her violin performances and rushed her to the hospital. But also the man who tried to blackmail her into turning against her father, then abandoned her to state care when he got a promotion out of state. The man her father considered dangerous.

One of those men must be real, but they couldn't both exist.

Resisting the tender memories of her uncle, burying the friend beneath the beast, Sasha had allowed her father to be the hero, the martyr who went to jail to protect important scientific research. Chuck, by default, became the villain. But what if she misconstrued? What if Chuck had been right? What if Bassel's mother's accusations were true?

What if Sasha had kept valuable scientific research from the world to humor a narcissistic, delusional man?

"My father demanded my loyalty without giving me any justification. And I gave it to him," she said as they drove to the market to find Octavia. "What if I was wrong?"

"I sometimes wish I'd had a little more faith in my mother. She wanted me to believe in her conspiracy theories. Maybe she was right about some of it, but how does it matter now? She obsessed to the point of losing her standing in the scientific community. It's all she talked about. This conspiracy she could never find evidence to support. She and I had a big fight years ago. Who cares? So what if Lawrence Severn spread rumors about her work? He's in prison. What would proving it now do for her? I probably went too far, but I told my mother to stop obsessing about it or move out. Two days later she took off. She's been bouncing in and out of my life ever since."

"Maybe our parents are destined to let us down," Sasha said. "And we are destined to fail them in return."

"She disappears for months, sometimes years. At least three times I've convinced myself she must be dead, then she all of a sudden pops up and wants to meet for dinner." Bassel's hair blew across his face as they drove. "She always finds a new lead, new proof, but none of it ever amounts to anything. It's not like I don't love her, I do. But she is impossible to be around sometimes. Laser-focused on outing the truth, or whatever she believes to be the truth."

"You're okay with me looking for her?"

"I want to know why your dad thinks she could help you. She's exasperating, but she's my mom."

"Is it okay if I talk to Octavia alone?" Sasha said as they pulled into the parking lot.

"Okay. I'll get us some breakfast. Come find me after you talk to her." Bassel squeezed her hand before they got out of the car.

The smell of fresh bread wafted through the stalls. As she worked her way through the crowd, Sasha waved at a young folk singer with bright red hair breathing life into the waking market with his guitar.

*What do you love?* Her father's words spun through the air.

The community that had risen from this abandoned parking lot gave Sasha hope, a reason to believe. To love.

Octavia sat, as always, under the partial shade of an awning fixed to the ground with iron spikes wedged through the crumbling macadam.

"Morning, beekeeper's daughter."

Sasha sifted through a box of mismatched bike parts and flipped through a worn paperback aptly titled *Tattered Novel.*

"You read that one last month."

"Right." Sasha picked up a different book.

"Something's on your mind." Octavia crossed her arms and pursed her lips. "Out with it."

"I'm looking for someone."

Octavia held a hand up to shade her face from the sun and squinted at Sasha for a few seconds. "I'm going to need a little more info."

"I'm trying to find Dr. Kamilah Maher. I thought some of those people you told me about, the ones who think bees exist, might help me find her." Sasha rocked back on her heels and tried to sound as casual as possible.

Octavia picked up the book Sasha had been looking at and stared at the back cover for a few moments.

Sasha's heart pounded as she tried to hide her urgency. Her headache throbbed behind her eyes. An argument over prices broke out at a nearby table.

Octavia kept her head down, focused on the book. After a long silence, without lifting her head, Octavia looked up through her furrowed brow at Sasha.

"Who's asking? The beekeeper's daughter? Or Dr. Maher's son?"

"You know her?" Sasha said a little too loudly, and Octavia scowled at her. "You know who her son is?"

"Eyelashes? Yeah, I know. I hear things. What's your business with her?"

"We have some mutual acquaintances."

"I bet you do," Octavia said.

Sasha leaned closer to Octavia and lowered her voice. "Tell her my dad told me to find her. It's important."

"Now, this is getting interesting." Octavia put her book down. "What are you getting yourself involved in?"

"She has the number. Tell her it's urgent."

"I'll do what I can, but I wouldn't go talking to anyone else about—about whatever it is you're up to."

"Don't worry about me."

"They found Leah." Octavia leaned over the counter and lowered her voice. "They're calling it a suicide, but it's bullshit. She didn't kill herself."

"Oh, God, I'm sorry," Sasha said. "Halle knew her too."

"This is serious shit you're messing with. I don't want you disappearing on me too."

"Why would I disappear?"

"Do you know how my husband died?" Octavia asked.

"No." Octavia never talked about her personal life. The mention of her husband made Sasha uneasy, as if she were prying even though Octavia brought it up.

"Neither do I. In fact, I don't even know if Horace is dead. All I know is he disappeared."

"Disappeared?"

"After reporting he'd seen a bee."

Sasha's mouth felt dry. She felt dizzy and leaned on the counter.

"He reported it and never came home. That was three years ago."

"I'm sorry. I didn't know."

"Dr. Maher was Horace's friend. They were both involved in an underground organization hell-bent on proving bees still existed. I thought they were both full of shit, until he came home with that damn bee."

"He saw a bee?"

"I saw it too. He wasn't crazy or delusional," Octavia said. "Is there anything else you want to tell me?"

Sasha shook her head.

"Scary things happen to folks who challenge the official version of the truth," Octavia said. "Or talk about bees."

"I didn't say anything about bees."

"Be careful. That's all I'm saying." Octavia shook her head and returned to reading her book.

# Thirty-Five

## SASHA, AGE 23
### JUNE 10

Don't get your hopes up. My mother has a talent for disappearing. What are we going to do if we can't find her?" Bassel drove faster than Sasha would have liked on the way back to the farm. Every pothole in the crumbling road rattled her teeth, exacerbating her headache.

"I don't know. I can't stand the idea of doing nothing, but reporting the hive feels risky for so many reasons."

Sasha's phone vibrated with a text message.

*We will be at the farm tonight at 7. Tell eyelashes she wants him to be there.*

It seemed too easy. Less than fifteen minutes had passed since Sasha mentioned Dr. Maher's name to Octavia.

"Looks like we won't have to make this decision alone. She's coming to the farm tonight."

"Octavia?"

"Your mother. Octavia says she wants you there."

Bassel didn't say anything, but his knuckles turned yellow as he strangled the steering wheel.

He pulled into the driveway and walked toward the porch stairs.

"I need to show you something before your mom gets here." Sasha walked backward down the driveway toward the workshop. Bassel followed.

Sasha walked inside the workshop and climbed the ladder to

the hayloft. Dust from decades-old hay gathered in the eaves and swirled in the stuffy air. She lifted the tarp to expose the honey frames as Bassel cleared the top of the ladder.

"Seriously?" Bassel's face broke into a slow, wide smile.

She broke off a two-inch piece of honeycomb and placed it in Bassel's palm. "No one else remembers this the way we do."

Bassel held the wax up to see the light pass through. Honey oozed out of the ruptured cells pooling in his hand.

Sasha put a chunk of honeycomb on her tongue. Bassel lifted his hand to his mouth, licking the honey from his skin. He closed his eyes and sucked on the wax. Sasha imagined him scrutinizing the sugar content, admiring the complicated mix of wildflowers.

He leaned closer and kissed her with a softness barely more than air. She licked the honey on her lips and inhaled the sweetness on his breath. Common memories hovered in the air they shared, infused in the sugar passing between their lips and tongues. She wanted to know everything about him. Did his fingertips buzz when he thought of the bees?

"I'm glad I found you," he whispered, his lips millimeters from hers. He pulled back and looked at Sasha. "I'm sorry I wasn't honest with you from the start."

"Are you worried about seeing her?" Sasha asked.

"I'm angry. I've been trying to contact her. I even hung flyers in the market once, but they were ripped down a day later. She couldn't be bothered to let me know she was alive? My mother is brilliant. She can be warm and charming. But she's also selfish and self-absorbed. Her work always came first, and when her career fell apart, her obsession with your father and conspiracies became her number one priority." A vein in Bassel's forehead pulsed. "I'm glad she's okay, but I'm furious with her."

The afternoon sun cast a pool of light through the round window at the end of the hayloft, illuminating the honeycomb, creating an illusion that the amber glow came from within the comb itself.

Sasha had always imagined the fabric of time as an infinite block of honeycomb, with endless hexagonal chambers filled with wax-sealed moments. Stacked together, the cells remained isolated, but if they ruptured, the memories would ooze out and merge.

"What if we have a second chance with these bees?" Residual sugar sizzled on Sasha's tongue as a warm rush rose from her toes through her chest to her throat. A swarm of memories, some of which weren't her own, pulsed in the air.

"I think that's the reason my mother has never backed down. Her compulsive, never-ending need to understand what went wrong is tied to her hope that we can do better in the future."

"What did your mom tell you about those alleged secret projects?" Honey seeped out of the broken wax, filling the space where she had broken off a chunk of comb minutes earlier. Trusting Bassel was a risk, but she recognized his longing to understand his past, a past that, in ways she couldn't yet identify, intersected with her own.

"She said the Department of Agriculture wanted to suppress the evidence in your dad's missing research. She talked about those documents like she was hunting for Atlantis. The truth existed, even if no one else believed."

"Maybe she was right," she said.

For the past year, Sasha and Bassel had been circling around each other, trading books, flirting casually, all while sharing an overlapping history Sasha was unaware of. Trusting Bassel felt dangerous a day before, but now, he felt like a vital partner. She needed him if she wanted to uncover the truth about her father, about his mother, about which one, if either, had been right.

But was she letting her feelings for Bassel get in the way of rational thinking? Those eyelashes, the crooked smile, the tenderness of his lips. Heat burned under her skin.

Sasha reached behind the honey frames and pulled the remaining journals out from under the tarp. She tossed them to Bassel. "There were more journals, but last year, someone stole the rest of the documents from me. I've been waiting every day since for her to come forward with them. She missed a few and I found them the day before I got stung."

"You've known about them all this time?"

"I promised him I would never tell anyone, although I never understood why this research was worth going to prison over. I haven't had a chance to read through them because of the bee sting. He references a genetics project, but I don't understand the details. Feel like helping me read through them?"

"Holy shit." Bassel flipped through one of the notebooks. "I think I wanted to find out my mother made all of this up. But maybe I've been gaslighting her all this time."

"Let's go through them and see what we can figure out before your mom gets here."

They lay on the floor sifting through the charts, seemingly incoherent notes, and observations.

After several hours of reading the journals, Bassel stood up and stretched. He paced back and forth.

"So, your dad participated in a genetics project, and he regretted it. I don't understand why. From what I can tell, he lost faith in the project at some point. He tried to stop the experiment, but someone released the modified bees without his permission; he doesn't specify who did it, or what the ramifications are, but it feels catastrophic from his language."

"That's what I think too." The welt on Sasha's neck raged with heat. She lay on her back and closed her eyes, unable to push away the image of the swarm escaping through the emergency exit of the apiary. She scratched at her skin until she felt blood under her fingernails.

*If only she understood what she has done.*

Sasha's stomach tightened as unwanted thoughts crept in.

She wished she could go back in time and stop herself from digging up her father's research, finding the honey frames, seeing that bee. She wanted to drink Ian's mediocre beer and spend her energy worrying about asparagus crowns, not about protecting what might be the last beehive in North America. The more she read in the few notebooks she had in her possession, the more questions arose, and without the rest of the journals, she had no way of finding answers.

"My mom can be an irrational pain in my ass, but she's a genius. She'll know what all of this means."

Sasha wasn't sure she wanted to understand.

"What does this mean for this hive I found? How did they survive? And what will happen to them—or to me—if anyone finds out?" Sasha put the notebooks down on the dusty hayloft floor and placed the microscope in front of her in a pool of light flooding in from the window. Careful not to touch it with her bare skin, she used a piece of paper to place one of the dead bees on the stage.

The battery for the tiny light surprised her by working when she flipped the switch.

The coarse adjustment knob turned with the precise amount of tension her fingers remembered. She shifted the corpse until the edge of the wing came into view. She turned the fine adjustment with slow, feathery movements until the smooth edge of the wing came into focus.

She imagined the waxy tobacco-tinged smell of her father leaning over her shoulder.

The edges of the wings were straight, like the good ones her father showed her so many years ago. She examined the other bees she had found in the forest, confirming each one had straight-edged wings.

*Those other bees never should have existed.*

She joined Bassel and lay on her back, staring up at the rafters as she mined her memory for other clues her father might have left her. Her mind wouldn't quiet. The tire swing, the mustiness of the bunker, the honeycomb in the woods, burnt potpie, the heat of Bassel's breath on her neck.

She slid her hand into Bassel's and inched closer until her shoulder pressed against his. The heat of his skin stilled the humming in her fingers. Her mind quieted until all she could hear or feel was her heartbeat and his.

"We need music." Bassel sat up suddenly, startling Sasha.

He fumbled with his phone and turned on an old song Sasha's father used to listen to in his bunker.

"Dance with me." He pulled Sasha up by both hands. As the tempo picked up he drew her close.

"A colony survived, and they found you. You. They found *you*." He took her hand and spun her around.

He wrapped his arms around her waist, her back against his chest. His warm breath in her ear sent chills down her arms.

"What if they really are back?" he whispered.

Sasha pulled away from him and broke off another piece of the honeycomb. She held half of it up to Bassel's lips. He sucked the honey from her fingers. Sasha put the other piece in her mouth. She danced with her eyes closed, savoring the drip of honey down her throat. She opened her eyes to see Bassel watching her. She put an arm around his neck and kissed him, the honey on his breath hinting at memories they shared and memories that had not yet happened.

She slid a hand up under the back of his T-shirt. Their feet splashed in a pool of waning light filtering in through the window.

Bassel dragged two fingers though the honey and painted a sticky line from Sasha's lower lip, over her chin, down her neck to her sternum. Starting from the bottom, he worked his way up the trail of honey with his lips, his tongue, his breath.

They fell asleep curled up in the loft, bits of crumbled hay clinging to their skin.

Sasha woke to her phone buzzing. The sun had moved beyond the window. Shadows blanketed the loft. She slipped out from under Bassel's arm and dressed before checking her phone.

*Where the hell are you?* Ian texted.

It was almost seven. Bassel's mom and Octavia would arrive soon.

Bassel wrapped his arms around Sasha's waist to pull her back onto the quilt.

"Your mom will be here any minute." She allowed him to pull her back down. The crunch of crushed grass shifted comfortably under the quilt. "I didn't warn my housemates."

"I've been looking for her for almost two years." Bassel leaned over her, his lips searching her neck for traces of honey. "I can wait a little longer."

They could stay in the loft and hide, Sasha imagined, surviving indefinitely on honeycomb and each other's bodies.

A car pulled into the driveway, passing the workshop and heading toward the house.

Sasha untangled herself from Bassel and stood up to collect her father's notebooks.

"Should we bring the journals? I think we need to lay everything on the table at this point. I'm going to bring some of the dead bees." Sasha transferred half of the tiny corpses into an envelope and tucked the jar with the remaining bees under the tarp with the frames.

Bassel watched her from the quilt, bits of hay stuck to his bare chest.

"Come on." Sasha threw his shirt at him and smoothed her hair.

Bassel laughed.

"What?"

"Are you nervous about meeting my mother?"

"Yes." She picked bits of straw out of Bassel's hair as he buttoned his jeans. "I'm very nervous about meeting your mother. She might have answers to the questions that have kept me awake for the past twelve years. And she might hate me because I'm my father's daughter. I have no idea what to expect."

"I'm nervous too. I can't decide if I want to hug her or give her the silent treatment. I revert back to a teenager when I'm with her."

"Ready?" Sasha asked.

Bassel buttoned his shirt and kissed her one last time before descending the ladder.

# Thirty-Six

Gino, Halle, and Ian stood with Octavia and another woman on the porch as Bassel and Sasha approached the house.

The long braid, the petite but powerful frame, ripped open an unhealed wound. Sasha didn't need to see her face. Millie stood with one arm around Halle's waist. Halle beamed and waved with flailing arms for Sasha to join them.

Sasha stopped walking and yanked on Bassel's arm. "Crap. Do *not* talk about bees or my father's research in front of that woman. I'll get rid of her before your mom gets here."

Bassel stared at the scene on the front porch, his mouth hanging open.

"Remember when I told you about the asshole who stole my dad's research? That's her. I can't fucking believe she had the nerve to come back here."

Sasha had imagined confronting Millie, yelling at her, shaming her. But the flash of anger quickly dulled as a sliver of hope edged in. She had an opportunity to reclaim the documents and understand what her father had been hiding.

Sasha took a deep breath to calm the long-dormant rage. If she acted forgiving and gracious, maybe she could persuade Millie to return the notebooks.

"Come on." Sasha took Bassel's hand and tried to pull him toward the house, but his feet remained firmly planted. "I need to talk to her before your mom gets here."

Bassel didn't move.

Ian, Gino, and Halle stood with their backs to Sasha and Bassel, talking with Millie. Millie, however, stared past them, her eyes locked with Bassel's.

"That *is* my mother."

"Wait, what? Millie's your mother?" Sasha flashed back to the eerily familiar voice on the phone. *Sasha?*

"Shit." Bassel wiped a hand over his face. "I'm so sorry she did that to you."

"Millie can't be your mother."

As Millie turned her gaze to Sasha, a flood of betrayal, anger, and sadness at the loss of her friend rushed through Sasha so fast she couldn't disentangle the conflicting emotions. The setting sun framed the farmhouse in a rusty halo embellished by the haze from a distant wildfire.

"Why didn't you tell us Millie was coming?" Halle called to Sasha.

"She let you call her Millie? She hates American nicknames," Bassel whispered as they approached the house. "Such a fucking hypocrite."

Millie's eyes darted back and forth between Sasha and Bassel, her face showing no emotion.

"I see you all know my mother." Bassel spoke in a gruff voice Sasha didn't recognize.

"No way," Gino said. "Sasha, did you know this?"

"Not until just now." Sasha glared at Millie with a ferocity she hoped burned her former friend's skin.

Sasha walked past Millie without acknowledging her. She went inside and took a seat at the table she had built months earlier out of salvaged wood pallets.

The others followed her inside.

"Kind of odd how you and Bassel both have hay in your hair,"

Halle whispered in Sasha's ear as she sat next to her. "I want details."

"I didn't make enough dinner for seven people." Ian squinted a silent reprimand at Sasha for not warning him about their guests.

"We brought food." Octavia reached into a messenger bag slung across her chest and pulled out a block of cheese wrapped in paper, a loaf of bread, and a bottle of home-brewed potato vodka.

"Now we have a party." Ian's demeanor brightened.

Gino helped Ian bring dishes and a pot of rice and beans to the table. Halle brought glasses for everyone.

Millie's eyes flitted around the room. A dry sink drained through a hose into a gray-water basin outside. A light bulb powered by the turbine washed the room with warm light. Millie offered Sasha a thin smile in appreciation of her handiwork.

Halle's mural on the wall opposite the fireplace held Millie's attention longest. Part family portrait, part historical document.

The day after Millie left, Halle had sketched Sasha and her garden into the mural. Sasha often touched her finger to the likeness of her own body as she passed by, reminding herself she was home.

The seven of them sat in silence for a few minutes until Gino coughed to break the tension.

"We missed you, Millie." Gino splashed vodka into her glass.

"I came because Sasha asked to see me," Millie said with a businesslike demeanor.

Millie's year-old betrayal stung with a raw edge.

Halle and Gino exchanged confused looks at Millie's formal tone.

"My father said you're the only person who can help me." Sasha narrowed her eyes, enjoying the small fist of power she held over Millie.

"What do you need help with?"

"How do I know I can trust you? You lied to me. You stole from me."

Millie pursed her lips and said nothing.

"What did Millie steal?" Gino asked.

Sasha trusted her father's judgment. If she wanted answers, she would need to take a chance on Millie. But it didn't mean she had to forgive her.

"I found bees."

Millie looked unimpressed.

Sasha took the envelope out of her pocket and dumped the contents on the table. Six dead bees lay in a pile.

Everyone but Sasha leaned over the table. Six perfect little creatures. Golden grains of fresh pollen peeked out of the pollen baskets on their hind legs. Millie put her hand over her mouth.

"Holy shit," Octavia said.

"Where did you find these?" Millie asked.

Sasha leaned back and made Millie wait. "I found a whole hive."

"Where?" Millie slid one of the bees onto a piece of paper and held it closer to the light.

"We've been preparing for this. I just, hell, I never thought it would actually happen," Octavia said. "We need to move the hive ASAP and get it to the safe house."

"Where is the hive?" Millie asked again.

"I want the journals you stole from me and an explanation about why you took them and disappeared. Then we can talk about the hive."

Bassel winced.

"Am I missing something?" Gino asked.

"You didn't tell them?" Millie looked surprised.

"Tell us what?" Gino said.

The low-watt light bulb struggled to illuminate the room as the sun set on the back side of the farmhouse.

Millie held Sasha's stare for a few seconds and straightened her already stiff posture. "I always knew who Sasha was. I came to the farm to search for those documents, but Sasha discovered them first."

"So, you stole them?" Gino said.

"I never shared the journals with anyone." Millie reached into a bag by her feet and dropped eight worn notebooks on the table with a thud. "I needed to know why your father lied about me and sabotaged my career. But there was more to the story than I realized. Your father's actions had nothing to do with me."

Millie paused and took a sip of vodka.

"After the *A. mellifera* emerged as the last reliable agricultural pollinator in North America, everyone wanted to know why they survived rising temperatures and drought when other bees were dying. Other species began filling the holes in the ecosystem and devastating crops. So Big Ag companies developed more and more pesticides, more fungicides, which turned our soil into a toxic soup."

"Everyone knows this," Sasha said.

"*A. mellifera* were well suited for big monoculture farms, they were resistant to drought and many diseases, and because we raised them in managed hives, we could treat them with antibiotics, antivirals, and antifungals native species didn't have access to."

"This isn't news to anyone," Sasha said.

"Hear Kamilah out. There's more to the story," Octavia said.

"They outcompeted local Hymenoptera, and worse, they spread disease," Millie continued. "Remember when everyone started putting beehives on their roofs and in yards? All those backyard beekeepers put pressure on local pollinators. While everyone was screaming *save the pollinators,* what they meant was save the honey bees. No one fought for the flies or mosquitoes or moths. There was no public outrage about the loss of wasps until we lost the fig trees they pollinate. No one cried about the invisible native pollinators which couldn't compete. Honey bees emerged as the invincible heroes. Until they started dying too."

"Cue the big money," Octavia said. "The US government doubled down on the honey bees. So what if they were squeezing out the remaining native species? As long as we had plenty of almonds and honey, nobody cared. We still don't know what put us over the edge. Was it pollution? Rising temps, drought, pesticides, altered weather patterns, or all of them combined? But suddenly we were left with *only* the beast of our own making: *Apis mellifera.*"

Octavia put her hand up to indicate a pause. She tossed back the rest of her vodka and leaned forward, her elbows on the table. "So, the Department of Agriculture created a genetically modified bee designed to be resistant to specific agricultural chemicals."

Sasha dug her fingernails into her thighs under the table.

"They intended to patent the modified *A. mellifera* and require anyone relying on honey bees for pollination to pay a licensing fee for the pesticide and the bees, forcing all farmers, including farmers from other countries, to license bees from the US government," Millie said.

"My father," Sasha said.

"Yes, Lawrence engineered the modified *A. mellifera*," Millie said.

"Our ag system was too big to fail. One-third of our food relied on pollinators," Octavia said. "Without the bees, we were left with a small number of crops—mainly grains, corn, and legumes—to feed the world."

Halle walked over to a basket by the couch and picked up a green sweater with a large hole burned through the back. She yanked on a piece of loose yarn and began unraveling the weave while perched on the arm of the couch, her attention fixed on the conversation at the table.

"To be fair, Sasha, I don't think your father had any idea about the plan to license the bees, at least not at first. He thought he was protecting food security," Millie said. "He tried to stop the release of the modified bees. He wanted more time to study them, but someone released them without his permission. Once in the wild, they were indistinguishable from the natural population."

"But here's what no one expected," Octavia said. "When the GMOs mated with natural populations, their offspring were sterile.

In less than a year, the honey bees were extinct. At least we thought they were," Octavia said.

"I thought you were a literature professor," Halle said to Octavia. A puddle of kinked green yarn pooled around her feet as she continued to dismantle the sweater.

"My husband disappeared after reporting he found bees. I educated myself about the collapse of the honey bees, and the rumors some survived. That's how I met Kamilah."

"Why are we trying to save honey bees if they're the villains?" Gino asked.

"Back up. Don't conflate the *manipulation* of bees with the bees themselves. Remember, this wasn't the bees' idea. Their purpose is to collect pollen and nectar, make honey, and raise their babies. US corporations profited from importing the bees from other continents to serve our agricultural machine," Octavia said. "Don't blame the bees, blame the machine."

"What do we accomplish if we save this one hive?" Ian asked. "If it's just to make a political point, it's not worth the risk."

"It's never just been about saving the bees," Sasha said. "We're trying to save ourselves."

"But there are still some native pollinators out there, right?" Halle asked.

"Of course. There are species of flies and mosquitoes, among others," Millie said. "But for agricultural purposes, they can't fill the gap left behind when the honey bees declined, in part because *Apis mellifera* had already edged out the local competition, especially in areas with heavy agricultural activity."

The light bulb above the table crackled and fizzled out, leaving them in shadows. They only had two more light bulbs left. Octavia had promised to procure more, but they were hard to find in a region where few people had power.

The sudden darkness quieted the conversation. The swish and snap of yarn unraveling sped up as Halle worked faster.

Ian went into the kitchen to get matches. He lit three brown tapers stuck in wine bottles and arranged them on the table.

"Why did they release the modified bees if Lawrence believed they weren't ready?" Bassel asked, his voice barely above a whisper.

Sasha fought off a sense of dread that had been building since Millie mentioned the experimental bees.

*Someone released them without his permission.*

"We don't know for sure. It's not in Lawrence's notes," Millie said.

The timeline seemed fuzzy in the dark, the edges blurred by the vodka. Had her father tried to sequester his own bees in the apiary before he launched the public campaign? Had he isolated Sasha's bees to protect them from exposure in the wild? Or had he wanted to protect the wild from the unnatural bees he had been hiding? The timeline spun in her mind but wouldn't come into focus.

Sasha had lived with the shame that she had possibly contaminated the last living bees. But had it had been much more?

*If only she understood what she has done. If only she knew.*

Her mouth felt dry, her hands sweaty.

She closed her eyes and imagined the swarm of bees escaping through the emergency exit door. Alcohol seeped into her bloodstream. The dimly lit room contracted around the table; the air felt like it was congealing around her.

*You never opened that door.*

But she *had* opened the door. The buzzing in her fingertips spread across her palms and up her arms.

She had always assuaged her conscience by telling herself she hadn't really doomed the last bees because they were already dying.

But the truth had been much worse.

Sasha had unleashed the beasts that doomed the last reliable pollinator.

And her father knew. Why else would he have asked her to lie about releasing the bees? He had been advocating to move bees indoors before Sasha released her bees, but maybe she let loose the modified bees at the wrong moment, just as they were dying off in the wild.

Sasha swallowed down a wave of nausea. Her father chose jail to protect her as much as himself.

The dancing candlelight illuminated the faces around the table in flickers of light and shadow, heightening the conspiratorial feel of the conversation.

"As soon as he realized someone released the modified bees, he launched a desperate campaign urging beekeepers to move hives indoors, hoping some would avoid contamination," Millie said. "But he couldn't tell anyone why because the project was classified. It was impossible to recall the modified bees, so the only thing to do was hope the hybrid populations would die off naturally, and that if enough people sequestered natural populations indoors long enough, they might outlive the GMOs.

"To the rest of us, it made no sense to move bees indoors. I became Lawrence's most vocal critic, but he had powerful supporters who initiated a campaign to discredit me," Millie said, the decades-old pain fresh in her expression. In the shadows, the dark circles under Millie's eyes looked purple. "Your father sacrificed me, my work, and my reputation for the hope some bees would survive. I think, perhaps, he sacrificed you, too, Sasha."

"Some bees did survive." Bassel pointed to the bodies on the table.

"True. But are they modified or natural?" Millie asked.

"Does it matter?" Halle asked. "If they can pollinate, who cares?"

"It matters. If it's proven these straggler populations are the result of a genetics experiment, people will eventually discover the US hastened the demise of the last reliable bee," Millie said. "The US didn't cause the Great Collapse. Pollinators were already dying off. But after we lost *A. mellifera,* our last hope, millions of people starved. Humans always seek someone to blame. The individuals involved will do *anything* to prevent this story from getting out," Millie said.

"When they do find straggler bees, they can't determine if they're genetically modified without taking them to a lab. It's easier to destroy the bees and silence the people who saw them." Octavia's chin trembled.

"Like Leah," Halle whispered.

"Exactly," Millie said.

"Before we say anything else, everyone needs to understand the stakes. If you want out, leave now. No judgment," Octavia said. "The next steps are illegal. We'll be risking our jobs, potentially getting arrested, or worse."

"If it's so dangerous, why are we talking about this?" Halle asked.

"Because the upside is enormous." Octavia threw her arms open wide, hitting the lifeless light bulb hanging over the table. "What if these crazy little survivors staged a comeback? What if we didn't need to rely on humans to pollinate our food anymore? We could save millions of people from starving."

"We need to move the hive and hand it off to an underground organization that will keep it safe," Millie said. "But we're going to need help. If you don't want to be involved, you need to go."

Bassel reached under the table and grabbed Sasha's hand.

"If there's a chance we could restore food security for millions, I want to at least try. But that doesn't mean all of you need to be involved," Sasha said.

Gino and Ian exchanged glances. They both looked over at Halle, who gnawed on her cuticles.

"What about Beatrix?" Halle said. "I'm so close. You're asking me to risk my chance to bring her home. I'm the only person she has."

"We aren't asking you to do anything," Octavia said.

"You three should leave." Sasha ran a finger over the grainy wood of the table, unable to make eye contact with her friends.

Halle stood up and walked over to her mural on the wall. With her back to the group, she touched her finger to the outline of the house, tracing the ridge of the roof, the rail on the porch as her distorted shadow danced on the scene she had painted.

"I'm in," Gino said.

"We can't risk our jobs," Ian said. "What about your meds?"

"Don't make this about my health. That's not your decision. I've done a lot of shitty things in my life. This is my shot at doing something worthwhile, something good," Gino said. "You're always talking about how this isn't a life because all we're doing is surviving. Let's do more than survive."

Halle ran a hand over the swaying grasses she had painted and followed the motion of the wind with the backs of her fingers. She took a charcoal pencil from the box of Sasha's father's art supplies. Kneeling in front of the mural, she began sketching the outline of a figure.

Halle's drawing took the form of a young girl running with outstretched arms through the grass. She smudged the charcoal lines with her thumb and stood back to inspect her image of Beatrix.

Halle returned to the table, her fingers black with charcoal.

"The risks are real. I'm not going to pretend otherwise. But if it works, if we can save this hive, we have a chance at altering the future, not just for us, but for everyone. We could help a lot of people. We could also end up in jail. Or dead." Octavia stood and poured another splash of vodka in everyone's glasses. "We need to know, right now, who's in."

Gino looked at Ian and raised his eyebrows. He put a hand to Ian's face and traced the chisel of his cheekbone.

"If there's a shot at putting a dent in the number of people starving, then I'm in." Ian swallowed his vodka in a single swig and slammed his glass on the table.

"Beatrix deserves a better world to grow up in." Halle tossed back her vodka and pounded her empty glass down next to Ian's. "I'm in too."

The old house creaked, its weary bones strained under the

weight of history and time, of secrets, love, betrayal, and hope. This house, this land, these friends. Gratitude swelled in Sasha's chest.

One by one, Bassel, Gino, Octavia, and Millie drained their glasses and slammed them down. Sasha added her glass with a final thud that shook the table and rattled the windows.

# Thirty-Seven

## SASHA, AGE 11
### JULY 15

"Do you believe they're gone?" Sasha asked her father the night before the trial as he walked her up to her room to say good night. "Forever?"

"Think like a scientist." His red-rimmed eyes drooped at the corners, his eyelids leathery with wrinkles forged from a lifetime of long days in the sun. "Evidence says the bees are gone."

"But is it possible some survived? What if I find new evidence?" Sasha ran her fingers over the chinked chair rail running the length of the hallway, closing her eyes for a few seconds and guiding herself by the familiar scars in the soft wood like a map under her fingertips.

"Always consider new evidence if you find it. If any did survive, it would matter *which* bees survived. The key is in the curve of the wing. Remember the scalloped edge on some bees? Those bees were no good."

He followed her into her room and sat on the edge of her double bed with a patinaed brass frame, the same bed her father slept in as a child and his father before him. He tucked the covers in around Sasha the way he did when she was little.

"You can never talk about the bees escaping. Do you understand how important this is?" He rubbed the edge of Sasha's floral curtains between his thumb and forefinger. Her mother tried to steer Sasha toward a more whimsical design, but Sasha insisted on the hydrangeas and roses, which reminded her of her mother's flower garden. As he fingered the fabric, Sasha could tell he was thinking about her mother too.

"I understand."

"Chuck told you they offered me a deal. If I admit to conducting research on those last bees and I turn over the documentation, they promise to give me a sentence of no more than two years, probably less. I know you don't want me to go away longer than that."

"I don't want you to go to jail at all."

"I doubt I'll be able to avoid jail time. There's no way I can deny I broke the law by keeping those bees in the first place. But it's important they *never* know a swarm escaped. You can tell the truth about anything else. Just not about the bees escaping or about the bunker."

"You told me all this already."

"I can't explain why right now, but protecting my research is much more important than protecting me."

"But I'll be alone." The anguish in her own voice scared her. She couldn't let him disappear for thirty years.

"I know I shouldn't ask you to lie. And I know what it will cost you if I go to jail for a long time, so ultimately, you need to decide for yourself."

"Okay."

"You can't look at me during your testimony. You don't want it to seem like I'm coaching you."

"I know."

"And if I look angry or upset, don't let it change your mind. Say what you need to say. If things don't go well—I don't think they are going to go well—I want you to make me a promise."

"What?" Sasha burrowed deeper under the covers. What more could he want from her?

"I want you to remember to seek out beauty in the world, always. I see so much of your mother in you, and I love that. Your mom had a brilliant habit of assuming the best in every situation."

"Like her jar of hope." Sasha curled onto her side. Her father never talked like this about her mother, and it made her squirm.

"Exactly. She always recognized the need for balance. She noticed the ways the world tried to correct itself when things swung too far in any one direction. Including me. I often swing too far. I want you to look for the beauty in small things and seek balance in what you take, what you give, and how you live. I wish I had done more of that myself."

Sasha's pillow absorbed the tears she didn't want her father to see as she tapped three times on the nightstand.

"I love you too, Little Bee." He leaned over and hugged her.

Sasha felt her father's heart pounding in his chest and wondered if he was afraid for himself, for Sasha, or for the entire world, now that the bees were gone.

# Thirty-Eight

## SASHA, AGE 23
### JUNE 10

I wish we could determine if these bees are GMOs," Millie said after they had all agreed to help move the hive to the safe house. *Those other bees never should have existed.*

Sasha closed her eyes and focused on the image of the bees she had examined under the microscope in the hayloft. No scalloped wings.

"They're not modified," Sasha said. "Dad taught me how to tell them apart under a microscope. I didn't realize it at the time."

"How did you examine them under a microscope?" Gino said.

"I have one in the workshop."

"You do?" Ian, Halle, and Gino all said at the same time.

"These bees are not modified. I'm certain."

"We need to expose the genetics project before more hives are destroyed. This story demands outrage. No more lies. No more cover-ups," Millie said.

"Are you outraged on behalf of the bees or yourself?" Bassel asked his mother.

"You're being naïve," Octavia said to Millie. "Don't you think some of those other people—like Leah—thought they had enough evidence to come forward too? I've been waiting a long time to prove Horace right. I'm not going to ruin this by going public then disappearing like he did."

Millie's knee bounced under the table, but her face remained calm.

"But they didn't have my father's missing research. We do. All of it. I have the notebooks Millie couldn't find." Sasha turned to Millie. "You missed a couple."

"Sasha, I'm sorry—"

"Not now," Sasha said.

"You're the only one who knows where the bees are," Millie said. "Do you want to expose the truth or are you comfortable perpetuating the cover-up? I want to find out who released the experimental bees and hold them accountable."

Sasha didn't know what she wanted.

Her fingers felt cold. Her tongue felt too thick to form the words she promised never to utter. The world already believed she had contaminated the last known hive, but now they would know she had released the very thing that might have destroyed the bees' chance at survival. And everyone would know she had been lying about it for twelve years.

She had never spoken that part of the story.

*You never opened the door.*

She worked so hard to unremember.

Flimsy light from the three candles cast angular overlapping shadows into the corners of the room. She couldn't hold the story alone anymore.

*Be brave.*

"After I got stung the day I broke into my dad's apiary, I opened the emergency exit and a swarm escaped." Sasha could feel the humming of the bees around her, hovering over her until her father found her. "It was me, not my dad, who deserved the blame. I released the genetically modified bees."

The truth flowed like honey, easy and slow. She couldn't take it back. She didn't want to.

No one spoke for several minutes. She put her head on the table and listened to the creaking of the house. She should have laid down her secrets years ago.

"You're wrong." Millie searched through one of the journals on the table. "According to Lawrence's notes, the modified bees were released more than a year before the day you got stung. He was waiting until they died off in the wild. He intended to release his natural bees, but you did it for him, and at exactly the right moment."

Under the table, Bassel squeezed her hand.

"When you set those bees free into a world without GMOs, into a world that had already banned toxic agricultural chemicals and fossil fuels, you gave that final colony their freedom and a chance," Millie said.

"How can you know that's what really happened?" Sasha said.

Millie cleared her throat and read from one of her father's journals: "'Little Bee set them free, and it almost killed her. They entered the world the first of their kind all over again. One last hope. If only she knew what she had done.'"

Muffled voices around Sasha formed a cloud she couldn't make sense of.

"You didn't destroy the last colony, Sasha. You saved them," Millie said.

Bassel tightened his grip on her hand.

"The Department of Agriculture took over the creation and distribution of queen bees a few years before the Great Collapse. But your father didn't know the department was quietly sending out genetically modified queens to beekeepers all over the world. By the time your father found out, it was too late. He couldn't undo the damage. When those modified queens mated with the natural bees, they produced sterile offspring and the global population of *Apis mellifera* collapsed within two years."

He knew.

Sasha—and the entire world—believed she destroyed the last chance for the last bees. He let her carry the guilt alone.

She was eleven again, enduring the relentless taunts from her classmates. She was eighteen, with a newly changed name, trying to keep her head down so no one would know her history.

Alone again, adrift.

The crush of Millie's betrayal piled on top of her father's deceit.

"I need some air." Sasha stood up so fast her chair toppled over backward. She walked across the room and slammed the front door behind her as she sprinted toward the forest.

He knew.

Branches whipped across her face and shins as she slashed through the overgrown path. Stumbling over rocks and roots, she imagined her younger self pummeling down that same path, furious at her father for forgetting her birthday.

She burst into the clearing where the bones of the apiary loomed over the tangled meadow, her body, like her mind, once again returning to the place that refused to release her.

Her father allowed her to be angry with him, to resent him, to shoulder shame that did not belong to her.

Sasha sucked in a stuttered breath as relief slammed up against her rage.

*I did not kill the bees. The Collapse is not my fault.*

Her life could have been so different. She could have had friends, excelled in school instead of hidden. She could have gone to college, built a life. Instead, she walked her days alone, haunted by a cloud of bees darkening every room she entered.

She forced the door to the apiary office open, brushing away the tangle of vines. Inside, her eyes adjusted slowly as she made her way toward the airlock leading into the apiary. The rubber seal along the edges of the door, now stiffened from age and heat, screeched against the concrete floor as she pushed the airlock door open.

She stepped into the windowless chamber. The door slammed behind her, and her ears popped at the suction. Because the airlock lacked light and sound, Sasha used to believe the room existed outside of time. She used to hurry through the chamber as quickly as possible, worried she might get lost in time if she stayed too long.

Standing in the dark chamber as an adult, Sasha wondered if she had been right. What if time moved differently in this place? What if she opened the door to the apiary as the eleven-year-old child full of rage, instead of the adult crumpling under anger and shame?

What if she could walk into the apiary and do it all differently?

She wouldn't wear her mother's ridiculous high-heeled shoes. She wouldn't trip and bump the tray of sugar water, startling the bees. She wouldn't panic and swat at them. They wouldn't fear her. And they would not sting.

She would not open the emergency exit door.

Her father would not rush her to the ER, thereby exposing himself to arrest when they discovered his illegally kept bees.

He would not go to jail.

With her arms stretched out in front of her, she inched through the chalky air toward the door. The knob stuttered, the dusty air choking the inner workings of the handle. She leaned into the metal door, and the pressure in her ears released with a pop.

She stepped over the threshold into the remains of the apiary. The monstrous frames arched over her head like a forlorn rib cage, picked over by scavengers. She stood, once again, in the belly of the too-familiar beast.

Wind whipped the shredded ends of torn fabric in a rhythmic pounding like water lapping a shore.

She yelled up through the hulking steel arches, through the tattered ceiling into the star-strewn sky. She filled the unbound chamber with all the wordless heat smoldering inside her. The soles of her feet sizzled in her shoes as she howled until her throat burned raw and the disquieting silence rushed back in.

Sasha could not go back and undo the past, but a new question rattled her now: Would she change anything if she could?

If she hadn't gotten stung, would those bees have ever been released?

She didn't deserve the burden her father placed on her eleven-year-old shoulders. The truth, however, might have been a heavier weight. If she had known the truth all this time, would she have traded her father's last hope for the bees for a chance to set him free? For a chance at an easier life?

Sasha lay down on her back on the compacted sand floor and stretched her body out like a starfish. She spread her fingers and pointed her toes, taking up as much space as possible. A distant hum tingled in her fingertips. A perfect G.

They had never been her bees. They were wild and chaotic, the cleverest architects, the most tenacious survivors, hiding and biding their time. The buzzing in her fingers tingled up her palms as she drew in a long quiet breath.

The bees had survived. And so had she.

"Sasha." Millie's voice rang out over the shush of footsteps in the shifting sand as she approached. Millie paused next to Sasha and sat on the ground next to her. "I've hurt a lot of people with my obsession to uncover the truth."

Wind snapped loose sails of the roof fabric like a cracking whip.

"Bassel told me what my father did to you."

"It's no excuse for stealing from you. I wanted to reach out and apologize so many times, but I couldn't face you."

Moonlight sliced through the damaged roof. Time and grief had carved more lines in Millie's stern face than one year should have earned. Sasha saw herself in some of those lines.

"We could have gone through this together." Sasha's chest ached as she imagined how much easier the past year would have been with Millie to share her burden. "I would have helped you sort through the journals. You made me believe you cared about me, then you got what you came for and left. Every day since, I've woken up afraid I'd see a headline exposing my dad's research. And me."

"I promised you I wouldn't tell anyone."

"How do I know you won't steal whatever info I share with you now? How do I know you won't sell it to the highest bidder or turn me in so I end up in jail like my father?"

"You have no reason to trust me, but I do care about you, Sasha. I can see Bassel does too."

Millie waited for Sasha to respond, but she did not owe Millie absolution.

"The attacks on my credibility were lies and your father did nothing to counter them. I didn't know it, but my opposition to indoor apiaries threatened his last chance to save the remaining *Apis mellifera*. I'm angry he didn't trust me, but there was much more at stake than my hurt feelings."

"It was still cruel," Sasha said.

"Let me take those bees to the media and expose everything. We don't have any more right to the truth than the rest of the world does. I have a trusted friend at a news station. I think she could get us on air tomorrow."

"No way. I've spent my whole life dodging attention."

"I can do it alone. I won't bring you into it."

"It's too risky. You've seen what happens to people who speak out about bees."

"I'm surprised you care about what happens to me."

"I was angry because you hurt me. You stole from me. But that doesn't mean I want you to get hurt."

"It's my risk to take. Your father assumed he knew better than everyone else. Discovery behind closed doors denies the scrutiny of the public. It would be arrogant of us to continue the cover-up. How can citizens put their trust in something if it's never explained to them?"

"I'll think about it." Sasha stood up and brushed the dust from her shirt and pants and left Millie alone in the apiary.

Warm candlelight flickered from the window as she approached the house. She could almost imagine her parents inside, waiting for her to get home for dinner, ready to scold her for staying out after dark.

They all stopped talking when Sasha walked inside.

"You okay?" Bassel looked over Sasha's shoulder. "Did she follow you out there?"

"She's fine. I left her at the apiary."

"I wish you'd told us," Ian said.

Sasha walked over to the mural Halle had painted on the wall. Millie's figure blended into the edge of the forest, not noticeable at first. There, but not there.

"You talked to her?" Bassel asked.

Sasha nodded.

Footsteps climbed the porch stairs, and Millie walked through the front door. She paused in the foyer and joined them in the living room.

"How could you do that to Sasha?" Ian said.

"My dad did some shitty things to Millie. She was searching for the truth. Just like I was."

Millie gave Sasha a grateful smile.

"Millie thinks we should expose everything. My dad's research, the genetics project, the cover-up. We should hear her out."

"We need to move the hive before the ag department finds it. And they *will* find it," Millie said. "Octavia and I work with a group that's prepared to extract rogue hives and move them to remote locations. There are pockets in North America where we hope the GMOs never made it, isolated colonies that could have survived undetected. Now with environmental conditions improving, we're getting more reports of bee sightings. Our goal is to get to these colonies and move them out of public view while they reestablish themselves. We have a safe house ready to take this hive if we can move it."

"There are other hives?" Ian asked.

"We haven't located any yet, but we will," Octavia said. "We aren't sure why, but the number of sightings has been increasing over the last few months, so I'm optimistic."

"Hold up," Bassel said. "It would take years, decades, if ever, to build a pollinator population to a level that would have a meaningful impact on food security. I'm not defending the genetics project, but if this story gets out now, people will lose faith. They might rise up against the glass farms, which are the only thing keeping this country from starving right now."

"But we'd be giving them hope in something bigger," Millie said.

"Hope won't feed people." Bassel paced back and forth in front of the mural. "We need to work in the margins until we have enough stable pollinator populations."

"Why do you presume *we* can handle the truth, but no one else can?" Sasha repeated Millie's argument.

Surprised to hear Sasha siding with his mother, Bassel opened his mouth to speak, but stopped and shook his head, throwing Sasha an annoyed glare.

Sasha turned to Millie. "When do you want to move the hive? Assuming I tell you where it is."

"Tomorrow night. I'll deliver it to my contact who will relocate it. As soon as the hive is secure"—Millie glared at Bassel—"we go public with the whole truth."

"I'm with Bassel," Octavia said. "What would be the point of exposing this before the bee population is more stable?"

"Covering up secrets is what got us here," Sasha said. "And if we don't expose it, they'll keep destroying hives to hide the truth. We expose the truth, and there won't be anything left for them to hide. The bees will be safe. They'll have a shot."

"Who thinks we should come forward with the bees, the journals, the whole fucking truth?" Halle said.

Millie, Sasha, and Halle raised their hands.

"This isn't up for a vote," Octavia said.

"Who thinks we should move the hive then wait to see what happens next?" Bassel said.

Gino, Ian, and Bassel raised their hands. Octavia reluctantly put her hand up, too.

"Okay then, let's stop wasting time arguing and make plans to get the hive out of here," Bassel said. "But we keep quiet for a little longer."

Millie's shoulders slumped for a minute, but then she stood up straight. "I have a list of materials. The network is arranging a vehicle for me to transport the hive. We've been preparing for this for years, hoping one day we'd find a hive before authorities located it first."

"I'm not letting you go by yourself." Bassel tried to maintain an angry facade as he spoke to his mother, but tenderness seeped through the cracks.

"No. We follow the the plan" Millie said. "I designed the hive-relocation protocol so only one designated person bears responsibility for the hive. It's safer for all of us that way. I'm going alone."

After they cleaned up the meal, Sasha went outside to get some air. Millie stood on the porch, staring at the garden she and Sasha started together.

"Do you want to see it?" Sasha asked.

"I'd like that." Millie followed Sasha.

Millie squatted down to admire the raucous tangle of pumpkin vines sprawling beyond the edge of the garden, curly tendrils climbing tall stalks of grass and bending them toward the earth. Dozens of male flowers did their evolutionary duty of opening a few days before the female flowers to attract pollinators so when the female flowers opened, days later, the bees would know where to go. Maybe the bees in the woods had already discovered the feast.

But, if Millie's plan worked, the bees would be gone when the female flowers opened.

Just as asparagus was the first vegetable up in the spring, pumpkins lasted the longest into the long winter. Sasha could continue pollinating her garden as she had for the past year. But for the first time, she had hope that in the future, real pollinators might return.

Millie looked at the pumpkin flowers and nodded, acknowledging Sasha's thoughts without words.

"We're running out of time. Let me take the envelope of bees to my friend at the station," Millie said. "If we suppress the truth, we become part of the lie."

"I want justice too, but this seems too risky. And besides, we voted."

Millie folded her hands into a pensive fist and held them to her chin.

"I'm going to see my dad in the morning. I need him to know I understand and that I forgive him."

"It's healthy to let go of anger and grief, but don't let him off the hook. I've spent my whole life being manipulated by lies told by men who thought they knew what was best for me. All because they didn't trust the public. Yes, there will probably be riots and outrage. But there *should* be outrage. People *should* be angry."

Despite their past, Sasha felt a solidarity with Millie. They had both been pawns in a cover-up they didn't understand.

"There's so much beauty left in this world. It feels like we're giving up on it," Sasha said. "I want to believe there's hope."

Sasha thought back to the nights she lay staring at the ceiling in her dorm. Her obsession with finding the truth gnawed on her, made her skin tough from the inside as she contained her rage by day, fed off of it at night.

A decade's worth of shame and loneliness roared inside her with the same urgency she had felt when she entered her father's apiary on her eleventh birthday. She had wanted to flip over the hives and scream until she had no breath left.

"You'll wait until after we move the hive? We can't tip them off about it until we move it, right?"

"Of course. We relocate the hive, then I expose everything."

"And if they arrest you?" Sasha asked.

"Then it's my responsibility. I won't take anyone down with me."

"Where will you take the hive?"

"It's better if you don't know." Millie stood up and stared down into the valley of glass shimmering under the starlight. "It's not sustainable. These houses are made of glass, and it won't take much to shatter them. The system's already showing cracks. This isn't a long-term solution."

She grabbed Sasha's hand, transmitting her rage and hope in a fierce burst. "But if the bees survive and multiply, we have a chance—a small chance—to change the path we're on. We could have a meaningful impact on life on this planet. We can't just sit around crying about what we've already lost or fearing what might happen. We have to believe. We have to act."

Sasha thought back to her father's words the day they moved the last hives into the apiary.

*Allow yourself to fall in love with what is real, with what exists, with what might exist. And fight for it.*

"Okay," Sasha said.

"Okay, what?"

Sasha took the envelope of bees out of her pocket and handed it to Millie. "Let's burn it all down."

# Thirty-Nine

## SASHA, AGE 23
### JUNE 11

Her father's thin hair was damp and neatly combed when Sasha arrived at the hospital the next morning. His signature eyebrows dominated his brow, with coarse wiry hairs sticking out in all directions. Sasha touched her own eyebrow, cursing her father for bequeathing her all the wrong legacies.

"What are you doing here? You're grounded." He scowled at her, his forehead crinkling to envelop his wild eyebrows in heavy folds of skin. He rubbed the arthritic knots on his knuckles with a rhythmic motion. "I don't want to catch you in the apiary again. What were you thinking?"

"Dad, the bees are gone. Remember? You live here, in this hospital, now."

"I *never* would have agreed to any of it." Anger burned behind his eyes, but under his rage she saw a flicker of pain, a vulnerability he rarely displayed.

Hugo put a hand on Lawrence's shoulder. His touch calmed Lawrence, triggering a twinge of jealousy in Sasha.

"Can I have a minute alone with my father?" Sasha asked Hugo.

"I'll be right over here." Hugo moved to the far end of the room, out of earshot.

"I brought you something." Sasha took a deep breath and tried to suppress the anger at her father that had been roiling since the previous night's revelations. She opened a glass jar containing a chunk of honeycomb, broke off a dripping piece, and handed it to him.

"Oh, thank God." He rolled the honeycomb around in his mouth for a few seconds, squinting as he scrutinized the viscosity.

Sasha surveyed his face, trying to determine if he was with her in the present or the past.

She offered him another piece of the honeycomb.

He chewed on the wax slowly, turning it over with his tongue.

She positioned herself so Hugo couldn't see what she was doing and pulled out an envelope with two dead bees.

"They're the good ones, the ones with straight-edged wings," she whispered.

Her father breathed in and out several times as if employing a practiced relaxation technique.

"It's happening." His eyes brightened and he dumped the bees on the table before Sasha could stop him. "They found you, Little Bee."

"Dad, stop. Someone will see." Sasha maneuvered her body between the bees on the table and Hugo.

Lawrence picked up a single bee between his thumb and forefinger. He fumbled at first, but managed to hold the creature so the stinger pointed down.

Sasha shuddered at the shiny barb and pulled her hands back from the table.

"Put them back in the envelope, Dad. Please."

With a trembling hand, he maneuvered the bee to the space between two knuckles on his opposite hand and drove the stinger into his skin. He flinched, closed his eyes, and smiled. His eyes appeared clearer and more focused when he opened them. He repeated it with the other bee on his other hand.

"Did you find Dr. Maher?" Her father's voice dropped an octave and he seemed like his old self.

"I talked to her yesterday," Sasha said, surprised he remembered the conversation.

"And you showed these to her?" He kept his voice low and leaned his head toward Sasha's.

"Yes. She told me about the genetics project."

Her father kneaded his knuckles.

"She said you tried to stop it. Why didn't you tell me about this back then?"

"The less information you had, the less likely you were to tell someone. If no one knew to look for the bees, the better their chance of survival."

A flush of shame rose up her neck. She had done exactly what her father feared when she led Millie to the storm cellar.

"I could live with you being angry with me, but I hated the idea of you knowing I created those monsters. The best way I could protect the bees that escaped was to make sure no one knew they were out there."

He put his stiff hands on top of hers. The heat rising off his bee stings stirred warmth in the welt receding on her own neck.

"Are they in the woods?" he asked.

"Near the creek. Dr. Maher is taking them to a safe house."

"Sounds like a big project."

Sasha smiled, thinking about the projects her father used to assign her as a little girl. Talking to her father about the bees in a public space felt risky, but conspiring with him again felt good.

"You did what I couldn't do."

"What couldn't you do?"

"Let them go." He chewed on his lower lip for a moment.

"I believed it was my fault they died. You should have told me."

"I regret that." Her father's posture stiffened, but the expression on his face did not change. He rubbed his knuckles with increasing pressure and speed. But his eyes remained fixed on the window. "But we have work to do now. No looking back."

"Love what exists, what might exist." Sasha repeated her father's words back to him.

"And fight for it." He smiled, and for a moment he seemed like his younger self.

Sasha wanted to curl up on her father's lap the way she had as a young girl, to breathe in the scent of tobacco and wax. This was too much responsibility. Too much risk. What if she failed? Was she risking her family's security for nothing? What were the chances that protecting this one hive could affect the future of the world? She felt silly for imagining she could wield such power.

"It's your time, Little Bee," her father said as if reading her thoughts. "I know you can protect them."

"How do you know?" She longed to believe him.

"Because you already did."

The buzzing in her fingertips traveled up her arms. She felt the resonance of the cloud of bees hovering over her the day she lay dying outside the apiary, marking her location so her father could find her in time.

"I'm proud to be your daughter." She leaned over and hugged him, promising herself to remember the feel of his papery cheeks, and the smooth skin stretched across his swollen knuckles. She wanted to remember all of him.

"I always knew you'd grow up to do amazing things," he said as Sasha leaned back in her chair. "Your mom and I were just talking about it the other day."

Sasha let her father stay in the past with her mother as she kissed him goodbye. This was her battle now.

Lost in memories of her mother, Sasha didn't notice a man leaning on an SUV near her bike when she exited the hospital.

"Hello again, Alexandra." The familiar voice startled her. Two men dressed in dark suits got out of a second, identical SUV and positioned themselves on either side of Chuck.

Chuck stepped away from two security officers to approach Sasha as she fumbled with her bike lock.

"Did you follow me here?"

"What makes you think I'm here to see you?"

"Then why are you here?"

"Your father's my oldest friend, my brother-in-law. I like to check up on him when I'm in town. Make sure he's safe."

"He's locked down in a hospital. You can't get much safer."

"True. I guess I'm sentimental. Did you have a nice visit?"

"I thought you were going back to DC."

"Change of plans. How are things at the farm? I'd love to stop by sometime. So many wonderful memories of sitting on the front porch with your family."

Part of her wanted to give in to nostalgia and sit on the porch with Chuck while he nodded off to sleep as the sun set. It would be easy to allow him to take her under his wing and protect her. But the cost of Chuck's protection would be letting go of ever learning the truth. It would mean turning her back on the bees, her father, and her friends.

"Is everything okay?" Perspiration glistened on Chuck's broad forehead.

"Seeing Dad like this is hard."

"Your mom would be so proud of you. You know that, don't you?"

Sasha clenched her jaw and swallowed. She couldn't let him see her emotions. Despite her father's warnings, Sasha found herself dangerously close to throwing her arms around Chuck and sobbing.

"I'm in town for a couple more days. Do you think we could get lunch or coffee?"

"Is this about the contract? I'm going to sign it. I'm looking forward to getting started."

"I'd prefer to catch up in a non-work setting and chat, like the old days." Chuck opened and closed his fists repeatedly, as if worried Sasha would dismiss him. Sasha suspected his entourage carried weapons in case anyone threatened the assistant secretary of agriculture.

If they searched her, they would find the envelope with the dead bees, which would be enough to detain her, arrest her possibly. Chuck had always annoyed her, but she never believed him to be dangerous, but this version of Chuck with his security force and political power scared her. She shook off the momentary tenderness and steeled herself.

"What do you say, Alexandra? Let me treat you to lunch."

*Do not get in that car. Do not get in that car,* she yelled silently at herself. *Think of Leah. Do not get in that car.*

"Sounds great, but can we do it another day? How about the day after tomorrow?" Sasha tried to sound cheerful and keep the tremors out of her voice. "Could we go out for pancakes, like the ones you made me at midnight that time? Do you remember that?"

Chuck put a hand to his heart and smiled as if touched that she remembered the pancakes. "I'd like that. I'll reach out, and we can plan something soon."

Sasha's fingers struggled to work the combination on the bike lock as Chuck and his guards watched.

"I can give you a ride if you need one."

"I'm fine. The lock's temperamental sometimes." The lock popped open on the third try.

"With your promotion, you might be able to afford a car, you know."

"That would be fantastic." Sasha held up a hand to wave goodbye without turning to face him as she pushed off on her bike.

Sasha looked over her shoulder every few minutes on her ride home to make sure no one followed her. More specifically, she watched for two shiny black SUVs. She stood up on the pedals, pumping her legs harder up the familiar hills.

Had Chuck really been visiting her father, and if so, why now? Or was he following Sasha? Was he trying to intimidate her?

Her pulse roared in her ears as the entrance to the farm came into view. With one last look over her shoulder, she turned onto the driveway, unable to shake the feeling someone followed her.

# Forty

## SASHA, AGE 23
### JUNE 11

Everyone owed Octavia a favor, but no one could find a chain saw.

Bassel and Octavia had cobbled together everything else on Millie's list of equipment needed for the hive extraction, but without a chain saw, none of the other supplies mattered.

"There's no way we can cut through the trunk with this." Sasha held up a hand saw that Octavia had picked up at the market.

"Unless you have a better idea, this is all we've got," Octavia said.

Sasha often imagined her life on the farm as circles stacked on top of each other, touching in moments that spoke to each other in unexpected ways. Her past, her present, her future, in constant conversation.

"I do have a better idea." Sasha sprinted to her mom's workshop. Inside, she repositioned the ladder from the hayloft against a rafter where Uncle Buzz, her grandfather's two-person saw, hung.

The six-foot-long tool dangled in the air, warbling and singing, as Sasha climbed down the ladder, careful not to let the rusty, but sharp, teeth swing toward her body.

Sasha's parents used the saw to cut down small trees for firewood.

*Push, pull, push, pull.* The hypnotic rhythm appeared effortless as they sliced through tree trunks. After her mother died and Sasha took up the other end of the saw, she realized that falling into perfect sync with another person wasn't so easy.

Every August when they left the cabin for the season, Sasha and her father had chopped a stash of wood to dry over the winter and spring. Sasha savored the mindless repetition of splitting and stacking and splitting and stacking.

Every summer when they returned to a woodshed full of split logs, Sasha sent up a silent thank-you to her former self for the blisters and splinters she incurred so they could light a fire the first night back.

Carrying the saw in front of her with one hand grasping each of the two wooden handgrips, she paused in the doorway of the barn to watch Octavia and Bassel loading gear onto the truck.

She scratched the toe of her boot against a patch of lichen feeding on the exterior wall. The green and white scales grew thick around the base of the building, extending upward as if the feathery pattern creeping up the skin of the barn was clawing the wood back into the earth.

Nature strove to reclaim all its parts. Abandoned vegetable fields teeming with wildflowers and dancing grass. The meadow hiding the bunker slowly transitioning into a forest. The lichen helping oak planks return to the dirt from which the tree grew generations ago.

Sasha scratched a small circle into the lichen to give air to the wood underneath.

It takes time, but nature always wins.

This farm, this home. The trees, grass, and soil. Constantly breaking down, constantly rising back up.

The minty green of the lichen with flakes of white stood out against the gray boards in a perfectly balanced color palette that stirred an ache in Sasha's chest.

*There is so much beauty in this world.*

She closed her eyes and pictured the inside of the hollow tree, the bees, the wax, the honey. *So much beauty.* An entire world lived inside that hollow tree, a society of creatures who tended, fed, and cared for each other, who kept a tidy home and protected their leader. They took what they needed and gave more than they took.

But there was more at stake than a single colony of bees. Food systems might stabilize if bees reengaged in pollinating crops. The world could step back from overreliance on grains, corn, and soybeans, which don't require pollinators, to feed the planet. Less hunger, less poverty, less war.

As Octavia and Bassel loaded gear onto the truck, Sasha wondered if she would ever lean against the barn again. For the past year, Sasha's primary goal had been to stay with her newfound family in this house, on this land. She'd found the home she had been searching for. Now, with everything she cared about at stake, her purpose finally felt clear.

*Fight for it all.*

In contrast to the neat edges and perfect angles of the honeycomb, the farmhouse drooped, showing its age in the rotting side boards and moss-damaged roof shingles. The few remaining shutters hung aslant. The wooden porch steps bowed under the feet of all the people Sasha had loved most in her life.

Tufted layers of forest and hills and valleys framed the house, filtering out the rest of the world. No greenhouses visible from Sasha's position. No pollinators, housing barracks, or encampments of the homeless and desperate.

She checked her phone again for a message from Millie. She should have returned to the farm by now. Sasha scratched a circle into the lichen on the barn wall with her fingernail. She rubbed the leathery scales between her fingers as she walked down the driveway to join Bassel and Octavia.

Octavia maneuvered a bolt of mesh fabric onto a cart. Seeing the preparations in motion gave their theoretical plan life, which simultaneously terrified and invigorated Sasha.

"Where is everyone? We have a lot to do," Octavia asked as Sasha approached.

Sasha noticed a liquid-fuel cap on the side of the truck, a straggler that hadn't been converted or scrapped.

"No chip." Octavia pointed to the fuel cap. "We needed a vehicle
no one can track. We have a full tank and several hundred miles'
worth of ethanol in fuel containers in the back."

"How was your dad?" Bassel said.

"In and out of lucidity, but mostly good. Chuck—Charles—
Skinner was in the parking lot when I came out."

"What the hell?" Octavia dropped a box.

"He claimed to be visiting my dad. I mean, Chuck's my uncle, my
mom's brother, which might make it seem normal that he'd visit,
but as far as I know, they haven't spoken since the trial. I'm pretty
sure he came looking for me. Until a couple of days ago, I hadn't
seen or talked to him in eleven years. But today, he acted chummy
with me, as if we chatted all the time." Sasha looked up the driveway again. "He knows I live here, which gives me the creeps."

"The sooner we move the bees, the better." Octavia looked up at
the sky. "They could be watching us right now."

Gino, Ian, and Halle pulled into the driveway. The usual relief
Sasha experienced when her housemates returned home felt mag-
nified by a thousand.

"We have all the gear on Millie's list. But I don't know where the
hell Millie is," Octavia said. "She said she'd be here an hour ago."

"I haven't heard from her either." Bassel paced next to the truck.

What if someone found the bees on Millie?

"Why are you all so glum?" Gino put on the beekeeping veil
and pulled Halle up onto the bed of the truck with him. "This is a
historic moment. We are doing something positive, adding to the
greater music of the universe."

Gino whistled a cheerful song and danced with Halle. They
stood on the edge of something enormous and dangerous. A quiet
hum of fear and excitement sizzled around them.

Déjà vu tugged on Sasha as she remembered hauling the box

frames onto her father's truck and hiding bees in the same woods from which they now intended to extract them.

A distant haze of ash from a fire burning a thousand miles away turned the horizon a noncommittal shade of grayish green.

Every few minutes, Sasha caught Bassel looking up the driveway.

Sasha's phone buzzed with a number she didn't recognize. She let it go to voicemail, but the caller didn't leave a message. Her phone buzzed again from the same number.

Sasha motioned for everyone to quiet as she answered.

"I'm looking for Sasha Butler," a woman said. "This is Dr. Leonard, I treated her in the ER recently."

"This is Sasha. I'm feeling much better. Thanks for checking in."

"I'm glad you feel well," she said. "But I need you to come back to the hospital right away."

"I'm fine, really." Sasha didn't remember seeing a female doctor the day she got stung.

"Your blood work showed some irregularities, and I should run some more tests. It's, well, important." Her voice sounded strained.

Sasha didn't respond right away. They must have detected the bee venom in her blood. If so, they knew she'd lied about getting stung. The Department of Agriculture operated the urgent care center, which meant her medical records belonged to the government.

"Ms. Butler, are you there?"

"Okay, sure. I can come by tomorrow after work."

"It would be best to come right now. We can send a car for you if you like."

"That's thoughtful, but I don't need a ride. I can be there in two hours."

"Okay. But please don't delay. It's quite urgent. When you come in, ask for me at the front desk and I'll come meet you."

"Thanks for letting me know. I'll be there as quickly as possible." Sasha attempted to sound appreciative.

Sasha hung up. Her phone buzzed again, but she ignored it.

"Who was it?" Bassel asked.

Sasha's mind raced. If she went to the hospital, police would likely be waiting to arrest her.

"Sasha?" Gino jumped down from the bed of the truck and touched his hand to her elbow. "You're shaking."

"The hospital wants me to come in. They found an urgent problem with my blood work. They must have detected bee venom in my blood. They know I lied about getting stung."

"You aren't going, are you?" Octavia asked.

"No way. The hospital's part of the system. I'm sure they already shared the lab results. That's probably why Chuck followed me."

"We need to hurry up then, before they come looking for you like they did Leah," Octavia said. "Where the hell is Millie?"

Sasha opened her phone to see a message from Millie.

*There are rumblings about a hive in the area. Journo friend says Ag Dept knows someone found a hive, don't know where, but have leads. Ag sending out armed sweep teams + National Guard. I had to do something to distract. Tell Bassel I'm sorry. You have to do this without me.*

What had Millie done?

"Hey, Bassel. I need to show you something." Sasha's fingers turned icy cold as she reread the message.

Before Bassel responded, Ian shouted, "Oh, shit! It's Millie, she's on the news."

Bassel jumped down from the bed of the truck, and they all gathered around Ian's phone.

Sasha felt queasy as Ian played the video clip.

"Our government has been lying to us about the extinction of honey bees." Millie stared into the camera. "Some survived, but they don't want us to know. They don't want to expose the fact that the US government developed and released an experimental genetically modified bee that interfered with the natural population and resulted in the collapse of the last known pollinators in North

America. They are afraid finding these bees will confirm the existence of their genetics experiment."

The journalist appeared flustered, unprepared for Millie's revelation. The camera zoomed in close on the bees in Millie's open hand.

"I suspect I will be arrested, or I will disappear like all the other people who have come forward with proof bees still exist. But I want you to see them, to understand that we have been lied to. There are bees in the wild, and we need to protect them, not destroy them, as our government has been systematically doing to shield themselves from culpability."

"And where did you find these bees?" the reporter asked.

"In a forest about thirty miles north."

The farmhouse was ten miles south of Millie's location. She was giving them a head start to move the hive.

"I also have possession of the missing research belonging to Dr. Lawrence Severn, the Last Beekeeper. His meticulous notes document the experiment involving genetically modified bees and prove that the US government withheld information from other nations so they could secure a patent. To be clear, our government attempted to patent the last honey bee for profit."

"And where is this research?"

"It's in a safe location. If anything happens to me, the research will be automatically sent to several media outlets."

"How can you be sure the documents are authentic?"

"When they examine the handwriting, content, and DNA, it will be very clear the notes are the missing documents the science community has been speculating about for years. I made multiple copies and placed them in several locations with specific instructions. If I go missing the documents will be released immediately."

Millie was lying. Sasha had all the journals stashed in the hayloft.

"Everyone should be outraged by these lies," Millie said. "Demand answers. Demand accountability. For the bees, for me, for all the people who have reported bees and mysteriously disappeared.

I want to see people standing up, marching in every city. We won't be lied to anymore. Look at this little bee. I need you to trust me. I'm designating you to act now."

"Okay, that's enough, turn it off," an off-camera voice shouted. The camera wobbled and fell to the ground in a blur of feet. "Dr. Kamilah Maher, you are under arrest for—" The video cut off.

"How did she get those bees?" Bassel clenched his jaw, the muscles in his neck tensed.

"She promised she wouldn't do anything with them until after we moved the hive," Sasha said as the sting of yet another betrayal settled in.

"And you trusted her after everything she's done? She's only in this for herself." Bassel glared at Sasha. "How do you not see that?"

"We had a plan," Octavia said.

Bassel glared at Sasha. "I'm leaving. I need to find my mother."

He started to walk toward his car, but Octavia grabbed his arm.

"She wants us to move the hive," Octavia said. "That's why she lied about the location of the hive and why she called for protests. She's trying to stir up trouble so resources will be spread thin tonight."

"How are we supposed to move the hive without Millie?" Ian said. "She's the only one who knows the plan."

No one responded.

"Does anyone else know where Millie planned to meet the contact person or who the contact is?" Halle asked.

"It's always been safest to keep contacts on a need-to-know basis for our safety and theirs," Octavia said. "I'm going to make some calls. In the meantime, we need to move fast. Millie gave us some cover and a distraction. Let's not waste them."

Bassel beat his fist on the hood of the truck, leaving a dent in the rusty metal.

Sasha laced her hands behind her head and squeezed her elbows in front of her face. She had ruined everything. Again.

Sasha's phone rang. She checked it, expecting to see the hospital's number.

The caller ID read CHARLES SKINNER. Her heart thumped hard, stealing her breath for a moment. She held up the phone for the others to see as it rang four more times then went to voicemail.

"We take care of the hive, then we find Kamilah," Octavia said.

Sasha's phone rang again. She turned it off without checking the caller ID.

"I helped my dad move hives. I know what to do." Sasha tried to sound more confident than she felt.

"I'll help," Bassel said without looking at Sasha.

"Bassel, I'm sor—"

"Not now," Octavia interrupted Sasha. "You two make up later."

Within minutes, they finished loading the truck. Bassel joined Octavia in the cab of the truck, while Sasha, Gino, Halle, and Ian sat in the bed with the gear.

How could Millie do this to her again? Worse, how could Sasha have let her?

*Fuck you, Millie.*

The hospital knew Sasha had been stung. Chuck knew where she lived. And now Millie was in real danger because of Sasha's recklessness, but indulging her wounded feelings would have to wait.

Sasha closed her eyes and pictured her father lighting the smoker, binding the mesh around the opening of the hive. A rolling hum swelled in her throat as she tried to remember the joy of being with the bees without fear.

*Love what's in front of you.*

Octavia revved the engine, which churned out a puff of vapor as the old truck sputtered to life. The growling engine rattled her teeth and knocked loose a bit of courage.

*Be that fearless, angry girl,* she willed herself.

Octavia looked over her shoulder through the cab window at Sasha and mouthed "Ready?"

Sasha nodded, although she did not feel ready. *Don't forget Uncle Buzz,* her mother would have whispered. The saw lay flat near Gino's feet.

Across from Sasha, Gino sat cross-legged with his back against the trolley. He stared off into the distance and rubbed the mesh of the beekeeping veil between his fingers.

Halle nodded at Sasha with slow, exaggerated bobs of her head, as if she needed to convince Sasha they were doing the right thing. Halle believed in the future. She believed in goodness. And with each slow nod, Halle telegraphed that faith to Sasha.

"We can do this." Ian leaned his head close to Sasha's, his eyes glowing with the same deep blue as the cloudless evening sky.

The hum in Sasha's throat and the rattle of the truck merged into one single vibration inside and outside of her body.

*You have the entire world, Little Bee.*

Just as Octavia put the truck in reverse, a black SUV tore into the driveway, blocking the truck from going anywhere.

# Forty-One

## SASHA, AGE 11
### JULY 16

Sasha sat in a small conference room with Chuck and a lawyer before her father's trial began. The room smelled like burnt rubber and furniture polish, although she didn't see evidence of either.

"Sasha, please." Chuck nudged her leg, suggesting she stop kicking the leg of the metal table. "Do you understand what the lawyers explained to you?"

She kicked the table harder.

"If you're hiding something, you are not protecting your father. You will be sending him to prison for a long time."

Sasha crossed her arms over her chest and refused to make eye contact with Chuck, whose breath grew increasingly raspy and rapid as he spoke.

"The prosecutor agreed they will ask for minimal jail time for your father if you tell them where he hid his research. Do you understand?" Chuck mopped the sweat from his brow.

"You explained this a million times already," Sasha said.

Chuck stood up and paced the small room.

"I can't change what your father did, but I can at least help you. We can help each other."

Sasha wanted to scream at him to stop talking.

"I'd love for you to stay with me. Or I can stay at the farmhouse with you. Whatever you want. Until your dad is released. It could be two years, if the prosecutor gets what they want. But if he gets the maximum sentence, you'll be an adult by the time he comes home."

Sasha rubbed her bare arms, wishing she had brought a sweater.

"We can get through this together. What do you say?"

Sasha forced a smile.

"You'll tell the truth?"

"Of course."

Chuck and the lawyer exchanged patronizing smiles.

"Can you tell us now, so we have an idea what you're going to say? Practicing out loud helps you gather your thoughts, so you don't stumble over your words when you're on the stand. You won't get a second chance," Chuck said.

"You don't need to coach me."

"No one's coaching you." The lawyer stood up and tapped a finger on his watch.

"Okay," Chuck said. "Ready to go in?"

Sasha allowed her uncle to take her hand and lead her into the courtroom.

She closed her eyes and conjured an image of her bees as she placed her hand on a Bible and swore to tell the truth. In her mind, the swarm billowed like smoke as it passed through the open emergency exit door.

"I solemnly swear to tell the truth, the whole truth, and nothing but the truth, so help me God." Sasha reminded herself God did not live inside a book or a building. God resided in trees and soil and wind, none of which existed in the sterile courtroom.

"Alexandra, can you tell us about the day you got stung after entering your father's apiary?" asked a tall lawyer with light brown hair hanging loose around her shoulders. She had pale skin and dark red lipstick that drew attention to how thin her lips were.

"I don't remember much." The truth pressed against her chest as the first lie formed on her lips. Above her, the mass of bees hovered, as if waiting for her to join them. Her body stopped fighting for a suspended, endless moment when she no longer needed air.

"I bumped into a tray of sugar water inside the apiary." Sasha focused on the lawyer's gold lapel pin in the shape of a rabbit. "I wasn't looking where I was going. Sugar water splashed all over me. I tried to wipe it off, but I was covered in sugar and the bees swarmed around me. I panicked and swatted them away. I don't blame them for stinging me."

She coughed, remembering the mouthful of dirt when she fell facedown on the dusty floor.

"What did you do next?" the lawyer asked.

"I screamed for my father."

"Were you wearing protective gear?"

"No."

"Why not?"

"I didn't plan to go in. I just wanted to find my dad."

"Did you know protocol for entering an apiary includes wearing full-body gear to protect the bees from contamination?"

"Yes."

Reporters' pens scratched against paper so fast she thought the friction might set their notepads on fire. People already blamed her for contaminating the last colony, which died shortly after they were relocated to another facility. They blamed her father for keeping the bees without permission, and for allowing his daughter to infect the last colony.

"Why did you go to the apiary in the first place?"

"To find my dad."

"And why were you looking for him?"

"It was my birthday, and he was late for dinner." Sasha snuck a glance at her expressionless father.

Sasha sat up straighter on the awkward bench, which lacked rungs to rest her feet on.

"So, you were angry at him?"

"No."

"I would have been angry if my father missed my birthday dinner."

"I guess I was kind of mad." Her father's words echoed in her mind. *You can tell the truth about everything else.* "Actually, I was really mad."

Chuck nodded at her with approval she did not want.

"Did you have a special attachment to the bees?" the lawyer asked.

Her bees. She loved her bees. The memory of wanting to flip the hives over shamed her.

"Yeah, I guess. I mean, I grew up with them."

Sasha closed her eyes and imagined the swarm hovering over her as she gasped in the tall grass. The bees waited above her, marking her location so her father would find her. The bees saved her.

Sasha stole a glance at her father. *Tell the truth about everything else.*

The lawyer kept smiling at Sasha, as if they were friends having a casual chat.

"Did you agree with your father that the bees should be kept indoors?"

Rows of reporters took furious notes, as if Sasha's ideas about indoor apiaries mattered.

"We made the world unsafe for pollinators. We had to try something."

"And who told you that?"

"Don't you pay attention to the news? They're dying. I mean, well. They died."

"Alexandra, did you release any bees the day you broke into your father's apiary?"

"I had a reaction to the bee stings. I couldn't breathe. I don't remember anything until I woke up in the hospital."

"You didn't open the door?"

"I was unconscious. How could I open a door?"

"Answer the question. Did you open the door and release any bees?"

"No."

Her father had lifted her out of the grass into his arms and sprinted toward the truck. Sasha had wanted to call out to the bees as the swarm lit off toward the forest.

This was it, she remembered thinking. Her father was too late to save her, but at least her bees were free.

When she remembered the moment, it seemed impossible to have held so many thoughts in her head while her body fought to stay alive.

*Be free.*

If only she had tasted the royal jelly her father had offered her, she would have been their queen.

Her mouth felt dry, and she tried to swallow, but choked.

"Would you like some water?" the judge asked.

"Yes, please." Sasha gulped down the water handed to her by a court officer. She was lying in court. Couldn't they tell by looking at her? What would happen to her if they found out she lied?

"Did your father work at home often?" the lawyer asked.

"Yes."

"And who looked after you when your father worked?"

"I'm eleven. I don't need a babysitter."

"Did anyone else help out, give you rides, look out for you?"

"Just Chuck."

Chuck gave her a smug smile that made Sasha want to scream. She clenched her jaw.

"Are you referring to Charles Skinner?"

"Yes."

"What is your relationship to Charles Skinner?"

"He's my uncle. My mother's brother."

Chuck touched the corners of his mouth and smiled with exaggeration, suggesting Sasha should smile, too.

Sasha pressed her hands together between her knees and forced a smile.

"He's also my godfather."

Chuck's chest puffed out when she claimed him as her godfather.

"Can you tell us about Charles Skinner's role in your father's destruction of the final bee colony?"

"Your question doesn't make sense."

"What don't you understand?"

"Nobody *destroyed* the bees. Well, actually, we *all* destroyed the bees. Climate change and chemicals and stuff. It took a long time. Not one person."

Sasha watched the jurors' faces, most of whom stared at their laps, picking at their cuticles or pretending to jot down notes. They looked guilty. They should be on trial—everyone should be on trial—for destroying the world.

"Please answer the question, Alexandra," the lawyer said.

"My dad *loved* those bees. He didn't kill them. And he didn't kill hope. Maybe he didn't do enough to save hope. But what did *you* do?"

The jurors squirmed. If they found her father not guilty, they would have to confront their own culpability. It would be easier to lay the collective blame on the final misstep, rather than the countless failures leading up to it.

"Miss Severn, I'll repeat the question. Can you tell us about Charles Skinner's role in your father's destruction of the final bee colony?"

"Chuck had nothing to do with our bees." *I will not betray my dad for you,* she screamed silently as she held Chuck's eye contact and maintained the torturous, lying smile for as long as she could bear. Courtroom cameras clicked in rapid fire, capturing the smile that would haunt Sasha in newspapers and magazines for years after the infamous trial of the Last Beekeeper.

Chuck pressed his lips together as if touched by her admiration.

Her father sat up straighter and flashed a real smile, not a forced smile for Sasha's benefit. His eyes shone brighter than they had in months. Her father still had hope, and if he could believe, then so could Sasha.

"Did your father ask you to lie about any parts of your testimony?" the lawyer asked.

"My parents taught me not to lie."

*You will be sending him to prison. You will be all alone.* Chuck's warning echoed in Sasha's mind, drowning out her attempts to keep her breath steady.

"Yes or no, please, Alexandra. Did your father instruct you or coach you to lie to this court?" Sasha hated how often the lawyer inserted her full name into the questions.

"No."

"To your knowledge, did your father ever hide his research anywhere other than in his study or at the office?"

It would be so easy. *It's in the bunker in the field behind the apiary! It's all there!* And her father would be home in two years. Her whole life up until this moment was fixed in her mind. Her mom, her dad, the farm, bees, vegetables, the forest, the tire swing, the workshop, the bunker, the porch stairs, lavender, and honey.

The images spun at her with a clarity that muted the dissonant hum of the courtroom.

She tried to conjure an image of a different future, but her mind froze, unable to imagine a single scene of what life might be like if her father went to prison for up to thirty years.

Sasha's breath rushed through her lungs too fast.

Her father touched a finger against the side of his nose. Was he apologizing? Or was he telling her he forgave her before she even betrayed him? He folded both hands under his chin.

Maybe she'd imagined the gesture. He might have had an itch.

Sasha held all the power but didn't know how to use it.

She looked around the room, at the slithery smugness on Chuck's face, the slump in her father's shoulders, the eagerness on the lawyer's face as she awaited Sasha's answer.

Her father gripped the edge of the table in front of him, bracing himself for Sasha to tell the lawyer about the bunker.

She had to decide.

Until she took the stand and observed her father's reactions, Sasha hadn't understood. But from her vantage point on the witness stand she saw what everyone else missed.

Her father had hope.

And that hope lay buried in the bunker.

"Miss Severn, are you aware of any other locations where your father might have kept research?"

Her fingers buzzed.

"No." The lie slid out effortlessly.

"Do you have any knowledge of bees having escaped from your father's indoor apiary on or around the date you were stung?"

*This is bigger than you and me, it's important in ways I can't explain to you right now.*

"No." She wanted to put her feet on the floor, to feel the ground under her feet. But she didn't want to squirm in her seat and reveal her discomfort. Everything solid shifted, becoming malleable, unreliable. The wooden seat might splinter to pieces. The ceiling above her might dissolve and float away.

"You're certain you don't know of any *secret* hiding spots or favorite places?" The lawyer scrunched her face up and pulled her shoulders up toward her ears as she emphasized the word "secret" as if the trial were a silly game and Sasha a silly child.

*I know what it will cost you, so ultimately, it's your decision.*

"I'm certain."

Sasha stole a quick glance at her father. He looked down at his lap, the corners of mouth curling up as he tried to mask his pride.

He rapped his knuckles lightly three times on the table in front of him.

Tears burned Sasha's eyes as she tapped her fingers on the rail between her and the lawyer. Three times. Her father lifted his chin and gave a nearly imperceptible nod.

"I have no further questions."

Chuck jumped up from his seat and stormed out the back of the courtroom.

The heat drained out of Sasha's body. Her fingertips turned icy. She couldn't turn back.

Sasha was alone, and she had no one to blame but herself.

Sasha ran over to her father as the courtroom cleared out. She wrapped her arms around his waist, breathing the wax and honeysuckle deep into her lungs.

"You were very brave." He wiped at her tearstained face with his thumb. "I'll be right here. We'll get through this."

Days later, after a jury found her father guilty, the judge read the sentence of twenty-five years, with the possibility of parole in eleven, in open court. Sasha would be twenty-two at the youngest. She would be an adult capable of caring for herself.

Panic brewed in her gut as the social worker walked toward them. Maybe she could run after the lawyer with the red lips and tell her she forgot about the bunker. Was it too late?

"Your father won't be coming home, you understand that, right?" the social worker said. "You'll be living with your uncle Charles for the foreseeable future."

Sasha would never forgive Chuck for urging her to betray her father. Never.

"One last goodbye." The social worker took a step back, giving Sasha and her father privacy. People lingering in the courtroom watched them, but Sasha did not care.

Her father pulled her in for a tight hug. Her body melted against his torso. She closed her eyes and imagined him disappearing like the cloud of bees.

"I'm so proud of you." His voice cracked at every syllable as he fought to hold back the sobs surging in his chest.

"What if I don't have anything left to love?" Sasha's chin quivered as she spoke.

"You have the whole world to love, Little Bee. Promise you won't spend your life grieving over things you already lost. There is still so much beauty in this world."

He kissed the top of her head. She threw her arms around him and refused to let go until the social worker pried her off and the court officer took her father away.

"We can rebuild," her father said over his shoulder as he walked away. "We are not the last."

# Forty-Two

## SASHA, AGE 23

### JUNE 11

The driver of the black SUV slammed on the brakes, churning up a cloud of dust as the car skidded in front of the farmhouse.

"This is on me." Sasha stood up in the bed of the truck. "Say you didn't know about my plans, that you were trying to stop me. They already know I'm involved, but the rest of you can walk away. I never should have gotten you involved."

"Stop it with the martyr act. This isn't about you anymore," Gino said. "We understood the risks."

The SUV's driver's-side door opened. As the dust settled, Chuck emerged, running awkwardly toward the truck.

"Why didn't you answer your phone?" he huffed.

Sasha stood up and looked over Chuck's shoulder at the car, expecting to see his security team, but the car sat empty.

"They know about the hive." Sweat beaded up on Chuck's forehead.

"What hive?" Sasha tried to stay calm. Gino, Halle, and Ian stood up next to her.

"We don't have time for this." Chuck's comb-over fell across his forehead, exposing his shiny, pink scalp. "We all saw Dr. Maher's video."

"Is she okay?" Bassel asked.

"I don't know where she is," Chuck said. "There's a warrant out for your arrest too, Alexandra."

"I haven't done anything," Sasha said.

"Tampering with pollinators is illegal."

"How can you tamper with something that doesn't exist?"

"I know you don't trust me, but please hear me out. Dr. Maher lit a fire. People are angry, they're already protesting downtown, and not just here, but across the country."

Bassel shook his head, but a small, proud smile flickered on his lips.

"None of my friends have done anything wrong. If you keep them out of it and release Millie, I'll talk to you," Sasha said.

"The hell you will." Octavia slammed the truck door and marched toward Chuck. "You aren't taking Sasha anywhere."

"Wait." Bassel tried to get between Octavia and Chuck. "Do you know who he is?"

"Of course I do." Octavia nudged her way past Bassel. "Last time I saw my husband he left our house to meet his pal Chuck to show him the bees he discovered. Horace never came home, and no one has seen him since."

"I never saw Horace that day. He didn't show up," Chuck said. "Octavia, I've told you this before, I never saw him. I assumed he changed his mind. A week later I heard he was missing."

"But you told someone else that Horace had bees," Octavia said. "It's the same damn thing."

"I didn't know they would look for him. I didn't know."

"That's right. You kept your head down and climbed the ladder," Octavia shouted, spittle flying as she choked down rage. "We aren't letting you take Sasha in."

"You think I'm here to turn you in?" Chuck looked hurt.

"Why else would you be here?" Sasha said.

"To warn you. You're my niece. They know you lied about getting stung. The hospital alerted the department when they detected bee venom in your blood work. There's been a ton of sightings in the area, and now with Kamilah going public, they'll be desperate to silence all of you. You're an easy target. The daughter of the Last

Beekeeper. They have proof you lied about having contact with bees."

"I know about the GMOs," Sasha said.

"We can talk about the past later." Chuck looked down at his feet. "Right now, we need to salvage what stability we have left. Kamilah's revenge mission will make things worse for people already struggling."

Sasha looked around at her friends. "We can't let him leave. If we're going to move the hive, we have to take him with us. There are six of us and one of him."

"No fucking way," Ian said. "That's kidnapping."

Chuck wiped sweat from his face and paced in a circle. "Not if I go willingly. I'll help you."

"Give me your phone," Sasha said to her uncle.

"Sasha."

She held her open hand out to Chuck.

Chuck handed his phone to Sasha, who took the battery out and put it in her pocket before returning the device to him.

He inspected the gear in the truck. "Is it nearby?"

No one answered him.

"You." Octavia pointed at Gino. "You're responsible for watching Skinner. He rides in the back with you all."

Gino saluted Octavia.

"I need to get something from my car." Chuck walked toward the SUV.

"I don't think so." Gino stood between Chuck and the car door.

"It's for Sasha. It's important. Get it yourself if you don't believe me. There's a white box on the front seat and an envelope."

"EpiPens." Gino handed the box and the envelope to Sasha.

"I worry about you being near bees. I didn't know if anyone else would think to bring them," Chuck said.

Sasha remembered the day of her recital when Chuck bought a bouquet of bright pink carnations because he knew her father would forget. Sasha felt a rush of regret over her lack of gratitude.

"You should read that." Chuck gestured toward the envelope in Sasha's hand.

She pulled out a small square of folded paper, worn and dirty on the edges and folds. The age didn't match the crisp new envelope it came in.

Sasha unfolded the note and recognized her father's handwriting.

"Your dad left this for you the night before the trial started, but I found it first."

Sasha read the letter silently, imagining the words in her father's baritone.

*Dear Sasha,*

*I want you to know that whatever decision you make in court, it is the right decision. And anything that happens after—or that already happened—is not your fault. I'm sorry I put you in the position of having to make an impossible choice on the stand.*

*You have a sharp mind and the ability to see what other people overlook. And more importantly, you have a natural ability to find solutions others cannot imagine.*

*Remember the night we beat on the tire swing with the leg of that broken stool? I have never been prouder of you. You smashed the stool because the old story I told you about nothing being able to break a three-legged stool was a flawed fairy tale. You are too smart for sugar-coated happy endings. Instead of letting my flawed story break you, you broke the story. I felt your strength with every blow you landed. Instead of using your anger to be mad at the world, I hope you will use your passion to make our broken world a little bit better.*

*No matter how much we have lost, no matter how much we grieve, there is still so much in this world to love. Find the beauty and the hope, and fight for them.*

*I'm sorry I failed you, that I'm not at home with you now. I made reckless and arrogant decisions that threatened the existence of not just our bees, but our future. I tried to stop it, but*

*I was too late. Chuck made the final decision, but I am the one who set things in motion. He and I both bear responsibility for the consequences of our choices.*

*I hope someday you will understand your actions may have given the bees—and us—our best shot at surviving. Please don't let grief over what we have lost blind you to the beauty in front of you. Don't second-guess yourself. And don't look back.*

*I love you,*
*Dad*

Sasha read the heavily creased letter three times, running a finger over the familiar script. These words would have mattered to her. She would have read them over and over as she lay awake in bed as a child. She would have memorized every sentence and repeated them to herself like a mantra.

"How could you keep this from me?" That lost, angry little girl had needed these words of reassurance. She needed to know he didn't blame her, that he forgave her. He believed in her. "My father went to prison, and you stole his words from me?"

"He implicated me. You would have asked questions and I couldn't live with you knowing I betrayed Lawrence like that."

"What did you do?" Sasha asked.

Gino put a hand on her arm to calm her, but she shook him off.

"I overrode your father's recommendation. *I* ordered the dissemination of the experimental bees despite Lawrence's warnings that we needed more time to study them. If you had read this back then, you would have started asking questions, and I couldn't risk you finding the answers. It was reckless of your father to endanger you with this information."

"We don't have time for this now. Work out your family drama later." Octavia glared at Chuck and got back into the cab of the truck.

Ian helped Chuck into the bed of the truck and the others squeezed in around the gear.

"I intended to give the letter to you when you were old enough, but I couldn't bring myself to do it. I didn't want you to hate me. I'm sorry," Chuck said as Octavia drove toward the edge of the woods.

The truck hit a deep pothole, and everyone lurched. Chuck lost his balance and fell over, hitting his head on the wall of the truck bed. No one helped him as he sat up, a trickle of blood escaping a cut above his eyebrow. Octavia looked through the window in the cab. She caught Chuck's eye and glared so fiercely Sasha felt the heat burning in her friend's eyes.

"You let my dad take all the blame, publicly and privately."

The truck lurched again as Octavia slammed on the brakes at the edge of the forest where Sasha and her father had crouched down in the dark, hiding from Chuck the day they moved Sasha's hives.

"If you read this letter, then you knew all along that I lied. Why didn't you just turn the letter over as evidence during the trial?"

"I was ashamed that I stole your letter, but I guess the real reason is that no matter how frustrated I was with you, I admired how much you loved your dad and how much he loved you. I hoped that you'd come to trust me, and you'd tell me where the documents were on your own, without me bullying you into it. I'll tell you everything you want to know. I promise. But right now, we need to get the hive out of here before they find us."

"You are not part of *us*. The only reason you're here is because we don't trust you enough to leave you behind." Sasha tried not to think about the day Chuck sat with her while they set her broken arm. He allowed her to scream and never once told her to calm down. *Sometimes we need to scream to let the pain out,* he told her.

Sasha's whole life since her father went to prison had been an exercise in holding in a scream.

They unloaded the gear and removed stones to clear an opening in the wall at the edge of the woods. The trolley bumped and stuttered over the uneven ground.

Sasha carried the roll of mesh under one arm and fell into step next to Bassel, who did not acknowledge her.

"I'm sorry I didn't tell you I gave the bees to your mom. I believed her that she wouldn't show them to anyone until we moved the hive to safety. She promised me."

"How could you trust her after what she did to you? My mother always has an agenda and she's only loyal to herself. I've been trying to find her for almost two years." Bassel stared straight ahead. "And now she's gone again. Why couldn't you wait like we agreed?"

"I'm mad at her, but I understand what it's like to feel lied to and manipulated. Your mom wanted the truth to come out. She's waited a long time."

"Tell yourself whatever you want if it makes you feel better," Bassel said.

Sasha wanted to throw her arms around Bassel and tell him how sorry she was, that she thought she was doing the right thing.

Her phone buzzed in her pocket. The hospital. Sasha silenced her phone.

"We have a decision to make," Octavia said. "I can't find anyone to transport the hive. I don't know who Millie's contact was or where the safe house is. We have enough fuel to drive about four hundred miles. But after that, we have no guarantees we can find more ethanol or a place to secure the hive."

"If you can't get it to a safe location, don't bother trying." Chuck panted trying to keep up. Sweat soaked the armpits of his shirt. "Millie directed them north, but they're deploying National Guard troops to expand the search."

"So, what now?" Ian said.

"We keep going," Sasha said. "We'll figure something out."

They trudged on in silence, stopping to clear branches and rocks for the trolley.

"I looked out for you when I could." Chuck caught up to Sasha. "When you and your friends applied for jobs at the glass farm, I made sure all four of you got positions in the first round."

"Great. I'll add more nepotism to the list of baggage I carry."

"I drafted the policy urging local authorities to stop evicting squatters from abandoned properties near glass farms nationwide. I mean, I did it because it's smart policy." Chuck's shortness of breath amplified the desperation in his voice. "No one lived on the abandoned farms. We needed workers in the greenhouses. So, yeah, smart policy. But I did it because I knew you moved back to the farm."

"I've never wanted you pulling strings for me."

Even in his shadowed profile, Sasha could see the wounded look on Chuck's face.

As the group maneuvered the trolley deeper into the forest, the sound of rushing water rose above the crunching of leaves underfoot. They passed the path leading to the spot where Sasha often went to play her violin in the middle of the stream. She spied the stand of fireweed where she had seen a bee the previous year.

She sucked in a sharp breath at the realization she most likely wouldn't be there in the spring to harvest the tender asparagus-like fireweed shoots, which they counted on to give them a long-overdue dose of vitamin C after their meager winter diet. A warrant for her arrest awaited her when she came out of the forest. If she didn't run, she would likely be caught. How did Millie expect them to relocate the hive with no plan and nowhere to go?

Would Ian know where to find the fireweed without her?

The energy and excitement motivating Sasha an hour earlier had drained away. Millie had been arrested, Sasha didn't trust Chuck, and Bassel refused to look at her.

Sasha felt herself reverting to the scared, angry little girl. She wanted to run. She couldn't be responsible for the last beehive. Not again.

How hard would it be to leave, to start over somewhere else and make a new life for herself? But imagining goodbye hurt worse than the prospect of getting arrested or of losing the bees.

They were a family, and she had worked so hard to find them. *Find the research. Understand the truth. Rebuild a family.*

She had achieved all the goals her younger self had set, but she couldn't hold on to any of it.

As the sunlight dimmed, a chill descended over Sasha, gripping her with a firm understanding that there was no way out. No way to save the bees, her chance at a relationship with Bassel, or the family she had established. No way to rescue Millie. Authorities would take the bees. By morning, they would most likely be evicted, possibly arrested. Or worse.

Why couldn't Millie have stuck to the plan and waited until they moved the hive? Despite her anger, Sasha felt a burning solidarity with Millie. They had both been deceived. They both loved the bees, not for their economic value but because of the complexity and the beauty of their existence. And they were both exhausted by people in power keeping secrets.

Millie saw the big picture. She always had. When Sasha first saw the video, she felt the familiar sting of betrayal. Once again, Millie had gone back on a promise to Sasha. But while everyone else remained angry with Millie, Sasha couldn't help admiring her steadfast commitment to the truth above all else.

Millie's video clip had diverted authorities with misinformation about the location of the hive and her call for protests. How did the others not recognize the sacrifice Millie had made?

Bassel only saw the danger his mother was in. And he blamed Sasha.

She simultaneously longed to console Bassel and berate him, but she kept her distance. Bassel needed his anger to shield himself from the fear that his mother might not return.

Lost in self-pity, Sasha caught a toe on a root and tripped, landing facedown in a bramble of broken twigs. The fall knocked the wind out of her. She didn't try to get up. Maybe the forest would absorb her back into the ground the way it was reclaiming the barn and the farmhouse. A primal desire to melt into the earth, to escape the aftermath of her decisions, pinned her to the ground.

Someone knelt next to her and placed a hand on her back.

"On your feet," Gino whispered in her ear. "It's time to save the world."

# Forty-Three

## SASHA, AGE 23
### JUNE 11

Gino helped Sasha into a sitting position and brushed the dirt and dried leaves from her clothes and face.

"You are Sasha Severn Butler, player of mediocre violin music, daughter of the Last Beekeeper, and you need to protect these miracle bees."

"I can't do this."

"You're already doing it. We're all here hunting bees in the forest—possibly facing kidnapping charges—because we believe in you."

"I believed in Millie and that didn't get me very far. I trusted her. How could she betray me again? How could I let her?"

"I don't think she betrayed you. I think she's counting on you," Gino whispered. "Watch this." He opened Ian's phone and played a loop of a section of Millie's video in which she held the bees in her hand and spoke as the camera zoomed in on the bees.

*Look at this little bee. I need you to trust me. I'm designating you to act now.*

*Look at this little bee. I need you to trust me. I'm designating you to act now.*

*Look at this,* Little Bee. *I need you to trust me. I'm designating* YOU *to act now.*

Millie had been talking directly to Sasha, handing her responsibility for transporting the hive.

Gino took both of Sasha's hands and pulled her up. "Now take us to the bees."

Sasha walked alone in front of the group, her pulse quickening as she approached the clearing with the hollow tree. The welt on her neck itched with growing ferocity.

How did Millie expect her to transport the hive if she didn't know where to take it?

They walked in single file, taking turns with the trolley in the rear, the crunching of leaves and twigs the only sounds.

"We're almost there." Sasha stopped to put on her father's over-size beekeeping suit. The shushing of the fabric as she walked distorted the sounds of the forest. Inside the suit, she felt separate from the others, alone, as if no one could see her.

"We're here." She pointed at the tree, a dead pine trunk that had broken off about six feet above the ground.

"Peek inside if you want to see them before we wrap the hive." She gestured toward the chest-high opening to the hollow. "One at a time. Move slow, no sudden motions. And don't block the opening to the hive."

Octavia, Gino, Ian, and Halle each took a turn peering through the opening to see the golden layers of wax cells swelling up from the bottom and dripping down from the top.

Sasha tried to quiet her breath and tame her fear so she wouldn't stress the bees. After adjusting her veil, double-checking for any possible gaps, she looked inside the hive and estimated the depth of the cavity based on how far up the honeycomb rose.

The smell of honey and wax bombarded her with the desire to giggle, to dance, to scream from the elation of swinging so high her bare toes grazed the leaves above her. Everything around Sasha shimmered in the evening sunlight, the green of the maple leaves so bright, it almost hurt to behold. Sasha longed to spread her arms wide and spin until she fell to the ground.

Bassel approached the hive last. He laid his hands on the tree as if touching a religious relic. He licked his lips and closed his eyes for moment. Sasha held her breath, awaiting his reaction, knowing he would feel the same rush of emotion and wanting to experience it with him.

His breath hitched as he peered inside. He pressed his forehead against the tree trunk. "They're real."

"Bassel, can you handle the smoker?" Sasha asked.

Bassel didn't answer but walked over to the trolley to find the smoker and lighter.

"Then we'll wrap the opening to the hive with mesh. Halle and Ian, can you do this? Bind it with duct tape so there aren't any gaps over the opening."

"On it," Halle said.

"Octavia, Gino, and Bassel, can you secure the trunk so it won't fall over when we cut through? We need to attach it with straps to surrounding trees so it will stay upright. I have no idea how to do this part."

Sasha marked a circle around the base of the trunk, tagging where they needed to cut.

Halle and Ian unrolled the four-foot-wide band of mesh and wound it tightly around the trunk, blocking the bees from entering or exiting the hive. Sasha sensed the bees' fear mounting as Halle secured the fabric with several rounds of duct tape.

Chuck and Bassel took thick nylon straps and wrapped them around the trunk. Octavia and Gino secured the other ends of the straps to nearby trees, winching the bands taut so the trunk would remain upright, supported by the straps, when they cut it down.

They worked in silence, finishing the preparations more quickly than Sasha expected.

Octavia and Bassel took the first shift of sawing through the trunk. No one spoke as the rusty teeth of Sasha's grandfather's saw chewed through the wood, slowly, slowly, slowly.

After fifteen minutes, Octavia and Bassel put the saw down to rest. Chuck took up one end and Gino the other.

Sweat beaded on Chuck's forehead and soaked his shirt.

"You should take a break." Ian offered Chuck a drink of water after a few minutes.

"I'm fine," he huffed.

Ian grimaced at every stutter of the saw, ready to jump in if anyone got hurt. His hand strangled the shoulder strap of his first-aid kit.

"That outfit suits you." Bassel stepped up beside Sasha.

"You're talking to me?"

"My mom understood the consequences of her actions. It's who she is." Bassel puffed out his cheeks and released the air in a long slow stream. "I finally found her, and now . . . And now I don't know what. I'm angry. But not at you."

The forest swirled with the earthy scent of humus and decay. The breaking down and the rising up of life. Bassel put an arm around Sasha's shoulders, and she leaned into him, wishing the fabric of the beekeeping gear weren't between them.

The ferns, the great hemlocks, the bees. Her friends. Every bit of love she had for her found family, the farm, and the forest invigorated her. The fear and grief that had been the filter through which she experienced life for the past twelve years were loosening from her bones, shaking away and regathering like a storm cloud.

*Love what's in front of you and be willing to fight for it.*

Sasha spent eleven years searching for something to love. And now, for the first time in her adult life, she had a lot to fight for, a lot to love in the farm, the house, and the people who lived there.

But that wasn't what her father meant. He wanted her to look up, see the trees, the mountains, the swans, the deer. The bees. It all made sense now. Fighting for her family meant being willing to believe in something better. They were all linked. They all deserved a chance to do more than survive.

The scent of burning wood rose from the friction of the saw blade carving through the wood.

Chuck lost his footing and went down hard before anyone could catch him. Gino, on the other end of the saw, fell backward as Chuck let go. Sasha watched the slow-motion slip of the saw, the drag of the ragged teeth over Chuck's thigh just above his knee, tearing his pants, ripping his flesh, the gush of red.

His wail, guttural and resonant, hung in the air, swelling, expanding to fill in the spaces between the trees, the people, and the bees.

Gino jumped up, unhurt, and crawled toward Chuck.

"Somebody give me their shirt," Ian shouted as he opened his medical kit.

Gino tore off his button-down shirt and pressed it on Chuck's wound as Ian tied a tourniquet around his thigh.

Sasha felt as if her body moved at a different pace than everyone else's, as if she were watching the scene, but not part of it.

"Stay with me, Skinner." Ian tightened the tourniquet a few inches above Chuck's knee.

Chuck howled.

Color drained from Gino's face as he watched his shirt darken with Chuck's blood. Gino unconsciously pressed one hand to the scar on his own side, hidden under his T-shirt.

Sasha knelt beside Gino. "You okay? I can take over if you want."

Gino shook his head and continued pressing on Chuck's leg.

"The bleeding's slowing, but I can't stop it entirely," Ian said.

Sasha walked into the forest resenting the man lying on the ground bleeding out into the earth. He enraged her, tormented her, annoyed her, but now, a desperate desire to save her uncle surged through her body.

*I wanted to make sure you weren't the only one without pretty flowers.* Had she thanked Chuck for the flowers at her orchestra performance?

"We're going to get you to a hospital." Sasha knelt beside Chuck.

"I won't be the one who ruins this." Chuck winced as he spoke. "Not again."

Ian cut open Chuck's pant leg, and Chuck moaned loudly.

"He's going to bleed out if we don't get him to a hospital," Ian said.

"Move the bees first." Chuck struggled to get the words out.

Ian grabbed a twig about three-quarters of an inch in diameter and held it to Chuck's face. "I want you to bite down on this. This is going to hurt." Ian unfurled a second tourniquet from the military field kit and secured it around Chuck's upper thigh inches from the first tourniquet.

"Bees. First," Chuck growled around the branch clenched in his jaw.

"I'll take care of Chuck," Ian said to Sasha. "Finish your job."

Bassel walked over to the saw and picked up one end. Sasha took the other. In her peripheral vision Ian yanked hard to secure the second tourniquet, twisting it tighter in sync with Chuck's moaning.

The first few drags of the saw felt unsteady; the teeth stuttered across the wood pulp without finding a solid grip. Sasha's hands shook. This effort seemed doomed. They had no one to take the bees, nowhere to take them, and if they didn't hurry, Chuck could bleed to death.

"Find the rhythm, Sasha," Gino said. "You both need to be moving together."

They faltered again. She paused to wipe the sweat from her face.

Halle took over for Gino and maintained pressure on Chuck's wound.

"One, two three, four." Gino clapped the rhythm for her the way he beat rocks together when she played violin in the woods. "One, two three, four."

Bassel fell into tempo with ease, but Sasha struggled to time her pulls with Bassel's release.

"Come on, Sasha, focus," Bassel said.

Sasha started humming a tune Gino had taught her on her violin. Vibrations in her throat and chest felt warm and powerful. She could feel the bees near her, buzzing with urgency.

"There you go," Gino cheered as they pulled several strokes in perfect sync.

The rattling of the melody warmed her throat, the tremors of her breath in communication with the distressed bees. But the more she worked, the harder her breath came.

Sawdust hung in the dry air. Sasha choked, the hum caught in her throat. She pulled the saw with aching shoulders, her heels rooted into the ground. Her breath came heavy until she could no longer hum under the strain.

Gino caught her eye and began to hum. The deep, rich vibrato seemed to move from Gino to Sasha, but she couldn't hold the low tune in her head over Chuck's cries and Ian's instructions to Halle and Octavia.

"Louder," Sasha called to Gino.

But the churning wood, the chatter, her own breath conspired to drown out Gino's song, and she felt disconnected from the rhythm, the saw, and Bassel.

She stutter-stepped and recovered.

After a few minutes, Gino stopped humming. Sasha felt the immediate absence of his song. But only for a few beats.

Gino's posture changed; he positioned his feet shoulder width apart, his hands by his sides with outstretched fingers, still covered in Chuck's blood.

No one but Sasha noticed.

The sound started on a deep note as if it were rumbling up from inside the earth. Gino's velvety tenor unfurled into the forest as he closed his eyes and spread all the fingers on both hands wider, as if summoning the wind. The words poured out of him in rich Italian, sending shivers across Sasha's skin.

Her body fell into rhythm with Bassel's, and the saw sliced through the tree with fluid grace.

Gino's voice wrapped around her, moving inside her and through her. She ached from the anguish tearing him open.

Sasha dug in with her heels and her shoulders. She and Bassel held each other's gaze as they plowed the saw through the tree trunk. She could feel Bassel's heartbeat resonating across the blade of the saw between them into the palms of her hands.

"Gino?" Ian said.

Gino kept his eyes closed against Ian's reaction to hearing him sing.

Heat from the friction singed the wood, burned in Sasha's arms and back.

"You're close," Octavia shouted and steadied the tree trunk as the saw chewed through the final millimeters of wood.

Gino's song expanded with a crescendo that powered Sasha's tired muscles.

As the saw broke through and the trunk swung loose, dangling from the straps suspending it between two trees, Sasha and Bassel both dropped the blade and fell to their knees. Octavia settled the trunk, which swung like a pendulum over the stump.

Gino stopped singing and the woods fell silent. Chuck no longer made any noise.

"Is he going to be okay?" Sasha crawled over and took Chuck's hand.

"I slowed the bleeding for now," Ian said. He had packed the wound with gauze and lashed two branches to either side of Chuck's straightened leg so he couldn't bend it. Octavia held the wounded leg in the air, and Halle held up the other to keep the blood pooled in his torso. "We need to get him to a hospital."

Gino, Octavia, and Bassel carried Chuck while Sasha, Halle, and Ian maneuvered the cart with the tree trunk strapped to it through the uneven ground of the forest.

The thrum of the hive's angst rattled her fingers. Her breath morphed into a hum warming her throat and chest. The sensation swelled in her shoulders and rippled down her aching arms. She squeezed her fingers tighter around the grip on the cart to get closer to the vibration. She wanted to calm the bees, to tell them they would be fine.

The cart hit a stone and threatened to tip. Sasha lurched backward and threw her weight against the tree trunk. Bassel joined her, his shoulder against hers as they stabilized the hive. Sasha let her forehead rest against the tree trunk, the mesh of the veil pressing into her skin.

"They're scared," Sasha said. The heat of furiously beating wings fanned the perfume of honey through the fabric trapping the bees.

They resettled the cart, tightened the straps holding the trunk in place, and trudged forward.

Sasha fell back to walk near Chuck. His eyes were closed, but she could tell by the occasional wince that he clung to consciousness.

"The Backup Plan," Chuck said, his voice strained with pain.

"I remember." Sasha tried to force a cheerful tone. "We had some great times there."

"You can do this." He opened his eyes to narrow slits. "Not Dr. Maher. You."

The potbellied stove in the family room and a small dining table with two chairs. The plug-in, two-burner electric plate tapped into the solar panels. On chilly nights, she had wrapped herself in a heavy quilt patched in colors of wildflowers and infused with the spice of woodsmoke. The precise weight of uneven batting and thread-worn cotton hovered in her memory.

"I can't." Despite her protest, Sasha knew she could do it. She could take the hive to the cabin where she had spent so many idyllic summers.

The icy water from the hand pump in the kitchen tasted like the mountains. Sasha had slurped it straight from the spigot, letting water roll down her chin and chest as she savored the hint of river stones and moss.

"You'll be safe there. I owe you and your father this." Chuck's eyes rolled back in his head, and his eyelids closed.

But how could she leave the farm, her friends? Sasha had spent eleven years making promises to herself. Rebuild a family and understand the truth about her father's hidden research. She had finally achieved her goals. How could she walk away?

"Chuck? Can you hear me?" Sasha squeezed his hand.

"There's a larder. Your dad rubbed off on me." Chuck half laughed and winced in pain.

"You aren't seriously considering this, are you?" Gino whispered to Sasha. "It's a terrible idea."

"I know exactly where to take them. Besides, I can't stay here. They know I lied about getting stung. I'm sure I'll be tied to Millie's media blitz. Best case is I lose my job. Worst case, we all get evicted, I get arrested or go missing. There's no scenario where I walk away from this if I stay."

"You don't have a great track record when it comes to bee stings," Gino said.

"I'll be more careful." Sasha's mind spun as she spoke, the ideas forming at the same rate the words touched her tongue. "I'm the only person here who knows how to get to the cabin. I know how to set up the solar panels, how to get the water pump working. I know how to take care of bees."

"What about *our* future?" Gino asked.

"If we aren't willing to fight for what is still good in this world, how can we imagine a future?"

"You're a shit sometimes. You know that, right?"

"I love you too."

Her younger self, the girl who desperately wanted more people, more love in her life, would have been grateful to know she no longer perched on a two-legged ladder or a three-legged stool. All the people she could see had entered the forest this day fully aware of the risk, because they believed in Sasha. She wanted to stop time and absorb every face, sound, smell, and vibration of the people she loved. She had everything she had ever wanted, but when they exited the woods, it would all slip away.

She imagined the large galvanized-steel tub they used to bathe in at the cabin. Her parents put pans of water on the woodstove and filled the tub out on the back porch. The tub must be there somewhere. Sasha imagined filling a steaming bathtub in front of the woodstove and reading while she soaked.

She had run through fields, picked berries, and helped her father prune the apple and pear trees and the grapevines. They must have grown into a wild, unruly mess by now.

*These are walnuts.* Her father had scooped up a handful of nuts. *They store well if you keep them dry.* In the spring he had taught her how to find fiddleheads before the ferns unfurled. They planted sunflowers and came back months later to see the seedlings burst forth into flowers the size of dinner plates. Every year they multiplied. Sasha had loved following her father spitting sunflower seed shells on the ground as they walked.

Sasha had been a wild thing at the Backup Plan. She ran, climbed, swam naked. Her heart pounded at the memory of sprinting toward nothing, wildflowers skimming her fingertips.

*What if I don't have anything to love?*

*You have the whole world, Little Bee.*

Wildness swelled inside Sasha, teasing her, reclaiming her.

Sasha had more to love in this world than at any point in her life. But having more to love meant having more to lose.

# Forty-Four

## SASHA, AGE 23

### JUNE 11

When they made it back to the farmhouse, Ian and Octavia flattened the seats in the back of Chuck's car to transport him to the hospital while Sasha sat with Chuck, holding his limp hand as he drifted in and out of consciousness.

"Keep him awake." Ian joined Sasha next to Chuck. "You knew, didn't you? About Gino."

"Give him a chance to explain."

"He doesn't need to explain anything to me. His voice. It's the most beautiful thing I've ever heard."

"Chuck, look at me." Leaves in the big oak tree chattered as a breeze blew through the branches. Sasha didn't feel the air move, as if her body was out of sync with what was happening around her. Nothing felt real except Chuck's clammy hand in hers. "Uncle Chuck, open your eyes!"

She stared at the beaten-down version of her uncle possibly dying in front of her. Sasha dug deep for the hate, the rage. Chuck's normally colorless face appeared almost translucent, his lips a watery gray in the moonlight.

*Hate him*, she urged herself. He had taken so much.

*Whatever decision you make in court, it is the right decision.*

Her father's permission could have freed her to tell the truth and bring him home. Life would have been so different.

But she never would have met Halle, Ian, or Gino. Not Octavia.

Not Bassel. And the hive. What would have happened to this hive if she hadn't been there to see the bee? Would someone else have found it? Would it have been destroyed by a weak government afraid to admit their mistakes?

*Don't look back,* her father whispered in her ear.

Sasha looked up to see Octavia standing in front of her.

"Sasha, are you listening? This is important." Octavia's voice sounded far away although she stood inches from Sasha.

Everything was slipping away.

"We're ready to move him into the car," Octavia said.

"Be still," Ian said to Chuck as he and Octavia lifted Chuck off the ground to put him in the back of the car.

Chuck moaned loudly.

"The night of your last violin performance, Lawrence discovered I'd been creating and shipping out the genetically modified queens without his knowledge. It's why he missed your concert," Chuck said weakly. "I'm sorry."

"We all did what we believed was best at the time. All of our decisions—the good ones and the bad ones—brought us here, to this hive, to this chance." Sasha tried to convince herself more than Chuck. "Maybe it's time we forgive each other and think about what's ahead. Maybe it's a better future because of those decisions and the ones we're making right now."

"I love you, Alexandra."

"I love you too, Uncle Chuck." Sasha tapped her finger to the side of her nose, and Chuck smiled weakly.

Ian slammed the door as Chuck's eyes drooped closed.

Helicopter blades chopped the air in the distance, punctuated by sporadic bursts of fireworks being set off by protesters blocking the road between the market and the farm. Videos of the protesters showed barricades of burning tires across the road, providing cover for Sasha to escape. The roadblock would also force Octavia to drive an extra five miles out of her way to get Chuck to the hospital.

"You sure you can do this?" Sasha asked Octavia. "You two have a complicated history. You're going to get him help, right?"

"I think he's probably telling the truth about Horace. But even if he isn't, I wouldn't let him die. Horace wouldn't have wanted that. I'll get your uncle to the hospital. I promise," Octavia said.

"Thank you."

Octavia opened her backpack and handed Sasha three paperbacks. "Take my emergency stash."

Sasha hugged Octavia, not bothering to read the titles. This time, Octavia hugged her back, a warm embrace, infused with all the possibilities Sasha wanted to believe in.

"I'm proud of you, beekeeper."

"Not the daughter anymore?"

"*You* are the beekeeper now."

"Can you get your hands on a ham radio?" Sasha asked.

"Of course I can. Why?"

"There's one at the cabin. I'll monitor it every night from nine to nine thirty until I hear from one of you." Sasha handed Octavia a folded piece of paper. "These are instructions on what to do and how to identify me. You should memorize it and destroy my note."

"It might take a while to find a radio. But don't give up on me. I'll find you," Octavia said.

"I'll be there every night," Sasha said, confident for the first time in her father's belief that hope and beauty and a future existed, not just for the bees or the world, but for herself.

# Forty-Five

## SASHA, AGE 23
### JUNE 11

After Octavia left with Chuck, Bassel and Gino lashed the handcart holding the tree trunk in the bed of the truck. Sasha practiced setting up the ramp and maneuvering the cart down from the truck bed by herself using pulleys and jacking up the cart to set the tree upright when she found a suitable location.

"I'm going inside to grab my things." Sasha pressed her hands together to suppress the shaking.

Gino followed Sasha up the porch stairs.

"I know you feel like this is your responsibility, your destiny or something. But you are not responsible for fixing your father's mistakes," Gino said.

"I know."

"We promised we were going to stick together, no matter what." The muscles in Gino's jaw quivered. He turned his back to Sasha and faced the mural on the wall.

"I'm not abandoning you."

"But you're leaving."

"Not forever."

"You don't know that. If you come back, you'll be arrested, or worse you'll disappear. Is one hive of bees worth risking everything?"

"It's not one hive. It's not even about bees. It's about everything.

Maybe we can save this hive, maybe they'll rebound as a species. Can you imagine what that would mean for the world?"

"It's a lot of risk and sacrifice for a long shot," Gino said.

"What if five people saved hives? What if twenty or a thousand people did something radical because they had hope? Look at the protesters Millie inspired. They're taking risks. If we aren't willing to fight for what's in front of us right now, what chance do we have for a better future? A generation ago, it seemed impossible we could ban coal and oil. But enough people fought to make it happen. I know there's a chance this will all be for nothing, but I can't give up. Even if it's just this one hive. The bees deserve a chance. We all deserve the chance."

Through the window, they saw Ian sprint up the hill.

"Where are you going?" Gino called as they followed him outside.

"I'll be right back," Ian yelled. He loped up the hill toward Sasha's garden. In silhouette against the blue-gray night sky, he dropped to his knees.

Minutes later Ian jogged back down the slope with something in his arms.

"Can someone get a wet towel to wrap the roots?" Ian panted as he approached his housemates on the porch. He extended his arms to Sasha and presented her with six asparagus crowns, clumps of soil clinging to the tangled roots, the fronds drooping across his arms, stained with Chuck's blood. "You can replant them, right?"

"That's perfect," Sasha said.

Following Ian's lead, Halle grabbed a spade from the porch and dug up two lavender plants, some mint, basil, thyme, and oregano.

Gino brought a wet dish towel out and swaddled all the roots in a bundle like an infant.

The light bulb in the family room illuminated the house with a thin amber glow. Sasha inhaled deeply to fill her chest with lavender, bracing herself for the ache the perfume always triggered. Instead, she felt the warmth of her mother's hand on her shoulder.

How often had she cursed the wobbly banister and the mold growing in the attic ceiling? But the old farmhouse had remained steadfast through freezing-cold nights when Halle, Ian, Gino, and Sasha slept huddled by the fire. Maybe memories and love held the house together. Flying on the tire swing. Beer chilling in the creek. Her mother braiding her hair. Wishes made on lights reflected off distant glass.

Halle jogged toward the truck with Sasha's mother's seed jars, which she positioned on the passenger-side floor. Gino carried two large rolls of fabric Sasha had sliced from the apiary walls to tent over the garden in early spring. He tossed the bundles into the bed of the truck to cover the hive.

Sasha's warped tire swing swayed under the oak as it always had. Would any of this be there when she returned?

Halle emerged from the farmhouse with sacks of clothes and bedding. The skirt made of Sasha's curtains hung over the top.

"Why are you moving your stuff?" Sasha asked.

"We're leaving tonight too," Halle said.

"You can't. How will I find you?"

"It's not safe for us to stay here. Octavia has one room available at her boardinghouse. It's cheap. I'll have to bunk in a room with the lovebirds for a while"—Halle looked over at Gino and Ian—"but as soon as another room opens up, I'll have my own space. Octavia said I can claim it as a legal address and petition for Beatrix to move in with us."

Sasha looked at the dangling shutters and sagging porch, the tire swing and the overgrown lavender.

"It was never about the house," Halle said, as if reading her mind. "I love this place. But it's just a house. The real miracle is us. And we'll be waiting for you."

"Promise?"

"Promise."

"I want to meet Beatrix."

"You will." Halle lifted one foot off the ground and planted it against her inner thigh, her balance never wavering.

"Even if they can't find me or the hive, there's going to be blow-back on all of you," Sasha said. "I want you all to say you didn't know anything about my plans. You were as shocked as everyone else. Be angry with me. Make them think I'm all alone with no support."

"You are so your father's daughter." Gino laughed.

"I wish I could say goodbye to him," Sasha said.

A fallen oak branch about the size of a baseball bat lay on the ground near her feet. She picked it up and walked over to the tire swing.

Raising the bat to her shoulder, she adjusted her grip and swung. The wood collided with the tire, sending a surge of energy through her arm and shoulder.

For all the years she had been alone.

She swung again.

For the guilt she had carried for releasing the last bees. The tire twisted and wobbled as it absorbed each blow. She didn't turn around, but she felt her father standing next to her as he had the night they beat the tire with the stool leg.

*Don't let grief over what we have lost blind you to the beauty in front of you.* The impact reverberated in her shoulders and her back.

*Don't second-guess yourself.* Her body, the swing, and the branch fell into perfect synchronization. She timed each blow with the arc of the tire swinging on the rusted chain.

*Don't look back.* The last blow took all the energy she had left, and she fell to her knees.

Sasha wanted to go back in time and sit with her childhood self in the courtroom, her feet dangling in the air, her heart breaking. For so long she had carried the anger at her father. She blamed him for abandoning her. But in reality, Sasha made the decision to lie herself.

Even if she had read her father's letter before the trial, she would have lied for him. Her eleven-year-old self recognized that something bigger than losing her father was at stake.

Sasha always resented that her father had sacrificed her for his bees. But in reality, it was Sasha who had sacrificed her father for hope. The truth hit Sasha hard as the lies she shielded herself with fell away.

Remembering the glint of pride in her father's eyes as she upheld his story in court filled her with determination and the belief she could finish what her father had not been able to.

*Thank you for believing,* she whispered into the ear of her younger self.

Halle, Gino, and Ian knelt beside her, folding her into their arms, enveloping her in the feeling she had been chasing her entire life.

Sasha wanted to soak up every detail of the farm. The naked light bulb dangling from a wire in the kitchen. Halle, Gino, and Ian had cheered and carried Sasha around on their shoulders the day she connected the wind turbine and brought light into the house. Sasha often returned to that memory when she had trouble sleeping. The feeling of being needed, of being loved.

Sasha untangled herself from her friends and ran inside the house one final time. She grabbed a piece of the art paper she had given Halle and a pencil. She scribbled out the best version of a map to the cabin she could manage. Like a bee, Sasha always knew how to find her way home, but could she transmit the information for others to follow? She closed her eyes, remembering the precise details of the landmarks, the roads, the angle of the sun.

She folded the map and put it in her pocket next to the letter from her father.

Bassel walked into the living room and paused in front of Halle's mural. His eyes lingered on his mother standing at the outer edge of the painting.

Everything in Sasha's body hurt. Her shoulders ached from sawing through the tree and from hitting the tire. Blisters stung her fingers. Sasha welcomed each minor hurt as a distraction from the ache in her chest.

"How can you be sure you can find the cabin? You were just a kid," Bassel said, his eyes fixed on his mother's likeness.

"My celestial compass never fails."

"When will you be back?"

"It might be a long time. There's enough ethanol for me to get to the cabin, but not enough to get back." Sasha stood about two feet from Bassel, her body stiff and aching. She would feel it in the morning. She couldn't imagine what morning would look like. Or any morning after.

"So, how—"

"Octavia knows how to contact me on a ham radio. We'll figure the rest out." She avoided looking him directly in the eye, afraid she wouldn't be able to leave.

"Get the honeycomb out of the hayloft and give it to Gino, Halle, and Ian. Octavia can sell it for them and use it for Gino's meds and Halle's legal costs when she petitions for Beatrix. When your mom comes home, tell her to show you where the bunker is. When things calm down, if they calm down, you can come back and open it up. There's a lot more honey down there."

"I'll save some for you." Bassel held her tight, and the humming quieted. Her mind stilled. She could do this.

"I have to go." She pulled away from him.

"Sasha." Bassel grabbed her hand as she started for the door. "I want to come with you."

"You need to save your mom." *Yes,* she begged him in her mind. *Come with me.*

He kissed her forehead, and for a few seconds she allowed herself to feel safe.

She pulled her face inches away from his. "I don't need you."

"I know."

"It's a small cabin."

"I like small cabins."

"Stop." Sasha put her hands on Bassel's chest and pushed him away. She couldn't ruin his chance at a normal life, a career where he could make a difference.

She could read, garden, sleep late, forage. She would be okay.

She picked up the last of the bags of gear from the ground and threw them in the truck. Gino had packed up some emergency canisters of unopened flour, bags of jerky, and sacks of lentils, and rice.

She would be okay.

Hazelnuts and berries. Mushrooms and fiddleheads. She would be fine.

"This isn't about you," Bassel said. "This isn't about your legacy, your father's or my mother's. This isn't revenge or redemption or glory. It's about the future, for all of us. I can help with the bees. What if you get stung?"

"Octavia brought me a bunch of EpiPens. Besides, I'm not going to get stung."

"Are there box hives up there?"

"No more boxes. If these bees are going to make it, it will be on their terms. They don't want to be in pine boxes any more than we do."

Sasha ran her hand over the hood of the old pickup truck, similar to the one her father taught her to drive when she was a preteen. Rust crawled across the dented metal and holes in the running board. The gritty paint reminded her of the wind in her hair, the rattling in her bones as she bounced in the back of her father's truck, his arm out the window, letting his hand ride the current of air like a surfer on a wave.

"Will you check on my dad and make sure they're treating him well? Tell him I love him, and I'll be back as soon as I can." Sasha handed Bassel her folded map. "I'm not much of a cartographer, but it's the best I could do on short notice. When things are safe and you know your mom's okay, you can come."

She reached into her memory, trying to picture the layout of the cabin. A woodstove next to the small dining table. The rough-hewn kitchen cabinets she helped her father hang when she was eight. It could be home. Sprouts to grow, a garden to tend, fish to catch, books to read from the library her mother had curated.

"Sasha."

"This isn't goodbye." She put her arms around his neck. His eyelashes brushed her skin as he kissed her. The taste of honey and the promise of a future lingered on his lips. Not goodbye. He pulled her closer, but she wriggled free of his embrace.

"I have to go." She climbed into the truck and slammed the door shut.

Not having driven since she was eleven, she pressed on the accelerator too hard, and the wheels spun, kicking dirt into the air and clouding her view of Bassel and the others as they waved.

The bees didn't scare her. Or the cold or the hunger. It was the looming hours. The noiselessness and the expanse of time that lay in front of her. It took so long to find a family. And so little time to leave them.

But not really leave.

She stroked the cracked leather of her violin case on the passenger seat. After a decade of dedicating herself to finding the truth and rebuilding a family, she had achieved it all, only to let it go.

Maybe she would climb trees again the way she had as a little girl. She could skinny-dip at midnight and sleep until noon if she wanted. She could sleep all day on weekends.

Weekends.

The word would lose meaning and context. No weekdays. No weekends. No one to make plans with. When she conjured the texture of the heavy quilts on the bed, Bassel appeared next to her in the vision.

Her heart pounded and she looked in the rearview mirror.

Bassel sprinted down the middle of the driveway behind her.

She slammed on the brakes, jolting the hive so it banged against the back of the cab as Bassel ran toward her.

She stopped the truck in the middle of the driveway and jumped out. Bassel's arms felt like home, like the future and the past in one moment. She smelled the woodstove they would light together. He tasted like the river water and the stars that hung so thick above the mountains that she believed as a girl they might fall on her tongue like snowflakes.

He embraced her with an urgency so bright she felt for an instant as if she were breathing through his lungs.

"I'll find you, I promise," he said.

She thought of her father's journal entry. *They entered the world the first of their kind all over again. One last hope.*

Bassel's smile pushed all her imagined loneliness into a far corner. In her mind, he lay beside her in the grass while she played music for the bees. He chased her through the woods as they foraged for fiddleheads in early spring. He rested his head in her lap as they read at night.

She could see it all reflected back to her in Bassel's eyes.

They were the first beekeepers and the last.

But not really the last.

Together, she and Bassel could be the first of their kind all over again.

"Hurry." As she kissed him, all her hope and fear tangled with the energy coursing through her body from pounding on the tire swing. Her fingers buzzed with the promise of the bees, and she knew the sensation wasn't her imagination. It never had been.

If she succeeded, if these bees survived, maybe the world had a chance to survive, too.

Sasha got back in the truck.

As the truck growled and backfired, the smell of burning ethanol triggered a memory of bouncing over the fields in her father's

368    JULIE CARRICK DALTON

truck, ten-year-old Sasha sitting on two cushions so she could see over the steering wheel, a block duct-taped to her foot so she could reach the pedals.

"Ease up on the gas," her father had shouted as she bounced over a pothole, but his smile told her he didn't want her to ease up at all.

Dust kicked up behind the truck, rising like a smoky phantom. She imagined the cloud soaring above the road, the fields, the treetops, and merging with the clouds stirred by other secret beekeepers hiding in mountains and hollows and valleys, biding their time, tending their charges until the world was ready to welcome them—and the bees—back home.

# Acknowledgments

In her comments on an early draft of *The Last Beekeeper,* my editor, Kristin Sevick, noted that I talk about bees the way other people talk about puppies. "You need to remember not everyone thinks bees are adorable," she advised.

I take Kristin's advice 99 percent of the time. She's a brilliant editor, but there was no way I could back down on this. Bees *are* adorable! I'd always had high hopes for *The Last Beekeeper,* but Kristin had raised the stakes. I was now determined to tell a great story *and* help readers (and Kristin) fall in love with bees.

When I first started keeping bees, everything about the practice delighted me. The hum that surrounded me when I opened a hive, the smell, their fuzzy little bodies, the twitch of a single exuberant bee. I built my own box hive, donned the gear, read books, and consulted with experts. I fell into the trance of watching bees come and go from the hive the way I lose myself to the flames of a mesmerizing campfire.

Then I watched all forty thousand bees die in a single day.

What had I done wrong? I read, studied, and tried again. I restocked my hive, and the bees thrived. Until one day, the following year, they all died again, in a single day.

The pattern didn't fit the numerous diseases and parasites afflicting bees. The sudden pile of corpses was not characteristic of colony collapse disorder. Although I didn't use chemicals on my own lawn, I'm convinced the bees were unintentionally poisoned by someone else's lawn products.

The second loss stirred a deeper grief than for just my own bees. If my carefully tended hives were struggling to survive in the toxic soup of suburban landscaping, what was happening to the local pollinators? That worry morphed into the plot of *The Last Beekeeper*.

*The Last Beekeeper* focuses on honey bees, but really, it's about all the pollinators we are losing, including the less charming wasps, mosquitoes, and yellow jackets. We need them all.

I owe a special thanks to beekeeper Alisha Gruntman, a professor at the Cummings School of Veterinary Medicine at Tufts University, for helping me create a plausible scenario for the collapse of the honey bee population in my novel. Alisha, you are the bee's knees!

I'm lucky to count Dr. Ginger Barrow as a close friend and advisor. She has counseled me through numerous medical emergencies—both real and fictional. Thank you for always having time to talk about gashes, rashes, broken bones, and acceptable amounts of blood loss.

I never could have finished this book without the encouragement and commitment of my agent, Stacy Testa, at Writers House. Every writer should be so lucky to have an agent who gushes when she loves your writing—and doesn't hesitate to tell when a scene you wrote is, well, a little cheesy. A fantastic editor, a savvy professional, and a kind friend, Stacy is always levelheaded, even when I'm not. She talks me through difficult moments with the steadfast confidence in me that I often lose sight of.

I owe an enormous thank-you to my ever-patient editors, Kristin Sevick and Troix Jackson, who suffered through numerous rewrites which included some wildly disjointed elements I now cringe thinking about. Thank you for saving me from myself. I feel so lucky you recognized the diamond in the rough (draft) and helped me chip away at the extraneous bits to find the story as I was always meant to tell it.

I'm fortunate to work with a talented and dedicated team at Forge Books, including Devi Pillai, Lucille Rettino, Sarah Reidy,

Jessica Katz, Alexis Saarela, Jennifer McClelland-Smith, Linda Quinton, Eileen Lawrence, Anthony Parisi, Ariana Carpentieri, and Libby Collins. I love being part of the Forge family. And a special thank-you to my fantastic publicity team at BookSparks.

I'm grateful to have the support of several writing communities, including Tin House, Bread Loaf, Tall Poppy Writers, Grub-Street, Novel Incubator, Writer Unboxed, Climate Fiction Writers League, and Wonder Writers, the world's best Slack support group. The camaraderie and friendships I've found among other writers have been the most precious part of my writing journey.

Thank you to my Season Six cohort of Novel Incubator for your feedback on the early pages of *The Last Beekeeper*, and a special shout-out to sixer Pam Loring for asking the "what if" question that opened my story up to possibilities I had never imagined.

I'm so grateful for my Tin House mentor, Paul Lisicky, the first person to read a full draft of *The Last Beekeeper*, and to my Tin House workshop cohort, who helped me shape the way I wanted to tell this story. Thanks also to my Bread Loaf Environmental Writers Conference mentor, Robin MacArthur, and my BLEWC cohort for your thoughtful feedback. Thank you, thank you, thank you to my Novel Incubator readers, especially Michelle Hoover and Elizabeth Chiles Shelburne, for seeing past the messy parts and convincing me there was something worth fighting for in my very drafty first draft. And to my early readers: Angie Kim, Matt Bell, Amy Brady, James Bradley, Rebecca Scherm, Sim Kern, Nancy Johnson, and Sarah Penner, thank you for your kind words and encouragement.

I'm grateful to the many early champions of *The Last Beekeeper*, including librarians Ron Block, Carol Anne Tack, and Terah Harris; booksellers Pamela Klinger-Horn and Mary O'Malley; and super-readers Francene McDermott Katzen and Annissa Armstrong. I've yet to meet any of you in person, but when I do, brace yourselves. I'm a hugger.

To my super-talented literary bestie, Nancy Johnson, how did

I get so lucky to find a forever writing friend like you? You are my bookish rock and literary soulmate. Weekly Zoom calls with Nancy and Sarah Penner helped me finish this book during those endless months of COVID-19 lockdown. I cherish our friendship and our mighty Accountability Trio. Sarah, your vision and mind-blowing work ethic inspired me on my most difficult days. The texts, calls, and Zooms with Nancy and Sarah, while we drafted our sophomore novels side-by-virtual-side made the pandemic a little more bearable.

Milo Todd, my talented writing partner and dear friend, thank you for being my sounding board as I battled through rewrite after rewrite. You always offer rock-solid advice, and just as importantly, you know when to step back and listen so I can talk through my plot problems and find the solutions myself. I'd be lost without your friendship, wisdom, and incomparable power of the pun.

The day Jennifer Berg Dardzinski, my oldest and dearest friend and my most dedicated beta reader, told me she loved *The Last Beekeeper,* I breathed an enormous sigh of relief. Ever since we were kids, I've always counted on Jen to give it to me straight. Jen is so committed to my books that she even donated her birthday to Sasha.

And to my parents, Ross and Barbara Carrick, thank you for always believing in me and for being my biggest fans. Thank you to my in-laws, Pat and Rich Dalton, for your never-ending support and fabulous dinner parties. And to my sister, Susan Jarecha, thanks for always calling (often accidentally via butt dial) at exactly the right moment when I need a good, long sister chat.

To my kids—Mikaela, Bronte, Chaney, and Everett—you never fail to inspire me. I left a little something for you in these pages. Search for the books discussed in *The Last Beekeeper.* Each of the made-up titles is dedicated to one of you. I'll let you figure out which book is yours and why.

To Sean, my husband of thirty years, you are still the hero in my stories. Thank you for your unwavering support and patience. We still have so many chapters left to write. I love you.

And lastly, thank you to the bees, wasps, bats, birds, yellow jackets, butterflies, and other pollinators. I think you are *all* wildly adorable.